THE CONSIGLIERE

A NOVEL

DONNA MASOTTO

WEST MARKET PUBLISHING
SAN DIEGO

Pam, It was my pleasure to meet you at the festival! Celebrate life today and always!

Donna Masotto

This is a work of fiction. Names, characters, businesses, places, events, locales, and incidents are either the products of the author's imagination or used in a fictitious manner. Any resemblance to actual persons, living or dead, or actual events is purely coincidental.

Website and cover design: Carousel Agency
Technical Applications: Doreen DeAvery, DeAvery Litigation Graphics
Ebook Formatting: KDP Amazon.com
Photographer: Bauman Photography, San Diego

Special thanks to Variety Recording Service, New York, NY.

Published by West Market Publishing
San Diego, CA 92101
www.westmarketpublishing.com
www.theconsiglierenovel.com

Five Star Reader Reviews

Reviewed By Romuald Dzemo for Readers' Favorite

The Consigliere: A Mafia Lawyer's Quest To Choose Love Over Revenge by Donna Masotto is a mesmerizing story filled with drama and very compelling characters. One of the important members of a mob, the Consigliere, is hit by tragedy, losing his eight-year-old daughter, and now he feels the irresistible call to set his life straight. Declan Quinn wants to find his long-lost sister and start a new life, but he must face his mafia boss. Help comes from unexpected places and Declan takes the road less traveled to confront his past and face his demons. Follow him on this unnerving quest as he struggles to reconnect with the child he once was and to find redemption. Follow him as he rediscovers love, but does he have what it takes to love and to break free from a life of crime?

Donna Masotto has crafted a story that is as inspiring as it is entertaining, starting with the protagonist's colorful yet troubled childhood, with an abusive father who drank himself from one jail cell to the next. With a mother dead and Shannon gone, Declan has to forge his own path. The story is filled with emotion and the humanity of the characters comes out neatly through the narrative. The author allows the religious, albeit the spiritual, to intermingle with the mundane, exploring human nature from quite unique angles. The psychological dimension of the novel caught my attention from the very first page and I became keen on finding out what made Declan the man he grew up to be, the secrets to his success, and the sudden, overwhelming desire to change his lifestyle. It's a story of a man's journey back to himself, but it is also a story of love that liberates from within. *The Consigliere*: A Mafia Lawyer's Quest To Choose Love Over Revenge will appeal to readers who enjoy well-crafted crime novels. It is riveting and thoughtfully written.

Reviewed By Ankita Shukla for Readers' Favorite

This is not just another mafia story—you know, the kind of stories that glamorize the mafia world and celebrate murder as if it's a rite of passage. No, Donna Masotto's *The Consigliere* is an eye-opener for everyone who has strayed far from love. When Declan's mother was murdered, he had to make a choice: either surrender to his anger and hatred for his father and choose the path of revenge or allow his love for his sister to embrace him and move on to live a good life unlike his father's. Many of his well-wishers tried to counsel him, but he tuned them all out. His act of vengeance did not bring him the peace that he had anticipated because you cannot fight the darkness with darkness. The author's style of storytelling is really smooth and engaging. Declan's journey from keeping secrets to "removing the thorns with telling" is fascinating and enlightening. Honestly, I had not expected a book with a mafia background to be this gripping; however, that is what it turned out to be and much more!

Reviewed By K.C. Finn for Readers' Favorite

The Consigliere is definitely painted with the same palette as The Godfather, and fans of Mario Puzo are certain to settle into Donna Masotto's world nicely. What I particularly enjoyed about *The Consigliere* was the amount of compassion and emotion worked into the story, from furious anger to terrifying grief, and those moments were when I was so hopeful for Declan's future and the prospect of his new life ahead. There's an exploration of what the word 'family' actually means, in terms of the mob and in terms of what people are willing to do to help those whom they love, and I thought that was very intelligently handled with compassionate side characters and multi-faceted 'villains'. Highly recommended.

Reviewed By Trudi LoPreto for Readers' Favorite

Declan Quinn is the main character in *The Consigliere*, a mafia lawyer trying to escape his life of crime. The story goes back and forth between the past and the present and his hopes for the future. Declan had a hard and troubled childhood, a sad and difficult life, and is attempting to right the wrongs and live happily ever after. We follow Declan on his journey, laughing and crying right beside him. His married life is in trouble; he is on the road to forming a close relationship with his son, Andrew; he is mourning his lost daughter; trying everything he can in searching for the sister he has not seen in many years and making plans to visit Ireland and his grandfather. This is all happening while his mafia boss is hunting him down, wanting to kill him for leaving the business.

I really enjoyed reading *The Consigliere* by Donna Masotto, and while it was about the mafia and inspired by The Godfather, it is so much more than that. I felt love, bravery, absolution, pity, fear, mercy and more as I traveled along with Declan, his family, his friends and his enemies. Each page was an exciting adventure that pulled me right into the story. Donna Masotto was truly inspired and took that inspiration to a brand new high. This was so much more than just another book about the mafia – it was the story of a boy making bad decisions and the effect it had on the man for his entire life. *The Consigliere* is well written with characters that you want to get to know better and a plot that never stops being good. I highly recommend *The Consigliere* to be read at your earliest convenience.

For Jaxon James

Sleep, with a smile on your face, in the arms of
St. Ann of Hemet.
We promise to live by your code always.

For Judy
Your voice is in our hearts forever.

THE CONSIGLIERE

A MAFIA LAWYER'S QUEST TO CHOOSE LOVE OVER REVENGE

A NOVEL

WEST MARKET PUBLISHING

SAN DIEGO

PROLOGUE

"We feel the thorns of the past. We remove them with the telling."

~ Declan Quinn ~

When my little sister and I were young, our mother would sing to us of how the green grasses of Ireland danced in our eyes. "Greenies to greenies," she'd sing staring into our eyes, as hers were a similar, unfathomably deep emerald color. "The green grasses of Ireland dance in your eyes, oh how the green grasses of Ireland dance in your eyes, please no cries, no cries, as the green grasses of Ireland dance in your eyes." Of course, the singing was embellished with her charming Irish accent, as we'd shout for more songs until our eyelids got heavy and sleep would close our days. The song was her nightly refrain to us as our father was habitually gone, drunk, carousing with his buddies in the speakeasy, located in the basement of our tenement house.

The nightly routine of hearing my mother's angelic voice blanketed us from our dad's rants on most days, but it wasn't until the night before my thirteenth birthday that our lives fell into a downward spiral. The songs and singing all stopped at that point, as my mother was murdered and I became resolute to avenge her death.

Two weeks after her passing, on a bitter cold night in February 1933, my friend, Tino Nusco found me lying on the freezing, concrete basement floor of our old elementary school on the Lower East Side of Manhattan, beaten and bloodied by the man I had sworn to kill. When Tino found me, I was burning with fever, extremely dizzy on my feet, and inches from death. He dragged me up the stairs, laid me in a wood-wheeled cart and pushed me down the street to Father Carmen's rectory. Father simply blessed my forehead ready to leave me in the hands of God.

I was just another orphan with no way to pay for a doctor. He must have pitied me, giving me sips of water, covering my shivering body with his own jacket, as he spoke to me in his thick Italian accent. "Oh dear, Declano, we have been looking for you for two weeks, you are sick." Chilled to the bone, he tried to warm me by slipping his gloves on my hands. "I am so sorry about your sweet mother, but she is in heaven now with the blessed angels."

"Where's Shannon?" I asked, my voice hoarse.

"Don't worry, your sister, she is safe. The sisters in the convent are watching her. It's good Tino found you, now you and Shannon can take the bus with the rest of the orphans in a few days."

I tried to jump to my feet but was too weak and felt dizzy. "No, I can't leave. I have to find my father and kill him," I said, and then began to cough so hard it quickly turned into dry heaves.

Tino stood behind me holding the handles of the wheel cart looking ready to push me the twenty blocks uptown to the hospital if he had to. "Hey, you may be Irish, but you're my friend. I know people around here who will help us find her killer, and then we can corner him in the alley…"

Father Carmen interrupted and in haste readjusted his jacket to cover my body. "May Jesus have mercy on you both. You are just boys. Do not speak of killing."

"That scum killed my mother. He deserves to die," I said, stripping off the jacket, trying to get up, but my legs still refused to work and my eyelids were sticking together like the crusted clams Tino and I caught in nets off the docks near the Brooklyn Bridge.

"Hey Father Carmen, doesn't Jesus say, 'an eye for an eye?'" Tino asked, interjecting as he punched his fist into his other hand.

Father took both his hands and placed them on Tino's shoulders. "No, he tells us to turn the other cheek. You must let the police take care of Declano's father. It's not for you to judge him. Only God in Heaven can save his soul."

I tried to muster up strength. "Save his soul? After I kill him, he will burn in Hell for what he did." With great effort I tried standing again, but the dizziness I felt was like restoring balance after riding the Cyclone roller coaster at Coney Island. But this day was far from the illusionary escape of a carnival, as the freezing cold on my face was sobering, and the thought of life without my mother—daunting. I realized the task of sending my father into the netherworld was going to be more difficult than expected if my eyes didn't heal and my legs stayed weakened.

Then Father Carmen's spoke further about that night and brought another element into an already horrifying situation. "Declano, this doesn't change what happened, but I must tell you the truth. The police investigation said your mother was beaten badly, just like he did to you, but your father didn't kill her. It was a terrible accident. Apparently he used his apartment as a wood shop to make clocks and furniture, so it was full of scrap wood with nails sticking out of them. She fell onto several, large rusty…"

For the third time that morning my head began to spin, as I recalled the whole fretful scene from two weeks ago. "He killed her. I don't care what some police report says, and look what he did to me," I said, interrupting him, even though I knew the story given to me was partly true, as that night his apartment was a mess of wood and scraps all over the place. When I found her, the side of her face and neck were punctured, as without a doubt, my father slapped her around causing her to fall onto protruding nails sticking out of the scrap wood. It was like seeing an inverted crucifixion, as instead of her body being nailed onto a cross, the nails sticking out of the wood planks, stabbed into her like daggers.

Father pushed Tino aside, put his hand on my forehead, and stopped me from speaking. "He is burning with fever. Be strong. Declano, your sister needs you. Sister Mary Catherine tells me Shannon cries for you every night."

"Shouldn't he go to the hospital?" Tino asked.

"Yes he should, but they will not take him. An orphan has no one to pay for doctors, perhaps the nuns in the convent can…"

Tino interrupted and lifted the wagon using its long handles and began to move me. "My dad will pay for it. I know he will."

Father Carmen took the wagon handles from Tino. "Go, Tino, run for your father. I will take Declano to the hospital. Meet us there." He pushed me to a busy street corner, whistled for a taxi, and helped me to my feet. Putting my arms into the sleeves of his jacket without caring they were two times my size, he readjusted my oversized gloves, as we jumped into the back seat. Tino closed the door of the taxi and ran in the opposite direction.

I don't remember anything else until I woke in the hospital with patches covering my eyes; they burned and stunk of the medicine the nurses dropped inside them.

Two days later, a bus full of orphans came to pick me up at the hospital. I sat in a wheelchair pushed by a nurse at the top of the hospital steps. A familiar nun I knew from the convent walked off the bus wearing her usual long black habit and head garment that surrounded her chubby face. "Declano, come with us, I brought a nurse along so she can care for you. And your sister, don't you miss her, son? She has cried and cried every night for you and is saving you a seat. Look at the window there…" she said, then stopped herself realizing I couldn't see through my eye patches. "Can't you hear her? We've all listened to that sweet thing calling for you for two weeks now. Please join us before she cries herself sick."

I heard her calling my name from the bus window. "Declan, Declan—the moon, the moon—Daddy can't find us on the dark side of the moon," she said, repeating our imaginary game we'd play when enduring our father's abuse.

Wheeling myself away from the nun and the busload of orphans, I wished to be deaf as well as blind for the moment, in that Shannon's cries cut into my heart. As my will was focused on my agenda, I ignored my sister's cries. Getting on board the bus was not an option in my plan, and for sure I wasn't going to weep like my sister for the entire population of New York to hear. Traversing on the dark side of the moon would only serve me alone; it was too late to get my family back. My sister would be better off without me and could live in the light of a new family's love. She was too innocent to witness another killing, I thought, and never saw Shannon again.

When Father Carmen came that night to my hospital room, he was angry. "Declano, why are you still here? You let the bus leave without you."

"I'm not going. I can live on my own."

"Boy, you are only thirteen. You need a family."

"My family is gone. I should have saved them." I thought of Signore Attanasio's revolver that he kept hidden in the safe at his shop, thinking how I could have saved my family if I simply shot my father that night. "I need a gun," I said, under my breath.

Father walked over, close to the side of my bed and whispered into my ear, grabbing my hand firmly. "Shh, you will alarm the other boys in this room with that kind of talk. You are not a murderer. Remember how you helped your mother and sister for many years? Most eight-year olds play in the street and trade baseball cards, but not you. The day I moved you into the safe house with the Attanasio family, you set aside your childhood. Working odd jobs, you helped your mother pay for rent, clothes—everything. Be proud of that."

I wasn't in the mood for optimism. "Yes, Father Carmen, I took care of us while my father drank himself into one jail cell after another. Look what good it did. Mother is dead and Shannon's gone."

"It's tragic. At least you had five years of peace living with the Attanasio's. You did well tutoring their children. I saw them all in mass and was impressed how quickly they learned to speak English after you and your mother moved in with them."

I tried to open my eyes, but could only see a shadowy Father Carmen through the patches as he stood next to my bed. How could he talk about tutoring and homework when my mother was dead? I thought. "So how did he find us?"

Father leaned closer to me and whispered, "I don't know. Perhaps he picked up gossip in the bar. I told the sisters in the convent to never give out any information about your whereabouts to anyone calling for you."

I shrugged. "Word leaked out from someone in the tenement I bet."

"I suppose, but we never wanted him to find you. You were so happy living with the Attanasio's—it was a blessing. And, if you don't mind me noticing a young love, Declano—I think you have a crush on one of those girls. Who is it?" He was toying with me, and I knew it, as he waited for me to answer. "It's Sal Russo's beautifully sweet daughter Judy, right?" he asked, using Judy like a carrot to bribe me.

It worked for a moment, as hearing Judy's name distracted me from my thoughts of revenge. "It's more than a crush, I wanted to marry her someday." I paused thinking of her sweetness. "So you've heard her sing at mass?"

Father Carmen clapped his hands together, seemingly happy to speak of a joyful topic instead of a vengeful one. "Oh yes. Her voice is like the angels singing. I just spoke with them over the phone. They said Judy has been very upset about you—you must want to see her. I can bring her here…"

I grabbed the sleeve on Father's jacket to pull him closer and whispered. "No. Don't. Everything's changed now." I pictured Judy coming to see me with my eyes all patched up and couldn't bear the thought. "Judy can have any boy. She doesn't need someone whose father is a murderer and a drunk. She's gone from my life now too."

Father Carmen whispered back. "What kind of talk is that? You are not your father. You must get well and remember who you are—your mother's boy, and a child of God. Don't let what your father did turn your soul into darkness, my son. I will talk to the Attanasio family again, they would be glad to take you in, and then you can go back to the parish school at St. Ephrem's with the rest of the Attanasio kids again. You are a special student there, all the teachers' favorite."

I shook my head and said nothing. My heart was closed—my old life gone. Judy needed to be free to follow her dreams without me, I thought.

Father Carmen said prayers placing his hands over my eyes.

His words fell silent to my ears. I had one plan and God wasn't in it. God didn't protect my mother who prayed to him every day. I was done with praying and decided at that moment any belief in a God was useless, so I knocked Father Carmen's hands away. "Don't pray for me, Father. It won't change what's happened."

"In time you will see how in suffering comes wisdom. For now, Declano, you must follow the light…"

"What light? All I see is black. Black from these blasted eye patches—I don't need them. I don't need God. I don't need anyone." I tried to rip the bandages off my eyes.

"Stop." Father Carmen held me down. He was stronger than I expected. Two nurses came running. One made me swallow some pills, put cold rags on my forehead, and fixed the bed covers while the other adjusted my eye patches. When one of the other boys in the room moaned and a smell in the air told me he had crapped his pants, the nurses let Father and me alone again as they tended to the other boy.

In the meantime, the pills had begun to calm me. I felt relaxed, able to make my case in a way that Father Carmen might understand. "Father Carmen, my father took the light away. He murdered it, how can there be wisdom in suffering? Suffering is seeing my mother bleed to death on the floor of his filthy apartment. He cannot go unpunished. Until I even the score of what he did, things will never be right."

"Don't speak this way. It was all a terrible accident. Follow Jesus, the light of His love will save you."

I shook my head at his foolishness. No preaching could help me—not even from Father Carmen. Why couldn't he understand? I thought. "He kidnapped them, hit her so hard—it was no accident. How can you say that? I need to talk to Tino. Can you call him for me?"

Father wasn't hearing any of my plans. "No. I will not make that call. Your mother never liked that boy. Besides, Tino is three or four years older than you. I will see if Signore Attanasio and his wife can pick you up tomorrow, they carry the torch of Jesus' love in their home. You lived there a long time, just stay away from Tino Nusco, he's headed for jail himself soon."

"Tino saved my life and his father is paying for this place. I owe them," I said, drowsy.

"You owe them nothing. Tino is trouble, he and his two brothers are always in scuffles on the streets."

I must have fallen asleep, as when I woke up later he was gone. I itched to escape from my hospital bed, kicked off the sheets, disgusted by the smells of medicine and bodily excrements. I needed to get out of there, find my father in that speakeasy, and slit his throat. The Attanasio's would never help me do that, but Tino would. I had the nurse look up the telephone number to the Nusco residence. She dialed and gave me the phone.

Tino and his father came to visit me the next day. I still had patches over my eyes, but I could feel the soft silk of Signore Nusco's suit sleeves when he shook my hand. I could picture him in a hat, suit, and tie, just like he always wore to morning masses at Old St. Patrick's. Back in those days, I was a mere kindergartener when Signore Nusco would sit in the pew behind us every morning for daily mass. She tried to hide my father's wrath behind a lace veil, but people knew she was a beaten woman, poor, and alone with two children to care for. These days were etched into my psyche like the word liberty engraved on the new silver coins he gave me.

Back then, generous, Signore Nusco would slip coins into the pockets of my overalls after mass. "Take care of your mamma, mio figlio; hide this money from your pappa. Be smart," he'd say as he poked my chest with his fist.

This was a regular occurrence for three years, until Father Carmen moved us to that safe house in Brooklyn. By then I had three small bags full of silver coins collected in a knapsack hidden under the floorboard beneath my bed.

On this day, Signore Nusco was at my side again ready to help. "You're a good figlio, Declano, a smart boy and always following my big boy Tino around town. Do you remember me?" he asked.

I was nervous around him when he'd give me coins years ago, and this day was no different. My voice shook as I responded. "Si, I remember you and saved all the money you gave me."

He laughed and patted my shoulder. "Si, when you were a little boy at St. Patrick's Church, you'd shy away from me," he said, tousling the hair on my head. "Never meant you no harm boy."

"I never shied away from you, just didn't want my father to…" I stopped, wanting to rip the patches off my eyes thinking of my father. "You gave me silver coins every day in mass. I hid them from my father just like you told me. When Father Carmen moved us across the river, Signore Attanasio helped my mother put all the money in the bank. Mi ricordo tutto, Signore."

He laughed. "Ah si. You're the Irish kid who speaks Italian. Maybe you should go back to live with the Attanasio family in Bay Ridge son. I know them. They are good Italians. I'm sure you can get your old job back. Didn't you work for Sam the butcher on Fifth Avenue?"

Still trying to sell my case, I said, "Yes I did, but that's over. I was hoping you would give me a job. I work hard, Signore Nusco, and I can pay you rent. I helped my mother pay our bills for five years. I loved to work and did anything my bosses asked me to do—at two jobs. I worked for Signore Attanasio delivering groceries and for Signore Russo at his paving yard, washing trucks on weekends. Let me work for you now."

I could sense Signore Nusco moving around my bed to speak closer to me as he whispered. "No, son, my work is not what you are used to."

"Then I can teach your boys how to read better and write essays, like I did with the Attanasio kids—helped them at night with their homework, too. You'll see," I said.

He smiled and patted my shoulder. "Yes, you did good work there. Those children are at the top of their classes now. Tino get's his high school diploma this year, but is getting F's, you can help him, yes?"

I shook my head and smiled. "No F's anymore if I'm helping him, Signore Nusco."

"Good. Help Tino to better his grades, but you are too young to work for me in my business. Do you know what work I do?"

The patches over my eyes were driving me crazy, as here I was asking for a job while on my back and desperate. But, I pleaded nonetheless. "Yes, I know. Please, Don Nusco, you can help me do what I need to do."

Again Signore Nusco leaned closer to me to speak. "Does this have to do with your father? Tino told me you were searching the streets to find him."

Tino punched his fist into his free palm once more. "Yes, let's kill the bastard!"

"Quiet Tino!" I heard him smack his son either on his hand or head.

"Signore Nusco, if you give me a job I will give you my loyalty—as my Don." I felt for his hand, searching to kiss it like I had seen other men do when they walked by him.

Tino fumbled with the intravenous bag and line attached to my forearm. "Tell him Declan. Tell him what you told me. You want to take your father down for what he did, let's kill the God damn bastard. Just say it, Declan. You want that dirty drunk German dead."

I heard Signore Nusco slap him once more. "Leave this room. Leave right now and wait outside the door. There are sick boys in this hospital room."

I heard them scuffle; frustrated I was trapped behind bandages. Their shoes moved fast on the floor and the door shut hard. It was quiet when Signore Nusco returned to my bedside. He whispered into my ear. "Are you sure your father is responsible for your mamma's death?"

"I'm sure. His name is Axel Hauser," I said, excited that finally an adult acknowledged my intent. I spoke with urgency. "Father Carmen told me the police took him away to jail again. Now the police say he didn't even kill her. He did. I saw everything that night. I will go with you right now and we can find him together."

"Okay. Aspetta, aspetta, you must wait. We will settle everything once you are stronger. My wife and I liked your mamma. It is a sad thing that Teacher Hauser is gone. St. Patrick's school was never the same without her classes and music."

His words roused my frustration more, so I spoke with even grater urgency. "I should have killed him back then, back when I had a chance, but now it's too late."

He dismissed everything I tried to say. "You were just a small boy." Then, I felt him grab his jacket off the covers at the foot of my bed and set to leave. "Come stay with us, you can sleep in Tino's room on a cot for now. I will talk to Father Carmen. These lousy doctors here don't know how to heal you. My wife can use her Italian medicine to clean your eye infection. With fresh herbs and fish oil from Sicily, she will get your eyes back to good health again. You can stay in my home for as long as you like."

"Take me with you now. Get me out of here. My mother was taken to this hospital barely alive, then left to die because she couldn't pay. The nurses tied my sister down that night and gave her a shot as she screamed for our mother. They scared her half to..." I paused and regrettably inhaled more aromas of disgusting bowel waste. "Ah, forget it." I felt dizzy, and tried to cough out the toxins in my lungs. "I hate the smell of this fucking place. Please, get me out of here." I ripped off the blankets and tried to lift myself from the bed—frustrated that yet another man could hold me down with greater strength.

He covered me again with the bleach smelling blankets, placing a no nonsense grip on my arms. "No, Declano, not tonight. I must prepare a place for you and speak to Father Carmen. I'm very sorry about your mother; she was a good Irish lady. I will come for you tomorrow," he said, and left me there.

Later that night, the nice couple that owned our safe house in Brooklyn came to visit me. During our five-year stay with them, I came to know Signora Attanasio as Zia Anna; she was your typical chubby Italian mamma and practically a nurse herself. She stood next to my bed asking the doctor about my medication and gave me a knitted hat and foot slippers. When she tried to help by showing the nurses how to use a special eye cream she brought, the fresh peppermint scent tempted me to climb back into her love.

I could hear Signore Attanasio's loud voice joking around with the nurses in the hallway, when he finally walked into my room; his banter stirred the sleeping boys in their cots. "Father Carmen called. We want you to come home with us. My customers at the shop are all asking where is my tall, handsome, redheaded Irish son, and Sal told me he wants you to come back to work in the truck yard on weekends, he even said you're old enough to work with the crews," he said, as I could hear Zia Anna whispering something to him. "Yes, my wife says, everyone misses you, especially Judy. She hasn't stopped crying since you disappeared."

My heart stopped when hearing her name. "Judy. Stop teasing me about her. Is she really asking about me?"

Zia Anna answered. "Of course, she is. Three boys at school invited her to the winter concert, but she sat at home all night crying until that Nusco boy finally found you. I even sewed her a new, burgundy taffeta dress, but she refused to go without you."

I shook my head. "She shouldn't have missed it. I'm no good for her now. It's Shannon you should have taken home with you. Rosy and Elizabeth always loved to braid her long red hair. Why did you let her go off in a bus full of crying orphans?"

Zia Anna began to cry. "Oh, Declano. We would have kept you and Shannon together, but we weren't given a choice. Everything happened so fast. Before we knew it, that bus was gone and so was our little Shannon. Father Carmen is trying to find her for us. We will try to get her back, or at least get an address to send her cards and letters. Oh sweet Jesus, little Shannon off somewhere alone with strangers. This is a terrible world sometimes."

Signore Attanasio patted his wife on the shoulder. "Don't cry, Anna. I know you would take in all the kids off the street who need a home and find a way to feed them, but we can only do what God allows. Come now; let's leave this boy to rest. Get well, we will come back for you tomorrow and bring you home. Okay, Declano?"

Their love tempted me, but my heart was too hardened to accept it—not even for Judy's sake. If Father Carmen was right, that they carried a torch for Jesus' love, my darkness shut it out. Any chance at love had left me now that my mother was gone.

With all my strength, I asked them to leave. "Shannon should stay with her new family and I am going to live with the Nusco's in Bensonhurst now. Thank you for everything you did for us."

Zia Anna had become like a second mom to me and cried hearing my words "No Declano, please, your home is with us. Your mother was like a sister to me, all the children love you and Shannon. What will I tell them? You are like a big brother to Frankie…" She stopped and blew her nose.

I shook my head wishing they'd stop tempting me. "I'm sorry, I must settle the score with my father. Please just leave. I can't say anything more. I can take care of myself. You won't ever understand, so just go."

She adjusted my bedding. "And what will we tell Judy. You must know that she loves you."

I shook my head once more. "No, she can't. We can't be together. Everything's changed now. Please just tell her I said good-bye and will write to her once I can see and write again—I will hear her beautiful voice no matter where I go." My tears finally came, wetting the bandages and causing Zia Anna's peppermint ointment to intensify up my nostrils. I knew Judy would never be mine.

"Now listen here, Declano." Signore Attanasio moved closer to my side, lowered his tone, and I could smell his butcher shop meats in his breath. "You are not going to live with the Nusco's, that family is trouble. Signore Nusco is a good man, but his business is not, and his three sons are worse."

I had to defend my friend's loyalty. "Tino helped me and saved my life."

Signore Attanasio raised his voice. "Tino? Forget about that kid, he's too old for you to be hanging with around town. You must stay away from all those boys. Come home with us, it's where you belong—and don't forget, the Bum's are in spring training now for the season opener soon, we have a box seat set just for us."

I pictured his son Frankie and I eating peanuts at Ebbet's Field and was of a mind to listen to them, as Zia Anna rubbed more peppermint ointment under my eye patches. "We're not the only ones who love you." Zia Anna said coaxing me further. "Your grandfather in Ireland, Professor Quinn calls our house every day asking me about you and Shannon. He told me he calls the hospital too, trying to talk to you. Son, didn't the nurses tell you he called?"

It was true my Pappy called the hospital every morning and each time I told the nurse, "No, I'm sleeping." How could I tell my grandfather that a man, whose blood ran through my veins, killed his daughter? How could I ever face him? Until my father was dead, I could not speak to my Pappy.

I tried to wipe off the minty cream from the top edge of my cheekbones, refused any topic of my Pappy calling, or of our seats at Ebbet's. "You both need to go. I've made up my mind. I'm moving in with the Nusco's, so don't come back."

They finally left me alone. I was glad my eyes were covered in bandages so they couldn't see my tears. My thoughts were with Judy—she did love me. It wasn't only a childhood crush after all.

Throughout the night, I wondered what to do about telling Pappy my decision, weighing three options in my mind. The safe house was out, as they'd never help me find my father, and the second choice looked even bleaker, a trans-Atlantic ticket back to Ireland in the middle of the depression—deemed impossible from my standpoint. So with intent, I didn't answer Pappy's calls, as he'd try to come and get me in New York, get mixed up with my vendetta, or put a stop to my plans altogether. So moving in with the Nusco's became my last and only option.

The next morning, the nurses rolled my hospital bed closer to the window as they spoke about how the rare sunny winter day might help the eye infection burn out of my system. I lay under the beaming sunlight all morning, and by the time the tray of uneaten oatmeal bowls were carted out of my room, Tino and his father came for me.

I willingly left that awful place to go and live at their home in Bensonhurst. They gave me my own bedroom with a small bed in the corner. I couldn't see the size of the room due to the patches still covering my eyes, but I walked around it and could tell there was much empty space around me. I instantly missed the Attanasio's and my family.

The next day, two men carried in empty bookshelves and a huge desk. Signore Nusco ordered the men to place the pieces in a special corner next to the large window overlooking the street.

"Hey, place that desk near the window so the neighborhood can boast how the Nusco boys study night and day, and soon, we will fill these bookshelves with all the great English books you see in the library."

One morning, a few months later, as the spring warmth filled the air and the scent of flower blossoms gave a reminder that new life had returned after a deadening winter, I sat on the front patio overlooking Ocean Parkway on the corner of Avenue U. Signora Nusco walked over to me and put one last drop of her magic saline into my eyes after she slowly removed the eye patches. I closed my eyes once more on her command as she rubbed a fingertip full of herbal oil over my lids. I opened them to warm sunshine and was overwhelmed by an array of budding red maple leaves sprouting from a row of trees lining the sidewalk, readying to explode on their branches as they climbed around the black iron fence surrounding the Nusco's home.

This restored vision gave me strength, with a will enough to begin plotting the murder of my father, Axel Hauser. I took pleasure in thinking how the murder should be carried out.

For the rest of the school year, Signore Nusco pulled me aside after dinner each night and thanked me for speaking English with his sons and helping them get their homework and book reports done. I finished my Eighth grade year at a different parish school closer to the Nusco's home and visited the local library every week just like my mother and I did with the Attanasio family. I tutored and read many books to Signore Nusco's three sons, Tino, Ricco, and Marco after school. They particularly liked The Good Earth and Goodbye Mr. Chips, and gave good effort to read excerpts along with me. Then each night, after receiving their father's praise, I would ask him about the issue of my father. His answer was the same every time. "You must wait, Declano. The time is not right. Finish school, then we will talk." Signore Nusco was a happy father, bragging about us all the time to the principal at our school. "My boys will go to college, next year Tino will start and the rest of them will follow. You will see, one day they will be congressmen and senators."

I knew the right decision was made on where and with whom I should live when listening to him dream of the future. I still wondered about Shannon and hoped she had fared well with a family unknown, but knew she didn't need a brother like me. Letting her go was the right decision, too, I thought.

Still wanting to stay connected to my Pappy, I wrote letters to him occasionally, being careful to ask Miss Emily from the library down the street to mail them using the library's return address. She was gracious to hold the letters he sent in return at her reference desk, as Signore Nusco was very private about us ever mailing anything using his mailing address, so we honored his rules. In my letters, I fabricated my situation with the Nusco family, telling him they were a happy and loving Italian family like the one I stayed with before. He didn't catch on, until much later, when my letters stopped coming.

On his last day of high school in mid-June, Tino boasted about finally graduating and bought himself a cigar to celebrate. But there was no celebrating for me. Sure my school year had ended, but my focus on vengeance never stopped. So I took the bus to Signore Nusco's office alone. I couldn't wait any longer to implement my plan.

Signore Nusco sat in a large, dark leather chair behind a cherry mahogany desk, writing notes and looked up at me in surprise when I walked in. "Declano, what are you doing here? Isn't today the last day of classes?"

"Yes, it is. I've helped Tino finish high school like you asked and in four short years that will be me—but now I'm here on business," I said, taking a seat in front of his desk.

Clinching his hands over the top of his head, he leaned back into his desk chair and sighed. "This is about your father," Signore Nusco said, frowning at me.

"Yes," I said.

"Son, you must be sure about this. A father is always a father—no matter what," he said, while twisting the large gold ring with the big diamond on his right hand, a habit of his when he was thinking hard.

Determined, I said, glaring at the ring on his finger. "A father? He doesn't deserve that title. He's just a murdering thug who beat my innocent mother to death and tried to do the same to me. If Tino hadn't found me, I'd be dead too. He's my father by blood only. I can't sleep thinking about how he took everything from me. Everything—my mother, sister, my whole life."

He leaned towards me. "Yes, he is a bad man and definitely was the wrong man for your mother, but a boy doesn't kill his own father. It's an evil thing. You should forget this. Go play baseball like the rest of the boys in the street and don't listen to everything Tino tells you to do."

I became indignant and practically jumped out of my seat. "Tino doesn't tell me what to do, and Signore Nusco, I'm not a boy anymore. I'm a man and a man takes care of his family. I need to find him and make him pay…"

Signore Nusco sighed and nodded, adjusting the customary blood-red rose pinned to his lapel. He took out a cigar from the pocket on his suit and lit it looking out the window onto Mulberry Street. "I already know where he is, this Axel Hauser. He's in the state penitentiary doing time for a manslaughter charge. I have a man inside watching him already. Perhaps it's time he pay your father a visit."

I immediately stood up at the suggestion, grateful once more for the acknowledgement. "Thank you. I want him dead or beaten within inches from death, so he knows what it feels like. Have someone take him out, like he did to my mother and me."

Signore Nusco tapped his cigar onto the top of his desk, but said nothing.

Feeling a sense of accomplishment I added, "One more thing—I don't want to use the last name Hauser anymore. You've done so much for me, I think it would be right to change my name to Nusco."

He smiled and placed the cigar between his teeth as he spoke. "No. My Italian name is not for you. You are an Irish boy. Honor your mother. Take her name, her father's name. What is her father's name?"

"Quinn," I answered, and as soon as I said it, the name fit like wearing a soft, seasoned baseball glove. "Do you know how I can change my name to Quinn?"

He struck a match and began to light the tobacco tip on his cigar. "You are a smart young man, figure it out or hire a lawyer. Better yet, go to school and become a lawyer, then you could go to court yourself. Perhaps then I would make you my Consigliere."

"What's a Consigliere?" I asked, taking a seat as I stumbled with the pronunciation.

He laughed and repeated the title with the proper pronunciation. "Con-sig-lee-air-ā, my right hand man and my legal counselor. The most important figure in my business."

"Would you really make me your Consigliere?" I said, trying to say it correctly. "So, you do want me work for you then?"

"No!" He laughed loudly. "You're too smart for my type of business, besides who's ever heard of an Irish Consigliere? No, Declano, you should become something grand. Become the President of this wonderful country. Can't you picture that someday? The sky's the limit for you. You have brains, mio figlio. Trust me, you don't want to work for me—you are un accademico, like your mamma was; she was the best teacher at St. Patrick's. How about becoming a professore? That would be a great profession for you." He stood up from his seat and smiled. "Come on, you should go celebrate with Tino."

Signore Nusco motioned for me to get up. He walked around his desk and put his arm around my shoulder as we exited his office. He walked me down Mulberry Street toward the bus stop. "Do your studying, help my younger boys now, that's all you need to worry about. Tino has the good grades to go to college because of you, in a few years it will be your and Ricco's turn, then Marco after that. Nice work helping them through all those classes this year. Book learning, it comes as natural to you as baseball, si?"

"Si, Signore, it does," I said, and shrugged. "But, Tino said he wants to work for you and not go to college. Didn't he tell you? And when I graduate, I will do the same."

He crossed his arms and was clearly upset at this news. "No, unless you want to get shot like the other thugs around here, my boys will never work for me, including you, Declano."

"But, Signore Nusco," I said, refusing to board the bus.

"Go. There will be no more talk about this," he said, firmly and watched as I reluctantly climbed the few steps onto the bus.

"Please, don't tell Tino I ratted on him about college in the fall. I will pay you back and do anything for you in return for helping me Don Nusco." I kissed his hand. "I will go to law school as you said, and one day—you will have an Irish Consigliere."

Signore Nusco smiled. "Well, as I said, that will never come to be, but I suppose stranger things have happened. Tell Signora Nusco I won't be home for dinner tonight. Hurry boy, your bus has a schedule to keep."

***

Later on that summer, on a hot, humid evening, Tino and I returned home after spending the day at Coney Island. Father Carmen was sitting on the porch of the Nusco's house having coffee and cookies, talking to Signora Nusco and two more ladies from the neighborhood, but was waiting to see me.

I walked over to greet him and shook his hand.

"I am glad to see you looking so well, Declano. Your eyes, they are healed now?" he asked.

"Yes, Father. Completely better, thanks to Signora Nusco's kind help." I nodded to her and she smiled back.

Father Carmen looked at Tino and me. "May I speak with you privately, Declano? I have news."

Tino walked up to Father Carmen and interrupted. "Hey Father C, bet you never thought I'd get my high school diploma." He shook off a sandy towel without a care the remnants got all over the ladies' dresses and into their coffee cups.

"And what college are you hoping to enter in the fall?" Father Carmen asked, dusting off the sand on his black jacket.

Tino sat down on the porch swing. "Uh, well …" He grabbed a handful of biscotti instead of replying, poured a cup of milk, and watched us walk away into the garden behind the house, out of range for others to hear.

Father Carmen waited a few seconds for two girls walking on the sidewalk to pass us before he began to speak to me. I waved to them with a wink and they rushed off giggling. "I'm here to give you some bad news about your father. I am sorry to tell you this, but he is dead, beaten badly a few days ago, and then hung himself in his cell last night."

I pretended to be shocked, but inside I felt triumphant, like one feels at the top crest on a rollercoaster before its descent. Then similarly, with the reality of what I had done, my heart sank into the pit of my stomach hearing this news crashing down on me. "Thank you for telling me." I said, without a tear for him and held my head low, not having the gumption to look into Father Carmen's eyes.

"I see no tears today, son. I worry for you, your mother would be saddened to see your once tender heart, turned cold," Father Carmen said, touching my shoulder as he tried to move my chin with his free hand.

I looked away at his mention of my mother, and fought tears. "Father Carmen, a man has to survive on these streets and to take care of himself. If you sense my cold heart, then so be it. He deserves to be dead with the other thugs in Hell."

He looked at me with suspicion. "You had a part in this, didn't you?"

I didn't respond and looked away.

"Well, a vengeful heart kills a man's soul—sending him into a bleak darkness. Remember that, Declano," he said, with sadness. "When you are ready to talk about your involvement in this, call me." He offered no more words or condolences.

I let Father Carmen walk to his car as he slowly drove away. I walked back in the opposite direction and could see Tino, still charming the ladies on the porch. He wasn't someone I needed at this time, so I turned and ran down the street trying to catch Father in his black Buick, but it was too late. He turned a corner and left me resolute with my sin.

For a few hours, I sat on a street curb in solitude thinking of my mother and of how she "would be saddened to see my once tender heart, turned cold," like Father said. I felt the gravity of the shame having been the author of my father's suffering and subsequent death, knowing how when my mother died, my noble spirit died along with her. Her death was the pivotal point between the Declan that was and the Declan that is. There was no returning to being her sweet little Irish boy who helped tutor immigrants, pay the rent, and push Shannon down the streets in her pram. And, although a gangster who treasures love doesn't quite fit the profile, the love that my mother bestowed on me was the purest form of joy I had in my life, and in that moment, I wished for it back.

Sitting alone amongst the smells of a dirty, muddied gutter, I could almost swear my mother's fresh rose bath powder filled the air instead. I remembered how when anyone who met her would stop to admire her crisp, authentic beauty; or of when she'd enter a room, it was as if she carried the sun's rays as they danced off her curls, coupled with the light in her deep translucent emerald eyes, brought delight to anyone graced by her presence. I thought of the many nights eating supper with the Attanasio family, as she'd walk around the table serving a ladle of sauce over our noodles, humming Irish ballads and teaching the kids English phrases every chance she could. Losing her was a loss to the whole community, a loss to having fun in learning, and a loss to simple pleasures like the Gaelic tunes she'd play on her flute after dinner.

I just sat on the curb, wishing she were still alive to tell me everything would be okay again, but was lost in regret and stuck without any family. And even though her beauty was one to never forget, I began to panic that my darkness would overcome the memory of her face.

Then through the chaotic street sounds, I heard a voice—not sure if it was coming from inside my head or from the ambient street noise. *Declan, please son, don't fill your heart with hate, go home—go home.* Could that be my mother whispering into my ears, I wondered, scared, yet warmed. But I quickly tuned it out, just like I had edged out the memory of seeing her face in horror as she bled to death in the mess of my father's apartment. So, to busy myself, I pitched a hand full of pennies to the curb with my thumb. Home? Where's that…? I thought. Just then the local bus zoomed past me as it headed eastbound toward Bay Ridge. It was too late to live with the Attanasios—too late to call Pappy, too late to listen to the spirit, too late for anything other than the cards I had chosen. From there on, I locked out the memory of her beauty, shutting out her voice for good.

A few days later after dinner, Signore Nusco tapped my shoulder, leading me to the porch outside. He roused his youngest sons off the swings and sat down, lighting his cigar. "Have a seat Declano."

I didn't wait for the others to leave. "If this is about Axel Hauser, I know he killed himself last week," I said coldly, as the food in my stomach was threatening to come up.

"Yes, I heard Father Carmen dropped by to see you. But you must know, my men roughed your father up good, but didn't hang him. He did that on his own."

"He was a coward, Signore. Your men did a good thing. Thank you." I swallowed down the lump in my throat.

Signore Nusco was more intent on smoking his cigar than to explain any details about my father. "Declan, I told you my work is a dirty business. Now, with this behind you finally, become a better man than me, better than men like Axel Hauser."

"I will be indebted to you, Signore Nusco, for helping me."

Signore Nusco let me kiss his hand and didn't respond. He just tapped the top of my head firmly. I walked off the porch and walked down Ocean Parkway and turned the corner at Avenue U, then kicked a can down the street, happy the noise of it hitting the road kept the spirits away.

Slowly it dawned on me nothing had really changed. My father might be dead, but this didn't restore the loss of the ones I had loved, and justice didn't bring me the peace I had hoped for—as guilt stepped in like an uninvited guest, bringing with it darkness worse than having to wear patches over my eyes.

Later that night, I lay alone in my bedroom, feeling more alone than ever before. I longed to have a friend like Judy and wondered if I'd ever see my little sister again.

PART ONE

BRIDGEPORT, CALIFORNIA

"When walking into the darkness,

it's best to take a guide."

~ Declan Quinn ~

CHAPTER ONE

THE LIE

Christmas, 1967

"There are only two races of men, decent men and indecent."

~ Viktor Frankl ~

I am an indecent man.

When my son recently asked me which type of man I was—

I opted to lie.

If the axiom is true, that peace follows justice, a time frame must be included into the fold. As three long decades had passed since the grief and consequential justice of 1933, and peace persisted to be a foreign concept to me. It felt like it was something locked inside a vault I couldn't open, as four vital treasures in my life were gone. I lost my mother, my sister, and my beloved Judy on the same day, and the final gem and ultimate treasure—my daughter, last year. How could any man be right after life stripped all his joys away? Father Carmen told me many years ago, time heals, but I had come to realize that the passage of time was no cure for the losses of the heart and for the pains trapped in one's soul.

On most days, and in all degrees of climate, I did most of my thinking under the large oak tree overlooking a pond on my ranch located at the base of the high Sierra Nevada Mountains, and wondered if darkness would always prevail over me.

One morning during the Christmas holidays, I sat and smoothed over the tan leather cover of a journal my oldest child, Andrew, gave me on Christmas Eve. I combed through its pages to a series of questions he wrote in his meticulous handwriting for me to answer. Even though my entries were blank, I wondered if perhaps at last the stars were aligned to set my pen to paper, to speak the truth, and begin to heal.

I looked up towards the house and saw my son walking down the graveled path with a pair of ice skates draped over his shoulder. Seeing him startled me out of a trance as I stared out at a frozen pond located at a base basin on our ranch.

"Merry Christmas, Paps. Do you like your gift? Please tell me you're going to help me out and write your thoughts down on those pages." He tossed the skates onto the rocky ground. "Come on, you're an alumni of Fordham and get the deep, intellectual approaches of the Jesuits," Andrew said, taking the journal out of my hand as he took a place on the bench.

"Hey, that's my book, give it back son," I said.

He handed it back in jest. "Come on, help me out Paps, I need your answers for my thesis project. And remember, you're the one who pushed me to get a Master's Degree."

I looked away from my son and flipped over the pages in the journal once more. Staring over the frozen pond again, I sighed with quiet laughter and thought, God surely had a sense of humor with me. As there I was, Declan Quinn, a gangster on a sabbatical, who had a son, a would-be seminarian studying philosophy with the Jesuits, who wanted me to answer ten existential questions on the meaning of life.

Indeed, I believed God punished men like me with irony. Using the scabs from our past to rip off our wounds without warning, he forced us to look straight at the sun and burn our souls of the sins we tried to hide. I understood the justice of it—I deserved to suffer for the life I had chosen and longed to laugh along with the ironic jest from the creator above.

But knew, only decent men had peace.

Nonetheless, life continued to move forward in spite of my mood.

As Andrew sat with me in silence, we watched a cluster of teens come down the path to prepare for their scrimmage on the icy pond. "So, can you help me or what, these final courses are killing me? And don't sweat it—I'll give you a month to finish." He looked at his younger brother in a group readying to play on the ice. "Hey Frankie, I'll step in for goalie if you need."

Frankie nodded. "Sure bro, but you might mess up your sacred, holy hands if you're not careful."

Andrew shrugged and didn't respond, seemingly too mature for banter between brothers.

On still mornings such as this, I loved how the majestic mountain range gave a backdrop of shadowy hews of pastel lavender gray with heavy snowcaps blanketing them, as they reflected onto the heavy pool of ice. Bundled against the cold, I watched the teenage boys dress in their various team jerseys.

Andrew draped his ice skates over his shoulder again, as he stood up to walk toward the ice. He wore a gray Mammoth Mountain sweatshirt, with a burgundy Fordham Rams baseball cap on his head, looking more ready for a game of baseball then hockey. He is full of charm, tall with a smooth, intelligent style, looks like my mother's side of the family. Slap an Irish brogue into his California accent, and you would have a clone of my grandfather, as his boney facial structure and deep-set emerald green eyes came from strong Quinn traits. Frankie, on the other hand, takes after my wife's family and looks straight off the boat from Italy. He's a dark, handsome, brawny kid, whose focus is more on hunting deer and chasing girls than doing his homework.

I held a pen in my hand, as the journal with Andrew's questions laid unopened on my lap.

Andrew looked at me with a defeated expression on his face. "I don't need your doldrums, Paps. Can see it in your eyes, you have no clue what to write, do you? It's too bad, too. Mom and I thought this would be a good project for you." Defeated, he cupped his hands like a megaphone at his brother who was doing figure eights on the ice. "Hey, Frankie. You afraid I'll show you up in front of your friends? Come on, let me play."

Ignoring the fact he and my wife plotted to get me into this corner, I shoved him gently. "Jump in, kid," I said. "You don't need permission from those punk high school jocks. You're a big graduate student now."

"I will. I'm just messing with him. Baseball is more my thing, anyway, just like you, Paps. I'll come back once school is done and pitch you some fastballs like old times. Okay?"

I took off my wool cap to comb back with my fingers what little hairs covered my head. "Drew, you're already pitching me strikes right over the plate with these ten curveball questions in this journal." I sighed. "Did you think of all ten of these yourself, or did Monsignor O'Shea concoct them up?" I asked.

"I did. Part of this project is to learn how to ask the right questions in the interview process. The questions, in and of themselves, are one-third of my grade," he said. "Are they too hard for you, Paps?"

I loved a challenge, and he knew it. "Nope, just thought I left Fordham and those uptight Jesuits decades ago."

"Hey, watch it," he said, punching my shoulder. "I'm going to be one of those myself soon. Use the other book I gave you to help answer the journal questions. When you get your responses to me, I'll write my thesis paper, earn an A, then enter the seminary in the fall."

For a moment, I thought I misheard. "What's this? Are you trying to throw another curve? What are you telling me?"

Andrew sat next to me, put his skates down again, and removed his baseball cap. "I'm sure of it now. I want to be a priest. There, I said it." He pointed at the house. "Mom's up there watching us from the kitchen window. She insisted I tell you before I head back to campus the day after tomorrow."

"So you told your mother, but left me in the dark. Why?"

Frustrated, Andrew stood up and grabbed a few pinecones from the ground to throw them towards the creek adjacent to the pond.

"Paps, come on. Are you so checked out of this family that you've become blind?"

I rubbed my hands together, annoyed. "Checked out, do I look like a library book or something, what's that supposed to mean?"

He took a seat to unlace his shoes. "You know what I mean. Perhaps you're the wrong guy for this assignment after all. I've been thinking of mailing it to G-Pap. I'm guessing he'd be honored to help me with this if it's too much for you."

I felt like a heavyweight, sparing partner had just jumped into the ring with me. "G-Pap? Did Pappy ask you to call him that?"

Lacing up his skates he said with a smile, "Yes. Great-grandfather Pappy, G-Pap for short. He writes me all the time at Fordham. Chances are I'll finally get to officially meet him soon. A group of us seminarians are traveling overseas to Ireland on a monastery tour and pilgrimage with Monsignor O'Shea after we graduate. Hey Paps, come to think of it, you should join us."

My jealousy worsened, knowing I was outmatched with this challenger, a literary man extraordinaire. "Go ahead kid, let your G-Pap swing at these questions, I'm sure he'd give you ten-thousand words by next week. And also, for the record, that Ireland trip and me won't work either, as I'd stand out like a sore thumb on a bus full of seminarians. So, no thank you on all of the above, okay. Perhaps your G-Pap is the better man for a pilgrimage, too." I said, beaten and jealous.

"Well, if that's the way you want it, but the thought of seeing G-Pap sure ruffled your feathers," he said.

I gave a better effort to mask my envy. "It sure is great you and G-Pap have a connection, send him this work son. He's all you have since both my parents are dead."

Andrew shrugged. "Well, I'd rather the journal come from you, but he's quite the academic. His poetry recommendations helped me get through a difficult creative writing class my junior year."

"Ah, yes, Professor Declan Quinn, that is. A poetic master of literary form, a genius with words, my mother was too," I said.

"Yes, but you never talk much about your Irish roots," Andrew said.

"No, not much," I said, and turned away.

"Well, it looks like Mom was right to have me try and get you involved with this project."

"Oh, what's she been telling you?" I glanced up toward the house and sure enough, there she was, looking out the window, staring back at us. "Look at her up there. All she does these days is spy on me."

Andrew stood next to me, wobbling on the blades of his skates, and glanced up towards the house to give his mother a loving wave with his baseball cap. "Can't you go easy on her Paps, you act as if you're the only one who's grieving?" he asked, adjusting his cap onto his head once again.

He was usually spot on with is observations, so I flipped through my book and grumbled.

"Let me see that," Andrew said, pointing to the companion book he'd given me with the journal at Christmas. I gave it to him while I held on to the journal, caressing its smooth tan leather cover once more. He flipped pages in the book until he found what he wanted.

The rising sun warmed our backs and the ice on the pond grew shiny and slick. I stood up and yelled to my younger son. "Hey Frankie, watch out down there, the ice is getting slick."

Andrew watched Frankie and his friends for a second and then showed me a page in his book. "See Paps, it says here that man can find happiness even in the depths of despair. '…to choose one's attitude in the throes of suffering,' I hoped you would read this before you answered the journal questions. Okay?"

I stared at him without comment, flipped through the questions again, and realized he was as crafty with words as his G-Pap.

He continued. "Sure, I'll admit the questions are deep, prodding, and introspective, but Frankl's work will bring you the needed mindset before you take a stab at them."

"Indeed. The death camp in Auschwitz taught him about man's capacity for suffering and death. Life can take good men out, this is true," I said.

He watched me staring blank into the journal. “Paps, if you don’t like my gift or the idea of doing this journal project, I’ll have to get you another Christmas present this year.”

I flipped through the pages once more. “No, don’t bother yourself. I like it. I just think a nice Cuban cigar in my Christmas stocking would have done the trick.” I pulled a fresh cigar out of the inside lining of my jacket, sat down again, and began to light it. “I don’t see what you’re trying to tell me though.”

“Just that I love you Paps.”

“And I love you, kid.” I inhaled oxygen into the cigar while holding a match to its tip and continued to speak with it between my teeth. “You know I’m already familiar with Frankl’s work. I read it in college right after it was published and I had just returned from the war. I have a hardcover edition, all marked in the margins on the shelf in my office. Viktor Frankl himself signed it when he spoke in New York that year. I found it was the rare read that made my heart sink while elevating my mind.”

He sat next to me again. “Paps, that’s great. I had no idea you met the famous Viktor Frankl. Monsignor O’Shea is using his work as the basis for our graduate seminar this spring.”

I held the book up, opened it to its correct page, and read him my favorite quote. “I remember one line that stuck with me. ‘There are only two races of men, decent men and indecent.’ Son, that line hits prejudices square on the head. In fact, it gets to me—especially when I’m staring in the mirror.”

“Perfect, Paps. I trust your reflection tells you you’re in the decent category?” he asked, with suspicion.

“Decent?” I paused, knowing I couldn’t tell him the truth. “Yes, of course, Andrew. I am a decent man.”

“Glad to hear that.” Andrew smiled and patted my shoulder. “Did you at least read what I wrote to you inside on the dedication page of your journal?”

I nodded and opened the journal to read the page out loud. “Paps, with all my love, Merry Christmas. Remember, ‘a wound is a place where light can enter’. Love, your son, Andrew.”

Surprised by my sudden emotion, I paused and took out my handkerchief. "If that statement is true, then my soul is primed for an illumination."

Andrew jumped off the bench, and quickly turned to me as he grabbed my cigar, standing with it to enjoy a few slow inhales. "Then examine your life, Paps, answer those questions and put the past to rest."

I watched him becoming a man right in front of my eyes. Could this process really be the remedy to put the past to rest? I yearned for peaceful slumber again, I thought.

I took the book out of his hand and he gave me the cigar back with a smile. I tasted the soft tobacco again, caressed the cover of the journal, and opened it. I stopped to read the first question out loud. "As you come to the crossroads of life, how do you evaluate which direction to take, and how do lessons from your past influence your decision?"

Andrew looked proud. "You've got to love the premise of it all, Paps. The crossroads of life."

I felt defeated once more. "I don't know son. It seems like Monsignor O'Shea should have his students answer these questions. See this first question applies to you, not me. My crossroads are behind me; yours are ahead."

"Okay fair enough, but we've reviewed them already last semester," Andrew said. "This semester he wanted us to pick a mentor to help us with this decision, this crossroad."

I stood up and looked at him from head to toe, as he was clearly a whole foot taller than me with skates on. "Indeed, you are at a crossroad. Why give your life away to become a priest, kid? You're a handsome man, you could have any girl on campus I'm sure."

He approached me closer, standing in a challenger's stance. "I believe it's my destiny to help people and to be of service. Besides, I don't ever want to marry, not after what I've seen of your marriage."

I challenged back. "Oh, what does a bachelor like you know about marriage, good or bad?"

He grabbed more pinecones to toss into the creek. "Marriage is a topic both of us are clueless about, Paps. Go ahead, work on the questions. No matter what age a man is, it's important to understand God's destiny for us."

I sat down with the thought of my destiny and sighed. "God's destiny. Is that what those Jesuits preach to you? Being a lawyer wasn't my destiny, son. I was born into a literary family, an academic one. My mother was an English teacher, my grandfather in Ireland, as you now know for yourself, is a well renowned professor of literature at the Catholic University in Dublin and was a writer for the Dublin Times for decades." I pitched a few pinecones off into the creek and reflected for a minute more. "If God's destiny had a part in my life, I'd be writing or teaching along side my Pappy somewhere." I shrugged. "Hey, does the good Monsignor at Fordham teach that sometimes destiny takes a wrong turn for some men?" I asked.

"He tells us it's never too late for a man to chart his path, as it's orchestrated by God," Andrew said, standing tall, looking as if he was a part of nature itself.

The topic was beginning to irritate me. "Andrew, leave my destiny out of this. Why do you want to throw your whole life away, kid? Priests make no money," I said, with mounting frustration.

"Wanting money in the bank isn't going to guide my path," Andrew said. "Have you ever heard of a life with purpose?"

I laughed with a shrug. "Ah, a life with purpose. Frankl would like that. Well, if your teachers at Fordham want you to interview a faithful, purposeful man—that's not me. I gave up on God for good when he took your little sister away."

I kept the cigar firm between my teeth, zipped up my gray parka, walked over to the creek, where a slow current fought a freeze, and picked icicles from the branches of a nearby tree. As I tossed them one by one, like spears into the cold veins of the earth, I put my ego aside. "Kid, go ahead, I'm sorry. Send these two books to your G-Pap. To be honest with you, I have no clue what to write in this journal and these fucking fingers can barely hold an icicle, let alone a pen anymore. You won't even be able to read my handwriting anyway."

Andrew walked up to me with care on the sloped ground, and took both my hands into his, trying to warm them with his black gloves. "Don't you believe in wool gloves, it's the latest thing in winter apparel Paps?"

I looked away and pulled my hands from his grasp. "Do you know my fingertips have been completely numbed ever since…?" I couldn't go on with the awful memory. "Should never have let it happen. That fence should have been built last summer, God damn it all."

Silence passed between us for a few minutes as my son watched for my next move.

"You're not the only one who feels guilty." Andrew took some icicles to toss into the creek as well, looking down as he spoke. "I should have helped you build the fence like mom wanted. Instead, I was too busy, bogged down with those damn Latin classes all summer. I miss her so much," Andrew said, looking unsteady on the skates while he bent down to double knot the laces. "Even though she was half their size, Aisling was a better hockey player than any of Frankie's pals here."

I grabbed another icicle and heaved it as far as I could. "You've got that right. She was one tough cookie with the boys."

My son began to cry, but tried to hide it from me. "I'll skate for her today. Kick some little boys' asses just for her," he shouted as he slowly skated in reverse towards the others wiping off his tears with the glove on his hand. "It's the same reason you need to answer the questions in that journal, they're for you—not G-Pap. If you can't do it for yourself, then do it for my baby sis."

I watched my son, as he spun around, and skated away, with smooth movements of a figure skater, and wondered how to help him with his pains when mine were buried so deep—by putting pen to paper? Possibly, I thought.

As I stood next to the creek, rubbing my hands together nervously, trying like I did to bring feeling back to my fingertips, my mind flashed back to that dreadful morning last February.

The winter sun was unseasonably warm the day before the accident. Aisling always longed for the earth to thaw, so this day was no surprise when she followed the sun like the face of a sunflower. She was a vibrant soul, born straight out of the mountains she loved, never resisting a chance to saddle her American Paint horse, Delilah, to take for a run when the trails would start to soften.

My wife Sofia woke me up from the sofa that morning, hysterical. She told me that Aisling wasn't in her room and that she hadn't come down for breakfast.

Frantic, I grabbed my boots, put them on without lacing, and ran to the barn calling her name. Delilah stood in the middle of the open barn, sides heaving, fully saddled. Her reigns were broken, and my daughter's lone rubber boot hung from one of the stirrups. Crystals of ice covered her legs and belly, telling me everything I needed to know.

I spun and ran from the barn down the icy trail. The stream at the base of our property, next to the pond sparkled with the sunrise and whispered gently without regard for my fast beating heart. "Aisling, Aisling!" I called over and over. The voices of my wife, my son, Frankie, and my other daughter, Patti, echoed behind me in the distance.

Our calls went unanswered. The Bridgeport Valley foothills that always watched over my wild redheaded horse girl, stood as a quiet witnesses to our panic, while we all ran about calling her name.

Kitchi, my Paiute Indian ranch hand, found her. He raced to me from the trail, steam escaping his mouth. "Come quick, Mr. Quinn, and bring an axe." I ran back to the barn, grabbed an axe, and followed him down the icy black-rock trail, about the length of a football field.

We stopped at the edge of the pond, shaded by a row of century-old pine trees where the air felt twenty-degrees cooler. Kitchi pointed at the new pond that his crew dug out the previous spring, now filled with frozen subterranean mineral water.

My daughter lay submerged under large broken frozen ice sheets; only her tangled legs were exposed on the rocky edges. I braced my legs on the pond bed and swung the axe hard onto the ice, breaking through to the freezing water and wood branches beneath. Then I waded in, frantic and found her, head down, and lifeless. Her legs were covered in slimy silt, keeping me from getting a firm hold. Kitchi pulled at her feet without success, until I saw that her arm lay trapped between rocks. With my body almost fully emerged in the bed of water and ice, I struggled for thirty minutes, working to remove the slippery, muddied rocks holding her down.

After finally freeing Aisling from the underwater rubble, I placed her frozen body blackened by silt in the waiting arms of Kitchi.

He laid her down at the water's edge, and gave me his hand to help me out. Near to frozen myself, in shock, unable to utter any emotion or words, I took Aisling into my arms again, and carried her gently back up the path to the house.

Sofia cupped her mouth like a megaphone, shouting at me from the barn, "What is wrong with Aisling? Is she passed out? Declan, oh my God!" Her questions echoed, then she screamed, "Why is she not moving?" Her screams cut throughout the valley as she ran to meet me at the front of our house. I couldn't see Frankie, but could still hear him calling out for his sister from another trail in the distance.

"Frankie, get down here. Now! The trail is dangerous up there." I hated the sound of my voice yelling over the limp body of my eight year old as her twin sister, Patti, still in her pajamas, stood on the porch, and stared at us in shock. I walked past Sofia, having no gumption to look at her, carried Aisling into my office, and closed the door.

Kitchi stood, like a shaman guardian to intercept Sofia, now frantic to get through the door. "Mrs. Quinn, please. You don't want to see her like this."

I could hear Sofia yelling at him. "What are you telling me? Kitchi! What is wrong with my baby?"

I ignored them while carefully placing Aisling on a bearskin rug in front of the fireplace. I wrapped her in cream-colored wooly blankets from the sofa, wishing they were still warmed from my own body heat from the night before.

I whispered, teeth chattering, surprised by the weakness in my voice. "You need to wake up, darling. This isn't happening, not to you. Let's take Delilah up to Virginia Lakes once the pass opens again." I reached over her, carelessly tossing logs into the fireplace. Sofia pounded on the door, begging me to let her in. But I could hear nothing of the pain of others.

This was my doing. I believed my sins had taken my beautiful child's life.

With both of our bodies frozen, all that was left was the warmth of my love. There were only a few brief moments we had alone together while I wrapped her with care with more bearskins. I walked to the fireplace and frantically tried to get two logs to ignite. "Kitchi, get in here and start a good fire." I wetted my hand with the little spit in my mouth trying to remove the lava silt all over her lifeless face.

Finally, Sofia burst in through the back patio door, followed by the others.

Knowing my battle was lost, I held and rocked my child trying to speak without success through a worsening, frozen body. "Sofia, please. Keep the children away. This is all my doing. God help me. We've lost our angel. Have Kitchi start a fire and fetch Frankie; he's still up the path on Quinn's Crag, the ice is slippery up there, damn it."

Then I saw Frankie, he stood in the back of the room looking as frozen and pale as his dead sister. Sofia moaned deep guttural cries, and Patti burst into tears. I couldn't make them leave, so I simply coddled our child in my arms. Sofia in haste opened a closet and grabbed more blankets. She took black beads from the pocket of her gray wool sweater and tried to pray the rosary with Patti, as Frankie stood over us, mute, and unable to move or cry.

Soon, Kitchi brought warm washcloths for us to clean and dry our child. He wrapped my hands as well and gently removed my frozen clothing. "Frankie, run upstairs, bring your father dry trousers and a shirt," Kitchi whispered, and Frankie took off.

Sofia and I cleaned her as best we could, removed the frozen clothes, and wrapped her body in the blankets. I dressed with Frankie's help and went back to cradling my daughter.

Kitchi walked to my desk to make phone calls. After his calls were done, he opened up a wooden carved box he'd given to me for my birthday; it was overflowing, full of dried sage leaves. Grabbing a hand full of the herb, he placed them in the concave side of an oversized hollowed tree bark on my desk. Lighting the sage, he sanctified Aisling's body as the herb smoldered, softly guiding the smoke over her entire body with his hand. When finished with his ritual, he added more logs to the fire, put sage leaves in, and then walked outside to my deck. Here, Kitchi chanted monotone verses of ancient tribes, motioning to Frankie and Patti to join him. Their chorus cut into my soul, speaking to the chamber of sorrows in my heart.

After what seemed like hours of a family prayer vigil, Kitchi and my children came back inside with quieted steps to tell me the police were here along with the coroner to take the body. Accidents had to be investigated. It was the law.

It was then my memory returned to the horrific night before my thirteenth birthday, the night when police and firemen came to take away my mother. I held her withered body that night as well, trying to revive it, wiping away blood oozing from her neck. She was an Aisling as well, in name and in character. They were both wild in genius, and both stolen from us. Perhaps I cursed my daughter from the moment of her naming, I thought.

After the police questioned everyone and Aisling was taken away, I picked up the phone to call Don Marco. I told him I quit. My role as his Consigliere was over. He sent me a condolence card along with a truckload of imported red roses for Aisling's memorial services. The card reminded me I was part of the core Nusco family, and the truckload of roses—a symbol. I could never quit.

Nonetheless, I was done.

Unfortunately, in Don Marco's world, no one quits on him.

CHAPTER TWO

AN EMPTY SEAT AT THE TABLE

Once Thanksgiving had passed, about nine months after we lost our daughter, Marco became very persistent when I took his telephone call. "Hey Quinn, come the first of the year, I will be putting you on a special assignment, I have a file for you to review…" Of course he was oblivious to the fact that our Thanksgiving table was minus one seat this year and my mood therein was—well, mushier than Sofia's mashed potatoes. But nevertheless, he sent a driver and an enforcer over to the ranch to pick me up. The enforcer hugged Sofia. I watched her weeping in his arms and was astounded by how she could be so naïve.

So, determined to end things once and for all, I got into the limo after having stashed a loaded gun into the lining of my jacket. Sofia had no clue I was a man with a target on his back, no different than the others who tried to leave the family before me.

Knowing Marco usually put a hit on someone from the backseat, I decidedly told the enforcer to ride in front as I sat in the back. I asked the driver the usual questions to test the waters just to be sure I wasn't being taken for the long ride to the hereafter. "Hey Anthony, we're old friends, right? Why do you do this? I already told Don Marco I'm done. I don't want to see him. Not today, not tomorrow, not ever."

Anthony shrugged. "Just doing my job, Quinn—take my sympathies about your daughter, though. My wife and I are sorry for your loss." He kept driving and shared a look with the enforcer, who tipped his hat at me with a look of sadness.

I didn't speak of my daughter. She was a sacred topic, so much so, I rarely mentioned her again to anyone, least of all to goons like these guys.

The gates of my ranch were adorned with a green painted, oversized wooden carved Quinn Ranch signage, and were opened and shut manually. Once closing them after we exited, the driver sped up the highway northeast to the Nevada border, winding up the curving mountain roads to the lake area. When we arrived at Marco's eighteen-story casino, the men escorted me up the elevator to a floor-to-ceiling, glass-paned windowed, penthouse. Marco's opulence showed no restraint, as his home and offices occupied ten thousand square feet of the entire top floor. The windows overlooked white snow groomed ski slopes, which were carved between pine tree carpeted mountains, with a massive blue lake below.

Don Marco met me with his usual gratuitous embrace. He motioned to a handful of men who were hanging Christmas lights around the windows, and asked them to leave. "Ritorna in due ore, come back in two hours," he said in Italian, as they set down their tools and moved the ladders to the side. Anthony stood by the door and saw them out, but stayed inside the office to guard the entrance.

Marco attempted to talk to me, but the only thing to do was turn away, as I was unable to face more darkness. When I didn't return a cordial greeting, he kept one hand on my shoulder. "Listen, Quinn, we were all very sorry you will have to celebrate the holidays this year without your daughter…" Don Marco tried, but couldn't remember her name. He walked away to fix a strand of lights and adjusted a ten-foot tall Christmas tree near the window. I watched him fumble over his words. "Well, the holidays will be tough to…"

I interrupted and looked straight at him, poking my forefinger into his chest. "Take my resignation this final and last time, and don't ever speak of my daughter again." I stepped away and grabbed a cigar off his desk.

Marco walked over to me and grabbed my shirt collar. "I've been patient with you long enough, Quinn. You. Will. Never. Leave. This. Family."

I pushed his hand off me. "Yes. I will. And I'm out of here, it's over between us—been over for a while now. Besides, this isn't about a so-called special assignment you have; this is about moving forward after…" I hesitated to mention this forbidden subject. "After Ricco—you knew I was against what you did, but you went ahead with it in cold blood."

Marco, unshaven and quite possibly hadn't hit the shower yet that day, walked behind his desk and took a seat, put on his pinstriped suit jacket as if it were a suit of armor. Sauntering over to a vase full of red roses, he broke off one from its stem. Then he took a seat in his oversized black leather chair. "Time to move forward, you're right. But, Ricco was a traitor. You know that, and now you want to be drowned in the lake too?"

I may as well use that rose as my target, I thought and crossed my arms thinking to grab my pistol right then, but knew a futile attempt to assassinate him was senseless. "Take me out now," I said, giving him the go ahead so he wouldn't take it.

He placed a cigar into his mouth and spoke with it between his lips as he adjusted the rose onto his jacket collar. "No one, not even you, can leave the family of their own will." Pouring himself a tumbler of brandy out of a crystal decanter on his desk, he grabbed a box of matches. "I've got accounts that needed your review six months ago." He struck a match to feed the tobacco tip of his cigar and said, "I want the work done now, and you'll be happy to know huge money depends on this." He walked over to the windows behind his desk and looked out over the massive lake below. "What's up brother—must move on after a heartbreak, didn't you learn that in the war? Besides, I never took you to be a whiner."

He provoked me, so I responded in kind to display my sheer intent. The brandy decanter sat within my reach, so I clutched it in my hand and heaved it toward Anthony, still standing at the wood, double-door entrance. It shattered, exploding a dark reddish liquid over the white marble floor. "Hey brother, there's some more whining for you to clean up," I said, and started to walk out.

But he was neither finished talking nor impressed by my rage as Anthony instinctively pulled out his gun. "Stop it right there. We've been a team since the early days after the war. My family took you in when you were a homeless and helpless kid. My father let you live with us because Tino wanted you around. You owe Tino and the entire Nusco family. Hell, remember, my mother even nursed your sick ass and my father paid for your elite Fordham law degree."

I listened to his list, but had heard enough and raised my right hand. "Objection your Honor. The GI bill paid for that," I said, relighting my cigar.

Marco walked in haste over to a large file cabinet next to his desk and opened a long drawer as he shook his head. "Fuck. Shut the fuck up, you bastard child. You would have been a hapless orphan without my family. You will not leave this family, so get that through your thick Irish head." He opened a file and showed me its contents; it was filled with the names of members in the city council, local business owners, and state officials. My role in the past was to wine and dine such people before we set out on another scam numbers deal or property acquisition. Marco motioned to Anthony to open the door. "Now go home and forget this nonsense of yours, and come the first of the year, get back to work—you do care about keeping your loved ones safe?"

All I could do was to give him a cold stare. "Remember, we keep our families out of the business. This is between you and me."

He took advantage that it wasn't my style to turn him in. On top of the fact that another untimely death at Marco's fingertips would have alerted the detectives already investigating him. As for the last two years, they'd been sniffing around asking about our brother Ricco's so-called drowning at the fishing docks. They even questioned me several times if I was suspicious if Marco had any link to my daughter's accident.

But, he didn't know what I would do to save my family. If he involved them, he'd force me to use the solid evidence I've collected against him in the event that this day would come. After Ricco's murder, I had had enough. So, I took a day, maybe two, to gather all the evidence I could, copied photos that proved to the world that Marco Nusco was the one who orchestrated Ricco's death. I gathered ledgers and affidavits, collected over decades, of scandals and many other crimes and murders. I then opened a safety deposit box at an obscure bank in Virginia City, Nevada, and hid the key in a secret lining in my briefcase. As soon as I held the key, I felt less trapped as Marco's Consigliere.

In spite of this, I simply wanted to leave the family. Quietly. No police, no lawyers, no bribes, no jail, or death. But then again, Don Marco trusted no one, and held no reverence towards life, least of all, a happy one.

CHAPTER THREE

TEN QUESTIONS

Looking back, Andrew's assignment came at a good time, becoming the proverbial crossroad before me. I kept reading his journal questions over and over from my usual seat alongside the creek and pond. "As you come to the crossroads of life, how do you evaluate which direction to take and how do lessons from the past influence your decision?" His challenge worked like a life preserver, begging me to grab hold and be rescued out of the quicksand of grief and guilt.

On this day, I sat watching the boys' roughhousing and laughed as they passed a black disc back and forth across the ice while aiming for their makeshift goal of dried pine needles and tree bark. It was difficult to separate the fact that Aisling's accident happened no further than twenty yards away. Then, as if nature itself moved my pen, I wrote one line below Andrew's journal prompt. "Life passes us by while the wind carries the tune of the spirit, its melody deafens the sounds of the earth, giving me no answers." Amused with the line on the page, feeling as if roles had been reversed between my son and me, I thought, had we reached a pinnacle in our relationship when he gave me this challenge? I respected this test in a way, and was proud of his cleverness, but did he have to use me as his lab rat? Nevertheless, he coaxed this stubborn mule into his stall for a grooming and I was forced, at least at this juncture, to let him hold the reigns.

Flipping through the journal, it was clear there was no escaping these questions:

- What defines you as a man: Goodness, success, community, or service?

- What brings you happiness: Pleasure, purpose, work, or love?

- Is happiness found within you or from extrinsic rewards?

I laughed once again at the notion of sitting with this book to write down answers intelligent enough for a graduate research project. Tempted to immerse the book in the trout stream, I began to think back on the events of my life that pertained to his questions and wondered if God had a plan for me all along. I asked myself, were Andrew and Sofia merely playing out their roles in a grand cosmic scheme? Whoever was calling the shots in this team of plotters, they knew my current state of existence—a man on an express train to nowhere. Together, they had crafted a clever nudge to pull me back into this world.

I continued to watch the boys on the ice, as one of them shot the hockey puck into the creek. I set the journal down, walked onto the rocky edge, grabbed the black disk and tossed it back to them.

Sitting back on my stump, I read the rest of the journal prompts:

- Do your sufferings lead you towards humility or rebellion?

- Do you believe your body is a temple of the Holy Spirit or a temple of pleasure?

- Do your sufferings turn you away from God or do they unite you to the Holy?

- When faced with conflicts, do you confront them or flee?

- Do you believe that you make choices or do choices make you?

- What in life causes you restlessness? And it can't be hunger, thirst, or lust.

I knew I was doomed. I would have rather combed through the stacks of case law, scheme ways to falsify evidence of a crime scene, and present it to a stoic judge and jury than answer these questions. Perhaps my son would have accepted my pleading the Fifth and closed this case altogether, I hoped.

Then, as if this team of schemers wasn't enough to nail me to a cross, another player stepped in while I wasn't looking, sending me a message from a dimension out of reach. *Declan, peace lies in the quiet crevices in nature.* My mother's spirit spoke in the wind. *Listen to the wind, my dear son, the whispers float to you from the Celtic Sea. It's where your light shines, secret mysteries are hidden within, if you dare to listen.*

I listened to her voice in stride, as hearing it had become a daily occurrence. So, despite hearing voices and watching a melodrama going on in my head, I continued to observe the boys playing their hockey game, thankful they were unaware of my inner struggles. Could Andrew and Frankie see their father was going insane—listening to voices in the wind? Splashing my face with freezing creek water, I continued my constant effort to regain sanity, as just that morning over coffee, I begged my wife, "Let's sell this ranch and move to the East Coast, buy a pastry shop or something. You can bake your grandma's recipes to your heart's content."

Sofia always shook her head at my nonsensical pleas, unwilling to run away. "Declan, we cannot escape or forget. And how can we leave our baby behind, alone in the cold earth?"

She was right, we would never leave this ranch for that very reason. And even though I didn't deserve her, I knew I had married well, to a woman who refused to give up on me. I couldn't figure out why she had stayed steadfast thus far. At the time, all I did to fill my days was tend my horses, chop trees for firewood, and tutor my children with their homework assignments, but I barely functioned otherwise. One day, in a fit of rage from seeing Aisling's empty and quiet bedroom, I stripped the walls clean, no more wallpaper, no more walls laden of running horses to remind us.

But nevertheless, Sofia was always after me saying, "Return to the land of the living, and how can you let your law practice go to waste?" She is a beautiful, doting wife, with Mediterranean bronzed skin, and a figure that would often lure men to stare, despite knowing I had the power to kill them for it. Like all mafia wives, she understood there was no talk of business. She trusted me; grateful my work got our bills paid and could buy her pretty things, like new lavender silk drapes in the dining room.

On that morning Sofia walked toward me from the house with a smile on her face. Her refreshing authentic beauty always provoked me to soften. "Sofia, what gets you out of the warm house smiling like you've got mischief up your sleeve?" I made room for her on the large boulder and together we watched the hockey game.

She fixed her scarf and cuddled closer to me. "Oh, nothing," she said. "Just thought I would watch the boys with you. They're so full of life, aren't they? I love seeing them together, being brothers as if Andrew never left for college," she said with a sigh. "Oh how I wish Aisling were here so we could be a complete family again."

I sighed with her. "I know. A moment ago Andrew said she was a better hockey player than any of those rough boys out there."

"That she was," Sofia smiled again, watching the boys as she put on a pair of black knitted mittens. "Declan, I need to talk to you about Andrew. Are you going to give his journal a try? You know he's depending on your answers."

I shrugged. "I don't know if I could wrap my brain around his questions too well."

She turned to gaze at me. "Why not use them for your own benefit then? Perhaps a journal like that would help you to…" She stopped. "Look, we've both lost a child, but I see more pain in you and I know you hide your thoughts from me. Perhaps writing in a journal can be a private escape for you to sort out…" She stopped again.

I stood up, annoyed by her line of questions, and gave her the oversized boulder to sit on alone. "I don't know what you're talking about," I said, trying to avoid the obvious subject she was alluding to.

She began to tear up. "You bury feelings so deep, it hurts me to watch you most days." She looked at me with such sadness, that I couldn't bear to meet her gaze.

I tried to deflect her concern and laughed. "Look woman, stop reading those stupid psychology books, you're starting to sound like one of those Transactional Analysis experts—I'm Okay, You're Okay, give me a goddamn break, nobody's 'Okay' on this planet, that's my analysis," I said, as she simply sneered at me while I gathered some pinecones to toss.

Her tenderness quickly turned to anger. "Well, I can't disagree with you more. Jeez Declan, read it sometime. It would be nice if you tried little self-reflection for once. It might help you find out why you've grown cold in our marriage, why you've stopped working, and why you only relate to living creatures with four legs and a tail? Other than fishing this stream in the mornings, sitting on this lousy stump of granite, and helping the kids with their studies, you've tuned out completely, especially to me. We don't even share the same bed."

I knew she had me in a corner, so I added sarcasm to assist my defense. "You say I relate better to the kids and to animals, so what? I can't help it." I tossed two pinecones into the creek and walked over to a batch of frostbit heather on the water's edge, pulling out a handful for her. "Here, Sofia, these will look nice on your nightstand. You can think of me when you see them and pray on your rosary beads that I come back to your bed someday."

She stood up, dried her tears with her scarf, walked over, and then slapped me across the face. "Yes, I will pray on my rosary beads, but not for you. You're a miserable man and it's time I was done with you. Go back to the casinos with your nightclub singers or drive down to Hollywood to see your so-called clients there. I know you are star struck on that Hollywood diva. Judy Winslow is her name. Right, Declan? You don't think I see the records you listen to and the playbills all over your office with that beautiful woman pasted all over them?"

She had me cornered even more. "So I love listening to opera arias and going to a musical when I'm down south. Crucify me again, Sofia."

"You love her, I'm sure of it."

Sofia began to cry, tossing it with anger. "I want you to leave. Go to your diva," she said, and walked away.

I looked over to the pond to double-check that the boys couldn't hear us. Lowering my voice and said, "You don't know what you want. First you scheme with Andrew to inflict this goddamn existential analysis project on me, and now you want me to finish it on the streets? I have my office here. I have my work. Right here. There is no other woman, no diva."

She continued to cry and took a seat a few feet away on the bench under a large oak tree. "You're lying. You love her, your Starlight Ruby Girl," she said with jealousy. "I found the Hollywood entertainment journal in your office. Sorry, I have to snoop through your desk to get to know my husband. The Daily Variety quoted you, her biggest fan, Mr. Quinn, the casino affiliate who gave Miss Winslow her stage name, Starlight Ruby. She's used that name for a decade now. Tell me. How long have you known your Starlight Ruby Girl?"

Shocked she spoke of my beloved; I tried to play it down. "Okay, Sherlock. So I'm star struck by a singer. What of it? Ask any man if they don't fanaticize about a famous beauty of the stage or screen."

Sofia had heard enough, fixed her scarf once more, and stood to walk back to the house. "You know her. It's no fantasy and I'm no fool. I'll let you stay here long enough to finish your journal. Stay in your cave and come out just long enough for food like you always do. When you're done, go to her. I'm finished with you. Finished dreaming of us, while you dream of someone else."

I removed my hat and finger combed the thinning strands of hair on my head once more. "Sofia, you never believe me. There's no other woman, but I will leave as you ask. I need to handle important business in New York anyway, and I'd like to get away from Marco, the bastard has been on my ass…"

She interrupted me. "Marco should be done with you as well," she said, and started up the path.

I continued to yell at her as she walked away, without a care if the boys heard me or not. "I wish he were. You are so in the dark when it comes to that miserable brother of mine. Don't for a minute feel sorry for him," I said, kneeling down and splashed more icy creek water on my face.

She walked back down the path to meet me halfway, looked at the boys and whispered still angry. "Just finish the journal for Andrew. Don't put it aside. I couldn't care less what you do with your brother. This project must take first priority," she said, ending up back on the bench, taking the journal into her hands. "He picked out this beautiful gift just for you. You probably haven't noticed that its soft tan leather looks like your favorite saddle. Andrew searched everywhere to find you just the right one."

Rising from my gaze at the creek, I looked at Sofia holding the journal, feeling guilty that I almost soaked it into the creek a second ago. "Okay, I promise. I will work on those questions for my boy. It's quite the step he's about to take. A priest of all things."

She calmed down thinking about our son. "Yes, it is and I know he will be an excellent one. A true man of God, unlike his father."

I put my hat back on, fixing it low over my brows and shook my head. "I can't agree with you more on that Sofia." I looked at my boys playing and couldn't get the word "decent" out of my head.

She softened, and walked closer to me. With rosy cheeks and snow chips in her curly auburn hair, I was afraid another slap was coming, so I turned aside. Instead, she took my face between her hands and stared into my eyes. "Perhaps within those pages you can begin to search inside your soul and come back to our marriage," she said, with pleading tenderness. "Then we'll see if the light comes back to those dead, deep emerald eyes again."

"Ouch!" I said, and gasped as I took her hands into mine to peal them away from my face. I knew she didn't realize her words had cut into me like the freezing cold in my bones. By saying my "dead eyes," she didn't know how they once danced with the green grasses of Ireland in them or how when my mother, whom she never met, used to sing to me, "Greenies to greenies," with eyes full of hope. She didn't know anything of this sweet memory, as I had never told her. But on this day, Sofia was there, holding my face in her hands, pulling me back into this harsh world. I tried to pull away from her. "Sofia, all I want is peace. Peace. Can you please give me that?"

She persisted. "I will, if you do the work Andrew has given you. Have you even opened the books yet?"

I stood straight, pumped my chest, and opened the journal. "Yes, I have. Look, one line. Happy now? Does this pass your inspection?"

She stood next to me, looked at the page and grimaced. "It's a start," she said. "Declan, you ask for peace. Okay," she said, patting her eyes dry again. "But I have one more question before I go and let you retreat to your cave." She paused to inhale fresh mountain air. "Who is Shannon? I have heard you cry for her in your sleep more than once."

I tried to pull my cap down again, far over my eyes this time. "Please stop. First you accuse me of being in love with a Hollywood diva, and now it's about someone else?"

She shrugged. "Just tell me who is Shannon."

I turned away, unwilling to answer. I couldn't tell Sofia or anyone about how I had abandoned my only sister—of how I let the last morsel of my family disappear from my life. This was a secret I tried to forget myself. No one needed to know the truth, I thought.

"Please, Declan. I don't want to argue, not here in such a sacred spot. I just wish for once you would be honest with me, but I see it's no use." She turned away and clapped her hands together, calling for the boys to clean up for lunch. I heard her crying as she walked back up the path to the house. I heard, but couldn't comfort her.

Instead, I opened my journal and wrote down a few notes.

Shannon. Light back into my dead eyes. Greenies to greenies. I thought I had forgotten the happy memories of our childhood. I thought I had forgotten all of it. Forgotten who I was—who I am. What I did. Forgotten about the path God once destined for me.

I hoped it was not too late to remember.

CHAPTER FOUR

PANDORAS BOX

Sofia's lunch bell rang, echoing off the mountains, reminding us men that our stomachs needed a dose of her warm meatball, sautéed green peppers, and mozzarella sandwiches. Frankie and his buddies darted into the house after throwing their ice skates onto the front porch, as they each took turns pulling on Patti's long braided pony tails while she quietly played on a redwood swing.

When she began to cry, Andrew walked straight into the kitchen, stirred the gravy for the sandwiches, and kissed his mother on the cheek. "Paps, you've got to stop Frankie and his goons from teasing her all the time. I used to get my ass kicked for doing shit like that around here."

Sofia removed her Christmas apron and finished stirring the meatballs, as she pretended to ignore me. "And you would get your mouth washed out with soap for using language like that in this house too," Sofia said, putting her apron over Frankie's head while pinching his cheek hard. "Frankie, go wash your hands, serve your buddies, and leave your sister alone for once."

Refreshed from the morning air, yet still feeling angst over the journal and Sofia's interrogation, I interrupted Andrew chatting with Frankie's friends at the table, "Come on, Drew, bring our lunch into my office so we can talk." I waited for him to follow me down the hallway as the aroma-enhanced steam lifted off the plate of sandwiches, and closed the door after he entered. "Your mother calls this my cave, but I manage to get some work done in here."

"This food looks great." Andrew said. He put down the platter on my desk and grabbed my worn pitcher's glove and an ancient looking baseball off the shelf. His habit was to toss a baseball into it hard whenever we sat and talked in my office. He flipped through the journal he gave me and checked my meager progress. "Can you get this back to me in a month?" he asked. "I have to present my graduate capstone project the last week in May."

I thought with Sofia and Marco on my ass, getting out of town might be a perfect plan. "Come to think of it, maybe I'll hand deliver my answers to you next week. A trip back east might be good timing, as your mother is getting sick of me hanging around here."

"Right, I noticed. Why was she crying?" he asked.

"Aw, she has some crazy ideas in her head, kid," I said.

"Well, if I could find a good woman like that, I'd sure treat her better than you do."

I grabbed a sandwich and took a healthy bite. "Oh, Mr. Priest-to-be, are we an expert on woman now?" I cleaned my mouth with a napkin and tried to steal the baseball.

Andrew protected the ball in the glove. "Look Paps, stop messing with me on the priesthood. Write your answers. Come to Fordham anytime. I'll show you around New York, better yet, you can show me the backstreets of the Lower East Side. If you come in the spring, we could take in a baseball game on campus or see the Yanks if they're in town. I might even try to swing a bat at one of your pitches off the mound at Fordham's Coffey Field."

"Ha," I laughed sitting down to finish my meal. "I see your grand plan now, it's about revenge. You still hate how you could never smack one of my curve balls."

His hand was massaging the ball in the leather glove like he was readying to put his plan into first gear. Sounding annoyed he said, "No, I gave up on that curve years ago. My only agenda is an A grade on this capstone project." He tossed the ball at me harder than I expected and I scarcely caught it in my bare hand. My son was raised on a horse ranch and was used to dealing with stubborn mules and wayward sheep, so I was not surprised when he pressed the journal issue again.

"Paps, there's a reason I chose you to be my interviewee, as it's no secret that you haven't practiced law for more than a year, fitting the mode of a man who's in search for meaning. Besides, how does

Uncle Marco allow you to hide in this cave so long anyway?" he asked taking a seat in my office chair to eat his lunch. When finished absorbing a few quick bites, he swung the chair around to look at my book selection on the shelves behind the desk.

Annoyed, I began to take a few bites of the food and sneered at him. "Let me handle your Uncle Marco. He is not who you think he is."

He took off his sweatshirt and hung it over a chair. "Don't cut me short on smarts, Paps, Italian gangsters never did fit your style. I'm not a punk teenager anymore, if you've noticed. Maybe I know more about your business than you think."

I got annoyed even more when he tried to get me to speak about my work. "Oh yeah? So what is it you think you know?"

"Well, I know Uncle Ricco was an avid fisherman and an excellent swimmer. He used to take me out on the lake for hours. You told us that he drowned accidentally. Come on, Paps, save the storytelling for Patti, Mom, and the cops." He took another mouthful of his sandwich.

I stopped him short. "You may be all grown up, kid, and a bit of a showoff, but you're off base. Watch it or I'll kick your ass back to Coffey Field right now. We will not speak of Ricco again. Got it?" I grabbed the glove and placed the ball in it, glaring at him until he nodded. Seeing him defeated on the subject of Ricco, I changed topics. "Are you going to start in center field again once the season gets going?"

"No. Last season coach put me on the bench and let the new starters take my spot, so I decided to focus on my studies for my last term," Andrew said. "As I told you, a group of us seminarians are going abroad this summer in Ireland. Come along with us, Paps, you can hang out with Monsignor O'Shea."

I shrugged. "Oh, that would be an odd combination, a priest would laugh coming face to face with this gangster."

Andrew was combing through a few books on the shelf. "No Paps, you're wrong, and hard-headed as usual. He helped me so much last spring semester after Aisling died, as a matter of fact. All the kids around campus bring him their problems. He's quite popular. I think he could really help you process what happened to Aisling, too. Do you know he was a Navy Chaplain on the Midway in the war? He would help you like he did for many tough guys…" Andrew fell silent. He noticed my copy of Frankl's, *Man's Search for Meaning* on the bookshelf and took it down. "So this is your copy. The one you said you marked up and had Frankl sign?"

I looked at him as if he just grabbed one of Sofia's fine china pieces. "Yes it is, his signature is right there, on the dedication page, and no thanks on introducing me to your Monsignor. Aisling is gone. No theologian can use his apologetics to get her back. I think it's best I leave my struggles here on this ranch for the land to settle."

He looked defeated, but then his eyes lighted up flipping through the book. "Do you mind if I keep this and use your notes for my thesis?" he said, as the book's loose handwritten notes fell out and onto the floor. "Shoot, I'll pick these up. Wow, you've written notes all over these pages. Nice—I didn't know you had it in you."

Together we fetched the random papers off the floor. "Sorry kid." I took the book and notes out of his hands. "This doesn't leave my office. It's precious to me. Like I told you, I read it right after the war in the same halls where you study. Everyone in the City was reading its account of the death camps in Auschwitz." Annoyed by his cockiness I asked, "What do you mean, you didn't know I had it in me? What did you think I did while at Fordham, is magna cum laude not good enough for you?"

In disbelief he walked over to look at my degree, framed on the wall. "Sorry about that, you just never act…"

I interrupted. "Like a show off?"

"Right, sorry about that." He asked graciously to look at the pages again, then flipped through it some more. "The salvation of man is through love and in love," he said, quoting Frankl.

"Yes, it's an amazing read, son. I'm impressed your Jesuit professors are using a Jewish man to teach about life, love, and suffering." He handed the book back to me and I read an underlined phrase out loud. "The angels are lost in perpetual contemplation of an infinite glory," and as I said the words, I imagined my mother holding Aisling in infinite glory somewhere in the heavens.

To cover up my sudden emotion, I walked to a wood stack next to the fireplace and threw two logs onto the fire adding two sage leaves to scent the room.

Still trying to sell his assignment to me, my son said, "Dad, when you flip through your journal, you will see I included the reading list and syllabus. We take three variables in life using the letter C. Monsignor O'Shea calls it the Three Cs Project: Conflicts, Choices and Crossroads. I plan to use your journal entries to formulate my thesis paper, so please be honest and consider the three Cs when you're writing your responses."

"The Three C's. Yes, I saw the outline. Interesting. Don't fret kid. I may not be a good father or husband these days, but give me a graduate school research project and I promise to come through for you," I said, and opened the journal. "See, I have one whole line completed already."

"Ooo la la, one line Paps. And you've only had this for a whole week already." Andrew smiled, but looked worried.

"Relax. I'm enjoying the notion analyzing my life's crossroads. I know you are definitely at one," I said. "Don't worry. I got this. Just for you. And count on me to be there when you present your capstone project as well."

Andrew put several notes back into the book and returned it to the shelf. Sitting with his lunch again, he blotted extra sauce with the end of a roll to finish his plate clean and smiled. "Great. Thanks, Paps. You'll do fine with the questions, I'm sure of it. My whole life I've watched you help people with their problems as they came in here with their heads hanging low. Every time, they'd walked away with their chins up and smiling. You can say this very room is a Three C's laboratory, so now you can help me with the decisions I'm currently making."

I listened and hoped to help him, but he was still ignorant about my work. "Son, I'm flattered, but this is no Three C's lab," I said with a laugh. "You need to know the truth about the sanctity of this office, all I did in here was find ways to manipulate evidence and scheme ways to advance our businesses. My job was to defend corrupt and immoral men in the court of law. Men whose minds worked with such evil, you would be astonished to hear them speak their thoughts out loud. My life's work must be far from what your professors are looking for."

Andrew finished drinking down a tall glass of milk. "On the contrary. It makes you a perfect specimen."

"Yeah, right," I said, pretending to fix my hair. "Cut me up in your experimental lab if you think it's helpful. Your life is all ahead of you. The last thing I want is for you to make the same mistakes I made at your age."

"Mistakes, regrets," Andrew said, and sighed. "You don't have to be your age to reflect on regrets," he said, taking the glove and ball into his hands again. "Dad, what I find astonishing is that you don't see how I am the one with regrets."

"Regrets? What on earth does a kid like you have to be regretful about?"

He shrugged. "Regrets over not being here to help build that fence for starters. I was gone, three thousand miles away at school, and lost my little sister. Have you ever stopped to think how we all have pains when it comes to regrets and mistakes?"

I stood corrected. "Yes, of course, I have. Losing our precious gem hit us all terribly hard. I know I've been an awful father and a worse husband. Your mother is finished with me as she should be. I hear her weeping at night. Do I offer her any comfort? How can I comfort you or anyone when I can't even help myself?"

Not wanting him to see the tears welling in my eyes, I walked over to the record player and started the turntable. "This is how I deal with my pain on most days, give it a try kid, and let's take our minds to a better place. Let me play you songs from a special friend of mine." Careful to adjust the arm, I placed the needle on the edge of a record, easing it into a groove on the black vinyl surface. "The voice of this woman is straight from heaven."

Together we listened, the aria taking me back as I breathed in the sage scented oxygen from the crackling logs in the fireplace.

Andrew's eyes beamed at me and he frowned a bit. "So is this the woman Mom thinks you're in love with? She says you have a crush on some nightclub girl in Reno or Hollywood somewhere."

When I didn't answer, Andrew took a seat in front of the turntable. "She does sound straight out of heaven," he said, staring at the black vinyl record spinning on the turntable. "Paps, you've made Ma good and jealous listening to this voice over and over. Are you aware of that?"

"Her name is Judy." I answered and pointed at the record cover.

He picked it up, reading out loud, "Judy Winslow. The Starlight Ruby from Positano, Italy—Live."

"Her fans call her Starlight Ruby. I knew her starting from when I was a boy living in Brooklyn. But, it's been a long while since I last saw her."

Andrew adjusted his chair, looking troubled. "Ma has good cause to be worried—she's a beauty." He stared at the record cover and flipped it over to see the list of songs. "Paps, I'm sorry to snoop—but, last night I couldn't sleep, so I came in here looking for you. I thought I'd find you with Kitchi near the fire, smoking cigars as usual. Instead I found you sleeping on the sofa, tossing your head on a pillow. You were in a deep dream or something."

"I remember. We chatted and had a shot of my finest cognac together, didn't we?"

"Yes, but do you remember how I startled you at first—you jumped up acting as if I had roused a bear out of hibernation, shouting another woman's name. 'Shannon. Shannon, stop crying so loud, Shannon?'"

"I do remember; you're lucky I didn't beat you silly."

Andrew crossed his arms. "Who is she, Paps, this Shannon in your dreams?"

I took back the album cover and looked once again at Judy in her ruby velvet gown.

"And I hope I didn't get you into trouble with mom, told her about it last night after it happened. You just were acting so weird, you scared me."

Annoyed once again. "You told mom I shouted out another woman's name. Great. Thanks, kid."

"So, who is she?"

I shook my head. "No one. It was just a nightmare. Nothing to tell."

"Dad, there's more to it than that. Mom says you've been having the same nightmare over and over lately. Always calling out the same name. She's someone important to you, but you refuse to talk about it. Don't you think it's time you come clean? You say you're a decent man, but a decent man doesn't need to keep secrets from the people who love him."

The word decent cut into me, like rousing a dead man in his grave, making me catch my breath.

Andrew's eyes stared into mine as he tried a rival tactic on me once more. "You need to trust me, man to man for once. Just tell me the truth." His arms remained crossed. "Who is this Shannon?"

The suspicion in his voice made me want to protect my innocent sister. "She's your aunt, my baby sister." The truth poured out of me. I sat down hard in my chair, shocked that I spoke of her to another human being. "It's a tragic story, son, if you must know. We were separated as kids, she was seven and I was thirteen. I've spent most of my life trying to forget about her, pushing aside countless memories," I said, staring at a framed picture over the fireplace. "It was your G-Pap who stirred it all up in my brain again, by sending me this sketch last year. It arrived here in a huge crate while you were off at Fordham last spring semester."

Andrew walked over to the fireplace and stared at the sketch for a long time. "I had no idea this came from him. It's mysterious looking, looks like a young boy in the midst of battle or something. Powerful. Where did G-Pap find it?"

"Your Grandmother Aisling drew it. She didn't have paint or colors, so she used the black coal out of the stove. This drawing was done many years ago, back when we all lived in a tenement on the Lower East Side."

"Sounds like there's a story to tell here," Andrew said, getting comfortable on the chair opposite my desk.

I nodded with a sigh. "Yes, it's a story. A very tragic story." I took the arm off the turntable and Judy's voice stopped in mid-stanza. Appropriate silence filled the room. "That piece of art arrived the month after we put your sister into the ground. Your mother thought it was a picture of Aisling. But I said, 'No. It's me.' My mother drew it when I was a boy."

"How old were you?"

"I was eight."

Andrew stood up and stared at the picture. "Gosh Paps, that's the same age as Aisling when she died. She looked just like you at that age. Gives me goose bumps all over." Andrew looked from me to the drawing and back again in amazement.

"Yes, it gave us all goose bumps when we first saw it." I told him. "My grandfather had no clue it would have had such an impact. He was simply clearing out his office, sent us art, relics, poetry books, and maps he had collected from all over Ireland. He retired from teaching at the Catholic University in Dublin last spring. Can you imagine he worked well into his eighties? You know now, he's back on his farm in Fethard, County Tipperary. This piece decorated his office at the University. I had forgotten my mother drew me at that age. When I saw it, all the memories, mostly sad ones, started flowing again."

"The memories of Shannon, too?" Andrew asked.

I nodded. "Yes, like Pandora's Box. Memories that were locked, I thought for good, began to surface. Shannon was the sweetest little sister, just like your baby sister—precious and beautiful to everyone who saw her. I protected her all the time. It was my job."

"Just like I did for my little sis—until…" Andrew said.

"Stop it with carrying any guilt about your sister," I said, taking his arm to console him. "Son, your relationship with your sisters is very reminiscent of Shannon and mine. But your childhood was a happy one. Yes or no?"

"Yes, for the most part, Paps. You could have been around more, I guess."

"Ah," I interrupted, "For Boy Scouts, baseball games, track meets. Right? I missed many of those. Guilty." I opened the cigar box on my desk, grabbed one out and smelled its fragrant tobacco leaves. "Well, if you want to hear my story, it begins with a very unhappy childhood, that is—until we moved away from my abusive father. Before those days, we'd hide under the bed or in the closet when our father would go on a rampage. Some nights, he'd force himself sexually on our mother and I would try to protect Shannon and distract her by telling stories of us playing on the moon together or on the fields of Ireland with our Pappy. 'Shannon, look at the moon,' I'd say, 'Let's pretend we are on the dark side of the moon where he will never find us…"

Andrew shook his head and frowned. "A sister? The dark side of the moon? I remember you used to have us look at the dark side of the moon all the time while we went camping. Paps, your life is such a mystery."

I walked over to the picture and stared at it. "Drew, I'm not a mystery. Those days are just too painful to remember. We had a tough life living in a tenement. My sister and I slept in the same bed and we'd hide under the covers, as I'd sing our mother's lullabies softly into her ear. 'Sing to me, of the fields in Ireland like mommy does, sing to me Declan like mommy. Tell me again about St. Declan's Wells with the magic waters,' she'd say with her sweet green eyes staring at me."

I walked behind my desk and sat, feeling the sadness of those times all over again and unbuttoned my wool cardigan and took it off, as my body heat began to rise. "Andrew," I said, and took in some fresh oxygen. "I had buried all the memories, kept them in a vault in my head nice and tidy. Then that picture arrived, at first we couldn't decide where the sketch should hang. Your mother wanted it placed over the grand piano in the living room where we could all admire my mother's artwork, but I negotiated to put it in my office over the fireplace here. But now, I look at it alone. Big mistake. It's like sitting in the dark with Shannon all over again as the ghost of my mother stares back at me night after night."

After the picture arrived, I started to flashback on the terrors of my childhood, and then, just like you saw last night, my nightmares began. Seeing the black charcoal sketch transported me to a place long forgotten. I remembered my mother, in her unbridled beauty drawing my portrait in our rat-infested apartment. As she drew the picture, she asked me to stand like a triumphant warrior. She caught the fierce look on my face that early morning when I stood over the passed-out body of my drunken father, wanting to beat him for what he did to my mother. The picture showed blades of tall black grass in place of my father's body lying under my boot.

"Dad, I can't stop looking at it," Andrew said, bringing me back to the moment. "You look war torn, yet victorious. It's beautiful. It almost makes me want to change my mind about the priesthood and give you a grandson who would look just like that boy."

The thought made me smile. "Now you're talking. Give me a grandson who plays baseball, and I will give you a hundred solid bricks of gold."

CHAPTER FIVE

THORNS

Andrew took a tour of my office as if he had looked at the walls for the first time. Next to my mother's sketch of me was another black and white picture. "So what's the story behind this eerie picture, Dad?" he asked, looking at another family heirloom from Ireland. "You as a child warrior goes as a great pair next to this old photo of some castle, is it from Ireland?"

"Yes, I have had that piece ever since I was a boy too. In fact, it belonged to my Pappy, but unfortunately, was stored, covered under my bed when I lived with the Nuscos. I bought this ranch because the landscape was the same, minus the castle on the hill of course."

He looked back and forth at the photo and the drawing. "Why did your mother make you look like a warrior?" he asked, intrigued.

Reluctant to tell the history of my life in much detail, I shrugged. "The story is not a pleasant one, but in light of your existential research paper, I suppose you should hear it. It's not something I ever planned to tell you. Our family history is nothing to be proud of—except, that is, for the remarkable artist who drew this." I paused, resolved to move forward, at least for the history books, I thought. "I suppose my mother's choice the night she drew this was to restore order out of the chaos we lived in. Viktor Frankl would have been proud of her that night, as you see my father was a drunk, a jealous drunk—and she'd been…" I took a breath, opened the box on my desk filled with dried sage leaves and removed a few. Taking in more oxygen I continued. "She'd been beaten up and practically raped by his bar buddies the night she sketched that picture of me," I said, taking a seat, feeling suddenly ill.

Noticing the fire burning low, I got up, put the sage leaves on the logs and walked outside to grab more wood, using it as an excuse to stall. I took more time to light my cigar, steeling myself before returning to supply the fire. When I returned, Andrew was there, waiting for me to finish the story, and I saw in his eyes that I must.

My sweater was thrown haplessly on the desk, so I folded it then dried my head with a handkerchief and continued. "My father drank most of what he earned and often ran afoul of the law. Whenever he was in jail, we stayed at the convent at the local church. Seeing our dire situation, a kind parish priest offered my mother a job teaching English at the school, so she now earned money to feed and clothe us on her own. One of the times my father got out of jail, he picked us up at the convent with a new suit on, all clean-shaven and sober. It gave us hope. The nuns helped us pack and sent us home. But, as soon as we entered our stagnant smelly apartment, he started in again with his true self. 'Goddamn it woman. This apartment stinks of dead rats and mice. Where the hell have you been for thirty whole days?' he said. Then later that night, he got good and drunk at the speakeasy in the basement of our building. The night my mother drew the sketch of me was the same night his buddies practically raped her."

"You were just an eight year old kid and witnessed this?" Andrew asked.

I rolled my eyes. "Yes, Shannon and I saw things children should never see." But the telling was becoming easier than I thought, so to entertain my son, I decided to use my father's German accent to tell the story in character. "Drew, bet you didn't know I could speak some German. 'Sie haben mich im Gefangnis wie ein gemeinsamer Dieb. They put me in the jail like a common thief,' my father said and continued, 'You all better watch yourselves or they will nab you in that paddy wagon, too!'"

Andrew listened fully, and took a seat, so I continued with the storytelling, standing up, using the layer of bricks in front of the fireplace as my stage. "'Hey, is that my beautiful Irish wife and my rat ass son?' he asked us as we entered the bar. 'My first day home and you leave all day to teach snot nose kids English.' He grabbed my mother, putting an arm around her. 'What about me, Aisling? I haven't seen a woman in thirty days, damn it. Goddamn. Goddamn. Sie haben mich im Gefangnis wie ein gemeinsamer Dieb. They put me in the jail like a common thief. I told you, Aisling, I'd give you the moon. Now finally here you are.'"

I sat down at my desk, opposite Andrew, and continued telling him the accounts of this night; it felt both strange and purifying to tell the stories. "I tried to pull my mother away, but some men pushed me aside and I fell on the spit-drenched floor. Mother twisted away from my father and placed my two-year old sister into my arms. 'Declan, upstairs quick, take Shannon to Signore Aimerito's.' I stood holding my little sister, scared, with my heart pounding out of my chest, but I didn't want to leave my mother behind. 'I am Axel Hauser, a master craftsman, not a common thug. Goddamn, goddamn.' He grabbed my mother's wrist then turned his back to take another gulp of bootleg wine."

The words flowed out of me, as Andrew sat as my captivated audience. "Andrew, accents were a part of my surroundings as the whispering winds blowing through the pine trees around here. So allow me to use my mother's delightful Irish accent to tell her side of this story." I took a moment and walked over to her drawing as if it were a shrine of worship. 'Declan, go now. Take Shannon upstairs,' my mother was frantic to get us out of harm's way, so I ran, doing as I was told, climbing to the third floor to leave Shannon with our neighbor. Then hurried back down to the bar. Like mother, I just wanted to get him home before the paddy wagon came to incarcerate him again. She whispered into my ear. 'I need to get Daddy home, Declan, and then we can feed him a big bowl of Signora Aimerito's noodles and gravy. Wait outside, I'll be out with him in a minute.'"

"Nice Irish accent," Andrew said, staring at me in amazement.

"Some accents you never forget," I said.

"What did you do next?" Andrew asked with rapt attention.

"I waited outside. My mother didn't come out of the speakeasy for a lot longer than one minute. She didn't come out for what seemed like an eternity. Men were stumbling in and out of the front and side doors to either have a smoke or to use the piss holes in the alley. I knew she wouldn't have forgotten about me in the street. So I worked my way back into the bar through a crowd of smelly men in suits and work clothes. Some of them accidently burned me with the butts of their cigarettes. It was so dark inside, all I could do to find my mother was to listen and follow the gruff voice and dialect of my father.

They were at a table in the corner lit dimly by candlelight. My father and four other men were hugging my mother as she tried to wiggle away. 'Ich würde dir den Mond geben, wenn du mir dein Herz gäbst, I will give you the moon if you will give me your heart,' he repeated that over and over as the men formed a circle around them clapping their hands above their heads." I walked back toward the fireplace, standing in front of the burning fire and sage smoke. "The men were grabbing at my mother and she slipped and fell. Then they took turns lying on top of her, rocking their bodies, on the filthy floor and grabbing her breasts, kissing her hard on the mouth, tongues and all. They drank some type of liquor putting the glass up to her lips forcing her to drink. When she spit it out, a few drops landed on me. I put my mouth to my arm to taste it and wondered how my father could love this awful drink so much.

Seeing all this, I shouted at the top of my lungs one of the few German words I knew. 'Halt! Halt! Please, father, please come home. Don't you see they're hurting mommy?'" My throat was strained from using their accents, so I decided to end the story and started to go outside for some fresh air.

"Dad, please. You can't end here," Andrew said.

I proceeded, but felt drained. "There's not much else to tell. She just sat down on the spit-dirtied floor and cried. When we finally exited the side door where the outhouses stood in their stench and filth, my mother wobbled out, trying to cover herself with her dress torn to pieces. She was shaken, but had enough strength to put her head over one of the four stinking piss holes in the alley, and coughed violently to vomit several times into it."

I stopped the story momentarily and reached for my journal to jot down these few words: We feel the thorns of the past. We remove them with the telling.

Andrew watched me with a curious and sympathetic look. "Jesus, Paps. That's rough. And you say that boy warrior sketch was drawn that same night?"

I shrugged. "The boy warrior, thanks kid. I like the sound of that. Yes, you can say I was a boy warrior that night. When my father finally came home that night, it was late, and he was obviously very drunk. I lay in my bed with the terror of it all, awake, and furious with him. He tried to kiss my mother again, so I jumped out of bed and began to punch him in his gut and legs over and over. He was so drunk I actually knocked him down, all sixty pounds of me, and then he passed out."

Andrew interrupted. "That's when your mother's existential genius came out?"

I laughed with an aching heart. "Yes, she was indeed an existential genius, son."

"Do tell. You may as well throw in the accent while you're at it," Andrew said.

With reluctance once more, I cleared my throat. "Sure kid. Happy to entertain you, albeit keep in mind, this telling is no Hollywood movie scene. I'm reenacting a painful memory, buried for almost half a century for good reason."

Andrew walked over to the journal, opened it and read my note out loud. "We feel the thorns of the past. We remove them with the telling."

"Thank you for the reminder. Let me give this my best shot, will you be here to stop me if I decide to shoot myself from this telling?"

"Tell the story Paps. If not for yourself, tell the story for your mother's sake, for the history books if nothing else."

He was right. This history must be told in my mother's honor. With Marco on my ass, who knows how long I would be alive to do the telling, I thought. So I relented, and got into character once more and took the stage.

"Okay, are you ready son?"

"Ready Paps, thanks."

I cleared my throat and continued. "'Oh, Declan, look at you, my brave son. You are a valiant warrior, an Irish rebel straight from my father's flesh and bones. You are so much like Pappy. You look like him, think like him. Why you even stand like him in this, your moment of triumph. He would be so proud to see how you protected your mother tonight.' I admit, I was proud, but I was still afraid for her, so I begged her to leave. 'Mommy, let's go back to the convent. Let's call Pappy to come get us.' But she would have none of it, saying as she dried her tears, 'you are so brave, Declan. Oh, if only I had paint and brushes, I would paint you in glorious color, victorious, having won the valiant battle over the Giant Axel of Orchard Street.'" She smiled then grabbed some charcoal from the kitchen stove. 'I have no paint, but I can still capture that look and send it to Pappy. Don't move,' she said, and began drawing. She walked over to our bed to check on Shannon, and then she returned to the kitchen and sat at the table to draw. I couldn't tell if the look on her face was of brilliance or insanity at the time.

"No, not insanity. Genius," Andrew said.

I looked at my son with affection, and then continued. "Do you think he's gonna die?" I asked my mother.

She laughed. 'Do the dead snore? He's passed out from the drink is all, but you did good to fight for your mum. Declan, I'm sorry you had to see all what went on in the bar.' She had me pose with a broomstick in my hand as she finished her drawing, then told me to pretend I was David after killing Goliath."

"I bet Grandma Aisling would have loved the Three Cs Project, she found a way to be happy even within her toughest struggles. She was at a crossroad and chose love." Smiling now, Andrew turned to write down notes at my desk.

"Yes, I suppose she did. I never thought about that awful night like that. I just wanted him dead. Perhaps your Grandma should be your thesis subject. Why don't you take this sketch with you to use as a prop for your capstone presentation?"

"That's not a bad idea," Andrew said, but got more serious. "How did she die? All you've told me is that she died too young."

"Too young, that's for sure, she was only thirty-three. She was all of those things you just described: an artist, teacher, and a genius. Killed by a stupid fucking drunk."

"You mean your father?" Andrew asked as he took off his baseball cap.

"Yes, him. He killed her, son. He kidnapped Shannon and my mother from our safe house and then killed her that same night."

"My God. Dad, why didn't you tell me? I never knew any of this. That's awful, awful," Andrew said, standing up to pace the floor. "I'm so sorry. Does Mother know any of this?"

I returned to sit at my desk, crossed my arms with conviction. "Nope. I never wanted to burden her or you kids. It was my tragedy to carry, not your mother's, and definitely not yours."

Andrew came back to the seating area in front of my desk. We sat in quiet for a while. He jotted down some notes and I got up to play the record again.

"Didn't you say Grandma's buried at the cemetery at Old St. Patrick's on the Lower East Side?" Andrew asked.

"Yes. The last time I was there was just before I left for the war." I paused to fix the needle on the record and wondered if it was time to make that trip. "Oh, and how I love that you are calling her Grandma by the way." I paused and walked over to the minibar to pour myself a drink. "The cemetery—that's a tough spot to visit. But, it's time to go again. Maybe you can meet me there when I go, perhaps as early as next week."

"Yes, of course. I'd love to do that. You can also take me on a tour of the Lower East Side, okay?"

I picked up the phone to call the airlines. "A nice tour is in order then. I will catch a plane in L.A. one day next week after sending you off for school. I'm hoping the church has records to help me find my sister."

"Aunt Shannon, right?"

"Yes, Aunt Shannon to you, son."

Andrew closed his notebook with excitement. "Great. So despite the fact that one of my ancestors was a blasted murderer, now I know I had a genius of a grandmother—and also, a lost Aunt

Shannon, who we might find again. I think this project is off to a good start."

I shrugged. "Yes, one of your ancestors was a blasted murder, I never wanted you to know that, but the women in your life are golden—focus on them," I said, and leaned back into my desk chair as I lost my thoughts in Judy's aria.

CHAPTER SIX

THE WRESTLER

In a few days, Andrew and I were packing the car with bags and books to supply the needs for his final semester at Fordham. As such, my jeep was filled to the brim, like it was when we moved him into his dorm six years ago. By default, I traveled with only the basics, a briefcase and an overnight bag. It was always exciting for us when we set him off to college.

I drove my jeep through the gates of the ranch and headed south on U.S. Route 395 toward Los Angeles. Andrew, in the back seat, was still packing, folding up a pile of clean t-shirts and underwear. His plane was set to depart the following morning and I planned to stay in L.A. for a few more nights to try and find Judy. "If we get to L.A. in time, I'll take you to the Del Rey Steakhouse for a nice slice of prime rib tonight."

"I'd love that," Andrew said, and rolled down his window to give us some fresh, cool mountain air.

"Take some clean air into your lungs, kid, it will clear your head to write that thesis paper. God knows the New York air doesn't smell like this."

"You're right about that, and I'm definitely more of mountain air kind of guy," Andrew said.

I looked at him by way of the rear view mirror. "Sorry to put you in the middle of all this. Your mother needed some space, it's perfect timing I suppose, you need my help with your research and I need to find out about my sister from the folks that managed her adoption. Maybe I will find an apartment near Mammoth Lakes after that."

"An apartment?" he said, shocked. "Don't worry, Mom will soften like she always does when you ruffle her feathers. You didn't see how upset she was this morning? Let her calm down. Use the

Duane Library on campus to work on your journal, and in a month or so, I'm betting she'll be ready to let you come home. You'll see."

I didn't want Andrew to worry about us. "Never thought the day would come when my son would be giving me marital advice. Besides, I deserve everything she dishes out. She should have kicked me out years ago."

Andrew smiled at that and said nothing more. We rode together in silence as he finished folding the fresh laundered clothing, appreciating the scenery. I always enjoyed the ride through the Owens Valley on 395 towards southern California with the snowcapped Sierra Nevada mountain ranges to my right and the Death Valley desert to my left. My family had ridden these foothills on horseback along the many trails to fish in the trout streams and lakes, and stargaze on campouts. When my daughter was just starting to learn to be a horse girl, at the tender age of three, she rode in front of me on the saddle. We'd bring the horses to the streams and she would pretend to pan for gold all over the Virginia Lakes region. When I looked out toward those foothills, I thought of her, my precious daughter, now one of the rare gems buried in the mountains, a fact impossible for me fathom.

Despite my disbelief, life continued around me with Marco making his demands. I took a call from him late last night, he prodding me to join him at a land developers meeting in Sacramento. I didn't give him any personal details or excuses, other than saying, "No. No meetings, no deals with land developers, and no padding the list of politician's bank accounts." It was my final answer.

But it appeared that Marco had neither mercy nor empathy for a grieving man, least of all, any license to a conscientious father. A black car had been following us for the last three miles. I noticed the vehicle when we drove through town as it was parked in front of the Court House, waiting behind a thick row of pine trees.

I continued to chat with my son casually in the rearview mirror and watched the black car approaching fast. "I'll get you to your plane in the morning and meet you in New York in a couple days," I said, thinking if Marco's guys were on my tail, Andrew was not going to be part of it. "You're right about Fordham's library, it's a great place to think," I said, trying to not stare too much into the rearview mirror.

"So looks like mom was right. That angelic voice on the records we listened to lives in L.A., right? You're going to see her," Andrew said.

I didn't answer. The black Cadillac was getting closer to us, and I saw the driver's face. It was Anthony, Marco's go-to guy, looking like he was alone. He sped past, cut in front of us, and then slowed down in front of my jeep with a signal for me to pull over to the slushy dirt roadside.

I pulled the car over and parked a ways off the pavement and onto the shoulder. "Andrew, don't you dare get out of this car. Finish packing. I'll be right back. Marco's goons have been on my ass for over a year now. Guys like him can't understand when a father loses a…"

"Let me help," Andrew said.

"Stay right here damn it!"

I grabbed the handgun in my briefcase and slipped it into my jacket pocket, got out, and walked over to Anthony standing beside his car, waiting for me.

He struggled to use a match to light his cigarette in the wind as he talked. "Don Marco is very upset again, Quinn. He wants to see you."

I didn't hide the pistol, kept it in plain sight with its handle showing out of my pocket. "I'm taking Andrew back to the L.A. airport, he has to start classes at Fordham next week. Tell Marco I'm busy." I felt the cold seeping into my shoes from the slushy snow and walked to drier ground, Anthony followed.

"Don't make this hard," he said. "And what's up with the gun?" he asked.

I turned to face him. "Come on, Anthony, you and I go way back, if I need this thing—you'll force me to use it." I held the gun in my hand.

"I'm sorry, Quinn, boss's orders."

I shrugged, put the gun back into my pocket, after seeing in his eyes there were no orders from Marco to hurt me. "Remember Ricco? Marco had that stupid fuck killed in cold blood—shot in the back, point blank, then dumped him overboard. I called them my brothers, but they're stupid on both ends of the bullet."

Anthony crossed his arms. "Stupid isn't the word for Ricco. He never even saw it coming, Marco had Porzio do it; I didn't want any part of that."

"You're part of it, still are—even now. Come on, Ricco was one of us. Marco stepped over the line. He's out of control. Anybody can see that. Even families on the outside know this was wrong. You're going to let Marco take out another one of us? Maybe next time, it's you—just because you didn't jump high enough to make him happy." I pleaded. "Come on, do me this favor—just say you lost me in traffic. Let me send my son off to college for his last semester." I tried to negotiate with him without raising my voice to alarm Andrew, who opened the car door to look at us. I told Anthony with no uncertainty, "He's a good boy, leave him alone."

Andrew got out of the car and looked at us confused. "Hey, Uncle Tony. What's up?"

"Get back in the car, kid. This is between me and your dad." He waited for Andrew to comply, but my son walked toward us.

"He's a good boy." I reminded him again, under my breath.

"Haven't seen you in a while Uncle Tony," Andrew said, coming closer, guarding his shoes in the slushy mud. "How is your beautiful daughter, Mary? Do you remember when you caught us behind the shed at the Christmas party when we first moved to Bridgeport? We were just little eighth graders then." Andrew's charm was undeniable. "Sweet Mary. She was the very first girl I kissed. Probably has a houseful of kids by now, right?"

Anthony nodded. "She's pregnant for number three. I wish you had married her, Andrew. Instead, she married some lazy ass cowboy from Reno who can't even count the change in his pockets." Anthony paused, looked at the vast mountains in the surroundings. "So, how do you like going to school in the Bronx, kid? I miss the East Coast."

I interrupted, changed my tone to that of a group of men having a happy reunion. I hoped Anthony would find it impossible to enforce Marco's orders in front of Andrew. "Hey look, Uncle Tony, it's great to see you, but my kid's got a plane to catch, so he can finish up and get that diploma he's worked so hard for. Tell your daughter she scared Andrew for good on girls—he's going into the priesthood of all things." I put my arm over Andrew's shoulder, thought not even Anthony would get violent in front of a future priest.

Anthony looked at my son from head to toe. "You want to be a Catholic priest? A handsome man like you?"

"Yes, sir," Andrew said.

"Don't priests take a vow of poverty and celibacy—a lot to give up? Makes me wonder if you're of Quinn blood. Don't you want money, horses, women, and a big ranch someday like your dad?"

Andrew shrugged and walked over to Anthony's car and leaned against it. "Money isn't everything. And women—well..." Andrew started to share, then stopped.

Anthony walked over, put his hand on my son's shoulder and smiled. "Some dreams require sacrificing other dreams. Right Quinn?" Anthony asked, winking at me.

Anthony always liked my son, and I counted on that. "Andrew that's real good, you take the straight road, not like us mamalukes. Women are nothing but headaches anyway. Maybe it's not such a big sacrifice." With a cigarette in his mouth, Anthony paused to smooth back his greasy, wind tattered hair with a small black comb.

"Quinn, I've got to take you with me. Andrew can drive himself to Los Angeles."

"No, I'm taking him."

"You're putting me in a tough spot. What do I tell, Marco?"

"Say you couldn't find me or we fought and you lost. See that snow bank over there? I could toss you into it myself or you could give yourself a nice icy mud bath. We could be all squared up with no bloodshed or feelings hurt. Tell Marco my son is on the wrestling team in college and beat you silly with a bag full of bibles and we got away."

"Come on Quinn." Anthony laughed at my foolishness. "You know the Don would never believe any of that."

Before I said anything else, Andrew, taller than both of us, took his Uncle Tony by the arm and tripped him into falling into the muddy snow pile at the side of the road. "There. How's that for a wrestling move?" Andrew said.

Anthony looked stunned, immersed in a pool of mud and black tar-filled snow. "Kid, you've got some Quinn balls after all." Then Anthony took a handful of wet soil and ice from the side of the road and rubbed more of it all over his face and new black suit. Standing up again, he ripped his white shirt between the buttons, removed his jacket, and pulled off one sleeve at the seam. Then he walked over to the rear of the car and opened the trunk, took out a crowbar, and started to walk over to us. He paused, thought for a minute, and then used it to bust open the rear window of his car. "Good luck with your graduation, kid. If you rethink the priesthood, my youngest daughter, Emma is as beautiful as Mary, and smart enough not to fall for some Nevada cowboy," Anthony said. "Even though you're only one-half Italian, I like you. You'd make a good son-in-law."

Andrew smiled. "I'll give her a call if I change my mind, Uncle Tony."

Anthony brushed himself off and tried to comb back his hair again, but couldn't find his black comb. "Go now. Marco will be on your tail. Be careful in those dark alleys in L.A. Are you coming back tomorrow night?"

"Just tell Marco we had words. I'll see him when I see him."

Andrew walked over to his Uncle Tony to say good-bye. "Sorry about ruining your nice suit. Tell Mary hello for me."

As Andrew reached to shake his hand, Anthony grabbed his forearm and threw him on the hood of the car. I rushed to his aid, but he just backed off and smiled. "Thanks, kid. The dent will add to my story. Here, do some more damage and puncture a tire for me," Anthony said, tossing the crowbar to my son.

Andrew obliged, brushed himself off, leaving several new scrapes, dents, and a flat tire. He dropped the crowbar and we left

Anthony with his beat up Cadillac. Cars and trucks whizzed by as we hopped back into our jeep. I looked at Anthony in the rearview mirror and hoped he wouldn't be stranded too long.

"We set a pretty convincing stage, I think. Let's hope it works and Uncle Tony doesn't have to suffer for it," Andrew said, as I turned on the engine. "I feel like a real gangster now, Paps. Would you say we're officially on the run?"

"It's only official for me, kid. They're not after you. I need to get you out of here, safe, and back to school. The last thing I want is for you to get caught in the crossfire."

I worried about Anthony, but said nothing to Andrew of my concern. Marco was quick to anger and he wouldn't like this, no matter how well we set the stage to paint him blameless. But it couldn't be helped at this juncture. My son came first, and my mind was set. I was going with him to New York to find Shannon, sit in the exhilarating library halls at Fordham, and figure out the answers to his questions. With hope, perhaps I would answer my own along the way.

First, in case Marco had me trailed with one of his L.A. guys, I had to make it look like Andrew flew back alone. So we stayed overnight in Los Angeles and did my usual routine when in the area. We had a nice prime rib dinner as promised and Andrew boarded the plane first thing the next morning. I stayed in L.A. set to find Judy. It was always a treat to listen to her singing live at her favorite Jazz clubs in Hollywood when in town.

I worked most of the day in the quiet of my hotel room on the journal questions and in the evening I searched out the voice of my beloved. Like any addict pursuing his fix, I needed to hear her voice again. Recordings pacified me, but seeing her live was intoxicating. Checking the names of the singers listed in the sultry jazz clubs at the concierge desk, I came up empty, so I drove around the Hollywood Hills and ended up at an obscure jazz stage and listened to a slew of second best artists. The Times Calendar section listed all the Las Vegas and Reno venues and didn't show her performing anywhere. "Maybe she's singing for a private party this weekend," a bartender said.

We used to meet at Donte's Supper Club on occasion, or I'd invite her for the day to stroll around Griffith Park, where we would talk about her family and how life would have looked had we stayed together, and of course, to stare at the stars. Nothing had changed. I was still chasing her, begging for a kiss and she refusing me. "Declan, stop. We're not children anymore. You're a married man with a fat gold ring on your finger."

I searched for her until midnight, and then retreated in defeat to the hotel. I thought to call her, wishing to stay a few more days, but knew I must go before Marco's men caught up with me. As it was, every black sedan or suited tough guy I passed, was a suspect. When was one of them going to unroll a rear window and pull out a weapon on me? I didn't want to look over my shoulder the whole time, and worse yet, had I found Judy; she might get mixed up with me on the run.

So I decided to board the plane to New York first thing in the morning and catch up with Judy when I returned. Anthony warned me about dark alleyways in L.A., but I would have to be just as careful in New York. Don Marco had goons in all five boroughs looking to earn a better spot in the family.

In the morning, as I settled in the plane for the cross-country flight, I asked one of the stewardesses for a telephone directory of the Manhattan area and jotted down the number of the Foundling Hospital. I looked out the window as we soared above the Pacific Ocean before banking eastward, wondering first if Judy was down there somewhere, and then thought about Anthony—did he fare well on the side of the highway and appease Marco with his story?

I used the time on the flight to work on Andrew's journal and before I knew it, the stewardess told me to prepare for landing. I checked for the slip of paper with the phone number in my suit jacket and patted it for good luck with the hopes I'd find Shannon soon.

PART TWO

FORDHAM and the LOWER EAST SIDE

"One never knows what could

happen down an alley."

~ Declan Quinn

CHAPTER SEVEN

FULL CIRCLES

Once in New York, I felt more at ease. I thought Marcos guys would have a more difficult time finding me in a city swarming with people. Just about very man walking around the terminal and on the streets of Manhattan and the Bronx wore a dark suit and fedora similar to mine.

Andrew was there to meet me at Keating Hall under the clock tower, the hub of Fordham University's campus. It bustled with students walking briskly down the labyrinth of icy sidewalks bordered by expansive lawns covered with foot high snow banks. The campus hadn't changed from a generation before, except the ivy looked thicker on the brick facades of the buildings with additional signs of growth spread out, as two new buildings were under construction. The working-class blue-collar workers plastering the exterior walls gave contrast with the privileged students carrying books of philosophy and engineering portfolios.

"What do you have there, Paps? Did you bring me an early graduation gift?" Andrew asked looking at the long rolled package tucked under my arm.

I handed it to him. "Consider this a late Christmas gift for you." He unrolled it and saw it was the sketch my mother drew of me as a boy. "I wanted you to have this. Maybe you'll think more about giving me that grandson who looks just like me." I crossed my arms, looking like a proud grandfather already.

Andrew was shocked to see what was inside. "Really, Dad, you're going to part with this prize piece from your office? G-Pap had it so beautifully framed, and you took it apart just for me. Are you sure?"

"Drew, we talked about how it would be a perfect prop to use for your thesis presentation. Sorry I couldn't manage to bring the frame too, it was hard enough to hide it from you when we packed the jeep. But, I'll keep its frame for you when you're ready to hang it in your own home someday."

"I can't believe you did this," he said, shocked.

"I'm happy you have it, feels like I'm passing the torch to you now, son. I've grown tired of looking at it and thought your professors would like to hear the story I told you."

"Oh yes, the story of a woman, sexually assaulted and humiliated on a bar floor, who found it within herself to use her pain as an existential source for creativity." He shook his head still gazing at the picture. "It's a story I'd like to share with them. Thank you. I will cherish this with all the care it deserves and carry the Quinn legacy with pride, Paps."

Listening to him interpret that night confirmed for me the significance of passing torches. "I spent many nights looking at it, a bitter reminder of something terrible. You helped me understand that she created this piece out of pure love for me that night."

"Yes, in the midst of her suffering, she made a choice, she did it for you and your sister, to protect you both," Andrew said. "I'm sorry I never got to meet her." As he rolled up the picture, he wiped his eyes dry using his shirtsleeve.

"Losing her was a great loss. But you've helped me see that through it all, she found a way give love despite the sadness around her," I said.

I dug another gift out of my briefcase.

"What's this, Paps?"

"My completed assignment. I told you I'd come through for you, kid. I finished all the questions on the plane. It's all in there. Good stories, sad case studies on the choices, crossroads, and conflicts of one man. This man. This man who can review his life in retrospect, just like you said."

Andrew flipped through the pages with his eyes wide in shock. "You haven't fooled around, have you—Magna cum laude Man. I can't wait to get started."

"Can you read my scribbles? I know it's messy handwriting?"

"It's fine. Really. Passes my inspection. Nice work, long entries. Thanks. It looks as though the apple doesn't fall too far from the tree, Paps."

"Oh, what do you mean?" I asked confused.

"You know, you're like Grandma Aisling. You found ways to give love despite your suffering," he said.

I shrugged, and felt my own tears welling up. "I can only dream to become a person like her," I said, and stole the baseball cap off his head.

"Hey, give me that back Paps," he said, and gathered his belongings, as I followed carrying my small duffle bag and briefcase.

I looked around the campus grounds and remembered the pathways well. Trading hats with my son, I gave him my fedora to wear as I slipped his cap on my head. "Your hat suits me just fine on this campus. Let's walk over to Coffey Field later—most likely buried under one foot of snow, right?" We walked for a bit and headed towards the Duane Library. "Perhaps we should go through a few pages of the journal together in the library first, and see if my answers are adequate for what you need."

I took a deep breath taking in the moist city air, having forgotten about the variety of scents of the East Coast. The mixture of the city streets, full of bus diesel fuel emissions and people moving around, all mixed with a surrounding forest, was a sharp contrast to the dry fresh aspen and pine scents I was used to in the high-altitude western mountain zones. I was not sure which I preferred.

"Dad, the jury was still out on whether you were going to work on the journal or not, but you came through for me with flying colors. Thank you again." Andrew smiled and shook his head at me. "You sure are full of surprises, glad you left the western bronco look at home. Honestly, I hardly recognized you. How does it feel wearing a suit and tie again and to be clean shaven?"

"Pretty good, actually. I wanted to make myself proper for all the young, beautiful women on campus, but what's with all the short skirts, and knee high boots? I've never seen so many sexy knees in my life. Perhaps I should be wearing the kilted skirt Pappy sent me from Ireland, rather than this pinstriped suit. What's up with the kids wearing torn up jeans and saggy t-shirts? I'm starting to think my rancher look would have fit in better."

He laughed. "When you came here in the late thirties, I bet you even had to wear a shirt and tie all the time," he said, as a handful of pretty, female students walked passed us who fashioned the hippy style of bell-bottom, hip hugging jeans, peasant tops, and long, flowing hair.

I smiled at them with a tip of my hat, but turned to take a hidden glance at their backsides, as they swayed like a metronome keeping time. Distracted, I said, "Yes, that's a fact. And my hair was cut short over the ears. The boys here, with their long hair, all look like Kitchi on the ranch. It looks like a London rock-and-roll festival instead of a Jesuit University," I said. "And girls on campus now. Forget about that when I came here."

"Yeah, girls, girls everywhere, the London fashions are all over the city. Someone's sure to throw some beads over your head, stick daisies in your hair, and hand you war protest posters if you're not careful," Andrew said.

It felt great to laugh. "Oh, great. I will look forward to that kind of torture," I said, as we came into view of the collegiate Gothic styled, gray stoned Fordham Library with an array of large white-framed windows on every floor, and a tall clock tower rising in its center. "Let's go inside, maybe it will provide us some cover from the sexy ladies and propaganda pimps."

"Absolutely. Did you have a favorite floor in the library for studying?"

I felt as if I had just returned home. "I did. Follow me, Andrew. You can see how your father handles himself in this building," I said, taking his cap off, as he did the same with mine. We traded hats again as we entered.

Crossing the threshold for the library, with the smells of aged books in leather bindings, caused my senses to go on overload, and I got dizzy for a minute. I stopped, took in the familiar air, and regained my equilibrium in a split second. "I have fond memories of being a student here. I was only seventeen as a freshman. When I decided to stay on for my law degree, I was barely twenty-one. I spent most of the free time with my friends, studying, hanging around the baseball field, and going to watch my girlfriend sing in Upper Manhattan. Then, in the middle of my first year of law school, Pearl Harbor was bombed, so most of us left to join the fight overseas."

As Andrew and I stood at the reference desk, waiting to reserve a private tutor room upstairs, we chatted. "That war was far different than today's. So, you shouldn't turn your nose at me when thinking about the seminary, as my graduate courses have kept me off the battle fields of Vietnam," my son said using a library whisper.

I nodded and whispered back. "You can say that again, that war is far different than what we fought for in Europe, if you hadn't used your college deferment, I would have had to hide you in Ireland somewhere for sure."

"Agreed, Paps, thanks." He signed a slip of paper from the librarian and put a pen inside his pocket. "So you dated that singer Mom's jealous of in college?" he asked, as we began to walk up the stairs.

"Nice guess. Yes, the records I listened to are the same girl I dated in college, but we were teenage sweethearts as well." I paused, cautiously. "Hey, are my secrets safe with you or will you be spilling out my stories to your mother the first chance you get?"

"Come on Paps. I don't deserve that. You know your secrets are safe with me," he said, and shrugged off my sarcasm. "It's so cool to be traversing the same grounds that you did as a student. But, I can't imagine leaving here to head off to a war zone."

"It was a different time. I didn't want to leave this place, but we did what we had to do to stop the Axis Powers of Japan, Italy, and the Germans. Aye, that bloody war was a far distance from the sanctuary of Fordham's campus, that's for sure. This is where my little world opened with possibilities, and now here you are, opening your mind in the same way," I said, with pride. "It's great to be back, brings me a new hope being on this campus, an optimism, just like I had when I returned from the war."

Andrew followed me up the staircase one flight to my old favorite corner in the library where I would sit for hours on end to finish research papers or review files on case studies. I reminisced. "On the weeknights, Judy and I would listen to records of the symphony or opera and drive the librarians crazy, as I'd usually have my baseball cleats on and would drag mud in from the field. Hey, perhaps while I'm here, we can venture over to baseball team room as well, let's see if they still have my picture on the wall with the Collegiate All-Americans—made that team in the Spring of 1939 and 1940."

Andrew shrugged. "It's still there Paps, Coach Sotto brags about you all the time, telling me I should be more determined like my father was as a player. You are welcome to hang out with me as long as you wish. Is there any chance you're planning to join me on that pilgrimage to Ireland, you don't have to drive with us on the bus, just pick up G-Pap and take a tour with him."

It sounded tempting. "You're softening your old Paps, Drew. I might join you boys. I would like to visit Pappy and see the parts of Ireland where my family came from that's for sure."

My son was delighted. "We should write to G-Pap to let him know we're coming."

My heart stopped for a beat at the notion of writing to Pappy on this topic. "Let's hold off on that letter just yet. I need to figure out some personal business in New York first. I have an appointment with a nun from the Foundling Hospital in the morning. She should have the information I need to find my sister," I said. "I can't visit Pappy until I learn of her whereabouts. It will be one of his first questions for me."

"Yes, Aunt Shannon. You will find her Paps, I can feel it in my bones," Andrew said, as we walked around the second floor library stacks of books and tables. Then he stopped at a row of glass windowed rooms deciding on which room to enter. "Why didn't you and Aunt Shannon go live with him after your mother died?" Andrew asked, signing his name on a sheet of paper taped to the door of one of the empty rooms.

"That is a long, long story. For now, I'll just say she was adopted in 1933 when she was seven years old to a family unknown to me. As you heard for yourself the other night, it's her voice in my head that haunts my dreams. Andrew, if I'm to find any peace in my life, I must find her."

"I'd be interested to join you for your meeting at the adoption center if you want company," Andrew said.

I loved the idea. "Of course, do that. You could even stay with me tonight at the Plaza Hotel if you wanted, have dinner in the theater district, and a warmed whiskey in the Oak Room after…"

Andrew interrupted me trying to keep his voice to a library whisper. "Oh, dinner tonight won't work. But, I'd love to join you tomorrow, if it's okay with you Paps. I can meet you at the hotel in the morning, as tonight at 8:00, a group of us guys meet in the library to study and compare notes on the Three Cs Project—they're going to flip out when they see all the work you put into answering the questions," Andrew said, as he opened the glass soundproof door to the tutor room.

"Tell your friends that the work was good for me, too. And tonight, I will get to bed early, as I wanted to be bright and fresh for my meeting with Sister Catherine tomorrow. If my memory proves me right, she's quite a character."

We settled into the small tutor room, closed the door, and sat in wood chairs at a round mahogany table. The rear walls of the room were covered in chalkboards full of mathematical equations and tiny bits of white chalk were left on trays. "Shall I take a stab at solving that equation, son?" I said, joking with him.

Andrew carefully unrolled the picture again and clipped it on the worn chalkboard. "This room isn't as cozy as your office, but let me try to set the stage again. Hopefully you will be game for some more of your storytelling."

I relaxed in my seat and reminisced while Andrew erased a portion of the math problem then fastened the sketch on the board "We all lived happily with my grandparents until I was in the first grade, often they would start in with violins and harmonicas while my Pappy told great stories, he's probably next to the fireplace entertaining a group as we speak. As soon as I find out Shannon's address, and hopefully track her down, I'll write him that letter to let him know I'm coming. It's a shame my work for Marco kept me too distracted to visit him all these years."

With the mention of Marco, my son took a chair and readied himself for more talk. "Sure. In your defense, Paps, Uncle Marco kept you at his beck and call. I remember a time we got back late from camping near Devils Postpile Monument and he was waiting for you with that serious look on his face."

I shrugged. "Yeah, I remember those days, too. I tried to protect you from my business with Marco. It wasn't easy, obviously I didn't hide it well enough."

"Yeah, I probably heard and saw more than you think," he said, pulled out his note pad and pen and then looked up at the picture. "So, as we said last week, Grandma Aisling had a moment of genius when she drew this."

"Yes, like you said, she found a way to transcend her pain by putting it into an existential art form that night."

"'Pain is God's megaphone to rouse a deaf world'—a quote from C.S. Lewis," he said. "In The Problem of Pain, Lewis posits that our sufferings can be used as an element of motivation. Without knowing, Grandma used her difficulties to dig deep within herself."

"And out came this magical picture. But, pain can cripple, too," I said.

"Okay. There's a choice, a crossroad to consider—to become crippled or motivated. Can you tell me if there was a time in your life when a suffering might have crippled you, but instead, you turned it into something positive for survival? Or did you succumb to the pain and let it cripple you?"

I felt comfortable being in the library and in the private quarters of the tutor room, but Andrew's question stopped me. At first I didn't want to answer. "Andrew, are you sure you want to know the parts of your father that are quite dark and sad?"

"Yes, I do. Absolutely. I'm not the peach-fuzz kid you think I am."

"Ha, that's for sure. I don't know one person on this earth who could trip up a guy like Anthony and get out of it without a black eye or dead."

"Yes, Uncle Tony's a tough guy. But come on—the question Paps, crippled or motivated?"

"Well, it's all in the journal, so you're going to read it anyway. But yes, in the midst of suffering, I did make a choice. However, unlike my mother, it wasn't a moment of genius like what you see on the wall there. Andrew, I let pain cripple me. I was thirteen and my mother had been murdered. All I knew was hate. All I wanted was revenge."

Andrew looked at me with crossed brows, folding his arms on top of the table and leaned forward to speak to me. "As difficult as this seems, it's great we are sitting here getting this story out, getting it down and out of your head. Your past is part of me. You can't hide it and I don't want to hide from it either. You say you sought revenge, can you tell me more..."

I stood up, interrupting him, and walked closer to the hanging picture and stared at it. "Very well. Brace yourself, being a soon-to-be seminarian and all, you're going to find out some things about my past that aren't very—Christ-like."

Andrew smiled and I saw a budding priest inside. "I think we're all pretty far from perfect, Paps."

His eyes were true and tender, his ears innocent, so I decided to give him a dose of the real world. "Okay," I said, still standing near to the warrior boy sketch. I crossed my arms, feeling like a professor preparing for a lecture, and put on my hat as if preparing for a journey. "Now listen up class, there's an entry in that journal that tells the tale of a thirteen-year old boy that scoured the streets on the Lower East Side of Manhattan one fretful February night in 1933, looking to kill his father.

CHAPTER EIGHT

A THESIS DISCERNED

Oh, I'm listening." Andrew stood up and checked the door to make sure it was sealed shut and returned to his seat.

I sighed, and then gave my son the truth of who I was. "This account is no fictitious tale Andrew, and might put the Brontë sisters to shame, I'm afraid."

My son's eyes lighted up as he grabbed a chair and took a seat.

I told the entire story standing. "It was a night with weather similar to what we have today, the snow banks were melting and rain had turned it all to slush. My mother and sister were walking home from school when my father kidnapped them. We were living in a safe house in Bay Ridge at the time. When I got home from my after-school job that day, it was dark out and the mother of the house was concerned why Shannon and my mother weren't home yet. So I looked for them everywhere, the library, the market, and the pastry shop on 86th Street. When the lady at the fabric shop told me she saw my mother talking to a man that fit my father's description, I immediately jumped on the bus to the streetcar. Once I finally crossed the Brooklyn Bridge, it was easier for me to literally run up Pike Street then to bother with the rapid transit system in Manhattan, so I traveled on foot the rest of the distance."

"How many blocks did you have to go?" Andrew asked.

"About fifteen or so uptown, running the whole way."

He shook his head. "Did you call the cops?"

"No. Cops scared me after seeing what they'd do to my father all the time. Truth be told, I was just a dumb kid and had no idea what I would find in his hellhole, let alone finding my mother inches from death and my sister crying on the floor in a pool of our mother's blood," I said, feeling ill.

"Oh God, Dad. I'm so sorry."

"Drew, if I had more brains than guts, I would have brought a gun."

Andrew took out his pen and paper. "Wow. A kidnapping, an uptown run, finding your mother and sister in a pool of blood, and a murder, all for a thirteen-year old kid to handle alone," he said, jotting down notes.

I shrugged. "Write it all down, most of it is in that journal anyway. It's a story for the books that's for sure." I stayed on my feet, feeling more powerful in this stance and removed my hat to give the truth its due honor. Telling this story had a new value to me, as my own mortality was now on the line, with Don Marco wanting me working for him or else. My story, my mother's story, and Shannon's story, they needed to be passed on to the next generation. This was my last chance. Mafia hit men in New York would've seen to my quick death without a trace. I could be dead in a week and this story dead forever, I thought.

Andrew had drawn a timeline in his notebook, so I eagerly partnered with him giving pertinent background information. "But Paps, see here, there's a gap to fill, it was during your safe house days in Brooklyn," he said pointing to his notes. "I've got the Warrior Boy from your Lower East Side days prior to 1928, but then here, we jumped to the night of your mother's murder in 1933—let's call that kid, the Lone Teenage Avenger."

I couldn't help myself and busted up laughing this time. His satire in the midst of my tragedy was killing me. "Happy to see you're enjoying this, Drew—so just how often does your G-Pap write you here, as that's the kind of shit he would say."

"Satire makes life tolerable. And yes, he writes me once a week. Guess I've got his wit in my genes—you do too," he said, completing his timeline. "Can you help me fill in the blanks from 1928 to 1933, before the Lone Teenager Avenger steps into the scene?"

I laughed again, appreciating a man who sought out the facts and placed them in order. "Satire and fact gathering—two assets for a man to have."

Andrew smiled. "Aye, got satire from G-Pap and fact gathering from you. Lucky me—the best from both of you, I guess."

"Thanks kid." I took his pen and wrote a few Brooklyn dates down on his timeline. "My Brooklyn days are stories unto themselves. Shannon was only three-years old when we moved there. It was a happy home. The Attanasio's had six children. When their firstborn, Mary Ann, was sent home from kindergarten because she couldn't speak a word of English, they asked around neighboring parishes if they had a nun to tutor their children. That's when Father Carmen put us together. It was a perfect barter of goods, we taught the family English and they in turn gave us shelter. It was in their home where I learned how a family could love each other, work together, and share food and laughter without the daily servings of insanity and fear."

Andrew kept writing notes without stopping or looking up at me, so I continued to speak. "Living with them was like a fairy tale when I stop to think about it."

"Aye." Andrew looked up and laughed. "Your mother was the damsel in distress and the warm loving arms of a big Italian family swept her off her feet." As he wrote down more notes, he asked about more details. "Their name was Attanasio, right? What were the first names of the owners there?"

"Signore Attanasio and his wife Anna. Saverio was his name for your records, and was known to everyone as, Sam. Shannon and I called the mom, Zia Anna, my mother and her became like sisters. Zia Anna joked with my mother that she was her Irish sister and my mother would say she was her Italian one."

My son was good at this, as his timeline looked like a board display in a courtroom trial. A jury would be impressed, I thought.

I got a big smile on my face watching my son work and thinking of the Attanasio family again. "Yes, as you said, they swept all of us off our feet with their charm and love. But sadly, like all fairy tales, it wasn't real. My father killed—literally, any notion of happily ever after." My smile was short lived.

"I'm sorry," Andrew said, getting serious again. "This must be hard to talk about, so I'm just going to keep asking questions and taking notes in the hope it gets easier for you. So, um…" Andrew reviewed his notes. "Did you move there after that night in the speakeasy?"

I nodded. "Yes. It was right after that terrible night in 1928. Father Carmen and a nun we loved, Sister Mary Catherine, arranged it for us."

"That's the sister you're meeting in the morning?" he asked.

"Yes, at nine o'clock sharp," I said.

He wrote it all down. "Thank you, Paps. Got it—thanks for filling in the timeline, you were blessed to live with them, even though it was for only five years." He paused for a minute or two. "Now—your father. I know it's difficult. But what's his story?"

The shift in gears was maddening, but to give respect to the details, I made it as brief as I could. "Well, I never say his name, but for the record books, it was Axel Hauser."

Andrew was shocked hearing for the first time how I had changed my name. "Are you kidding, it just dawned on me, Quinn is your maternal name, your birth name was Hauser?" he asked, writing down notes.

I shrugged. "Yes, changed it when I got my law degree a year before you were born. Quinn fits me well. Fits us well," I said.

"Agreed, it's just you're such a mystery," he said, shaking his head.

"Well, this project unlocked it, so you're stuck with me. I may as well give you the full serving now," I said.

"Serve it up, Mystery Man," Andrew said, with enthusiasm.

I laughed. "From Warrior Boy, to Magna cum laude Man, to Lone Teenage Avenger, and now, Mystery Man."

He busted out laughing with me. "True. I wonder what other characters you have hiding inside your psyche," he said, writing without looking at me. "So any chance I can hear the Axel Hauser story—can you stomach it?"

It was easier than I thought, so I delved into talking about the taboo character in my life. "He did have a good side, for the record," I shrugged, "crafted ornate furniture for a living and made us toys, like a wagon for Shannon. It wasn't bad all the time, as we'd pull her around town to shop and go to church everyday. But then my grandparents moved and the speakeasy opened in the basement of our building, and everything changed. I always felt bad for him in a way, as he'd grumble all the time about his father and brother in Germany who screwed him on some business issues or something like that. So, from then on, the routine consisted of my father drunk in the street with a police wagon picking him up with the other drunks. Father Carmen would come in the morning to take us to the convent. We'd spend on average two to three nights a week in the convent house to get a warm meal, a bath, and a safe bed. Days later, or sometimes months would go by, my father would come home from jail cleaned up, sober, wearing a nice borrowed suit and hat, looking refreshed and repentant. Father Carmen would make him promise he would never drink or hit her again."

"So priests got very involved in family life in those days, didn't they?"

"Oh yes, he even found carpentry jobs for my father throughout the Diocese. The priests and nuns became part of the family. The women loved them—the drunks did too. As I mentioned, Father Carmen bailed my father out plenty of times." It was difficult remembering it all. "The last time was my father's final chance to keep his promises, however, he blew it. He blew it big."

"So you moved away after the Warrior Boy night?"

"Yes. We moved the day after my mother sketched that picture of me." I stood to gaze at the photo again.

Andrew wrote notes and glanced at me standing next to the sketch. "Whew, that's a lot for an eight-year old kid to handle." Andrew summed it up.

I was grateful to my son and confident that this hidden story was given to the right man. "Yes, and like it or not, I remember every horrifying detail too. The morning after her assault in the bar, my mother went to work at the church school, battered and bruised again. Father Carmen had seen enough, and most likely had heard the nuns' pleas to save us, so he called us all into the rectory with a plan to move us away. I'll never forget that day with my mother sitting in his office, cuddling Shannon as we all cried. Father asked me to tell him everything that happened. So I did."

"You should be proud of that eight-year old boy inside you, speaking the truth no matter how shameful it was," my son said.

It never occurred to me to be proud of myself, but seeing my past through Andrew's eyes shed a new light. I looked at my watch; it was getting close to four o'clock. Since it was my first day on campus with my son, the jet fatigue from travel, combined with the contents of the story just told, I felt a need for some fresh air. "Let's take a break," I said, standing up. I walked over to the sketch, took it down, and rolled it back into the wrapping. "This room is getting stuffy. Let's take a stroll through the Eddies for some fresh air, then walk over to Arthur Avenue for an early dinner," I said, still familiar with the spots near Fordham to eat and socialize.

I put the picture under my arm and opened the tutor room door. Once again, the similar smells of books put my senses on overload. The intoxicating library air filled my lungs while I waited and held the door open for Andrew to finish his notes. "Hey Andrew," I said, with a library-styled whisper. "Jot this down while you're at it. Believe it or not, I'm okay to talk about this. When I told you about that night in the bar, then wrote about it again in the journal, it felt like I was plucking out thorns from my heart one by one."

He responded with excitement, and his classic Quinn high cheekbones perked as his green eyes brightened. "Really Dad?" he said, and sat back into his seat. "That's significant. I was concerned this process would feel like stabbing yourself with sharp painful memories."

I stepped into the room again and closed the door. "No, surprisingly not. The feeling is the exact opposite. Not a stabbing but a pruning. It's as if these memories were thorns stuck into my heart all these years and are finally being removed."

"That's a relief to hear and an interesting analogy. Sit for a minute Paps. Can you hang with me while I brainstorm out loud? Last week, I took an exam in my Italian class where all the words came from nature, you know, like plants and vegetables for example." He paused to think for a minute in silence as he dug into his book bag, retrieving an Italian paperback dictionary. Flipping quickly through its pages, his eyes got excited once more. "Hum, the word for thorn is spina. Pronounced speena."

"Spina, the thorn," I said. "And…" I said, taking a seat again.

"Yes, I think I'll use a new term in my thesis. Spina. How does Spina-therapy sound to you?" he asked.

I sat and listened, but couldn't grasp his idea. "Sorry, Mr. Existential Man. I'm lost. It's been a while since I've used critical thinking," I said, watching a growing excitement in his face.

Andrew continued. "Paps, I think we may have discovered a unique psychoanalytical technique. A process of pulling out thorns through the telling and retelling of painful memories," he said, and took time to write down more in his notebook.

I watched him write, wishing I could start my college years over. "Spina as the thorn. I like it."

Andrew looked up and nodded. "It's like Viktor Frankl's term Logotherapy—derived from 'logos', a Greek word that translates as 'meaning'. He attached that to the term, 'therapy', and study of man's search for meaning was born. I'll use Spina-therapy as the study of man's longing to tell and extract the wounds of his past—his thorns," he said, looking back at his notes. Andrew closed his notebook and looked at me for approval.

I got serious with my son, feeling honored to have witnessed his personal epiphany. "Perhaps you and your Spina-therapy will be world renowned just like Frankl's Logotherapy," I said, imagining where it might lead, maybe somewhere other than the priesthood. "Don't throw me out of here yet Drew, but you know what?"

"No what, Paps?" he asked annoyed, expecting more sarcasm.

Always a father first, I had to suggest. "You could become a psychologist and still minister to a congregation of needy folks like me. God knows I'm not the only one with painful memories. Many of my fellow comrades would benefit from telling their stories of the war traumas we had to witness. I don't mind being a guinea pig for your scientific discoveries."

"Paps, it's obvious you are not keen on my entering the seminary; but you're right. I'll admit a Spina-therapy doctorial research could open doors for me," he said, standing up and gathering his things.

Delighted, I got up and opened the door. "You are at a crossroads it seems, son." Andrew walked over to a table lamp and pulled its chain to shut the light. "Finish the research and see what Monsignor O'Shea thinks. If the world needs your Spina-therapy, doors will not only open for you, but tens of thousands of men and women would benefit from your efforts." I said, looking at my son, wondering when he passed me up in height.

Andrew's face lighted up with a fresh newness. "I will chat with Monsignor O'Shea about this soon, we will see."

I put a loving arm around him. "Either way you choose, do the right thing for your life. The beauty is that the choice is yours and no one else's." I gave him a huge hug. "I never officially thanked you for my Christmas present," I said, holding him into my embrace.

He smiled with tears welling in his eyes. "You're welcome, Paps."

With my hands on his shoulders, I smiled. "And since you've taken the role of the Quinn Family historian, on our way over to Arthur Ave, I'll tell you more about your Grandmother Aisling."

"Great." Andrew smiled, hugged me in return as we exited the tutor room. "The Quinn family historian. I like the sound of that."

"Indeed. Tomorrow, you and I will go visit her grave at St. Pat's Cemetery. Sound good?" I asked.

He smiled, looking excited about the research and the notion of delving deeper into the qualities of the existential genius he never got to meet. "Yes, I'm up for that. So, what did she look like for starters?" Andrew asked, in a quieted voice as we made our way back through the library hallways and down the stairs.

The question made me smile, and I stopped on the stairwell's landing and whispered into his ear. "Well, son, you already know. Your sister looked just like my mother." I pulled a worn photo of my deceased daughter out of my jacket pocket and showed it to him. Her soft pink skin and huge green eyes were so tender; it melted my heart every time I stared at it.

He took it from me. "Dad, it breaks my heart to see this, I miss her so much, and now you tell me she looked just like Grandma Aisling," he said, holding his hand out for my handkerchief as a few boys passed us on the steps.

He stared at the photo for a minute before returning it to me. I placed the picture back into my jacket pocket for safekeeping near my heart.

Exiting the library, we put our hats back on, walked along a large lawn in the center of campus towards Arthur Avenue, and enjoyed the fresh air. The field was covered in melting snow, but I recalled many lunches I shared here on the greens with Judy.

"This great lawn brings back many fond, yet bitter sweet memories," I said.

"We'll be here in May when I graduate. I'm looking forward to it being warmer then," Andrew said, turning his collar up against the frigid air.

Returning to the Eddies lawn was like coming full circle for me. The last time I stood in this sacred place was twenty years ago when I graduated in 1946 in the maroon regalia gown for my Juris Doctorate ceremony. Three years earlier, I stood here in cap and gown as an undergrad. A total of seven years of my life were spent at this university. At both graduation ceremonies I yearned to have parents attend like everyone else. Society can try to fill the void in an orphan's heart with foster parents, teachers, mentors, and bosses, but there is always a void when you're an orphan.

Being in this spot again, I felt the emptiness close in a full circle. My son and I were here together as I gave him what I longed for at his age. I wanted to linger here and remember, so an empty bench at the edge of the snow-covered field beckoned me. "Let's sit for a moment." I said, even though it was freezing and the bench was wet.

Andrew took the sleeve of his sweater and dried the seat off and sat next to me. "So who was here to see you graduate from law school?" Andrew asked, as if reading my mind.

"Just my girlfriend, Judy," I said, zipping up my jacket.

The mention of her name made me restless and I felt the need to move again. I stood up, fixed my hat, and readjusted my scarf. "It's too cold out here. Let's go grab a sandwich and a hot bowl of soup."

Andrew walked next to me with his hands deep in his pockets. "Was there an investigation on your mother's death?"

The question hit me hard—the answer complex. I tried to keep it simple. "The jury convicted my father of manslaughter, not murder. But he killed my mother. His apartment was full of wood scraps, so apparently after he smacked her around, she fell on a sharp wood stake full of nails. By the time I got there, around eight o'clock, it was too late for the medics to stop the bleeding."

I lit a cigar wishing I didn't have to go on with the telling of this awful night, but continued after seeing Andrew's wanting eyes. "My father was gone when I got there—he just left my mother, on the floor bleeding to death. When the medics put us into their ambulance, I carried Shannon. She clung to me, her arms around my neck tight, as if fear itself would killer her."

Andrew didn't respond and held his head low. Keeping his hands warm in the pockets of his jacket, he was all ears and heart to hear the rest of my story.

I continued with great trepidation. "Our mother died in the hospital an hour later. Father Carmen arrived some time around midnight. I could only think of finding my father, who was most likely drunk in a bar, oblivious to what he had done. So, when Father Carmen drove us to the convent, passing our tenement along the way, I jumped off the truck bed and ran straight into the speakeasy."

"To seek revenge?" Andrew asked, glancing over at me.

I held my head down, and continued walking. The cold sidewalks were nearly empty of pedestrians. "Yes. Let's pray your forgiving Jesus understands my will to kill that night."

"Well, there's a confessional for that. Monsignor O'Shea is a great man to hear a confession. I go all the time."

I stopped him, annoyed by his naivety. "Save it, Andrew." I said, irritated, my voice turning sharp. "Here's my confession to you. I'm not a believer in matters of God or forgiveness."

Andrew sighed, and stopped walking. I turned to face him and he looked straight into my eyes. "Where is your dad now?"

"Dead—hung himself in his jail cell," I said, with a mix of shame and satisfaction. "Thanks to me."

"Oh, what did you have to do with him killing himself?"

"You think I'm a decent man, don't you son?"

"Absolutely Paps. I do."

"Then let's just leave the details of my father's death for another day."

My son looked over at me with concern and continued to walk next to me in silence.

CHAPTER NINE

AISLING'S EPITAPH

After we shared a pizza on Arthur Avenue, the ethnic section of the Bronx a few blocks away from campus, Andrew walked back alone as I took the subway into the City. I checked into my hotel and went straight to bed, exhausted. If my son's psychoanalytical technique does takeoff with success, he will have to give his clients energy pills to take along with his treatments, I thought.

I woke thankful the Plaza Hotel lived up to its reputation of quality and had given me a night of restful slumber. The sunrise came early for me, easing the East Coast time change into my eyes through soft cream-colored sheers over the windows. I got up and searched my briefcase for the necklace I packed. The day we moved out of our tenement, nearly forty years ago, Sister Mary Catherine gave me a medallion of St. Michael the Archangel along with his prayer card. "Defend us in battle, be our protection against the wickedness and snares of the devil…" I recited the St. Michael Prayer from memory. Finding both items, I smiled at the memory of her placing the medal over my head as we all sat, homeless, in the bed of Father Carmen's truck, with only enough belongings to fit into one suitcase.

I remember that early morning move vividly as the sisters in the convent sent us off. "Wear this medallion in good health, Declano, be strong for the battles ahead, you are the new man of the family now," she said, as she waved goodbye, putting the prayer card into my pocket.

"Let's hope the snares of the devil stayed at Marcos' high-rise casino in the mountains," I said to myself, grabbing my briefcase and set to leave.

Andrew met me in the lobby, looking refreshed and eager to get our day started. I thought about Shannon all morning and hoped my search for her would bring me quick answers. We stepped outside and adjusted our jackets for the cold. Standing idle for a minute on the sidewalk, like two fish trying to decide if they should go with the flow of the current or to swim upstream, we decidedly walked uptown. "Let's find a spot for breakfast, Foundling Hospital is only ten-minutes from here," I said, enjoying the New York City vibe in my bones again. The air was cool, but dry, with snowflakes melting as soon as they hit the sleeves on my jacket.

It was good the streets of Manhattan were a sea of pedestrians, as Marco wouldn't ever find me here, I thought. The Central Park neighborhood areas were busy and the narrow streets choked with bulging trashcans and street vendors. The morning hustle of pedestrians with briefcases and taxis tapping their horns fit my mood. My mind was racing with thoughts of finally obtaining a name and address to find my little sister.

We stopped at a smoky diner across the street from the huge ten-storied state-of-the art building that made up the Foundling Hospital on 68th Street. "Leave it up to Sister Mary Catherine and Father Carmen to grow their stewardship for orphans into a giant force for lost families. They must serve thousands of needy children and their families now," I said staring up at the building. We took a window seat watching the action on the streets of Manhattan, while we ate fluffy stacks of pancakes and eggs, anticipating my nine o'clock appointment.

When we finished and paid the check, I looked out the window and spotted a nun, looking like it could be Sister Mary Catherine, standing on the Foundling Hospital's steps. We exited the diner, then walked to the corner and waited for the light to change. Crossing the street, I saw her talking to a driver in a green Dodge van parked along a yellow curb. Although it's been decades since I last saw her, there was no mistaking her for anyone else. She wore the all too familiar black habit gown that skipped precisely one inch above the concrete sidewalk.

Standing on the corner I could hear her speaking to the van driver. "Stay with your vehicle so you don't get towed," she told the driver. "We are waiting for two more." Not realizing that we were watching her, I smiled seeing how she looked completely the same. The only difference in appearance was how her black curls were now mixed with plenty of wiry grays popping out from under the black, boxed framed head cloth that draped over her shoulders.

The driver looked irritated. "Yes, I know, Sister, I was told to pick up you and two others this morning. Father Carmen is waiting for you at the rectory."

"They are set to arrive in ten minutes…" She saw us standing, staring at her and paused, looking annoyed. "Boys, move along now. Unless you have business here, this is no place for loitering."

The driver opened the rear door for her. "Driver, please let me wait here a bit so the two gentlemen can find me."

I stepped up to greet her.

"Is that you, Declano Hauser? Well, why didn't you say it was you? It's been too many years for me to remember your face." She gave me a closer look. "Oh, I see you still wear the St. Michael medallion around your neck. It really is you. So, has St. Michael proven to be your guide after you left us those many, many years ago?" she asked.

"Yes, he has. St. Michael has defended me in battle several times actually. I wore this just for you today and every day in the war. It's so wonderful to see you, Sister Mary Catherine. You haven't changed. I use my mother's maiden name, Quinn, now—dropped Hauser when I got my law degree," I said, giving her a hug.

She stared into my eyes with a tender look. "I understand. Quinn. It fits you better anyway. I wouldn't have known you if I saw you on the street. Oh my, have the years brought you too many worries, son? The lines on your face, if you forgive me for saying, show many lines of worry, but you were always the type to carry everyone's burdens."

"Worry lines…" I said, as she interrupted me.

"Yes, apart from those deep green eyes that so resemble your mother's, I wouldn't have known you at all."

I took a quick look at my reflection on the van's window as she approached Andrew.

"Oh, this must be your son." She greeted him, kissing both sides of his cheeks.

"Yes, this is Andrew. Son, meet the famous Sister Mary Catherine."

"Well Andrew, I would have stopped straight in my steps when passing you on the street. You are the true image of your father and grandmother combined. Don't you agree, Declano?" she asked, with her memorable Italian accent.

She was always completely animated and today was reminiscent of that. She walked the sidewalk, commanding a ten-foot radius around her. "Declan, your mother was like a sister to me and your son has her tender eyes. It was so tragic when we lost her," she said, and patted her eyes. "Andrew, your father told me over the phone you are studying to become a priest?"

Andrew smiled and nodded. "Yes, it's true Sister Mary Catherine."

"Heaven preserve us today!" She clapped her hands together then embraced Andrew again. "Well now, let's go see Father Carmen, are you okay visiting with him too today, Declano?" She gave Andrew her portfolio case to carry and took his free arm without waiting for my response.

I assumed as much, seeing the van that we weren't walking inside the Foundling Hospital. Andrew stepped up like the gentleman he was and helped her. "It's so great to meet you finally, Sister Mary Catherine. My father has told me so much about you," he said, helping with the length of her habit gown and gave me a wink.

"Oh, I trust not too many horror stories," she said. We climbed into the van with her as she continued talking. "When I telephoned Father Carmen that you were paying me a visit today, he insisted we join him at the rectory. I hope you don't mind we took the liberty to make arrangements for us to have lunch at his favorite place on Mulberry Street. You are staying for lunch?" she asked, as I got in the van to sit next to her.

"As usual Sister Mary Catherine, you are in charge," I said, feeling anxious about the mafia thugs that combed the streets near Mulberry Street. Would we ever get to the subject of Shannon's adoption, I wondered. But I complied, like the good little Catholic schoolboy again. "Lunch would be lovely. You even found Father Carmen for us. How is he? Still saying the Italian mass at noon? If I do my math right, he must be over eighty-years old."

"Oh yes, well over eighty for the record. He's officially retired, but is still keeping the parishioners happy at Old St. Pat's Cathedral. Many of them moved out of the Lower East Side, and yes, he still says the noon mass in Italian, but only on the first Sunday of the month with another mass at St. Ephrem's in Brooklyn."

"And he's in good health?" I asked.

"Oh yes, he's still very strong. You will soon see." She tapped on Andrew shoulder in the front seat. "Andrew, you will be in my daily prayers. The priesthood needs new young men to carry our church into the new era, especially to carry out the new Vatican Council's plans. Pope Paul is looking for men like you. Our church is changing for the good I think."

Andrew was humored and thanked her, turning to speak to her from the front seat of the van. "Sister, it would be a great honor to serve, just like you have done for decades. My dad told me you grew the New York family social services into what it is today."

"Yes, we started around 1875, and by the first part of the nineteenth century, we found homes for over one thousand children a year. Oh, Declano, how I wish we had you and your mother here today to help us pass on American culture and language to immigrants from all over the globe, they're not just from Europe anymore. Oh, how your mother made learning English fun with music, these new families would love her."

Always the chatting type, her black habit gown never could cover up her vivacious personality and it appeared she hadn't changed. "Declano, you know you were always my favorite. I can say that now, now that I'm old and gray. Father Carmen can't roll his eyes at me anymore for being so obvious with my favoritism toward hard working students like you."

I wanted to jump in with all my questions, but I held back. Sister Mary Catherine was having too much fun.

"Oh, I have to ask. Did you ever become a professor of literature? You were my best student in writing and reading. Please tell me you are the editor of a respected newspaper in California or an author with a loyal following."

"No, I'm not writing as a profession. I attended law school, against your wishes, remember?" I said, thinking how she and Signore Nusco went round and round debating my academic path after I graduated high school.

Her smile disappeared and she pouted. "Law school, yes, I remember now. I cried for weeks when you and Signore Nusco decided on that. So dry—with no poetry or prose for you."

I shrugged. "I should have listened. My life would have been very different."

My statement brought the smile back to her face. "Can you write that down? I will frame it for all my seniors at St. Joseph's Academy."

I laughed and nodded, remembering how for two years, after my sophomore term, Signore Nusco had a driver pick her up once a week at the convent to work with all of us boys near the library adjacent to Borough Park on Thirteenth Avenue. "Of course. Let me tell any of your students who aren't planning to follow your advice, how foolish they are. You always wanted us to be our best, I can drop by your Academy while I'm in town to chat with your seniors if you want."

She looked at the driver and pointed for him to turn right at the light while she continued to hold my hand in the backseat bench of the van. "You would? That's a date, Declano. I want my students to polish the talents that God bestowed upon them, and hearing that from one of my former students would personify that. That's all I want for them and of course they must to follow a righteous path," she said, and winked at Andrew.

The driver took the van south down Park Avenue towards lower Manhattan, buzzing past slow cars and honking at them.

"It feels great to be back in Manhattan," I said, my excitement growing. "Hey driver, before you turn on Mulberry Street, would you mind swinging by Washington Square Park and Orchard Street?" I asked, and then turned to Sister Mary Catherine. "I want to see my Pappy and Mammy's place real quick if that's okay, they had a quaint brownstone home on Twelfth Ave, after that, can we show Andrew my humble Orchard Street tenement, as this historical tour is part of a research project we're working on together."

"Oh, yes Sir. I was told by Father C to take you anywhere you wanted to go today," the driver said, talking to us via the rearview mirror.

"Declano, you must be someone else's favorite, too. Father Carmen is usually very persnickety about his precious green Dodge van. And Andrew dear, you must tell me all about your historical research work you're doing at Fordham," Sister Mary Catherine said.

I looked at a reflection of the van in a windowed storefront and laughed to myself. None of Marcos' guys would think to look for me in a parish van like this one, I thought.

When the driver approached Washington Square, I asked him to turn right on my grandparents' street. I wished to go back to the days when my Pappy would sit with me on the front brownstone steps, with my dog-eared innocence, telling me tales of his homeland Ireland. "One of these homes has to be theirs. They moved from this street when I was around six years old, so I can't remember which home it was exactly. Stop here, just for a minute driver." I jumped out of the van and walked up the steps of one of the homes and inhaled a nice breath of New York air into my lungs. I could still see my mother pregnant, throwing me a ball or sweeping the steps happy and singing Irish ballads. I sat on a front porch of a random brownstone home and wished once more I could simply blink to make time go back four decades.

I jumped back into the van and gave the driver the address on Orchard Street.

"97 Orchard Street?" the driver asked. "That's just a boarded up vacant building now." He drove a few more blocks, stopping in front of the dilapidated structure.

I had no idea why I wanted to see it again. As I looked at the boarded up windows, I remembered playing stickball on the streets with Tino, as my mother held Shannon in her arms, always with a look of longing on her face, wishing to go to Ireland and be with her parents again. I couldn't get out of the van, as the voice of my father shouting German rants from the speakeasy window still played in my head. "Move on, driver. I've seen enough," I said, feeling sick to my stomach. "We shouldn't keep Father Carmen waiting."

When we turned on East Houston towards Mulberry Street, I saw Father Carmen instructing two men shoveling snow off the steps to his door of the rectory. When he saw the van, he handed his shovel and gloves to one of the workers and waved his hat in the air at us. I opened the car door and he approached us saying, "Buon giorno. Declano Hauser, it's a delight to see you. It has been too many years since you visited St. Patrick's."

Jumping out of the van, I shook his hand. "Buon giorno, Father Carmen, it's been a long time. I go by my mother's name now, Quinn. The last time I was here was just before I left for the war. Your blessing that day and Sister's St. Michael's metal saved my life many times over."

"Happy to see you faired well, son," Father Carmen said.

"So good to see you, don't you ever age?" I turned back to wave Andrew over, proud to introduce him. "Meet my son, Andrew. You will be happy to hear he's a student in Fordham University's pre-seminary program."

Father Carmen took us on a tour of the grounds chatting the whole time with Andrew about his work at Fordham. "Before we go inside, the florist delivered new flowers this morning for the Blessed Mother statue in the garden. Would you boys like to join us in placing them at her feet with me?"

"We'd love to, Father," I said. "Andrew has never visited his grandmother's grave before, and I confess it's been so long for me as well. I'm not entirely sure I remember where to find it. I know she's buried close to the Blessed Mother's statue. Please Father, would you mind guiding us?" I asked, and stopped to buy two bushels of winter lilacs from a corner display.

Father Carmen and Sister Mary Catherine exchanged sad looks, and then he nodded and led the way. We followed them into the stone arched entrance to the cemetery where winter had stripped the trees bare and a cold wind blew giving me a chill. I knew my mother's burial plot was near.

When I saw her headstone, I removed my gray derby hat to cover my pounding heart. Father Carmen, Andrew, and Sister Mary Catherine, instinctively knelt in reverence. All three removed rosary beads from their pockets and began to recite a chain of prayers at her grave.

I stood stiff and in shock, seeing my mother's headstone for the first time. When I last visited her grave in the summer of 1943, just before I left for the war, there had been only a steel grave marker sticking out of the dirt with her last name on it. The stone was perfect and beautiful with the Irish Cross embossed on the left side. The epithet summed up her whole existence in ten words.

Aisling Quinn Hauser
June 2, 1900-February 8, 1933
Herein Lies One Whose Name Was Writ In Song

Who did this for her? I thought.

I interrupted her prayer with a whisper. "Sister Mary Catherine, did you have something to do with the making of this headstone?" She gave me her hand and I helped her stand, together we walked slowly to the kneeler under a huge, bare oak tree a few yards away.

Speaking in soft tones she said, staring at the gravestone, "No. Although, I wish I could take the credit for that one."

"Who then? Father Carmen? This is the most beautiful headstone that I've ever seen," I said, surprising myself as I started to cry.

Father Carmen, still on his knees in deep prayer, looked up at me, and slowly got to his feet. He walked over to us, using his cane, wobbling over the uneven gravesites while handing Sister another handful of flowers. "No. I am not the one responsible, but I remember the day it was delivered in a huge wood crate. I have the paperwork in my office. Her father came here after the war. He designed and bought this stone special in Ireland. If I remember correctly, I believe you are his namesake, Declano."

Shocked, my thoughts began to spin. "Yes, I am. But my grandfather never told me about this or of his visit to New York."

Father Carmen tried to recall. "No? Well, it's coming back to me now. Professor Declan Quinn of the Catholic University in Ireland. Yes, I remember. He had such a thick Irish brogue and very impressive, someone you meet once and never forget. You bear a strong resemblance to him, in fact. Forgive me, I assumed you knew about the headstone."

I was still very irritated. "No, Father Carmen. It's all a puzzle to me. I would like to get more information from you, if you don't mind."

"Fine, I'll pull her file and prepare us some tea and toast. I need to warm up these old bones by the fireplace, but you take as long as you need. We'll talk when you come inside," he said.

Watching him walk back toward the rectory, I felt a gnawing curiosity, coupled with the old bitterness rising in me like the trusted morning sun. I watched Andrew demonstrating a pure, unblemished dedication to a grandmother he had never met. My reverence, in contrasting shame, was anything but pure. In my head I heard the voice of Shannon's screams crying out for our mother, there was no quiet in my head. My thoughts defiled this sacred space. They came with the influx of the howling winds around me, and wreaked havoc into this peaceful setting. How could my Pappy come here after the war without contacting me? More than strange, I thought.

I wanted to follow Father Carmen right away to search in that file, but it was obvious that neither Andrew nor Sister Mary Catherine were planning on making this prayer vigil short. What was this disbelieving man to do, get on his knees and fake it at his mother's grave? Their dedication was admirable, bent knees in deep contemplation on the frozen ground, without a care or interference from the world around them. I wondered if their power in contemplation came from a true entity, or if they foolishly believed in something that didn't exist.

Sister Mary Catherine always joked to me when I was a boy. "Declano the doubter", she'd say. "Always questioning everything, and never satisfied." On this day, I looked at my son in total devotion, questioning nothing, yet believing in everything. He was at peace, while doubt zapped my strength. I couldn't ignore the confusion that robbed me.

Nietzsche was right, and said it best, "Whoever fights monsters should see to it that in the process he does not become the monster. And if he gazes long enough into an abyss, the abyss will gaze back." I saw, as clear as the winter sky, that I became the monster in order to defeat the monster, and had been gazing into an abyss ever since.

I had to contain my instincts and wait, in utter madness, while Father Carmen searched for the file and my questions got answered. But what to do while I bided my time—pray?

So, for Andrew's sake, and in honor of my mother's memory, I took another deep breath and listened to the wind blowing through the cemetery and made a respectable effort to contain myself. I imagined a twisted God above toying with me again as my son approached with yet another proposal.

"Paps," Andrew asked in a whisper. "Would you join me in praying a decade of the rosary? It couldn't hurt. It's only a decade. They even have cushions over there so you won't muddy your trousers."

Sister Mary Catherine slipped away, making a quiet exit to warmer quarters. I longed to escape with her, but my son was looking at me with such hope on his face. I hated to disappoint him, but the idea of getting on my knees was one I wasn't ready for.

I shrugged. "Well Andrew, I appreciate your asking, but I've got to be honest with you. It's been a long, long while since I've gotten down on my knees and prayed." I tightened my jacket buttons with difficulty. "And looking at that headstone makes it hard for me, kid. Can you believe it? Father Carmen said my Pappy came here and had it delivered from Ireland. How could he have come to New York and never tell me?" I saw Andrew looking at me, frowning, not accepting my refusal as I continued. "Come on, why don't we get inside and talk to Father Carmen about this, besides aren't you freezing your ass off out here?"

I stood up, fixed my scarf, ready to walk back, but Andrew turned away and got me a kneeler. He handed it to me along with his ebony black rosary beads. "Come on, Paps. This will do you good."

Unable to refuse, I got on my knees for the first time in ages. Andrew said the first half of the Hail Mary and I recited the second half. "Holy Mary Mother of God, pray for us sinners now and at the hour of our death." The words, stuck in my throat for forty years, flowed out like they did when I was a student in Sister Mary Catherine's classroom helping her teach the Italian boys to say the holy prayers in English. As I recited the prayers, I wished the words could transform my heart back to my former innocence, move the needle and restart the record of my life from the beginning. One thing I knew for sure, ten Hail Mary's weren't enough to restore my faith back to anything like my son's.

On bended knees, I felt our souls touching once again. "Greenies to greenies," I said to her in a whisper. "Together at last, greenies to greenies my sweet mother, do you see the green grass of Ireland dancing…" I had to stop speaking all together and wept on my knees next to her grave. Andrew moved away and sat on a bench in silence.

After ten or more minutes of devotion more than prayer, I stood and stretched out my frozen bones, happy an earthquake didn't erupt when this gangster got on his knees.

"You look more at peace. Nice job, Paps. Let's get you inside before we turn into ice for good." He put his arm over my shoulder. "Don't worry, with Grandma's spirit guiding us, you will soon solve all the mysteries that haunt you, Paps."

As I walked quietly toward the rectory with Andrew, I turned to acknowledge my mother once again with a sign of the cross. Of course, I didn't forget how to do that either.

Don't fill your heart with hate, no matter what this world can take. Our love must not be disgraced. My mother's spirit whispered in my ear once more.

I stopped, walked back a few feet alone, as if she beckoned me to hear an encore.

Declan, please son, turn away from darkness, go home—go home.

Home, I thought. "But, it was only home when you were here with me," I said, whispering back to her, wiping off my tears.

CHAPTER TEN

A TIME FOR PRUNING

When we entered the rectory, the warmth of Father Carmen's front office was a welcomed relief. I blocked out the fact my mother lay cold and frozen under the earth, so close and alone in the dark, just like my little Aisling at home. Cemeteries were places I tended to avoid.

"Come in, boys." Father Carmen said. "I'm having your family records brought here, it's no problem as most students we haven't seen in years come for their baptismal records or certificates of the sacraments. But you say you've never seen the beautiful headstone straight from Ireland until today, I find that strange, don't you?" he asked, looking confused, motioning for me to have a seat. "So, I asked Sister Elizabeth to fetch the receipts from your mother's cemetery plot, they will show what day we installed her headstone."

Sister Mary Catherine carried in a tray of hot coffee, tea, and donuts and offered them to us. "I know you've come from a cemetery, Declano, but from the looks of you—you appear to have just seen a ghost. Are you okay?" she asked, setting down the tray and pouring us steaming coffee and tea.

"I'm fine," I answered not wanting to be distracted from my goal. "Thank you, Father Carmen, for pulling the files. Yes, her beautiful headstone came as a complete surprise, and I'm very interested in getting the facts, but that's not why I came to New York. If it's no trouble for you, I also would like to see the records of my sister Shannon's adoption. I think, Sister Mary Catherine, we may have to go back to the Foundling Hospital for those."

Sister was warming her hands near the fireplace. "No. I brought her file with me. It's right here," she said, and walked over to her portfolio sitting on top of a corner table. "Like Father Carmen said, we're used to siblings like you coming to see the records on their families."

I took a thin manila file from her graciously, as if she handed me the secret code to finding happiness again. "Thank you so much for this." I froze having this information in my hands, pulled the papers out, and noticed my hands were shaking.

A memo, stamped on top of a pile of paperwork from the Foundling Hospital read:

March 3, 1946. Received by: Declan Quinn.

Several forms under the memo said:

Shannon Quinn Hauser / Date of Birth: February 11, 1926, New York, New York.

Adoption Date: March 24, 1933. Age 7.

Adopted by: Jason and Joan O'Scanlon / Buffalo, New York.

"What is this note here? That's my grandfather's signature," I asked, confused, pointing to the top of the file, but was reluctant to touch the paper.

Sister came over to look at the file in my hand and ruffled through the paperwork wetting her fingertip to flip through the stack quickly. "Oh, let me see that. Indeed, I remember now, your grandfather asked me for a copy of her file," she said. "I remember that day," she repeated. "He said he was going to see you. It was such a long time ago, I forgot all about it until now," she said.

Sister Elizabeth came in from the rectory office and handed Father Carmen another file. He glanced at it and handed it to me. "Here it is, the cemetery file on your mother's burial plot."

"Thank you," I said, and opened it, feeling light headed, my hands still shaky.

It read:

Aisling Quinn Hauser, Deceased: February 8, 1933.

Special Order: Imported Headstone Delivery

(Ireland Shipping Company/Galway) Received: March 1, 1946

On the delivery slip with the same signature in my grandfather's handwriting:

Received: Declan Quinn. March 3, 1946

I looked at Sister Mary Catherine and Father Carmen and tried my hardest to calmly request more information. "Would you please tell me what you remember of my grandfather's visit here?"

Father Carmen took a seat behind his desk and offered his recall first. "I remember he was excited when we opened the crate that day on the cemetery grounds. He stayed and watched as the groundskeeper laid it into the cement. He asked about you, of course, and I gave him the address of the Nusco residence in Bensonhurst. Didn't he come for you there?"

Sister too, remembered his visit. "Declano, I told him where you were living as well. I know he wanted to see you," she said. "So many folks came to me after the war looking for lost relatives. He was one of them. We were still in the smaller complex near St. Patrick's Parish then. He was so pleased when he opened the file on your sister, the same as the one you're holding right now. I assumed the two of you planned to track down Shannon together."

I looked at the date again on the top memo, it had Pappy's signature and a stamped date: March 3, 1946. I pieced the facts together in my head quickly. It was the first spring session after the war, when I stayed on campus finishing law school at Fordham and preparing for the New York bar exam. There was much going on in the mafia then, post World War II—mafia wars broke out all over the West Side docks and in the boroughs of New York. During this time, even Lucky Luciano exiled to Italy for his own safety. In the Bronx, outside of the campus' walls, it wasn't unusual to hear a street war and gunfire taking out a gang member or two. Tino was taking over running the business operations out of the Nusco mansion on Ocean Parkway, while Signore Nusco left the East Coast to establish a casino business in Reno and Las Vegas. The date on the forms was the same week of Tino's murder on the docks at the New York Harbor shipyard.

I pictured an Irish man, a professorial type, innocently walking up to the house asking questions about me right after Tino's murder. Instead he found a den of wolves at the gate, most likely in a frenzy of rage. Questions from outsiders never went well, let alone in a wartime situation on the streets. I figured they chased him away or worse could have happened. With no way of knowing I was at Fordham, he must have given up and flew home to Ireland.

Then I shuddered at the notion, what if Pappy got mixed up in that conflict and was hiding something, as he could have easily told me the story in the many letters over the years. I rubbed Shannon's file wanting to make a phone call to Ireland immediately, before lunch to get the facts. I was not a patient man.

Sister Mary Catherine snapped me out of my thought. "Declano, forgive me for asking. But…" She hesitated, speaking in a soft tone. "I remember distinctly, and now you're confusing me—but it was your choice to let Shannon go off without you on the orphan bus. We came for you at the hospital and I made sure to have a nurse on board for the journey, just for you. However, you refused to come with us. I have always wondered why. Was it that girl in Brooklyn you liked so much? Did you ever marry her?"

I put my arm around her. "I was changed after my mother died and Shannon didn't need an angry brother around. So I let her go."

"But, you were wrong, son. She did need you, Declano," she said, and took her white handkerchief out of her sleeve to dab at her eyes.

I kissed her cheek. "I'm sorry, Sister. You have no idea how much I regret that day. I think about her all the time and wonder how she is. Can you at least tell me how Shannon fared on the journey?"

Sister Mary Catherine stood to pour us more tea and coffee as Andrew took the kettle from her to help.

Father Carmen stepped into the conversation. "Declano, families were split up every day due to the depression in those years. There just weren't enough jobs to find for them or bread and jam to feed all the children," he said.

"Oh my, we had so many little ones to place." Sister agreed. "However, Shannon's adoption I remember specifically, because I delivered her myself to a farm near Buffalo. She was almost eight-years-old and the cutest little red head with her curly locks. Sister Elizabeth made a new green eyelet dress for her and she wore pigtails…" She stopped and took to her handkerchief again. "I will never forget how that dress made her eyes pop like emeralds."

"Do you remember the family who adopted her?" I asked.

"Oh yes. Sweet Shannon went to a beautiful family. Your mother would have been pleased. They had a farm and two twin infant boys. They wanted Shannon instantly when they saw her. Their daughter, who was the same age as Shannon, died from influenza the winter before. They waited all day at the church for our bus to arrive. When they saw your sister, it was love at first sight. Her curly golden red hair and freckled, fair complexion fit in so well with their family. When Shannon stood with them they looked instantly like a simple Irish-American family."

Sister took the file and read the forms again. "See, their sir name was O'Scanlon. I recall their family originated from Galway. It was important to them to find a daughter of Irish descent. I told them your mother was from southern Ireland, where was it your grandfather lived?"

"County Tipperary," I said.

"Yes, that's right. I knew he taught literature at the Catholic University in Dublin because your mother used to send him letters and packages all the time. I helped her mail them from our convent." She shuffled the papers in the file. "Yes, I remember. County Tipperary, Ireland. When the O'Scanlon family heard that, it sealed sweet Shannon's fate. I carried with me all of the paperwork needed to process the adoption, so she became Shannon O'Scanlon that very day," Sister said.

I sighed and thought back to that day and had to give them a not-so-rosy backstory. "The night our mother died, Shannon and I were left alone with those awful nurses who…" I stopped, wishing to never speak of this again, yet continued. "Then, I heard Shannon screaming from the bus weeks later when you came for me, but my eyes were infected and patched up, so I couldn't see what was going on."

When I lapsed into a long silence staring at the file, Andrew came over to whisper in my ear. "Spit it out. Shannon. You have nightmares about her. I saw it myself. Tell her, Paps, pull out those thorns."

I shook my head, conflicted between spitting out the truth and letting the memories hide to play their silent refrain in my head forever.

Sister attempted a rescue. "Declano, it was an awful night when we heard of your mother's death, one I will never forget too; she was like a sister to me. You are brave to return to this pain, most people never do, and become ill due to the suppression. I can appreciate when people like you come to us to track down their lost family and speak of the loss," Sister Mary Catherine said, yet hesitated to continue. "You did ask me a pertinent question about that day and are willing to peal back the scab, so I must tell you the truth." She took a deep breath and continued. "You see, Shannon was quite upset the entire ride upstate. The poor child, she saw her mother die right in front of her and never calmed down." Sister looked straight at me again. "However, you were a child too and a witness to this atrocity as well." She placed her hand on mine.

Unable to bear her touch, I stood up.

She continued. "You and Shannon needed each other. Of course, this is all water under the bridge indeed, Declano you two could have stayed together and been adopted as siblings. The O'Scanlon's would have welcomed you both, I'm sure of it."

Father Carmen listened to our conversation without comment, then left his desk, motioning Andrew to join him in the adjacent room near a wall of bookshelves. Sister refilled my coffee cup and sat next to me as I carefully put Shannon's file in my briefcase.

As if she were my guide, walking with me into a dark cave, I took her hand and decidedly spoke of the past and of the sadness I had held inside from this trauma. If Andrew's method held any validity, there was no denying it any more. So, with difficulty, I began to speak to Sister again. "I can tell you her crying voice haunts me on a regular basis. I hear it like a constant ringing in my ears," I said, in a shallow voice, the truth came of its own will. "First, she screamed for our mother in that stinking hospital, and then…" I stopped for a second or two. "And then, the terrible nurses tried to hold her down on a gurney to give her a shot as she was screaming for hours for mother to wake up." Sister listened without comment. "When you returned with her in the bus to pick me up at the hospital, her cries continued." I stopped and sipped down a shot of hot coffee. "Sister, if you must know, Shannon's cries haunt me lately, night after night."

She placed a tender hand on mine and sighed. "Yes, me too really. It was the one transfer that was the hardest for me to sign off." She began to cry. "Let's not worry about Shannon, she was placed with a good family," Sister Mary Catherine said, wiping her eyes dry with a handkerchief, however I could tell she was worried. "Tragedy came into your life and everything changed. It's time for you to find her. Like the wool interwoven in your sweater, she is a part of you and you a part of her."

Taking the cup, I sipped the hot restorative liquid and nodded in agreement. "Yes. That's why I'm here. I won't rest until I find her."

"Good. See that you do. And please write and tell me how she is doing, so I too can put her adoption to rest in my head," she said, and smiled through her tears. "And of course Declano, I'm always a teacher first, do you remember how I made you boys copy St. Paul's letters straight out of the bible until you had them memorized?"

"Oh yes, Sister. My group was assigned The Epistle to the Romans, how can I forget that one, I painfully remember those days," I said with a chagrin.

She smiled devilishly wiping her eyes dry. "Good. Then what does Paul tell the Romans in Chapter Five about man's struggles in life?"

Indeed those verses were ingrained into my brain, so I recited a few lines from memory, but rolled my eyes the same way I did in her seventh grade classroom at St. Ephrem's. "We can boast of our afflictions, knowing that afflictions produce endurance, and endurance, proven character, and proven character, hope, and hope doesn't disappoint," I said, surprising even myself and smiled with relief.

She was pleased. "Good for you, happy that ruler tapping did some good after all."

I laughed and gave her a hug. "Yes, you were tough, and my knuckles have the scar tissue to prove it, but we learned a lot from you that's for sure."

She didn't apologize. "Love is a tough discipline, son, most kids would just rot away without a firm line to follow. Nonetheless, I loved you, and saw so much potential there," she said, tearing up a little and grabbed her scarf. "I will pray that soon you and your sister will be joined together again as you were born to be, and again, don't forget to write me when you do."

Father Carmen and Andrew walked back into the room over to us with smiles and a plan for lunch. "This boy was always your favorite, and now look at you, upset that this one got away." He laughed. "Anyone interested in a nice hot lunch over at my favorite spot on Mulberry Street? Sister tells me two nice Irishmen are treating us today," Father Carmen said, throwing his arm over Andrew's shoulder. It was like looking at the beginning and the end of a priest's career path in one glance.

Appreciating a change in the action, I said, "We would be delighted. Thank you both for telling me about my grandfather's visit. The headstone is beautiful. So Irish, just like my mother. But let's put all this sad talk of the past behind us," I said, feeling better having told my story. "We must move along as my son here needs to return to his research at Fordham," I said. "Andrew, do you mind me telling them about your newest research idea?"

He laughed, and walked over to me, putting his arm over my shoulder. "Please do, Paps, it looks like you're my first success story."

"Well, I'm proud of my boy," I said looking at them. "Watch for the abstracts and methodologies of his research soon, you can read of his newest psychoanalytical approach of getting men like me to revisit the traumas of their past."

Father Carmen smiled. "Yes, Declano, your son explained to me his idea. I love it, in fact. I told Andrew to speak to Monsignor O'Shea about this, as I believe a therapeutic method like that is where people could go when the clergy is tapped out. Surely there's a good chance it could become the therapeutic discovery of the decade," he said.

We all exited the rectory, talking about Andrew's research, while my mind was focused on delving into the findings in my briefcase—and it seemed there was a grandfather in Ireland who had some serious explaining to do.

CHAPTER ELEVEN

DINNER AT NOON

We walked the few blocks to the restaurant on Mulberry Street. I missed the safety of the van and the rectory, lunch delivered would have been better, I thought. So I went back to looking over my shoulder checking to see if I was being followed. Father Carmen and Sister Mary Catherine kept up with us despite their ages and Father's cane. They chatted with Andrew, leaving me in quiet thought and planning.

To stay on guard, I felt down to the bottom of my briefcase and was relieved knowing my steel protection was handy. After a lifetime of crime, I knew my holy-clothed bodyguards wouldn't be enough to save me from Marcos' guys.

I was very interested to know what happened to my Pappy when he went searching for Shannon and me. Nothing, not even a brigade of Marcos' brawlers, would put an end to my search.

Father Carmen broke step with my son and Sister Mary Catherine, and moved closer to talk to me. "The restaurant is just around the corner, and lunch is on me today, Declano, never mind what I said in the rectory. Today is my treat and we will eat like the Italians do, enjoying our main meal at noon. You two Irishmen will live like Italians today and eat like only we know how, then take a nice nap at two o'clock."

He made me laugh and happy to be reunited with him again. When we approached the restaurant, I realized this was the same place Marco favored when he came to the Lower East Side. It worried me, but I kept quiet lest I spoiled the day for the others.

The doorman greeted us and gave Father Carmen a firm handshake, helping him with his hat and jacket. Sister Mary Catherine hugged the server as he led us inside to a table in the rear of the restaurant. I kept my hat on low, until we sat in our secluded corner. Walking in with Father Carmen was like being with the Pope of Mulberry Street, so for the most part, I felt protected.

I helped Sister take her seat. "Well, Declano, we must thank you again for this wonderful surprise today. Please, feel free to ask us anything about Shannon, absolutely anything."

I needed a drink. "Father, would you mind if I order a bottle of Chianti to share and some garlic bread perhaps?" I asked. "And please, this visit doesn't have to be all about me or my family. Tell me about New York these days. It looks like the struggles we had in the Thirties have almost vanished from these streets," I said, trying to make the best of the gathering as I put my patience to task.

Sister Catherine interrupted. "Oh, don't let all the flashy Cadillacs fool you. Poverty is still everywhere. We can barely keep up with the mothers trying to raise their children alone after losing their men to drugs, prostitution, and gambling."

Andrew took a seat. "Bless you both for all the service you do for the needy, I can round up a group of interns on campus to help you at the Foundling Hospital."

I sat quiet on the issue; embarrassed for the part I played in destroying families here in New York. When Signore Nusco was in charge of the business, we stayed away from pushing drugs. Not so when Tino and Marco took over leadership, drug trafficking, like heroin inside an addict's veins, became our main addiction giving us exorbitant cash at hand.

Father Carmen settled in at our table, grabbing a slice of garlic bread, and nodded at the server who showed him the label on the bottle of Chianti. "After all these years, I can't believe that finally Declano Hauser, oh excuse me, Declano Quinn, has come to visit us. You were heading off to fight for the Army the last time we saw you," Father Carmen said, and ordered our complete meal as if it were a dinner feast. "Waiter, please prepare my favorite speciale Positano antipasta con prosciutto con olives, e' per secondo, we'd like your best veal con marsala con rigitoni melanzane, per favore signore." The waiter took the order without writing it down. Father Carmen took the wine from the waiter and then opened the bottle with a corkscrew, twisting the cork until it popped. He smiled as he poured it for everyone, filling his own glass last. "So where did we leave off? Did you get everything you needed from the office?" Father Carmen asked handing back filled wine glasses to each of us.

"Yes, I think so. Sister Mary Catherine gave me copies of the files. Thank you for everything. I will call you when and if I get a hold of my sister," I said, and double-checked on the contents of my briefcase under the table.

"We will pray you find her safe and happy, Declano," Sister Mary Catherine said.

"And your grandfather too," Father Carmen said. "I'm sure you have many questions for him."

I let the notion of my grandfather slide without comment, as a trip to see him to get the facts was first on my agenda. We chatted for a while, drinking wine and enjoying Andrew's stories from campus, but I got quiet when the waiter arrived with an array of dishes wafting a full aroma of garlic and basil, as my stomach remained in knots since the cemetery.

Overwhelmed by the vast quantities of food and scents, I wished for my appetite to return and the stack of pancakes from the morning to settle. He set down each family sized dish onto the red-and-white checkered tablecloth then served generous portions to each of us. The server graciously finished, draping his white napkin over an arm and picked up the Chianti bottle, but Sister Mary Catherine held her hand over her glass and refused him topping it off with a smile.

Father blessed the food with a quick prayer as we bowed our heads to pray along.

We began to enjoy our lunch together and the Chianti was refreshing, but I felt obligated to clear the air with them, given my mood in the rectory was mixed with shock and emotion. They both tried their best to help my family, before tragedy intercepted their good will.

"Father Carmen and Sister Mary Catherine, I realize this is all from a time lost in oblivion, but can you both forgive me for running off when you tried to help us the night my mother died? I was just an enraged teenager, searching to find my father," I said, looking at Andrew with a look of warning, as he raised his eyebrows at me. If he brought up the Teenage Avenger, I'd surely kick him under the table.

Father Carmen took one bite of his food. "Oh, you remind me now. Of course we forgive you, son. But, Declano, if my memory serves me well, you were a teen looking to kill a man—your father of all things."

I looked at Father Carmen, old and worn from helping lost souls like me, and held my tongue as he finished his lunch serving. My father killed my mother. He needed to die—end of story. I was sorry for running, but not sorry for my intent, I thought to myself.

Sister Mary Catherine added her thoughts and tried to ease my mind. "What you don't realize son, is that you were just a boy when this tragedy hit you, there's no need for apologies today."

A server refreshed our wine and bread as Father Carmen gave him a stern look, so he got the message and left us alone for the duration to serve ourselves.

I continued. "Well, for the record, take my gratitude and my apologies today for all the years you helped my family. Come to think of it, perhaps a nice donation to the Foundling Hospital in my mother's name could be my penance for that night, right Father Carmen?" I asked, and took out my checkbook, put a nice hefty figure on the line, signed my name, and slid it across the tablecloth in front of Sister Mary Catherine.

She stopped eating, looked at the amount and almost choked on her food. "Declano, we can't accept this from you, it was our honor to help you and your family."

I slid it another inch closer to her. "I need to do this. Please, Sister, take it."

Andrew and Father Carmen smiled watching us debate the issue and continued to do more work on the food. Our reunion wasn't a place to speak of sons killing their fathers, so we left the notion of my rage and continued to speak in general terms on subjects like the problems that occurred with orphans abandoned on the steps of the rectory. I realized Shannon and I were just one of many sad cases they had to settle in those depression era times.

Sister got excited, sharing how she was going to put my donation to good use, asking me if I had a photo of my mother that she could hang at the hospital. I explained to her how I didn't have one, with regret. A picture, I thought. There must be one somewhere.

My thoughts kept returning to the date on the file and that of my Pappy's visit. March 3, 1946—Received by: Declan Quinn. Strange. Should I excuse myself and find a phone booth on the corner and place a call to Ireland now, I wondered.

As if he could read my mind, Father made a suggestion. "I could use some fresh air," he announced after taking one last bite of the Veal Marsala. He stood up, and pulled two fine cigars out of the inside pocket of his black jacket. "Declano, how about if we let Andrew and Sister chat about the problems in this crazy city. They can discuss his research and intern jobs over cannoli and espresso, while you and I step out back to enjoy these cigars. Sound good?"

I was relieved and grateful to him. "Fresh air sounds great," I stood up eagerly and pulled his chair away to help him stand, giving him his cane.

"Good," he said, taking my aid, and turned to Andrew. "Andrew, be sure to save me a cannoli, but watch out, Sister Mary Catherine here likes to steal delicious pastries for her novitiates at the convent." He patted Andrew on the shoulder and Sister pretended to slap his arm with her napkin.

"Oh, you go off now and we'll be sure to eat up all the pastries in this place so you can't have any," Sister said, and laughed loudly enough to turn many heads our way.

We all laughed together as I gave Andrew a look of confidence with a wink as I assisted Father in putting on his coat. "Well, if you're telling me Sister Mary Catherine is a thief, then for certain I am a candidate for hell," I said, winking at my son.

I put my arm over Father's shoulder, as he walked through the bustling kitchen. We exited the back door into an alley shaded under a flimsy, rusted tin roof where rancid trash odors assaulted my nose and rats scampered over the trash bins to hide inside the stacked boxes. This was the last place one would think to find a priest, but Father Carmen seemed completely at home as he put his hat back on.

One of the workers came out the alley door, threw out a bag of trash, and saw us. "Hey, Father Carmen, good to see you. That issue with my son is getting a little better. His grades are improving, too. You're a wise man, one of the good ones," he said, shaking his hand before returning to the restaurant again.

I sighed, feeling guilty. "Sorry Father, I feel bad we let most of that beautiful lunch go to waste. Maybe you can have them pack it up for your dinner tonight."

"Don't worry about the food, Declano, and Sister Mary Catherine will fully take your generous donation and use it for a great cause, just the water cost of that building alone would surprise you." Father Carmen brandished two cigars in his hand and handed me one.

With gratitude I took it, smelling its deep tobacco scent. "Um, this smells wonderful, thank you."

His eyes tried to read into mine and he didn't smile. "Let me be blunt, okay, Declano."

"Of course. I can take the heat," I said, surprised by his tone.

"Okay, this alley is a place for truth," he said, and put a cigar into his mouth and prepared to light it. "I know you and that Nusco boy set out to kill your father. Is that why you went to live with them? The Attanasio's would have taken you back for sure, they were a good family," he said, struggling to light the cigar.

I took a matchbook from my pocket to help him. "Let's leave old topics alone."

He ignored me, and I lighted his cigar as he inhaled oxygen into it while speaking through his teeth. "Then poor Sister Mary Catherine in there, she arranged for your little sister and you to go on the bus to a new family, and you refused again. You had revenge in your mind and it blinded you; but you were one of the good ones, always a straight A student. Then you got mixed up with that Nusco kid—what's his name again?"

"Tino." Shocked by the topic, my voice became filled with anger, and I couldn't hide it, despite being in the presence of a priest. "Tino had nothing to do with it, I set out to find my father for good reason. You saw for yourself how he always slapped my mother around. No one ever stopped him. You tried to help us, but even the police failed."

"Declano, life can bring us many challenges. It helps to talk about it to clear the air."

"Or to clear the cobwebs in my head," I said.

"Indeed, to clear it all up, if one's not careful, our minds can become tangled into a web we try to weave ourselves in."

I shrugged. "A tangled web—can't deny that."

He looked at me with concerning eyes. "Forgive me, Declano, for mentioning this, but your son told me what happened to his little sister, Aisling. That's a name given to her from a great woman. Your son is having a difficult time processing that loss, and I can see you are suffering deeply as well. Tell me, how you are coping."

The turn in the conversation struck me hard. "I wouldn't know where to start."

"Okay, how about if you begin by telling me why you haven't left your ranch nor practiced law since her death last year?" he asked.

I shrugged. "I just can't go there today with you Father," I said, and stepped back. "Did you and Andrew also talk about what clients I represent? It's not something many people know. Quitting my job isn't a bad thing."

Father Carmen nodded, and then relighted his cigar. "Declano, are you going to join me? A parishioner from Cuba gave me a whole box of these at Christmas."

I walked back next to him, gladly smelled the tobacco once more, put the cigar into my mouth taking my sweet time to light it and to speak of the topic at hand.

"Come on, Father Carmen, " I said at last. "You know the Nusco family, and that I've been part of their underworld syndicate all these years."

He nodded again but said nothing, forcing me to continue.

"So this all has to stop, right? All of the lies, the murders, and drug trafficking, the list goes on and on. We're damned, every last one of us. Right, Father?"

"There is always a way back to God," Father Carmen said.

I cut him off with a dismissive wave. "It's too late for me, and my sins were paid for with my daughter's life."

He stopped. "You believe Aisling's accident was what…? God's way of getting back at you?" he asked.

"Yes, exactly. It was my fault. I should have protected her, built that fence I promised my wife. I should have been there, been a better father. It's my fault. It's my fault entirely. God help me. My child is dead because I am an evil man. My father may have died in jail—but I was the one who killed him—you know that, too." I walked away and he followed me down the alley.

"Delano, son, what are you saying? Your father hung himself. What did you, a teenage boy, have to do with that?"

I stopped walking, turned and faced him. "I asked Signore Nusco to kill him for me. He had his goons at the jail rough him up enough, scare him, and tell him that the mob was after him for killing my mother. I wanted him dead and it worked."

Father interrupted. "He hung himself. What you did was wrong, but he hung himself."

"Maybe. Or maybe one of Nuscos' men did it for him. What the fuck difference does it make?" I paused. "Sorry about the language, Father. But he kills my mother then gets killed or takes himself out—either way my life isn't a pretty story to tell."

He paused and inhaled his tobacco. "A man can see life like that. We all encounter darkness, but remember there is much good as well. You have happy memories of your daughter. She lived, and her light will always be part of you. Is that not a gift from God?"

"Yes, there is no denying the happy times we had, I taught her how to ride a horse when she was only three years old."

He smiled at that, and stared at me through a long exhaled amount of tobacco smoke condensing in the cold air. "It's the Enemy who is making you believe your daughter died in payment for your life's transgressions," Father Carmen said.

"The Enemy?"

Father took his cigar and pointed it at me. "Satan."

I backed away, as if giving darkness a name carved a black hole into my core, like a branding on the hind of a horse. "Okay, then I believe Satan is right." I pulled out the photo of my daughter from my vest pocket. "See what I've done to my little angelic child? I'm the one who should be dead, not her."

We were near a row of empty tin trashcans and Father Carmen turned one over to make himself a seat. At eighty plus, his movements were slow and he was methodical with the use of his cane, which made me realize I was probably testing his physical endurance by standing out here in the cold. Still I stood there, staring at the photo, waiting for him to get comfortable on his makeshift seat.

He took her picture from my hand and stared at it for a long minute. "She looks like her namesake," he said, and took out a handkerchief. "I've got good news for you though, Declano. God doesn't work like that, not in the way you think," he said. "Sorry to break up the melodrama you've designed so tidy in your head." He blew his nose and wiped his eyes. "If God wanted Aisling, it was her time to go. Nothing you did or didn't do could change that."

I had heard enough of religious platitudes for the day, so I bent over and grabbed a bottle of soda out of a case stacked against the wall and threw it as far as I could down the alley, the glass shattering, but Father didn't flinch, nor did I. "God willed this, you say? What kind of God is that? You think God wanted to cut off her life at eight years old—in the middle of doing the joy of her life? If that's your God, I want nothing of him," I said, my heart raging out of my chest as I looked at the rest of the stack of bottles. I paused, tempted to toss the whole bunch.

Father didn't alter the rhythm of his tobacco intake as he continued to sit watching me. "So you prefer your God, one who seeks to punish rather than forgive, and especially, a God without love?" He shook his head at me, taking another moment and walked back over to me handed Aisling's picture back. "Son, shames in our hearts pierce like daggers. When you carry them inside, you die from within. Again, it's the Enemy's game, and he's good at it." He paused, enjoyed his cigar, looking at me with affection. "I gave you all your sacraments, from your baptism through your Confirmation at St. Ephrem's and look at you as if you were my own son. It would be my honor to help you through these struggles." He returned to readjust the dilapidated trashcan, made it sturdier for his seat and slowly sat on top of it again. Blowing smoke from his cigar, he said, "Last Sunday in my homily I spoke about the dangers of not standing up for our beliefs when we see injustice around us." He took his cane and used it as a pointer towards my face. "Declano, I know what happened with Ricco's drowning, it was in all the papers. So as the family's counsel, you let that happen, and it wasn't any accident—right?" His cane may well have been the barrel of a rifle, as the truth he spoke made my heart race.

I put the photo back into my pocket for safekeeping. "Don Marco wanted him dead. I arranged it as I always have."

Father Carmen nodded, showing no change in expression. "When a man like you does this, he loses his voice, and begins to speak the language of the tribe around him. Even though he may continue to live on in the physical sense, he begins to die from an internal death of the spirit. Your job is difficult. Marco is your boss, your Don, as you say. I understand the workings of the mob. You can't live in an Italian neighborhood like this and not hear and see all of it, even the dirty gangsters want their infants baptized."

"Oh, believe me, the mafia lurks close Father, watch yourself, often they use the Church as their cover. You see that black Cadillac parked over there? It's most likely trailing me," I said.

"Oh." Father looked over at the car, started to walk towards it, but the driver rolled up the window, threw the gears into reverse, and sped away with the tires screeching.

"You see. Don Marco's not too happy when someone wants to quit the family," I said.

"I see. You want out." He was happy to hear that. "I know you, Declano, you are a good man, which means you had to set your values aside to go along. I caution you to resist this death of the spirit."

"So put me in my grave then, Father Carmen, so this death will be complete and final."

"You want to die, Declano?"

"Well, you just saw for yourself there are those who want me dead. And yes, I've thought about ending it at times, by jumping off a cliff or something. But I have my kids. And I have a wife, though I'm not sure for how much longer, as I haven't been much of a companion."

"Do you love your wife?"

I didn't want to answer, and was starting to feel the cold. "We should get back, your cannoli is probably eaten by now."

He stayed seated on the trashcan. "Do you love her? Son, answer the question. Do you love your wife?"

I looked at him deadpan, and knew he was not going to give up until I answered. "No. I've never truly loved my wife. Sofia and I are more like business partners. We run a tight ship with great kids, twelve chickens, four cows, ten horses, five pigs, and the best tree orchard in the eastern Sierras. You'll have to pay us a visit the next time you're out west. You'd enjoy Sofia, Father Carmen. She's a good companion and knows me well. She hasn't suffered. I've given her nice homes to live in from Jersey to California. But the truth is, I have loved another women for many, many years." My confession continued.

"The sin of adultery is yet another thread in your tangled web," Father Carmen said.

"Not adultery. Love. We never did—that. It could have gone easily in that direction if the decision were up to me, but this woman wouldn't have me. I went to work for the Nusco family straight out of law school, and we broke up. She knew I was involved in a world of crime and wouldn't consider being a mob wife. Not to mention, her father would have kicked my ass," I added with a smile and walked over to the row of trashcans, flipping one over for myself, I placed my seat across from him.

"You met her in law school while attending Fordham?"

"No, we grew up together, childhood sweethearts you can say. We started getting serious while she attended the now, Julliard School of Music and when I was up at Fordham. You knew her family, remember?"

"No, I don't, sorry losing my memory these days son. Who again?"

"You remember. She's a Brooklyn girl, from Bay Ridge."

"Oh sure yes, I am starting to remember. You were good friends with those pretty Attanasio girls when you lived there. You had a crush on one of them. Remind me which one. Was she the one you dated in college?"

I shrugged. "No, the Attanasio girls were like my sisters. I liked one of their cousins, Sal Russo's daughter, Judy. She's the one I dated in college," I said, enjoying this topic, so I continued. "She moved to Hollywood after graduating from music school, and then we broke up. After that, I married Sofia and had four children, but Judy and I still stayed in touch. I've always loved her, suppose I always will. Father, she would never allow me to betray my marriage bond no matter how many times I showed up to tell her how much I adored her."

"Judy Russo. I see," Father Carmen said, and smashed the end of his cigar into the pavement, then grew quiet.

"I tried to look her up just before I came out here, but couldn't locate her," I said, trying to perk him up. "Did I say something out-of-line again, Father Carmen? It's true I'm a sinner. And have doubts about God's will and such. But at least, I stayed clean in the adultery category and will have a straight path to heaven, right? Whew," I said, tapping on his shoulder.

Father Carmen scowled at me, apparently not liking my sarcasm. He stood up and the wobbling trashcan tipped over, so he kicked it as hard as he could while bracing his other leg with the cane. Surprised, I jumped to my feet, and had to brace him from falling over.

"Are you okay, Father? Please don't show me your human side after all these years."

"I'm okay," he said. "Sometimes things get the best of me. And at times, life can stink as much as this alley. Let's go inside, Declano," he said, and walked back towards the restaurant with his head down.

"Wait. Why the sudden change? What did I say? You can give me my penance now if you like. I can take my sentence standing right here in the freezing air. What's it going to be, fifty or one hundred rosaries? Or maybe one-thousand Our Fathers?" I spoke fast and walked in front of him to make eye contact.

Father Carmen stopped and took both of my arms with his hands and looked into my eyes. "I'm just tired, Declano. I'm old and tired. Sad, that's all. Please. Let's check on Sister and Andrew," he said, his voice trembling.

I walked him towards the back door, and he sat down on a chair next to the rear entrance, acting as if he could not walk any further.

"Can I get you a glass of water? I hope my sins haven't taken you under. You don't look that great all of the sudden."

"No, no, it's not that," he said, taking off his black Fedora hat. "I'm sorry I brought you out here to hash out the past, it's surprising how much ministry I do in this stinking alleyway. But son, after what you just told me, I must tell you some terribly tragic news before we go back inside."

CHAPTER TWELVE

ANCORA IMPARO

Father Carmen stood up after a minute or two of rest, still wobbly on his feet. "Declano, your son, Andrew, is a nice boy, but he's taking on a difficult job. Times like this make me want to talk him out of it."

I put my arm around his shoulder. "Okay, now you're making me feel guilty. Apparently, our time together has been too much for you."

"No. Your visit today has meant the world to me," he said, tearing up. "When people like you come back to see me after so many years, it makes my life all worthwhile. Thank you for coming my son."

Relieved he had softened, I said, "No, it's I who should give thanks, from helping my mother find a job, to finding us that amazing family in Brooklyn, to right now hearing me rant." I said, taking his hand. "But you're obviously upset about something. Tell me this terrible news you're so afraid to tell me." I held his arm as he sat down into his seat again as I stacked a few wood boxes for my own seat and positioned them close to him. He fixed his hat onto his head once more and began to tell me the dreaded news.

"All right. I celebrated mass last Sunday at St. Ephrem's in Bay Ridge for the Italian community there, and afterwards, Saverio and Anna Attanasio were in the parish coffee room. They asked me to stop by the Russo house on Shore Road to give the Sacrament of the Last Rites to one of their loved ones."

I stopped. "The Russo's. I guess Sal is in his seventies now, but I hope he is still healthy."

"No, Declano, it wasn't for Sal," he said in a weak voice, removing his hat. "I administered Last Rites to his daughter, your friend, Judy. Son, I'm very sorry to tell you she has terminal cancer and is in the final throes of her long, losing battle."

I stood up immediately. "No. You must be mistaken. Judy? She can't be in the final throes of…" I began to pace the ground. "That can't be. She was fine the last time I saw her, just a few months ago—well, I guess that was over half a year now. But she was fine, as beautiful as ever and strong, singing at the Copa Room at the Sands." I set my cigar down on my seat.

Father Carmen shook his head. "It's no mistake. I saw her just a few days ago. She is not likely to live more than another week. The Russo family is in shock and your sweet Judy is in significant pain," he said, looking defeated. "I am so sorry. She is such a beautiful girl, such a vibrant spirit. It will be a terrible loss. I had no idea you and her were close."

I started to grab another soda bottle out of the stacked cases, but soon discovered Father Carmen, even at his advanced age, was still bigger than me, and stronger than I expected, when he grabbed my arms and held tight.

I started to cry and began to pace again. "But why, Father? Why does God take the good ones and allow them to suffer? First my mother, beaten like a street rat, then my angel daughter, drowned and frozen, and now God is taking beautiful Judy with some forsaken disease, and letting her suffer. They're innocent of evil. Why take their lives and not mine? How can God let this happen? Can you justify any of it?"

He shook his head, sitting back down exhausted. "I have neither the wisdom nor the words to explain the sufferings on this earth. All I know is that anything worthwhile in this world has always been intertwined with pain. The cross of Jesus tells us that. We can't run from this reality any more than we can stop this world's rotation around the sun. One can only trust in God's plan, and pull out the thorns of suffering, like your son said, and to discover their deep meaning."

I put my hat down on the makeshift seat, and with my fingers, brushed the few hairs on my head back, wanting to shout, but in Judy's honor, I toned my emotions down. "Forgive me, Father, but to hell with that. If God's plan is to teach us understanding through suffering, I want no part of it. I don't buy it, anyway," I said. "Really, Father. With all due respect, you can give your parishioners this verbiage if you like, but you promised me truth today."

"That's exactly what I'm giving you. Have you ever had a splinter in your finger, Declano?" he asked.

I sighed, looking at him, knowing he was sincere. "Yes, Father, I live on a farm, chop wood on a daily basis. Splinters are part of my life."

"Good, if you don't pull them out right away, what happens?"

I knew where he was headed. "They grow deeper," I said, putting my hat back on. Settling myself down onto my seat, I gathered my thoughts in preparation to delve into his beliefs, while trying to square them with mine. "Okay then." I swallowed my tears. "If God is perfect, all knowing and omniscient, why did he make our world a fucking chaotic place? Why let good people suffer? Is he a sadist?" I said, and didn't feel like apologizing for my language this time.

Father leaned against the wall, crossed his arms, and offered me a sad but patient smile. "These are questions man has asked from the beginning of time. You must find your own answers. What I do know is that you can't find peace by running away or throwing things like a boy. A man must accept life as it is, in all its complexities, with no clear solutions, no concrete answers."

More platitudes, I thought, and shook my head, unsatisfied. "I've done plenty of searching, for almost a whole year since my daughter's accident," I said.

"No answers yet?" he asked.

"Not one."

He walked closer to me again. "So, which answers fit your life? Darkness hasn't fit. Sin doesn't either. One way is through surrender, another way is to find light inside the darkness."

A wound is a place where light can enter, I thought, remembering Andrew's dedication page in my journal. I finger combed my hair back once more and put my hat back on. "I have failed in both the search for light and reject surrender. Surrender to me is the same as death."

He placed his hands on my forearms. "Not death. Life. Turn down a new path, one that could mend your broken life. Make a choice," Father Carmen said, putting his cigar between his teeth, and then clapped his hands together as if to snap me out of a trance. "Ancora Imparo!"

I smiled at the memory. "I remember that one. My mother used to preach it to me every day, saying 'Father Carmen says we are 'always improving, always learning.''' I nodded and had to smile with him as he had a triumphant look on his face, even through his tears. "Ancora Imparo." I said, shaking my head, laughing.

He wasn't finished. "The phrase isn't meant to be funny, it's meant to have us keep our heads up, not down." He continued. "Is Thomas Merton's No Man is an Island part of Andrew's curriculum?"

"Yes, as a matter of fact, that's one of the books in his reading list."

"Good. Get your mind into that work in particular. Merton speaks of suffering in ways you probably haven't thought of. For starters, he explains how suffering is useless when it changes love into hatred."

I paused holding my hands together trying to absorb his wisdom, but my thoughts were of Judy, sick and dying. "Changes love into hatred. That's a good one, and true. I will remember to read it when I get a chance. Thank you for your counsel, and I'm sure this is all good stuff, but I can't deal with it right now." Tears came again. "All I can think about is Judy. I've got to call her. I think you're better off saving these philosophies for the graduate students. It's a hard call for a man like me. I've spent most of my adult life rejecting the religious platitudes in Andrew's books."

Father didn't look disappointed in me, and I was grateful to him. "Maybe they're not for you, but give them a try. Keep an open mind. That would be a start."

I shook my head. "It would take your God performing a few miracles first, I think. He'd have to bring back my baby and stop the suffering of a beautiful girl in Brooklyn to make me a believer again."

"I hope that is not true, for it would mean all your suffering has been useless. Your mother's death and your daughter's would all be in vain then as well. Judy's too, if once again you change your love into hatred. It would be like your mother's death all over again, have you learned nothing from holding on to hatred all these years?" Father Carmen asked, searching my face with his gaze.

"What I've learned is how to survive. And that usually means, taking someone out before they take you out." I stood up and prepared to leave.

He wasn't quite finished. "Survive, at what cost? Hatred breaks men, no matter if their heart stops beating or not."

Still trying to leave, I shook his hand and hugged him good-bye. "Okay, I'll read the Merton work and get back to you on it the next time I come through New York. I promise."

He acquiesced and shook my hand goodbye. "Your boy inside, I see a lot of you in him," Father Carmen said, relighting another cigar.

"No, not me. Can't really say what rock that kid was born under," I said, and looked up the alley towards the street. "Is it fairly easy to hail a taxi around here?"

"In a minute. We must finish this first. I've been a priest for over sixty years, son. Believe me, I've heard it all before. Your questioning isn't unique. I have counseled hundreds of men in prison, who think just like you. So one more question before I let you go." He inhaled his fresh cigar and squinted from the smoke. "Are you sorry today for the sins of your past? All of them, from your involvement in the death of your father to your complacency when it came to Ricco?"

I shook my head at him. "Father, you are a man I respect and it hurt to tell you I did such things. But my father was a bum, as you well know, and he killed my mother. He deserved to die. Guess I'm just damaged goods, right? Damned to hell for good."

"But are you sorry?" he asked again without pause.

"I don't know—I need to think," I said, and looked for an escape. His question needed an answer though, so I paused. "For Ricco, yes—and for the work I did for Marco, yes. But, for my father, I have no answer."

He nodded, looking tired and old. "I'll let you go now, but can you drop by the rectory one more time before you return to California?"

Just to end his line of questioning, I complied. "Yes, I suppose. You are a stubborn man, Father Carmen. You still think you can save my soul, don't you?"

"It is not mine to save, but I trust you will figure it out yourself in time. Meanwhile, I have something to give you. Something the Attanasio's gave me many years ago to thank me for helping them find tutors for their children—your mother and you," he said, wagging his crooked cane at me again. "The item belongs to you anyway."

"To me, what is it?"

"A clock. A beautiful, ornate clock carved from mahogany wood from Germany. It's the only clock I've ever had that keeps the proper time," he said, with a grim smile. "They told me your father made it, apparently your mother…"

I shrugged. "Yes, I know about that clock. Signore Attanasio loved that thing and was always asking me to wind it up every week. But no thank you, I don't want anything my father made. Why would you give me something like that?"

"Because it belongs to you. We will never know if your father repented before his death. Axel Hauser was a broken man, possessed by resentments he carried from his own family in Germany, and then he treated these with the curse of the drink, instead of confronting his family face to face. I pray every day for men like him, incarcerated in jail, hoping they will confront their resentments, then repent and renew their souls," Father Carmen said gently. "Perhaps your father did just that."

My frustration clawed at me. I wanted to leave, but felt trapped by his compassion. I turned and kicked a random piece of trash down the alley.

"Look son, a priest like me hears more than he cares to working on these streets. If God ever offers me a chance to soften a man's heart, I take it," Father Carmen said, poking his finger into my chest. "Go on now. You better head over to the Russo's, as there's a beauty in Brooklyn who needs a good friend. Sort out your life, son. You're too good a man to let resentments eat away at you."

I smiled and nodded, but was only half listening, impatient to leave. "Father Carmen, there's simply too much to sort out. Forgive me, it just might be too late to save this man no matter how hard you try."

"It's never too late." He took my hands into his and pulled me back down onto the seat near him. Without letting go, he reached into his inside jacket pocket with a free hand and pulled out a small round silver case. When he opened it, I smelt the strong scent of oil mixed with a vast array of herbs. He put his thumb into the oil, and then touched my forehead with the butt of his thumb, making the sign of the cross. "This is the same oil I blessed Judy with a few days ago." His bottom lip was quivering. "You were bonded to each other as children, and now you are bonded in Eternity too."

Then, as if a damn broke in my heart, tears rolled down my cheeks in gratitude that my long love for her had been blessed. I leaned into his embrace and cried for a good while in his arms.

When finally exhausted of tears, I pulled away, smelling the herbal scent on my forehead. "Thank you for your blessing," I said, and saw he too had been crying. "I promise, you aren't through with this dirty sinner." I gave him one last hug, then stood and walked down the alley, intent on seeing Judy again.

Back out on Mulberry Street, I hailed a taxi, and then asked the doorman outside the restaurant to fetch my son and Sister Mary Catherine from inside. When Sister and Andrew came out and walked toward our taxi, I smiled at them and took Sister's hand as my son handed me my briefcase.

"It was wonderful seeing you again. By the way, did you wrap up the dessert for Father Carmen?" I asked her.

She laughed at my question. "Oh, yes. I wouldn't dare deny him. See him over there?" she asked, pointing toward Father Carmen standing by the door. "Look at him, he's acting like the Vatican guard to the neighborhood right now, but as soon as you leave, he'll go back in to enjoy his sweets with an espresso. Thank you so much for visiting us. This was a lovely morning and lunch indeed."

I received her affectionate hug, prepared to leave, but she had more to say. "Declano, your son Andrew is a delight, so intelligent, just like you. I could have passed on dessert altogether and simply visited with him."

Andrew interrupted to tell us he was going to say good-bye to Father Carmen.

"Hey son, tell Father Carmen that I promise to 'Ancoro Imparo'".

"Will do Paps." He laughed, knowing the expression was one of my favorites.

Sister waited on the sidewalk, and my words made her cries turn into laughter. She gave me a final hug goodbye. "Ancora Imparo. Oh, yes. I, too, remember Father Carmen using that one all the time—'of all perfectionist in the world…'"

Looking at each other, smiling as we said in unison, mimicking Father's accent, "…the great Michelangelo coined that phrase while painting the Sistine Chapel on his back."' We laughed and embraced a final time as I hopped into the rear seat of the taxi.

I unrolled the window as her long habit blew in the wind. Sister asked me if I had my briefcase and the file as we watched Andrew talking to the would-be Pope of Mulberry Street. The weather was becoming more frigid as my son headed back to us, guarding his face from a snowy gust to give Sister Mary Catherine one last embrace.

Looking back as we drove off, I saw Father Carmen take a puff of tobacco, tip his old black fedora, then smile as he blessed us with his right hand, motioning the sign of the cross in the afternoon air.

PART THREE

BROOKLYN

"Love and truth can never be silenced."

~ Declan Quinn ~

CHAPTER THIRTEEN

A VOICE ON THE TURNTABLE

"Driver, 1102 Bay Ridge Parkway in Brooklyn, please," I said, glad I remembered the address of the Attanasio residence, some numbers you never forget. I knew they could guide us to the Russo house on Shore Road. The light snowflakes from the early morning had turned into gusty snow flurries, so the driver turned on the windshield wipers.

Andrew looked at me confused. "We're going to Brooklyn? Great, feel like going to Coney Island in the dead of winter?"

I neither had the energy nor the humor for any more bantering with my son. As the taxi pulled into traffic, I felt a mix of emotions all at once, and suddenly felt nauseous thinking of Judy sick at home on the other side of the river, while at the same time, searched the road for that fucking black Cadillac.

"You okay?" Andrew asked. "Lucky for you the weather stayed mild for your visit with Father Carmen. One thing's for sure, that nun's a chatter-box, but you gotta love her, and it's a sure thing you were one of her favorites."

I took his hand into mine and he stopped.

"What is it, Paps?"

"Father Carmen told me tragic news," I said, my eyes filling with tears. "It's about my friend, Judy. She's here, in Brooklyn, and she's sick. So it looks like you're going to get to meet her, and I trust you to please, leave your mother out of it. Okay? Besides, it's not an affair like your mother thinks."

Andrew's reaction was of genuine concern. "Yeah, okay, don't worry, my lips are sealed. No matter what you tell me, or what I see. I promise I'll take it to the grave."

The nausea was getting worse. "The grave, please don't say that word. I've heard enough of death for one morning." I grabbed my stomach and succumbed to my nausea. "Driver, please, pull over, and hurry." I jumped out of the car and ran to the gutter and rejected some, if not all of the morsels of lunch we just had.

Andrew waited near the open door of the taxi and watched, as I paced up and down the sidewalk, motioning to the taxi driver to wait. I lost it again in a trashcan on the corner, and rushed back to the taxi before he could kick us out. Cars and buses were honking at us, totally uncaring of any trauma happening to me on the street. The taxi driver offered me his personal sympathies as well. "Hey mister, if you gots that nasty influenza that's wreaking havoc all over the city, you betta hop out now or I'll have your ass."

I just gave him a cold stare instead of killing him for his comment. Andrew looked at me with concern, but I didn't offer either of them any explanation, as all I could do was blow my nose and clean up with a handkerchief.

"Dad, I'm so sorry. You and Father Carmen talked outside for a good hour or more. Did he help you at all?"

Feeling slightly better, I unrolled the window and let the clean winter air in. "Believe it or not, yes, he helped me," I said, getting emotional again. "Guess you can say he's the father I never had. There is so much we talked about. He even blessed my forehead with some magical oil right there in that dirty alley. You can still see the oil right here, smell it." I took a fingertip to my forehead and rubbed some on the top of his hand. "The man's a saint. In some crazy way, I feel, what do you Catholics say, absolved? Look at me, can't seem to stop the tears either."

Andrew looked at me surprised and smelled the oil on his hand. "That was nice of him. It's never easy. I've learned that pain begets truth, truth begets light, light begets freedom, and freedom begets peace. The truth will set you free, Paps."

He regarded me with such hope, my mood lifted a bit. "I like that. Thank you, Andrew." I blew my nose again and continued to give a cold stare to the driver, who kept tabs on me in the rearview mirror. "Is that a quote from one of the books Monsignor has you reading for your three Cs project?"

"No, actually, it's a line I memorized from one of G-Paps letters."

I laughed. "Of course, poets run in our family. You'll never believe this, but I used to write poetry way back when," I said, with an aching heart, thinking of my young love with Judy as we wrote poetry and love letters to each other. I hummed my favorite one in my head, "my heart is true I swear by stars above you, come say you're mine, all mine." He watched me hum and smiled. The Brooklyn Bridge stood in its grandiosity ahead, and I knew we were getting close to my beloved.

And, if I didn't have enough on my mind already, six out of ten cars on the road in New York were black sedan Cadillacs, so it was hard to know if the black car from the alley was trailing us.

Watching the calming waters of the East River flowing below, we drove over the bridge into Brooklyn. There was no conversation between us, but my head was filled with thought and my stomach was settling at last. "Hey driver, swing by the site of the old Ebbet's Field on the way, will you?" I asked, blowing my nose.

I checked my trouser pocket for my lucky Walking Liberty silver coins and was confident to find them there as always. If Signore Attanasio was around, I wanted to show him how I had carried these for nearly forty years, I thought, smiling instantly remembering the love he and his wife gave us. I took them out to show my son. "Andrew, one day at Ebbet's Field, Signore Attanasio gave his son Frankie and me these two silver coins." I mimicked him and used a strong Brooklyn accent. "Boys, if you rub that coin every day until you're gray like me, you will always have good luck, and maybe marry a beauty like this one day,' he said, then kissed Zia Anna, or better yet, molested her. He never cared when Frankie and me would laugh when his mouth and neck got covered with her red lipstick." My mood lifted from the memory.

Andrew smiled, held the coins, and smoothed them over as if they could rub luck into his fingers too. "Geez Paps, these coins you flip all the time came from your friend from way back? And is that the same Frankie you named my brother after?" he asked curiously.

I laughed. "Yes, on both accounts, Frankie was my little brother at our safe house and his dad many years ago gave us the coins at a Dodger game. I wonder if Frankie kept his, too," I said, pointing to the coins. "See the inscription and the year, In God We Trust, Liberty, and E' Pluribus Unum 1928—'the three core values this country was built on'," I said, using Signore Attanasio's accent again. "Now they're all faded from the many times I rubbed them." Until I spoke of this memory to my son, I hadn't realized how much Saverio's lessons and his love for Zia Anna had affected me.

I asked the driver to turn east on Prospect Avenue, towards Crown Heights where the stadium used to be. In a few turns, we saw huge, newly built twenty-five story apartment complexes, housing some one thousand or more residents on the corner. "Well, it's a shame about Ebbet's. I heard that kids aren't even allowed to play baseball close by as too many windows were being broken, if you can believe that."

The driver agreed and grunted. "Eh, let's hope the Bums win this year after last year's heartbreak, they should've never left Brooklyn," he said.

Happy to have won his favor, I patted the driver shoulder. "You're right, they blew it big last season, and it's impossible to be a Yankee fan, right?"

"You can say that again," he said, grumbling.

Andrew looked outside. "Hey, do you happen to know the going rent there?"

The driver shrugged. "Eh, you can rent a triple for about 150 and a bunt or a flat for a hundred bucks or so. I was there when the wrecking ball demolished the place in February 1960, and cried with my little boy when a brass band played Auld Lang Syne. They were selling the old seats for five bucks a piece that day, so I thought, what the fuck, and sprang for two—had to drive overtime all month to pay for them, too."

"Ha, I bet your wife wanted to kill you for that," I said, laughing.

He shrugged and mumbled a few comments under his breath.

"Boy, what I would give to have taken you to a game here, but we can take in a weekend double-header at Dodger's Stadium after you come back home," I said.

"Count me in, too bad Koufax pitched his last season though, the Bums won't be the same without him," Andrew said.

We always bonded on topics of baseball. "Don't cut Drysdale and Sutton out, and don't forget, they need to avenge the Orioles somehow," I said.

"The worst showing I ever seen, losing four games straight—it was embarrassing man," the driver said.

I had to get back in the mode of combing the streets for Marcos' tag men, so I kept looking out the window. "I wonder if Signore Attanasio's retired now, if so, maybe he'll be home with Zia Anna. I hope you get to meet them; you'll be in for treat if you do. Who knows what would have happened if they didn't open their home to us when they did."

Andrew was curious. "You keep looking out the window. Do you think Marcos' guys are on our tail here, too?"

I looked closely at the cars following us. "Well, yes. There was someone parked in the alley trying to listen in on Father Carmen and me, until the good Father chased them off."

He sighed. "Damn Paps, they're like vultures hovering over prey. How can we get rid of them?"

"A vulture is right, but let me worry about that," I said. "It's nothing new to me, been doing this for over a year almost."

"But, Paps. I want to help."

"Thanks, but you can't, not when it comes to Marco." I needed to get my mind off of Judy for a minute. "Besides, this trip isn't just for me, you know, and I'm your father don't forget. Seeing Father Carmen worn out after all these years makes me worried now for you."

"Oh, and your profession hasn't worn you out?" Andrew said. "Sorry, but my decision is pretty much made already."

I shrugged off his comment. "Son, he's tired. Tired of trying to save souls who don't care if they're damned or not. I hadn't thought of it, but Sister Mary Catherine was right, you are just like your grandmother in many ways—along with looking like her and your G-Pap, she always kept hope, only hope for the hopeless. Then ended up dying too young."

Andrew sat without response and we drove into Bay Ridge in silence.

I broke the quiet, still watching the passing cars. "You can't stop me from wanting the best for you. You're making a life changing decision soon, and as much as I love and admire Father Carmen, he said it himself, being a priest is a difficult job."

"I'm not doing it because I know it's easy."

"Son, there's no question on what a hard worker you are, but the way I see it, that poor man has been carrying the burden of twenty-million confessions."

Andrew softened. "Believe me, I understand your worry, don't sweat it, besides it's cool you care at least."

"Perhaps it's time to be a better dad," I said, still canvassing the road.

"Do you mind me asking what's wrong with Judy before we get there?" he asked.

It was hard to say the word. "Cancer. My sweet Judy is dying of cancer," I said, and then imagined knocking on the Attanasio's front door, arriving unannounced, and suddenly it seemed like a very bad idea. "Now that I think about it, maybe we shouldn't go straight to the Attanasio's home after all these years." I stopped myself, realizing if we were being followed, the last thing I wanted was to bring my troubles into Bay Ridge. "Driver, please take me to the Police Department on Lawrence Avenue, circle around the block and come back to get us after ten minutes. Okay?" If followed, this would scare them off, I thought.

After the driver dropped us off, we stayed standing on the steps of the station until I was sure no one suspicious was following us.

"Paps, you really are watching out for us."

"Just covering all the bases, don't think those guys will look for us here."

We got back into the taxi in front of the police station. "Take us to Russo's asphalt yard on Fort Hamilton Parkway," I said, not sure if it was still there. "I think a better idea would be to go see Judy's father, Sal, at his office first. I hope the paving yard is going strong. I worked for him there for five years, but that was over thirty years ago. I would probably still be working there, or running the place for him, had I chose a better path."

Andrew shrugged his shoulder and elbowed me. "True. But then you would have never met mom and I wouldn't have been born."

I smiled at my boy. "Okay, you've got me cornered on that one Andrew. God saw to it that you were born as you have too much to offer this world."

"Thanks Paps."

Riding the streets of Brooklyn brought me back to my golden years. I started working two jobs at the age of eight, cleaning paving trucks on the weekends for Sal Russo, Zia Anna's cousin. On weekdays after school, I swept floors and took out beef fat and scraps to the large cans in the alley at her husband's butcher shop on Avenue U. "Andrew, you're about to learn about another chapter in my life, use these details in your timeline," I said. "It was the happiest time of my childhood. We were far away from my father reeking havoc all the time. Living with the Attanasio's, my mother and I tutored them in English, but for the most part, we sang, played games in the street, and ate like kings, even during the depression years of rationing." The reminiscing eased the knot in my stomach, and I wondered if Zia Anna was still making chicken dinners with what she called, "the chickens that needed a home" from the butcher shop's day-old poultry case.

"Driver, take Fort Hamilton Parkway down towards Ninety-second Street." I was relieved that my stomach had continued to settle, even though my heart still hadn't recovered, and happy the streets of Brooklyn were edged into my memory like lines on the palms of my hands. "Andrew, you're about to see where I learned to use a shovel, trowel, and pickaxe. It's the first place I built arm strength and felt like a man."

When we arrived in front of the gate at Sal's yard, it was obvious that he was still in the paving business. The old wooden sign had been replaced with a larger engraved one in metal, but the words were the same: WE PAVE THE WAY / RUSSO BROTHERS PAVING COMPANY, Established 1910. I smiled, seeing two beautiful German Shepherds running alongside the taxi as we entered the lot, barking in unison at our intrusion. A huge asphalt and concrete plant had been built on the site, and there were three rows of six blue Dodge trucks loaded with gravel and tools. Even though the weather was cumbersome, the workers in hard yellow hats toiled around the yard emptying a few truck beds full of asphalt.

"Looks like Sal bought the whole block to expand his yard. It's more than doubled in size, and of course he's got two Shepherds guarding things still. Let's see if we can break into his Fort Knox and say hello." It felt great to be back on the grounds of his yard and I was excited to see him again, despite the given dread in my heart.

Looking at my son, I felt he deserved to hear more about Judy and me. "Andrew, after my mother died, I broke up with Judy. Most people called it just a teenage crush at the time, but it was the real deal, and thanks to her persistence, we reunited in our twenties."

He interrupted, pulled out a small notebook and pen. "Again, tell me how old you were when your mother died?" he asked.

"Thirteen." I continued. "As I was saying, we got back together when she was studying music in Manhattan, she surprised me on campus one day to have a simple visit over coffee, 'one more time just for good-times sake,' she said. I couldn't refuse her anymore, and we met every weekend after that. I'd watch her sing at side clubs and parties and she'd come to watch me pitch at Fordham's baseball field. Ours was a rare love given only to few in life, but I let her go once more. This time I simply wanted her to follow her dreams. She was from a good, honest, hardworking Italian family, as you'll soon find out, and far too talented to settle for the life of a mob wife, even for me."

He slouched. "And you needed a woman like mom, who was happy to stay in the dark about Marco," he said.

"Okay, you badass seminarian. Don't think that of your mother, your mother was choice meat and a great woman, just got stuck with me. But enough said on that," I said, opening the front door of Sal's office building.

When Andrew and I entered, the receptionist in the front office told us Sal was in a meeting with his salesmen, but she would let him know we were here. She walked away disappearing around the corner. Moments later, we heard a booming voice down the hall telling everyone the meeting was being cut short. Salesmen in suits and smelling of cigarettes came walking past us, giving us curious glances. Next thing we knew, the amplified voice of the yard dispatch called out on an intercom overhead, "Leo, main office, Leo, main office. Sal says you have visitors. Leo, main office." The voice over the intercom speaker made me laugh, as it used to be me fetching people from the yard to go into the office. I was the boy runner and made a dime a day, and on Saturday's, he'd call me in to his office for a root beer break at ten o'clock in the morning.

We heard Zio Leo's gruff voice respond back over the intercom from the yard outside. "Okay Sal, five minutes, five minutes."

Sal came out to the lobby, greeting us with a big smile and handshakes with the same Italian hospitality I remembered and took us down the hall to his office. He still wore heavy black-rimmed eyeglasses, but had dark, puffy bags under his eyes. Short and stout, he hadn't changed too much from when he would tease me that he'd still be my boss after I passed him in height at thirteen. Dressed in a blue pinstriped suit with his tie loosened, he shook my hand; his palms always did feel like sandpaper from years using a shovel or trowel.

A conference table in the center of his office was scattered with ashtrays holding abandoned cigarettes and purchase orders from the meeting that abruptly ended. The walls were decorated with duck decoys, mounted hunting trophies, and photographs. One large framed picture showed Sal triumphantly holding a fishing pole and a big king mackerel, about two feet long. Mounted behind Sal's desk was the head of a wild boar with its eyes popping out looking straight at us as we stood inside.

Sal pointed at the boar. "I should hang you on the wall next to him, Declano Hauser. You disappeared from our lives without so much as a good-bye."

I was taken aback and not prepared to argue about decades old drama. "I was just a punk teenager, with no brains…" I said, not sure if he was being serious or not.

He continued. "Hell, it took you over thirty years to come back here. You think you're too high and mighty to come see us now that you're some fucking, fancy Nevada gambler? Seriously, my family was good to you, and you left without a word. I should punch your lights out. My wife and cousin Anna cried for weeks—and you broke my Judy's heart," he paused at the mention of her name.

I inhaled sharply, shocked at being scolded. No one had spoken to me like this since I was a young boy. At the same time, there was no question that he was right. "I'm sorry. What I did was thoughtless. By the time I recognized how wrong it was, I was too embarrassed to apologize. Look, angry thirteen year olds can fuck up their lives, and factor this in Sal, I was screwed up after my mother died." I raised my hands in surrender. "Kick my ass if you want, but if you could cut me some slack here, in front of my son, that would…"

Sal smiled at me and interrupted. "You know I'm just giving you a bad time. We loved you and we missed you, but we understood what a terrible time you had losing your mom." He turned then to Andrew. "I can see the family resemblance. Irish blood runs strong in the Hauser family."

I hadn't heard my father's name so much in one day and was irritated to hear it again. "We dropped that name in honor of my mother. I go by Quinn now, her maiden name. Meet my son, Andrew Quinn. He's studying at Fordham's seminary, thinking about becoming a priest. Not too bad for a product of the Nusco family of thugs. Right?"

Sal looked surprised. "What, a handsome young man like you, studying to become a priest? What a shame for all the girls in New York," Sal said, with a wink and put his hand over my shoulder.

"Quinn is a fine name. What Declan, your Nusco brothers didn't want to share their last name with you?" he asked, giving me a shove, and walked away. "Come, Andrew, let me show you my trophies. Are priests allowed to hunt?"

Andrew was taken in by his devilish charm. "It's a pleasure to meet you Mr. Russo. I will find a way to hunt with you even if the Pope himself tells me no."

"Good. And I'm sure your father here taught you to shoot a rifle?" he asked.

"Indeed Mr. Russo. We used to hunt all the time, before…"

Sal interrupted him and pointed at each hunting trophy explaining them in detail.

Once the tour was complete, Sal looked over at me staring at a large, gallery sized picture of Judy on the wall wearing a long burgundy velvet gown and smiled. "Well, Declano, if you came to ask for forgiveness, you know the Attanasio's and Russo's pretty well. We are as soft inside as pizza dough. We all loved you boy, especially my girl there. It's good you came back. Come, sit down," he said. "Tell me how that crazy Nusco family is doing. You look like you need a drink."

"Thank you, that would be great."

"How about a shot of homemade Lemoncello straight from Naples, or do you need something harder?" He pressed a red button on his desk and spoke into an intercom, calling for the Lemoncello and glasses, which soon arrived. As he poured and we sipped, he went back to asking questions. "So how's the Nevada casino business going?" he asked, looking like a high rolling gambler himself.

I didn't want to talk about money or casinos, so I walked around his office trying to find more pictures of Judy. Her soft feminine beauty stood in sharp contrast to the masculine décor and the pungent aroma of cigars and sweet pipe tobacco.

I knew he saw me staring at Judy's photograph, but he was holding back from talking about her, most likely wishing it were just a bad dream. Sal lifted his shot of the lemon liqueur, and Andrew and I raised ours, the three of us sharing a toast to our reunion.

Putting his arm around my shoulder, he said looking at Judy's grand photo. "Let's raise our glasses to Judy, a beauty isn't she, but remember Declano—I loved her first."

We all smiled and raised a toast. "To Judy."

"And may her dreams reach past the stars, too," Sal said, with tears welling in his eyes.

I watched him and knew it was true, and nearly broached the subject of her illness, but then heard the all too familiar deep, loud voice of Zio Leo. He was talking to the receptionist, his voice growing louder as he came down the hall toward us.

"What? Who's here? Are you kidding me? Declano Hauser? Here to see us? Does he know the Dodger Bums up and left us?" Leo yelled the last question as he burst into the room.

"Hey Leo, can you believe it after all these years? This kid here comes into my office looking for a job in the yard," Sal said, and gave us a wink.

"Don't hire him, Sal. This one will quit on you and leave without so much as an arriverderci." Leo shook his head at me. He looked the same as I remembered, short, heavyset and walked with a limp from a bout with childhood polio. He wore a blue work uniform, still the same, just grayer and weathered by time and the elements. "Declano Hauser, as I live and breathe, I wondered if the day would ever come that you'd walk into the yard. So what brings you back to Brooklyn now that you're a western John Wayne cowboy type?"

We shook hands and embraced. "It's great to see you, Zio Leo. How's Zia Giugno?" He lighted up at the mention of his beautiful wife as I introduced him to Andrew. "So finally, you come see us here in Brooklyn. You know Guigno and I came out west more than once over the years to see Judy in Vegas and L.A., but we only saw you that one time for Judy's birthday celebration. It all was so glamorous. I told Sal you acted like a bodyguard, watching over our Judy. Right Sal? You stopped worrying so much when you knew Declano was there," he said.

"Hum, stopped worrying, it's a hazard of the occupation these days," Sal said.

Zio Leo's boisterous personality commanded our attention. "Yes, Declano, you kept an eye on our sweet Judy. I was glad, but always told my wife you'd be better off leaving the damn Nusco hoodlums in Nevada and come back to New York where you belonged. So what took you so long, Declano, and what brings you back now?"

Sal interrupted, "Yes, we were so worried when Judy got all those singing shows in Las Vegas, with all those debonair suitors always grabbing at her, even Frank Sinatra was after her, but like Leo just said, having you around put her mother and me at ease. Never had a chance to thank you for that kid." He lifted his drink, gulped the rest of it down, and poured another, setting the bottle on the front of his desk for us to serve ourselves.

"Who wouldn't want to protect that talented Italian goddess?" Leo asked, pointing at Judy's picture on the wall. "Sal, play Judy's last record for them, it's straight from heaven," he paused, and I saw from the look on his face, he knew he had said too much. My eyes fixated once more on the walled photo. I already knew of the recording, every word and note, and wondered if Sal would tell me of his daughter's illness now, but I was hoping that somehow Father Carmen had it all wrong.

"Have you heard Judy's latest record, Declano?" Sal asked, looking at Leo with a silencing stare.

I took my eyes off the photograph and pretended to be looking at all of Sal's accomplishments on the walls. "Yes, I have. But I'd love to hear it again if you feel like playing it," I said, even though I feared my heart wouldn't survive hearing her voice.

"Great. Leo, have one of the office girls bring in a turntable, it would be appropriate for this reunion I think. You two were young lovers I know—snuck around and dated behind my back while she was in college, couldn't get anything past me," he said, looking at me with deep eyes of sadness.

But, what of her illness? Will he speak of it or must I ask? A secretary brought in the record player; Andrew helped to set it up and plugged it into the wall. Sal removed her album out of the familiar coverlet I had seen many times before, and gave it to

Andrew carefully, as if it were a priceless possession. Andrew took it graciously and placed the record on the turntable.

"Something terrible has happened to my dear sweet Judy," he said, speaking in a softened tone that seemed stuck like mortar in his throat. "Declano, Judy has been home for quite some time recovering from treatment after doctors found terrible cancer lesions in her body, it's Hodgkin's Lymphoma and she's terminal. She's home to be close to us, to her mother especially, now that she's fighting for her life." I took the news standing, but my knees failed me and I sank straight into a seat as the word cancer came out in the same sentence with the name of my beloved. My tear ducts, already warmed from the morning, overflowed again.

Andrew jumped in to rescue me, asking Sal for details of the cancer and her hopes for survival. We all cried when he told us her prognosis held little hope.

"She was working late nights and traveling back and forth from Vegas to Los Angeles," he explained. "She neither had the time nor the intuition to see a doctor when she started having symptoms, even though she was having difficulty singing and was wearing scarves to hide lumps on her neck. She ignored the early onset signs of the disease. When she passed out on stage in L.A., her friends took her to the emergency room. We flew out immediately and brought her home. That was nine months ago."

"I wish I'd known," I said. "I would have come sooner."

"Perhaps we should have called you, but she has been so sick from the chemotherapy and radiation treatments, she didn't want to see anyone. We were hoping the treatments would work, but she's still not in remission," Sal said.

Zio Leo walked over to me and spoke softly, "Go to her, please. Maybe seeing you walk into her room will help to get her well again."

"Yes, that would be a great idea," Sal said, being trapped by Leo's invitation, but looked at me with sleep-deprived eyes. "Leo's right, you should go see her. Who knows, perhaps if our Judy sees her sweetheart Declan, all will be right in the world again."

I nodded, wiped my eyes dry, feeling his pain, one I've experienced myself. A father who would do anything, give up everything if only it could save his daughter. I didn't know if I had any power to save her, but I was set to try.

He cleared his throat and wiped his eyes, regaining composure. "How about if you and your son come over for dinner tonight, we'll eat early—Italian style, yes?"

I sat numbed in his comfortable leather armchair. "Yes, that would be fine. We'd love that," I said, inhaling a deep breath before I spoke again. I stood up weakened, walked over to Sal, and took his hand. "I didn't get a chance to tell you we visited Old St. Patrick's Cathedral today and heard this awful news earlier. Father Carmen told me Judy was ill, so I came to see you right away. Didn't mean to hide it, I just didn't know how to ask about her. Thank you for telling me and inviting us for a visit. You have no idea how much I want to do just that." I rubbed my hands together feeling the numbness of my fingers again and remembered the pain of losing a daughter, as I looked at Sal directly in his eyes and held his hands tight. "Sal, it's the real reason for my visit today."

Sal and Leo looked at me, nodded with sadness, and with a glimmer of hope. Sal walked back to start the record, placed the needle into the black grooves and turned the speaker volume to high as Judy's voice enveloped the room. We all sat and listened as she sang, "I don't know why I love you, but I love you…" The notes and words were all memorized in my head, but I refrained from singing along, the way I usually did. Her clear sweet voice permeated into the hearts of all of us, every man in the room listening in quiet mourning, hoping a miracle would change her fate.

Sal picked up the phone to call his wife. Speaking in Italian, he asked if she was up for some surprise visitors. I stood behind his desk in front of a vast wall of noise silencing windows facing the truck yard as I watched workers outside as efficient as I remembered from thirty years ago.

Sal hung up and announced that his wife and Zia Anna were preparing dinner to include us. Again, with the same hospitality I recalled from my youth, Sal invited us to ride with him to his home on Shore Road, and promised that Signore Attanasio would meet us there. The house where Judy lay dying was only minutes from here. It hit me then that a lifetime of late nights reading existential philosophies on suffering could not have prepared me for the pain of seeing Judy near death.

Sal's car was parked in the back of the quarry yard. I was happy to stay off the main road where Marcos' guys could find us. Dejected on many levels, I thought to warn Sal about my issue, but didn't want to burden him with another stressor.

I drove in the passenger's seat and Andrew sat in the back. "Just keep your hat low and I will do the same. One can never be safe with Marco looking for you." I whispered to Andrew as we jumped into the car. Sal and Andrew spoke between themselves on the way to Shore Road and in the quiet of my mind I prepared myself to see Judy.

***

Note: Judy recorded and copyrighted this song in 1967. You may listen to it on YouTube: http://www.youtube.com/watch?v=7R-4fKuZihM&feature=email

CHAPTER FOURTEEN

LIPSTICK ON MY COLLAR

The snow had since stopped and the sky was clearing, but the temperature had dropped significantly, so the thought of a cozy night with the family I once loved was lifting my spirits, even though the reason I was here was far from a joyous cause.

We arrived at Sal's house around half past four. He pulled his car into the garage at the back of the property and was happy the driveway wasn't filled with cars. "I told Loretta to have everyone visiting today to park their cars in the street so I could buzz right in the back when I got home tonight. It's a hassle on most days, as I have to honk the horn to get visitors out of the house to move their cars and let me park. Andrew, perhaps you could give us a hand after dinner, to get the cars off of this street and back onto this driveway."

"Of course, Mr. Russo. Anything," Andrew said.

The home was a large two story, set high over the street on a corner lot with a large front yard. Made of red brick and gray mortar with huge arched Romanesque Revival windows, the home commanded passersby cause to look. From an upstairs room, a black wrought iron fenced balcony overlooked the Narrows waterway and the vast newly constructed Verrazano-Narrows Bridge.

A handful of kids were chasing each other up and down the front steps, when they saw the car, they all chased it up the driveway as we drove in. We parked and entered the rear door into a service room, kitchen area. I took a deep breath wondering had Judy and I gotten married, I too would have been blessed by the love shared within these walls. We would have enjoyed post-dinner music gatherings in the family room with all of our bouncing kids singing along.

Zia Anna wore a dirtied cooking apron and was first to greet Andrew and me. She told us she came over every day to bring care and food along with Miss Marie C. I recognized her as well, as she carried a basket of towels and waved to us from a set of stairs. Is that the very same woman who helped my mother the day we arrived beaten and tired so many years ago? I wondered.

Zia Anna hugged me and smiled, but I could see the years and stress had taken their toll. Still her chubby warm self, but she was definitely not the vibrant mama I remembered. She strained to greet us, "Oh Declano, how wonderful for you to come and visit our beautiful Judy. She was always telling us how you helped make her famous, but tell me, who is this young charmer with you?" she asked, as she took my briefcase and set it on the floor near the stove. She was never one to let someone go unnoticed or unwelcomed for long, reminding me I had failed to introduce her to my son.

"Oh forgive me, Zia Anna, this is my son, Andrew. He is going to Fordham University right now, studying for a possible entrance into the seminary this coming fall," I said, knowing all too well she would love to hear that a young handsome man was planning to become a Catholic priest.

"Molto bene, Declano. Molto bene, Andrew," she said, and cheered up, pinching his cheek and looked at me. "Declano, we just told Judy you were coming over, and of all things she asked us to fetch for her, was lipstick and her makeup bag. She made us all laugh at the thought of her painting her lips just for you. She always loved you, bless her heart. But, you need to prepare yourself. Our sweet Judy is withered down to just her skin and bones now. Please be ready for the shock of seeing that," Zia Anna said, looking at me with worried eyes.

I nodded and tried to brace myself.

She lowered her voice to a whisper and I wondered if she was still speaking to us or addressing God. "Such a terrible thing. I will never understand how sweet Jesus could abandon her like this. Why is this happening? Why?"

I tried to offer comforting words, something I just learned from Father Carmen. "Through suffering comes a deeper understanding. But, it is something I, for one, will never comprehend. Not when it hits in a home like this."

Zia Anna listened, then responded with many words into one breath like she always did. "Yes, this disease comes in the dark of night to the best of us," she said, and extended her arms open to hug me again. "Oh, Declano, you are so good to come. Seeing you today brings us some happiness, coupled with bittersweet memories. Oh, those days of you and Frankie playing stickball in the street seem so easy now, so carefree. After your mother passed away and you left, life for all of us took a down turn. We missed you, your sweet mother, and Shannon. In a flash of the night, you were all gone," she said, and began to ramble nervously. "Then my dear Saverio had to deal with the OPA, that lousy Office of Price Administration. Back then those damn politicians controlled the price of everything from an olive to a roast. The only way to survive was to deal with the black market, a world my Saverio always despised, but he had no choice. Maybe he'll tell you at dinner how we almost lost the store when we couldn't charge enough to pay our overhead and feed ourselves."

I heard the sounds of Sal and his wife in the kitchen dining area, moving chairs and dishes, as Zia Anna talked. She was helpless with grief, yet still wanting to be welcoming.

"Excuse me Zia Anna. May I put this briefcase out of the reach of the little kids in the house? It carries important papers you see..." I asked, handing the briefcase to her with a lump in my throat thinking of the pistol inside.

"Of course," she said graciously. She took the briefcase from me, opened a hall closet full of jackets on a rack and hats on the top shelf and turned to Andrew. "Son, please, use your tall legs to set your father's bag on the top shelf and just move the hats to the side."

I watched and swallowed an unsettling feeling in my throat as she continued to chat to us without a pause.

"It was smart you went to live with Carmella and Vincenzo back then. You seem to have fared well from them adopting you. We felt so terrible about what happened to your beautiful sweet mother, and poor little Shannon, sent away to be adopted by someone we didn't even know. Poor child. She was every one's little Irish sister. I'll never forget those precious red curls. We wanted you both to stay with us." She began to cry. "Oh, dear, here I am dredging up the past. I'm so sorry." She dried her tears with worn tissues from the pockets of her apron.

Relieved the gun was out of the way I grabbed her hands to still them. "It's all right, Zia Anna. You were always full of love everyday I lived with you, for this I am forever grateful. We must embrace the past. The past is why I'm here. I came back to find Shannon, picked up her file this morning at Old St. Patrick's. I promise we will be reunited at last."

She grabbed me into a hug. "Oh, Declano, I'm so happy to hear you say that. Love will prevail today. Your mother will dance in heaven the day you and Shannon are together again."

Turning to Andrew, she hopelessly searched for an answer. "Please shed some light on our sufferings today. Son, from what you've learned in your Catholic training at the university, help us understand these things, it would be such a blessing. It's all just too much for us, watching this terrible illness take our angel."

Andrew nodded. "I will do my very best, is there a place we can sit and chat?" They walked arm in arm through the rest of the house and to the front room overlooking the Narrows waterway with the high-arched bridge as a backdrop to the left. I followed them. The three of us stood near the window as Zia Anna pulled the drapes all the way open to watch the freight ships entering the Port of New York. We watched cars moving on the top layer of the bridge while construction on the lower lanes continued. A cool ocean wind wafting up through the trees from the water made us happy to be in the warm indoors. Down on the street, pedestrians and cars passed by, oblivious to our heartache on the other side of the windowpane.

Andrew sat with Zia Anna on a long brown sofa as she placed a warm green wool blanket across her lap, extending half of it for Andrew. "I do have a quote from last semester's Christian apologetics class that might help. Have you ever heard of Clive Staples Lewis?"

"Perhaps, but please go on," she said. "Does he make any sense of how God allows our angels to suffer?"

He took her hand and looked gently into her eyes. "Yes, he does, I've got the perfect explanation for you. 'God whispers to us in our pleasures, speaks to us in our conscience, but shouts in our pains: It is his megaphone to rouse a deaf world.'"

Listening to the tender voice of my son eased my own pain. I was lost in that moment, watching him hold sweet Zia Anna's hand, speaking from his heart, I knew he'd make a fantastic priest or therapist someday. As they chatted, I left them alone to look at an array of pictures on the walls and thought of how God shouts in our pains, but also saw how he was there in many moments of pleasures displayed on these walls.

The Russo home was beautiful, full of family photographs of life's celebrations. On the living room walls were pictures of baptisms, graduations, picnics, reunions, and weddings. There was a corner full of framed record albums with more portraits of Judy; she always looked glamorous under the lights of a stage.

I began to question if our visit was appropriate. Their home was a sacred place adorned in love and family. I chose another path for my life. Did I have any right to slide back into the world I abandoned, wanting to embrace my beloved? I hadn't earned passage into this haven, free of guilt and sin, after spending just one morning on my knees and receiving Father Carmen's blessing. I still felt and smelled the oil on my forehead and looked around, hearing some voices talking quietly in the kitchen and soft whispers from women in the bedrooms upstairs. I regretted my presence again and wanted to grab Andrew and flee down the Narrows waterway to avoid my past forever.

Before I made my escape, Sal and his wife Loretta walked into the room with a look of tenderness, carrying a tray of meatballs and assorted cheeses. Feeling trapped, I smiled and took the tray Loretta handed to me, and then watched her go back to the kitchen for something more. I stood there wondering what to do when Sal walked in with another tray full of rolls and olives.

"Would you like go upstairs with us to take this early dinner to Judy?" he asked.

"Yes, of course," I said, though filled with dismay, pushing down more nausea smelling food again. I wished I could have shed my skin like the snakes on my property and grow fresh scales to protect my aching heart, as when I dressed this morning, I hadn't prepared myself to see my beloved, and especially, to find her suffering. When Loretta approached us with a tray of sodas, her heartbreak looked too familiar. I regrettably knew if my experience had told me anything, their lives would never be right again.

The truth I knew was too painful to speak aloud, so I nodded in silence and followed them up the stairs, carrying the tray of Italian meatballs and cheeses. The women's voices grew louder, coming from one of the many rooms down the long hallway. Several women in skirts and dresses overflowed from one of the open doors.

A girl in a blue dress emerged and greeted Sal with an affectionate hug saying, "Oh Zio Sal, how did you know exactly what we were hoping for? Hot dinner is just what she needs in this chilly upstairs room. Judy had her bath and is sitting up now, so she might be ready to eat something, even just a bite or two might help." Her gaze fell on me. "So, this must be the amazing Declan." She shook her head slowly at me and her eyes were flirtatious. "You must be very special, Judy put on her rouge and lipstick just for you."

Sal introduced us. "Declano, do you remember Rosy, Judy's cousin? You were both living at 1102 on the Parkway at the same time. Declano and Judy courted throughout her college years in Manhattan," Sal said, looking down the hall.

"Oh yes, they were sweethearts at St. Ephrem's dances, too. And I know all about their college years," Rosy said. "Judy tells me everything. I remember you, my sisters and I used to fight over who was going to braid your sister Shannon's pretty red hair before school in the mornings," she said.

"Yes, sure. It was a busy house…" I said, as she interrupted.

"Fun times for sure. I also remember your mother. She was a fun teacher. I loved her flute the best. It's good to see you again. And how romantic for you to show up now after all these years." She spoke fast as her smile faded and eyes glisten with moist tears. "She needs you now, Declan. Please give her your tenderness, all of it. I fear only love can cure her now."

I stayed back somewhat down the hallway, feeling a growing panic in my stomach as I tried to steady the platter of food in my hands. The group of animated women gathered around Judy's bed wasn't something I expected.

Rosy asked, "Would you like me to take that tray?"

"No." I said, startling her. I thought I should have brought a gift, flowers, or something. I couldn't bear the idea of walking in there empty-handed. The plate of food was all I had to offer.

Feeling lost inside this sea of women, I looked at Sal for help. Thankfully, he understood my overwhelmed expression, and stepped in. "Ladies," he called out, and the feminine voices fell silent. "I know you all want to witness this sweet reunion, but we don't want to scare Declano off before he has a chance to see his old friend."

Miss Marie C interrupted too, and put her arm over Rosy's shoulder, speaking loudly over the chatter as she gave me a wink. "And Declano's extremely handsome, young, and unmarried son is sitting in the front room with your mother, getting an earful no doubt. Why don't you all go downstairs and rescue him."

Rosy smiled as the line of women all ages and shapes exited the room giggling down the hallway, followed by Miss Marie C. Sal leaned over to me keeping his voice low. "Don't worry. They're harmless. Andrew's perfectly safe with that group of boy-crazy females."

I chuckled at the scene, but was still holding the tray of food, and my feet seemingly stuck to the floor in the hallway, unable to budge.

Sal came over to me with an encouraging nudge. "Forgive my nieces, they have all been here almost every day helping their cousin. When you left in 1933, you missed the many new babies born at 1102. You won't believe this, but my crazy cousin Anna had many more children after you left Brooklyn. What is the count, Loretta?"

"Eight girls and three boys is the final score I believe," Loretta said, taking the tray of food out of my hands. "They have all been dedicated to our Judy, here by her side, giving her love and care as if she were their own sister."

Sal put his arm around my shoulder, applying pressure, still encouraging me to move forward, but my body wouldn't cooperate.

Then I heard her soft voice. "Please come in. Declan, it's been so long." Judy spoke in a fragile tone that cracked with weakness. Hearing her speak pulled me inside the room, like a fireplace entices one near when it springs forth its warmth.

Sitting up in bed, dressed in a thin jacket of yellow satin, her legs covered with cream colored blankets to her waist, she was reed-thin with sallow skin, pale but for her rose colored lipstick and rouge, but all I saw was my Judy wearing a knitted lavender hat to cover her balding scalp. She would always be my beautiful Starlight Ruby Girl no matter what.

I walked over to her outstretched arms as she took my face into her hands. "Declan. You look good. Give me some love, my darling," she said, releasing each word with effort, taking pauses in between to breathe.

I gave her two gentle kisses, one on each cheek, taking in the sweet, fresh powdery scent of her skin.

"Stand back, for just a second. Let me see you," she cried, with her chestnut brown eyes as huge as ever complimented by the softness of her cap.

I complied, heart-struck seeing her this way, and feeling a bit foolish posing for her inspection.

"Yes, you do look good. Now, tell me. Why are you here? Give. Me. Some good news," Judy said, struggling with each word as her long eyelashes wetted with tears.

"I am so sorry," I said, and moved beside her bed, caressing the soft blankets covering her. I had no words of comfort, no happy news, only sorrow. We stared at each other as tears rolled down our cheeks and embraced for what seemed like an eternity. I felt her heart beating, fluttering like a weakened bird against my chest. Her arms slipped, too feeble to hold on, and I gently released hold, for fear of bruising her frail casing of flesh and bones.

Sal and Loretta stood in the back of the room silent, holding each other crying.

"Mother, Father, please leave us be. Declan and I need some time alone."

Sal coaxed his wife out of the room. They had seen life fading in their child with no power to stop it. Loretta looked at me with such hope and love that perhaps I could magically extract the disease from her daughter with my friendship, so much so, I was compelled to move away from Judy's bed to embrace her mother. I looked at Loretta, trying to convey in silence that I would do whatever I could to get her daughter through another day. Sal squeezed my upper arm with a man-to-man display of trust.

"Enjoy dinner together and ring this bell if you need anything," Loretta said, still hesitating to leave.

"Thank you, Mama. We will be fine," Judy said, adjusting her hat with weakened effort.

I waited for her parents to leave the room and sat next to the bed on a small chair. She waited as well. Once the door shut, she opened her arms again.

"Oh, Declan, forgive me. I know you are a married man, but I need you to hold me. Hold me forever."

In the request I heard not so much about her needing to make up for the love we lost, but her need to hold on to life itself, as if I was the means, a source of healing, to bring her back to life. If only our love was strong enough to do just that. We embraced each other for yet another moment in eternity, as the fluttering of her heart melted mine.

Finally, she weakened again, and I had to release her to allow room for her lungs to fill.

"Declan, can you do me a favor, dear? Open the balcony doors. Mother is always afraid the cold air from the Narrows blowing in here will make me sick. Daddy put me in this room because it has a balcony over our front porch. It's so refreshing when the fresh salty air comes in. I love this room. Every morning he sneaks me out onto the balcony when Mother is still sleeping, and reads me the newspaper. It's such a thrill to watch the construction of the lower lanes being built on the bridge. You know ours is now the largest expansion bridge in the world, it took the Golden Gate Bridge off the top of the charts," she said with pride, and to my amazement, looked a bit stronger since we hugged. Hearing her talk about the bridge, reminded me of how we talked about current events when we had our own private time together in the city.

"And it is right in your front yard, dear one," I said, caressing her soft hand.

We heard voices down below us on the front porch, as the group apparently coaxed my son outside. Indeed, Judy's cousins were teasing Andrew just as Sal and Marie C expected.

"Maybe you should check on your son, Declan. Those girls will kiss him, tease his hair, and squeeze his cheeks until he dies of too much Italian passion. He better be careful not to fall in love with one of them," she laughed. I saw she loved her cousins and was happy for them to have a visitor as well.

I laughed and it felt great. "Just what he needs, the passion of Italian women is a good test to make sure he's on the right path. He's planning on entering the seminary in the fall. Funny, I was going to take him to see the Rockettes at Radio City, but this is so much better," I said, with a gladness I had forgotten was possible.

Judy rummaged through a small powder tote and touched up her gray skin with a blusher, making me reminisce some more, as it was always my sheer delight to watch her in the make-up room before a curtain call. "Oh, the Rockettes would be divine. But I must laugh at the notion of you with a son entering the seminary. I love the irony. How old is he then?" Judy laid a hand on her chest in delight, laughing, but it made her cough. She pointed at a glass of water on the nightstand.

"Just turned twenty-three," I said, as I retrieved the glass and hand it to her. I watched her take small dainty sips. "Andrew gave me an interesting gift this year at Christmas. It's a journal with ten questions he wanted me to answer, ten questions on my life's path."

Judy looked intrigued. "Oh my. Sounds like an exercise in soul-searching, give me an example of one of his questions," she asked, always a good study partner. She gave the glass back to me with trembling hands and I placed it next to the ignored platter full of food.

I hesitated, wondered which one to give her. Then took a risk with this one: "Do your sufferings turn you away from God or do they unite you to the Holy?"

She closed her eyes and seemingly contemplated the question.

I rambled on, nervous to tread on the topic of suffering as she lay in the midst of it. "I completed the questions for him on the plane over here, and then we reviewed some of them at the Fordham library yesterday. This morning, we visited with Father Carmen; he was the one who told me about you."

She smiled at me, listening, but her eyes were closed. "Yes, he blessed me with his herbal oils yesterday."

I decided not to tell her how he blessed me as well.

Her eyes remained closed. "Do your sufferings turn you away from God or do they unite you to the Holy?" she said opening her eyes. "Hum, tough questions huh? My sufferings have brought me closer to the Holy than I have ever been in my whole life. Without God's strength, I would have been dead already," she said with a whisper. "How did you answer that one Declan?" she asked, taking my hand as she closed her eyes once more.

I shrugged. "Judy, my sufferings didn't serve me well, and I'm far from an angel deserving any closeness to the Holy." I made light of the topic and didn't plan to give her the full answer, like I gave my son. "Hey sweetheart, wouldn't it be great if we could turn back the clock, start it all over again?" I asked. "Remember the wonder of our Manhattan days? I'd visit you when you practiced at the clubs downtown, I wanted to take you as my bride then and there, but knew you were out of my league. So I let you disappear into the lights of Hollywood."

She gently opened her eyes. "I knew full well when you went to live with the Nuscos that Tino would corrupt you. And then, before I knew it, you chose a bride, an Italian Jersey girl of all things. Please tell me you didn't honeymoon with her on the Island of Capri. You promised you'd take me there when we were young," she said, showing me a glimpse of her old sassiness.

"Every time I listen to your record, my mind goes to the Island of Capri with you," I said and kissed her hand.

"Declan, you were so stubborn, trying to act like a tough gang kid like your Nusco brothers all the time. But I knew who you really were, just a sweet Irish boy who had a crush on me."

"You brought the best out in me and never gave up, even after I moved in with Tino's family, you sent letter after letter."

She pouted as I melted some more. "Yes, letter after unanswered letter Declan. When you lived with them, you were cold as ice for a long time, ignored me and never wrote me back."

"Judy, your letters kept me going when I was alone at Fordham and I wouldn't have survived the long dreary nights overseas in the war if it weren't for your letters, at least I wrote you while I was in the trenches in France."

She began to cry. "Yes, I got those thankfully, but you have it all wrong. Writing to you kept me going, it just hurt when they'd go unanswered. When I surprised you at Fordham after the war, it was just like our teenage love days again."

"Let's go back to those days little one."

Her face glimmered with a soft smile. "Remember when I dropped the Russo name."

I laughed. "Yes, indeed you stayed strong with your dad on that Judy Winslow."

She smiled. "I'm still a Russo on the inside."

A lamp lighted her face and made her eyes sparkle, I looked at her as if a spotlight still shined on her. This moment became embedded in my soul and would remain with me to the end. I caressed her hand. "Judy, I have always loved you and always will, now and forever."

She squeezed my hand as hard as she could. "Please stay with me tonight."

CHAPTER FIFTEEN

ILLUSIONS UNVEILED

The door of the balcony had to finally be closed again, it was frigid outside as a rising half moon lighted the sky. I stayed with Judy at her bedside for the entire evening.

When Signore Attanasio came over for a late dinner, he brought Andrew up with him into Judy's quarters with another tray of cheese, olives, biscotti, and of course, a carafe of Zio Leo's homemade wine with a few empty wine tumbler glasses. We stepped aside at a sitting area adjacent to the bedroom to greet each other, as I didn't want to rouse Judy too much since she dozed off for a little moment of rest.

Signore Attanasio tried to use a lowered voice, but couldn't help himself and bantered with me in his usual loud Brooklyn accent. "Hey, stop stealing my niece all day Declano. The women downstairs said you are hogging our Judy all for yourself today," he said, giving my memory a sudden jolt with the familiar odors of salami and beef in his breath and on his skin.

I greeted him with a huge hug. "Hey Signore Attanasio, so good to see you after all these years. You're not retired from feeding the whole neighborhood yet? It looks as though Zia Anna is taking good care of you as usual."

He smiled, put black-rimmed reading glasses on and pulled out a small memo pad. There was a collection of items inside both breast pockets; one held a pack of Lucky Strike cigarettes with its red round label showing through, and in the other was a row of attached pens. He took a pen and wrote his phone number down, ripping a sheet off the pad. "Hey don't be a stranger and wait three decades to call us—there's this new invention called the telephone," he said, handing me his phone number.

"Got it, Signore Attanasio," I said, whispering, putting the slip of paper away. "Too much time has passed that's for sure, and I'll be sure to give you a call. Thank you."

"You better do that, and don't just say it, kid. You were like one of my own, and the only Irish son I ever had."

I smiled and loved to hear him say that when his customers would come in. "Any plans to retire yet?" I asked, feeling a bit awkward having Andrew near the bedroom of my beloved. It felt as though Sofia herself had entered my private world.

"What me retire and drive Anna crazy painting the house or something? Nah, it won't work for me to sit idle or try and find something to do with my days. Look at me, I'm a lucky man, have happy, successful kids, three fruitful businesses because Anna does my bookkeeping, and good health, due to low stress in my life. I give Anna all the credit for that though, as she was never one to nag or gossip—nah, she was always the peacemaker instead." He smiled, looking like a classic Dean Martin styled, handsome Italian, and filled up a glass of wine. "Of course she's still yelling at me when I come home with a new Buick or another fig tree to plant on our patch of grass in the yard, but for the most part, we run our lives like that fine-tuned Buick Riviera you see parked on the lawn," he said, pointing outside.

I laughed, remembering how he was always obsessed with cars and his tree orchard, and realized nothing had changed at 1102. "Hey Signore Attanasio, speaking of trees, tell Andrew here, your Florida palm tree story—I'll never forget that one." I left them to visit as I walked over to check on Judy, and then looked out the window at his shinny-waxed black car he parked halfway onto the front lawn, as the driveway was now filled with a line of cars. At the same time, I scanned the road for any other unwelcomed intruders, and hoped there was no possibility Marco would send his boys to look for me in Bay Ridge.

"Nice ride, Signore Attanasio," I said in a whisper. "What's the going rate for a car waxing these days, bet it's not a nickel like Frankie and I got," I said, tiptoeing my way back to him still trying not to wake Judy.

"Oh, I have my grandsons, Sammy and Matthew, helping me with that now," he said, as he continued to tell Andrew how he and Anna honeymooned in Florida and of how he drove home with a palm tree hanging out of the trunk of their car—and of how, when they got home to plant it in the front yard, how it died as soon as the ground froze that winter.

He laughed and put his arm around Andrew. "You have yourself a fantastic boy here, Declano, he laughs at my stories, too. You must have married quite well yourself, son. He's been counseling all the women downstairs on life, sounds like a philosopher or a priest already, I'd say. He tells us perhaps the seminary this fall?" He gave out another laugh. "Ha, I never thought a Nusco boy like you would be raising a religious man."

"A Nusco boy? I'm far from that these days, Signore Attanasio. But, yes you're right; he is more like his mother than the likes of me." I looked at Andrew with pride. "And for your information, you'd be glad to hear my Nusco days are coming to an end soon."

He crossed his arms and scratched the side of his temple and spoke even louder. "Oh, does Don Marco know about that? I know what it's like to get pressure from a mob boss—and you're his Consigliere. Yikes. Be careful when you try to take the straight road kid, once a mobster, the only way out is with a bullet straight to the heart," he said, poking my chest with his index finger.

I gave Andrew a look that he'd better not bring up what happened on the highway with Anthony, and he seemingly got the message. I wasn't going to comment on Signore Attanasio's banter nor tell him I was on the run as we spoke.

Then Judy started rustling a little, so I walked over to her and took her hand as Andrew stood at the entrance of the room with an awkward look on his face. "Come in here, quietly Andrew, meet my friend, Judy. I've spoken so much about her, you must feel as though you know her pretty well by now son." He looked uncomfortable, obviously having never seen a deathly ill person before.

Judy opened her eyes and smiled, her warmth eased his guarded approach as she stared at him speaking softly. "I feel as though I'm going back in time. Are you the Andrew your father has boasted about? Oh my, you are the spitting image of him at your age. I think I've fallen in love all over again seeing you. Let me look at you closer as I'm stuck here in this awful bed." Andrew leaned in closer, although very stiff as she placed her hands on his arms. She took his face and gently kissed both cheeks and whispered, "I heard you chatting downstairs on the patio with all my cousins, you poor soul. Have you been pinched by enough women to last a lifetime yet?" We all laughed as she seemingly softened Andrew's mood and began to act like her usual self again. It was true, we brought her joy being here today after all, I thought.

Andrew smiled and accepted her kisses with tears in his eyes. "Yes, your cousins have taken great care of me miss. It is an honor to meet you. My father tells me wonderful stories about you, and we listen to your records at home. I'm so sorry to see you suffering today," Andrew said, in a gentle voice trying his hardest not to lose it to tears.

Signore Attanasio interrupted, "Oh, son, please recite to Judy the C. S. Lewis quote you told all of us. I believe it will help our Judy understand what she is going through or why God is allowing it. Judy darling, he somehow gives a purpose to the madness of it all and puts it in startling language, just like a true Englishman would."

Andrew recited the quote once again. "God whispers to us in our pleasures, speaks to us in our conscience, but shouts in our pains: It is His megaphone to rouse a deaf world."

Judy listened intently to Lewis's take on suffering, but her response to the quote was even more profound. "We sing our heart's longings, we sing our heart's joys, but suffering brings us to an understanding, to a truth that lies at the core of our being," she said, coughing slightly into her lace handkerchief. She then, held up her hand as though she wanted to finish her verse, but trying not to cry. "At the core of our being, before we covered it with our illusions."

The room fell silent and no one spoke another word.

She spoke again after too much silence passed. "Illusions Declan," she said, and closed her eyes seemingly in deep thought.

When she opened them again, after a minute of our gazing at her angelic face, she spoke. "Zio Saverio, can you please go downstairs and fetch the *La Boheme* record for us? I want to play it for Declan tonight, and you can tell Daddy that today I will be telling my friend that his grandfather came to visit us—no more secrets, no more illusions," she said, to our surprise.

Signore Attanasio raised his hands so fast, like a police officer had just caught him stealing. "Oh, Madonna mia, now that's a topic I had nothing to do with—do you want me to fetch your dad along with the album dear one—this is his secret, not mine, so please, leave me out of this fight."

She rolled her eyes. "Don't worry Zio, but it's time I tell Declan the truth about…"

As I walked over to hold Judy's hand, Signore Attanasio practically ran out of the room before she could finish. "It should be in the stacks near the hi-fi in the living room," she said, trying to shout as he fled down the hallway. She smiled. "Boys, let's have a party tonight, listen to records and sing. My best friend has come to visit me, and I feel a lot stronger."

I smiled. "You're feeling stronger, darling?" I fixed her soft silk blanket and adjusted her lavender cap. "What did you say about my grandfather…?"

Not allowing me to pull the blankets up nor fix her hat, she abruptly pushed the blankets off and turned to my son. "Oh, and Andrew, please pour me some of Zio Leo's wine over there. I suspect that magical juice might be the elixir to cure me. Please, just a half glass though."

When we all had a glass in hand, I held up mine to lead the toast. "Let's have a toast to love and friendship," I said, as she and my son followed. "To love and friendship."

"And to truth," Judy said, gazing at the moon outside, taking a small sip of wine, and giving me her glass.

I placed her tumbler of wine on the nightstand, as we waited for Saverio to return—he never did, but a pretty, twenty-something year old girl, with flowing black hair came in holding the record.

"Here's your music, Auntie J, Nonno said you wanted this." Her sweet smile and huge brown eyes got the attention of Andrew.

Judy took the record album in her hands and smiled looking at both sides. "Hah, it figures. My Zio doesn't want any part of this story as usual. Thank you, Terri. Please, take this sweet handsome boy with you, okay. He doesn't need to be around an old dying lady like me." She turned to talk to my son. "Please Andrew, go on sweet one, entertain my cousins like you did so well earlier, and you'll like Terri, she's a student at Brooklyn College right now." Judy smiled, and set the album down on her bedding.

"Do you want me to play your record for you Auntie J?" Terri asked, blushing.

"That's okay. My friend is here, he will play it for me, go along now you two," she said, giving Terri a wink.

I took the vinyl record out of its cover, as Andrew was eager to leave with the pretty young lady. But first he walked over to kiss Judy good-bye. "My dad was right telling me that you are a special lady and a special friend. It's been my honor to meet you Judy," he said, and kissed her cheek.

She got teary eyed again. "No, son. The honor is mine. Go off now, have fun tonight with the Russos and the Attanasios, soon you will discover how we celebrate life with simple love and not so simple food."

"Celebrate life. I will remember that miss." Andrew leaned over to give her another parting hug and looked at me with a smile.

"And good luck finishing up your degree at Fordham, that college breeds fine young men and women, this I know from experience."

After the two left the room, I placed the album on a turntable sitting on the dresser. As the needle settled into the black vinyl, the overture began to envelope the room with its hypnotizing instrumental. Soon the air was filled with Puccini's first act, and gratefully Judy and I were alone again.

She became melancholy with tears welling once more. "I wanted to play this tonight for us, as this brings back a special memory for me. But truth is, I never passed the second round of auditions for the spring session at the Met that year, as I was frozen stiff during, Musetta's Waltz."

I didn't want her to cry. "Darling, with all your successes, you bring up the one time you…"

She put her finger to her mouth to quiet me. "There is something I must tell you about that audition—so, maybe just one sip," she said, pointing to her wine tumbler.

I handed her the glass and thought, this has something to do with my grandfather. Did he phone them after the war? Everything in me needed to delve into the particulars of what she wanted to say, something that scared Signore Attanasio enough to run out. I would ask the men about it later, I thought. I wanted to enjoy my friend as much as I could and knew her health came before any need of mine. "You should rest. Let's simply sit and listen to this together, let's sing…"

She interrupted. "Would you believe me if I told you your grandfather was there the day I froze auditioning for that show?"

I frowned. "No, now you're losing me."

"He was there—well not in the audience, but he heard my voice crack practicing the high C note," she said. With a sigh of relief, she continued, "Declan, as your friend, let me go to my grave in peace having finally told you the truth." She slowed to a whisper and called me closer to her bed. "Your grandfather came to New York to see us—here, at this house. As your friend, it's my duty to tell you all about it." Judy stopped and placed the handkerchief over her mouth to cough gently.

"Please darling. It's too late for old secrets," I said, feeling stuck between the need to hear more particulars and trying to protect her. "Besides, I know he was in New York after the war to place a headstone for my mother's grave, just saw it today at the cemetery for the first time."

I was relieved to make her smile again. "Oh, Declan. Good, I'm so glad to hear that, I imagine it's beautiful. We all loved your mother." She asked me for another sip of wine, taking in a drop slowly. "Don't you find it odd he never told you about his visit?"

"Yes, I do."

"He came after the war, almost twenty years ago, right? Strange," she said.

My tone turned stern for her benefit. "Yes Judy, it bothers me a great deal, but why is this your issue to fix? I plan to call him and straighten this all out. Please, I want no trouble for you my love, not now."

"It's okay. I'm stronger than you think. He came to see us for help—in finding you." She paused. "He was sent away from the Nusco home and was clearly upset about it, had letters that Miss Aisling wrote him showing the Attanasio's return address, at 1102 Bay Ridge Parkway. Was so distraught when the security guards at the Nusco's house forced him off the property and threatened him, that he came to us for…"

I had heard enough and struggled to stay firm. "Judy stop. I know he came after the war looking for me, and will talk to the men downstairs about this before I leave here tonight. I promise. You are my only true friend in this whole world. I beg you to stop."

She tried to gather up all her strength, squeezed my hand, and began to cry. "Daddy made me swear to never tell you this, he didn't want me ever to interfere with your family over the years. I am sorry. I never should have gone along with this. Never."

This sanctuary was the last place to bring up the past. "My darling, have some water instead," I said, as Judy graciously sipped it to quiet her cough. My heart was about to sink, and my mind raced to find a quick way out of this conversation. "Judy, your father was right to protect you. Some memories need to stay buried," I said, and caressed her blankets again.

"No Declan. Truth cannot be buried."

"Well, you're right about that," I said. My curiosity mounted, but again, Judy was not going to be the one to ease it.

She fixed her soft nightgown collar as it was slipping off her petite shoulders. "Please, don't treat me like a helpless patient. I'm so damn tired of being sick and weak. If you let me tell you about this, the burden of holding in this truth will be finally freed."

I was caught between a rock and a hard place like no other. "You're right, but let us men work it out later tonight. Your job is done, and the truth is out. You are so brave. Thank you, I didn't know about his visit to the States until today when Father Carmen showed me her headstone and a file with his signature on it."

She took a deep breath. "Okay, promise me you'll talk to my father tonight, and feel free to use our phone to call your grandfather in Ireland. Do it for me, please," she said, closing her eyes.

"Will do sweetheart," I said quickly, to put a stop to the topic. Whew, got out of that one, I thought.

She sighed and closed her eyes once more, seemingly used to speaking with her eyes this way. "Declan, can you stay here tonight so I can be with you again when the sun rises? We can sit together on the balcony in the morning watching the freight ships head into the City—I think the heartbeat of the whole world starts here in the New York harbor."

I hugged her, fixed the bedding again, as she felt for my hand. Taking her hand, I'd didn't respond to her request to stay the night as I knew her request was a rhetorical one.

CHAPTER SIXTEEN

A WHORE IN A BUSINESS SUIT

Declan, please play me the waltz."

I got up and looked at the record album and saw that the song was on the B-side, Act II, fourth song in, so I counted the dark lines on the vinyl and placed the needle at Musetta's Waltz. Even in the worst of times, this waltz had the capability to still the winds in a hurricane.

"Turn up the volume darling," she said, with her eyes still closed.

Together we listened and I visualize us on the dance floor again. After the song finished, I lowered the volume so we could talk some more.

It seemed the both of us visualized the same scene in our heads. "I dance with you every time I hear that waltz darling," she said, and motioned for me to sit her more upright in the bed. I adjusted three pillows behind her back as if she were a body resting inside a canoe. "Thank you, I want to stay awake as I've slept enough for a hundred bears hibernating in the woods." I fixed the pillows just right and placed her hands gently on top of the bedding. "Declan, all that mafia stuff scared me, I wanted to tell you about your grandfather, but didn't know what to do. This was why I kept this awful secret until now."

I caressed her hand. "Well, you'll be happy to hear, my days as Marco's Consigliere are over with."

She screamed with joy. "Ah, the brilliant lawyer finally sees the light," she said, and pulled me close for a hug. "Had you told me that twenty years ago, I'd be your wife today and your grandfather would be a regular guest in the Russo house."

It hurt to hear the truth of her words and of how I wished for the same thing. There was nothing I could do about it but to die inside, and then she stuck the knife in deeper. "Declan, forgive me for saying this, but the many days in this bed have given me plenty of time to think. I see everything now, especially regrets, they are as clear to me as Musetta's voice is perfect, and they stab me at night when I cannot sleep. But darling, you must see, keeping that secret changed everything for me—for us."

Good sense told me not to interrupt her.

"I don't blame my father for this, as he had his own reasons. But, I know if you were allowed to see your grandfather after the war, you would have left the damn Nusco family, left the crime underworld all together. Married me after college. No one even gave you a choice. I fought with my father all night when your grandfather was here, but he wouldn't let me call you." She began to weep uncontrollably.

I scrambled around her bed, trying to find a tissue, it was as if the house had just caught fire and I began to search all over for the extinguisher. With no way to fan the flames, I let her cry.

After a good few minutes, I took her face into my hands and kissed her as if we were young lovers again. I had no words to give, only my love. Together we cried and I felt as close to her in those moments than ever before.

"Keeping a truth inside is difficult, if not impossible," Judy said.

"Yes, you can say that again," I said.

"Okay." She laughed now and put a calm back to our reunion. "Keeping a truth inside is difficult…"

We laughed together and I started the album over again. "The truth always comes out despite our efforts at silencing it. Would you believe that I finally, after all these years, just told my son about my mother's death—and of how I have a younger sister? I kept that secret since 1933," I said, watching the record spin.

She motioned for me to sit with her again. "It's difficult, but freeing to get it out, isn't it?"

"Freeing is an understatement," I said, taking her hand, but I had to add one more thought to ease her regret. "I lived in such darkness after my mother died, so please love me anyway when I admit this—but, there's no saying I would have ever left the Nusco family when my grandfather came for me after the war."

"No? That hurts to hear that," she said, and frowned.

"As it does me to say it," I said, kissing her hand.

She sighed and closed her eyes for a minute.

I continued. "And, dear one, your father was right to protect you. What if you would have gotten caught in the crossfire of a gang war? And it was a blood bath in the streets at the time, I can't even entertain that thought…"

She looked at me with affection, and then stared out the window at the half moon for a while longer and sighed once again. "Then I guess we will never know, will we?" she said, continuing to look outside.

I gave her space with her thoughts for a minute or two, but still had one question for her. "The day of your audition at the Met, what was the connection with that and my grandfather?" I asked with a slice of humor.

"Well, that is where my audition fits in." She laughed a bit. "After your grandfather was chased away from your house, I told you how he came here with Zio Saverio to ask my father to call the Nusco home for him. You see, my father would have to call the Nusco's occasionally, regarding their subway contracts in the City, so we were happy to help your grandfather—such a dignified man, I remember him well." Judy lighted up thinking of my Pappy, but changed abruptly at the thought of that phone call. "Unfortunately, we hit a block wall when the threats came flying over the phone from one of your brothers."

I should have followed my initial instincts and never asked the question, I thought. "Please, darling, never mind, I'll get the details from your dad," I said. Why didn't I keep my mouth shut? I thought, kicking myself.

Nevertheless, she was excited to provide me the details. "We were forced to promise your brother that we'd take him straight to the airport the next morning. But when your grandfather pleaded with us to let him go to the Foundling Hospital first, we couldn't deny him that. So I took him with me into the City the next morning, our taxi driver dropped him at the Foundling Hospital and I headed to the West Side for my audition. He was so determined to find you and Shannon, so I'm sure he got the adoption records that morning."

She looked youthful and started to laugh some more when she inserted a happy memory. "The poor man," she said, blushing through her pale skin. "Professor Quinn had to listen to me sing, *Quando m'en vo* the whole car ride into the city. I must have broken his eardrums working on my high notes."

I finally made the connection with the opera and had to laugh with my friend. "My dear, if I know my Pappy at all, he was delighted to hear you sing. Oh, my darling, the vision of you singing with him listening, blows my heart wide open, secret or not," I said, kissing her hand a few more times.

Defeated in my efforts to keep Judy from having to tell me the details, I had one more question. "So who took my Pappy to the airport and when?"

She shook her head. "I don't know actually. He called to thank us for our kindness the next day and said he was staying in the City that night with his former colleagues from the university. He planned to catch the morning train to Albany, or some destination up-State to find your sister."

"Buffalo, she lives in the Buffalo area I think. She's the main reason I'm in New York, just picked up her adoption file this morning."

She smiled. "Oh, that is the best news I've heard in moons, Declan. I remember her well. We all fought over who would get to braid that long fire-red hair of hers, she was like everyone's favorite doll to play with. Sweet little Shannon, you must find her—she's what, about forty years old now, right?"

"Yes, she is. I've never been right without her—never been right without you." Kissing her forehead like I always did, I needed to down shift and collect a few more details like a detective gathering evidence "Forgive me, but did my brother ever follow up with you about getting my Pappy to the airport?"

She nodded with assurance, but still was sizably angry about it. "Oh, yes, as sure as the rising sun, someone in your family called my father at his office the next morning. Of course Daddy lied to him and said he left safely for Ireland early in the morning," Judy said. "We all respected your grandfather a great deal and gave him the dignity to do as he pleased with his time in New York."

She was agitated at the thought of Marco calling her dad, so I tried to divert her. "The Russos and Attanasios are a classy bunch and always did the right thing and stayed clear of the mafia. I must thank your father later for sticking his neck out for me like he did…"

Still agitated Judy interrupted. "Declan, how dare they call my father at his office and to interfere with your life, your grandfather and sister are your only blood relatives for God's sake—he had every right to see you," she said. "And aren't most of the damn Nusco brothers dead now anyway?"

Could I ever escape from my past I thought, and shook my head. "Yes, two of my three brothers are dead, both shot in fact, but please…"

Reaching for more blankets, as she seemed cold, I helped to add an afghan on top of her. She sighed. "Oh, you were just the trusted lawyer around to protect everyone and bail them out. I remember it all. None of them had any brains and they used yours to make them money. The way I see it, you were like a whore in a business suit for them," she said, and lamented some more. "It was a sad day for me when you moved in with that family. It was a sad day for all the Attanasios, Zia Anna cried for months about it. Why did you make that choice? Lucky you weren't shot dead too."

I shrugged. A whore in a business suit, I thought, and knew she was spot on with her analogy. "Please stop, Judy, not tonight." I craved the times we had and took her into my arms as she tried so desperately to be my strong friend as always. "Please, don't leave me now. Not like this. You don't deserve to suffer."

Then she invited me to lie next to her on the edge of the bed and into her arms. Once more, Judy and I held each other as if we embraced life itself.

We didn't talk for a long while and relinquished ourselves to sleep, wrapped together like petals on a rose in this position, wishing that all our choices could be changed. As if my body's strength supplied hers, she opened her eyes again after thirty minutes or so and was the first to speak. "Are you okay, Declan? All these years seem to have been hard on you." Even though she was sick and dying, she still worried about me, stroking my face with barely any life left in her. "I can see it in your eyes. Tell me darling. Tell me what is inside those deep green eyes."

I couldn't tell her of my pain when I was trying without success to remove hers.

"I know about Aisling," she said, with a whisper and tearful eyes. "I wanted to call you when I heard, but with Sofia…" She stopped herself.

I paused, closed my eyes wishing to sleep with her some more. "That's another topic to leave aside. It's too tragic, and you didn't need to call—I pretty much climbed into a hole after."

"I'm so sorry my darling. Talk about it with me."

"There's nothing to share, other than it was all my fault it happened."

"Your fault?"

"Yes," I said, fighting off tears. I slipped out of her arms and walked to the balcony doors, opening one for a clearer view of the moon, and as if I were a wolf howling at night to convey a long-distance message to my daughter, I retold the story. "Sofia hassled me every week in the summer and the fall. She wanted me to build a fence around the pond before the snow. My daughter was a fanciful horse girl and only eight when the accident happened." Even though it was difficult, I was relieved to speak of this with my trusted friend and continued, "Aisling slipped right into the ice after her horse threw her."

"Yes, you told me you had twin daughters, Patti is the other one, right?"

"Yes. Patti is the type to read, paint, that kind of stuff. But, Aisling, well, we couldn't keep her indoors. So I taught her to ride and gave her a few horses that were gentle walkers," I said, staring at the moon, as I couldn't face my friend when giving these details.

"Go on," Judy said softly.

"Sofia warned me time and time again. You see Aisling would always sneak out of the house…"

She stopped me. "Please Declan. Come over, climb into my arms, just once more darling."

At a snail's pace, I glanced at the moon once more, and then closed the balcony door, turning to look at Judy with a look of disgrace and shame. Would she think of me as a total and complete failure now, I wondered.

Her arms, weakened, opened slightly, and her begging eyes drew me toward her. I kneeled at her bedside, and put my head down into her delicate palm. "What's a father to do with all of this guilt on my heart?" I asked, picking my head up as she took my face into her hands again.

"If I could hold your face like this forever, would you promise to let your guilt go—to forgive…" She paused. "To forgive yourself. I need you to hold me forever Declan. I'm afraid to die alone."

I held her close again, as she lay helpless and weak in the bedding. "My love, I will never leave you."

"Let it go, then—be free. Be free. Your baby Aisling is free. I soon will be free. Promise me you will be free from the past and from all of this. I won't be afraid and will let my regrets go, if you can be free."

"And when the earth shall claim your limbs, then you will truly dance." I quoted Kahlil Gibran, the poet we'd memorize and recite together during our late nights in the library.

She smiled and a tear fell down her cheek. "Oh, you remind me now. I remember that one. I miss our late night poetry readings to each other. 'For what is it to die but to stand naked in the wind and to melt into the sun? And what is it to cease breathing, but to free the breath from its restless tides, that it may rise and expand and seek God unencumbered,'" she said, adding her own Gibran lines as if were a song.

"Oh, my Crazy Ruby Starlight," I said. "'Only when you drink from the river of silence shall you indeed sing.'" I recited Gibran once more and we embraced as the foghorns blew from the Narrows waterway. "Don't be afraid, my darling—sing, sing, sing.

Never stop." Then, as if a spirit entered my body, I began to sing to Judy her latest record, the one I just heard in Sal's office.

She listened to me singing with her eyes closed the whole time, thankfully, as I tried so hard not to let my voice crack between the tears.

She cried for the both of us. "Declan, you are a good man. Thank you for the gift of that memory tonight. Good for you, my Crazy Ruby Starlight Boy. You sang the Italian ending beautifully."

We hugged for a long while. "I will talk to your dad and uncle tonight," I said, "Thank you for your friendship and for your courage. Buried truth is painful to come out, but it's also very healing when it does. You are a brave soul, indeed. I wish you could come to Ireland with me. You could sing to my Pappy an Italian aria again," I said, and slowly stood up weakened.

"I would love to sing for him again," she said with a smile. "Stupid me, letting you go and marry someone else, can you just carry me out of here and take me to the Copacabana right now? We were destined to be together, just like tonight."

"Let's go my Ruby Starlight Girl."

"But destiny takes a turn when we're not looking," she said.

I sat next to her and wished to never leave.

Judy continued. "Sofia, that pretty Jersey girl, she gave you a beautiful boy didn't she. Promise me you will make things right with her. Do it for Andrew and your daughter. Do it for me."

"Yes, I will try. I may have blown it with her."

"She'll be there for you. I know—like gravity—you always return to her. Come on, my dear friend, let's face it—love is only for the stars in the sky to figure out. Life on this earth is too imperfect to experience a perfect love. We can't have the love promised to us in fairy tales, at least, not on this planet. No Declan. I will wait for you in the stars, my love. I will even wait on the dark side of the moon, where we can share our love forever and ever, just like you promised me as kids together," Judy said, pointing to the door with an unspoken request to look at the half moon raised high in the sky once more.

I opened the door again and looked outside. "The dark side of the moon. I can't believe you remember my silly games of star gazing with you in the summer."

"Oh, yes. We'd kiss behind Zio Saverio's truck and you'd tell me we could escape forever on the moon where no one would find us. I remember it all. But I was too busy being a sassy high school girl while you were still in the eighth grade playing your boyish games of kissing in the dark. I look back now and wish I could escape to the dark side of the moon with you, away from all this pain and sorrow."

I embraced her again as she held me close while I kissed her fragile neck and face. "Please Judy, don't wait for me in the dark, I don't live in darkness anymore. Wait for me in the light darling."

"Yes. The light. I can see it Declan."

I could feel her arms give way to the submission of her unconsciousness, where at last she closed her eyes and entered into the deep realm her dreams.

I wasn't privy to come along, so I let her go at last.

CHAPTER SEVENTEEN

A ROUND OF DRAW POKER

It was half past eight in the evening by the time I walked downstairs. A few young kids were sleeping on the family room floor covered in blankets and I heard people chatting in the dining room. I was tired and didn't feel like socializing. I could see Sal and his wife sitting alone with each other in the front room, and out of respect, I walked over to them. We spoke in brief and they were pleased when I reported that Judy was sleeping peacefully. I broke my promise to Judy, as there was no way I could bother them about my grandfather's visit at a time like this.

They left and went up the stairs to sit with her. I stayed, sitting in solitude watching the lights of the bridge outside and wished I could rest alone here all night. But the chatter in the other room was getting louder and I knew sleep wasn't an option any time soon. So I got up, walked towards the commotion, and found my son sitting with a group at an oversized dining room table.

Signore Attanasio and Zia Anna were talking to Andrew along with several others. Another handful of relatives sat at the other end of the table discussing the latest headlines out of a section of the newspaper. A half-full pot of espresso was there along with a scattering of empty shot glasses bearing the evidence of a liqueur that once filled them. "Come, join us, Declano, there's plenty of room. Prego, prego. Did my granddaughter get you the record you needed?" Signore Attanasio asked.

I laughed and took a seat next to him. "Oh yes, Signore Attanasio, thanks, it's funny you left us so soon though."

He looked nervous and lowered his voice so only I could hear him. "Ah, don't worry about the details too much kid, life doesn't have to be complicated now, does it?" he said, patting my back and then spoke to me in a normal tone. "Did you and Judy enjoy your reunion?"

"Yes, Sal and Loretta are with her now, she's sleeping peacefully," I said, showing him I got the hint, besides, Judy and I had covered it all anyway.

He smiled, happy that I respected his position. "Do you want a shot of anisette with your coffee?" he asked, filling my glass without waiting for an answer.

I hesitated. "I'm not sure how long we can stay. Andrew, don't you have to get back to the university?" I asked hoping we could leave. I was exhausted from wishing love could heal my beloved. I gave her all I had, as I was sure everyone at this table had as well. But it was not enough. Nothing would be enough. I looked at all the different faces at the table and wondered, was Father Carmen right about the notion of God's will, and were we all victims of some preordained course of action that no individual or family effort could alter? Nonetheless, I knew getting the answers to my uncertainties was like solving the mathematical equations on the blackboard back in Fordham's tutor rooms—all drivel with no point, and definitely with no solutions.

Andrew sat at the other side of the table, having a good time with the young girl who came upstairs and two other kids around his age. He reminded me what my mother used to do at the Attanasio's house, speaking half Italian and English in jovial conversations while drinking coffee or wine. "I feel like I've known this family my whole life, and these folks are giving me an earful of you as a boy. You just missed Frank. He had to run back to his pizza deli," Andrew said, accepting a slice of pie from one of the girls.

"Ah, the dishwasher at his shop near Prospect Park didn't show again," an attractive, robust woman in her thirties said, and reached across the table to give me her hand. "Hello there, you sure have caused a ruckus here tonight. My name is Julia. I'm Anna's daughter, the seventh in the line of all of us. Mama said I wasn't born yet when you lived with us."

Andrew waited until she was finished introducing me to several others. "Paps, Frank said you taught him everything about baseball. He's the guy you'd go to Ebbet's Field with, right?" he asked. "But he's no little brother anymore—more like a heavy weight boxer these days."

"Oh, he is, is he? Gosh, I'll never forget the days when we'd go to the Sunday games when the Dodgers were in town," I said, disappointed to have missed Frank. "Oh, too bad. I would have loved to see Frankie. So he has a pizza joint in town you say."

"Try two of them in Brooklyn and one in the City, Declano," Signore Attanasio said, looking proud.

"Oh, that's nice." My words were congenial but my thoughts were on Judy upstairs and on calling the telephone operator to look up a few numbers for me. I thought to call my Pappy, but wanted to call Buffalo first—a Shannon O'Scanlon in upstate New York was out there somewhere, and she would soon know me.

Signore Attanasio put his arm around my shoulder. "It's not easy to watch our beauty suffer, is it? You don't look that great, kid. Here, have a double." He poured me more of the liqueur in the crystal-stemmed shot glass already in my hand. "Judy and you go way back, way back. Un giovane amore batte il piu forte, a young love beats the strongest." He took out his handkerchief as Zia Anna stroked his hand. "I don't know what I would do without my Anna." He turned to her and pointed his finger up to heaven. "Don't you be getting any ideas about going to see the big man upstairs before I go. It's me who's buying that ticket first, you hear." He grabbed her face and delivered a long romantic kiss like he always did. I was happy to see that nothing had changed between them. "Anna, the two love birds even listened to Puccini tonight, so romantic isn't it?" He kissed her again.

I remembered learning about love when I first saw Signore Attanasio and Zia Anna together. After we moved in with them, I stood astounded watching when he would come in from work and Zia Anna would be doing her usual oratory from the kitchen sink or as she stirred a pot of noodles. Without fail, he would coddle her face saying, "Lei e' la donna piu'bella che abbia mai visto—she is the most beautiful woman I have ever seen," and then he'd plant one, or two, or three big, wet and juicy Italian kisses straight on her lips.

Zia Anna pretended to be annoyed, saying, "Oh stop, there you go again catching me in my bare feet," and he'd kiss her all over again. It was like watching the Italian version of James Garner and Doris Day, in *The Thrill of It All.* Their kids assumed such affection was commonplace. I knew differently. I loved to watch them in action, but it pained me too. Not seeing this affection between my parents hurt, but knowing that it actually existed gave me hope. I pledged to find a love like that and knew I had found it with Judy.

As I sat at the table watching the family interact, I was reminded of the first days we moved in with the Attanasio's. They gave us love, and in exchange my mother taught them English, using her flute to teach their children a new language through music. Mother would have Shannon and me sing Gaelic songs and they'd sing Italian ones, then we'd all sing in English together. After we moved in, music became alive in their home. Before then, they kept a piano covered with a linen cloth and used it only to hold framed photos or to hang laundry over. It frustrated my mother to see a perfectly good piano going to waste. So she uncovered it, moved it to the center of room and pulled Zia Anna out of the kitchen to accompany her on the piano while my mother played her flute. "Music is the universal language," she'd say. I missed Shannon more than ever in this setting, realizing the many good times lost from the choices I had made.

We chatted for a while as two girls exited the kitchen with a tray of teacups and a kettle, telling us they were bringing it upstairs for Judy and her parents, as yet another girl came to the table to greet me. "Hey Declano, I'm JoAnn, number eleven, and the baby of the bunch, try some of my special tea, and drink it warm, it's my own herbal concoction of beet juice, green leafy vegetables, and spices. We've been offering this to Judy every night, but now you're the one who looks ill. Please, allow me to help you, I promise this will make you to feel better," she said, as she added honey to her potion.

Zia Anna looked annoyed. "Oh, JoAnn. Leave this poor man alone, you and your secret herbs are for the birds. You will scare away Judy's friend," she said, then looked at Andrew and me. "Please, don't rush off boys, as your visit today has brought life back into this house."

I felt the pressure to stay and could see Andrew wasn't in any hurry to leave as he grabbed more dessert and refilled his coffee cup. I inhaled the steam from the revitalizing concoction of herbs and spices, and to my surprise, it calmed me.

"How about a nice cigar, Declano?" Sal asked, having returned to join us. "Let's go down into the basement to enjoy some sweet tobacco." He leaned over to whisper in my ear, "I'd like to hear your stories of the west."

"Is Judy still sleeping soundly?" I asked.

"Yes, indeed. We haven't seen her this peaceful in over a month. You've truly given her a gift tonight with your visit. Thank you," he said, with a smile and shook my hand.

Signore Attanasio stood up, walked to a large cherry wood cigar box next to the china cabinet, and selected one, smelling its aroma.

"Andrew, do you want to join us?" Signore Attanasio asked.

"Sure," he said, and turned to the women, "Do you mind ladies? Duty calls." He gave me a wink, smelling the long cigar given to him.

I sat in my own zone, with a feeling of numbness, as the steam from the cup of tea calmed me some more. Perhaps JoAnn was right and that the elixir would restore my mood, I thought sipping her elixir.

Unmotivated to join the men, I slowly drank the tea, but Sal persisted. "Come on, we're good Italians, we don't bite like the Nusco's." He waved me over to join them as if it were an order.

"Fine." I got up, gulped down the rest, as it burned and revitalized my throat, took a cigar and followed the men down the stairs to the basement. Even though I told Judy I would ask her father about my Pappy's visit, I wasn't planning on mentioning it again. I will call my Pappy and get the answers needed once I get back to the hotel, I thought calculating the time zone differences.

As my mother used to say, "when we hit our pillows in New York, the Irish are seeping their teabags to start their day."

We walked down a flight of steep wood steps to a huge room full of soft, worn sofas against the walls, covered in colorful crocheted afghan blankets, with folding chairs surrounding a large round wood table in the center of the room. The table had green felt fabric on top, grooves full of red, blue, and white chips to hold poker coins for betting, and boxes of cards sat in the middle. A few ashtrays were full of remnants from another gathering giving the stale stench of old cigarettes in the room. One item specifically caught my eye, as a phone was attached to the wall.

Sal resumed giving me another tour like he did earlier at the office. The decor was similar, with a few deer heads mounted on the walls. Sal had more stories to go with them. "Leo and his guys built this card table special for me last summer and glued the green felt fabric on top. It's a tight fit but the kids love to play down here. Every Friday night, as the women pray their rosary, Saverio comes over and we play a few rounds of poker with the men from the Knights of Columbus," Sal said. "Feel like a fair round of five card draw, boys? The buy-in is only five bucks, chump change for a high rolling Nevada casino man like you, Declano."

I really wanted to leave, or at least ask to use the phone, but Andrew jumped in eagerly, pulling out his wallet. "Absolutely, Signore Russo. Here's ten bucks for the both of us. This basement is fantastic, my pals and I are always looking for a place to hang like this."

Before I knew it, I was shuffling a worn deck of cards and dealt out five faced down in the round. As the game continued and Saverio discarded three of his given hand, a few women brought down more drinks and desserts and returned up the basement stairs. Two of them who were chatting with Andrew earlier, stopped to take a seat together on the top step to watch us and listen.

Andrew looked at them with a wink and whispered to me. "This could end up being an all-nighter. Sorry Paps."

"Watch it. Nusco secrets aren't allowed boys. Are you in?" Sal asked.

Sal and Saverio wasted no time to ask me questions as we took turns throwing in our bets to the center of the table. "So I feel somewhat safe now to ask you what I've always wanted to know about the Nuscos," Saverio said, as he motioned for the young girls to leave.

I frowned. "I thought we had a deal to not bring up the past, Signore Attanasio."

Perhaps it was the wine and safety of the basement walls that made him so brazen, I thought. His questions rolled off his tongue. "About the incident with your brother Ricco, what's the real story on that? And save the headlines or one-liners for the papers, kid. An accidental drowning, please spare us the bullshit," Saverio said.

"Yeah. More like he got a concrete life preserver for being such a wimp. So what really happened?" Sal asked, as the two twenty-something girls left the staircase giggling.

"What makes you think I know anything more than what was written in the papers?"

Signore Attanasio had one glass of anisette too much for sure. "Please, kid, cut the bullshit."

I looked at their honest faces, including Andrew's, and the concealing four basement walls, and was happy the young ladies closed the door at the top of the stairs. "Okay. Truth is Ricco was a traitor, a liability to the family. I'll give you the short list, of a long line of offenses. He befriended Marco's archenemy, Geno Rogerio, who took kickbacks in exchange for tips on construction bids. Geno's operation bid just under Marcos' and he won contract after contract that stole our solid customers, then Ricco doubled-down, and pocketed ten percent under the table as a kick back from the signers."

"Ouch. I'd have to kill the bastard too—that's stealing from the cookie jar," Sal said.

"Fair enough. But I wanted to send him to Wyoming or something, as the only thing the idiot wanted to do was to drink wiskey, fish, and golf anyway. Give him a ranch up north, I told

Marco, not the bottom of the bay for Christ's sake. Unfortunately, we disagreed and haven't seen eye to eye since. Ricco screwed up in many cases like this over the years, putting us at risk to blackmail, amongst other dangers. But he didn't deserve to die."

"So you and Marco are on the outs?" Sal asked, and got up to check the two small basement windows. "Hey kid, don't take it personal. I check the streets all the time for men like your brothers. You're not being followed I hope."

I stood up and walked over to the window near him. "Well truthfully Sal, I worried about that back in Manhattan, but we are all clear on this side of the river. They wouldn't think to look for me in Bay Ridge anyway. I guarantee it."

"Hum, a Nusco guarantee—not too reliable," Sal said.

"No. A Quinn one," I said, firmly.

"Right. A Quinn guarantee, not sure I can trust that either. So you are being followed, now, here? I sure hope your Quinn guarantee is solid," Sal said.

"It's solid," I said. "You think I'd ever consider jeopardizing Judy or your family?"

Sal half listened, unlocked a drawer and pulled out a gun. "Ah, Joey Fitz keeps my family safe every night, he walks a beat at the park across the street after he ends his rounds at the corner market. My father worked with the NYPD detective, Joseph Petrosino in the early part of this century. They got the mob to stop hassling good Italians like us. My father used to warn us always, 'If good men stop fighting the bad guys, then evil will triumph.'"

As I listened, feeling sizable guilt over my involvement with the evil side, I grabbed a tall liqueur bottle baring a Galliano label and filled a shot glass. I gulped the yellow liquid down to ease the bitter memory of Ricco, and to swallow my disgust in taking any part in Marco's schemes. Sal's father was right to work with the good guys, and being with these men helped me to remember who I was, who I was born to be at least. It was as if my life was being recalibrated, an initiation in reverse one could say, to take me out of the mob for good. Perhaps it wasn't too late to get my own family back and to be a good man again, I thought.

But death was close as well, with Judy upstairs and Don Marco looming for me in dark alleys across the river. Death edged close, forcing its fate on me. Shannon wasn't with me yet, but she was close. With her file just upstairs in my briefcase, she could be a mere phone call away.

Signore Attanasio snapped me out of my thoughts and took the deck away to shuffle and looked at me straight. "You're not telling us anything we didn't suspect, kid. A Consigliere doesn't oppose his Don's wishes, even if it means brother killing brother. You said your Nusco days are coming to an end soon. But this puts you in a fix, doesn't it?"

Andrew eyed me, but I ignored him. He put the tips of his playing cards over his mouth to hide—and as sure as he was working on a straight flush, he was biting his tongue as well.

Sal threw in his bet as he evaluated his deck hand and discarded one card. "He's in a fix alright. We've all been there, Quinn. It's just taken you over thirty years to see it. Believe me, every Italian in New York who wants peace has to deal with the mafia. We don't like it either, the labor union bosses have me by the balls most days, but I mind my own business and leave the city and subway contracts to—well, we won't mention any last names tonight. At least the grass is greener living on the right side of the fence, right Saverio?"

"And who's gonna mess with a Russo brother after what your pops did with that NYPD detective?" Saverio said. "Declano, you were there that night at the store when I had to face Don Vaccaro. Remember him? He led the Eighth Street gang in the Thirties. You were working for me at the time."

I laughed. "Indeed. I remember. You wrapped two revolvers in butcher paper and hid them in the freezer. We held watch all night," I said, tossing blue chips into the pot.

"That's right. I wouldn't pay the monthly protection money to Don Vaccaro's goons. So to teach me a lesson, they grabbed Frankie on his way to the bank to get coins for my cash register. The bastards left him stuck in a closet all night, tied up and gagged, then left the front doors to the shop wide open with the floor's sawdust blowing out to the street. When Don Vaccaro himself showed up that night at my house, I thought I was a dead man, my son too."

"I take it you paid the Don his money after that?" Andrew asked, reviewing his hand of cards.

Saverio put his five cards face down to talk. "We did. After that, we paid every month and minded our own business, just like Sal said. If Sal didn't send over twenty percent of his contracts to them, he'd be gagged and tied for good."

"So, Quinn, now you want out and to walk a straight path. It's not so bad, kid. We look happy. No?" Sal asked.

"Yes. Happy. But unfortunately, that's not an option for me anymore. They're not going to let me just walk away, take it from me," I said.

Andrew tossed three blue chips into the pot and asked Saverio for two more cards as Sal picked up his deck to review his hand. "I'm out for good, boys," Saverio said, tossing his cards into the pot.

"So how are you going to tell Don Marco to shove it without being put out to sea yourself?" Sal asked. "Has this been going on long between you two?"

Andrew grabbed a stack of winnings from the center of the table. "Straight flush. Sorry fellas."

I was over any talk of my brother, but respected these men, so I had to give them the truthful story. "Over a year."

Sal looked at me concerned. "I don't get it, so how does anyone accomplish dodging Don Marco for a year?"

Andrew interrupted counting his chips and had one too many shots of the liqueur as well it seemed. "Yes. The last episode was just a couple days ago on a California highway when we were headed for the airport."

I was annoyed once again that I could never escape from my past. "Got a little dicey, but we squeaked free, when you're raised by wolves, a boy learns how to think like one."

Signore Attanasio got defensive. "Wolves? Didn't have that living with us."

"Right. Thank you for that too, never even knew what love look like until I set foot in your home," I said.

Signore Attanasio laughed and enjoyed his cigar. "And you absorbed it like tomato sauce on bread, that is until we lost your mama. Sorry that had to happen, we would have loved to keep you all for the duration." He inhaled his cigar for a few more breaths. "So what's your next move with the Don of the west now, kid?"

"Good question. No answer yet, but I'm working on it," I said.

"I know what it's like to confront Marco Nusco, pulled one over on him after the war. It involved you, as a matter of fact," Sal said, oblivious that I just heard about the hidden secret.

"Oh," I said, trying to make eye contact with Signore Attanasio. "That's okay Sal, don't bother with the details. A little birdie already told me how you helped my grandfather after the war, if that's the story you're talking about."

"Yes, and I told Marco to fuck off and leave the professor alone," he said.

I smiled. "You're a good man, Sal, I appreciate your help."

"Did your grandfather ever find you and your sister after all?" Sal asked. "He sent us a package of homemade brown bread from Ireland after his visit, but never a mention about finding you."

"Well, he didn't find me—something happened and he never called or wrote to mention it. I haven't the facts yet myself to explain…" I said.

Saverio interrupted. "Details Declano. Remember what I told you about details, the Devil's in the details, and it's getting late. I have to get to the harbor side market at sunrise."

I was happy someone else noticed the time. "Sal, thank you for helping my grandfather. I won't ever forget it. That's a Quinn guarantee you can bet on."

To conclude this discussion and return to my agenda, I took the cash from my son, put his winnings back on the table, and set to leave. "Andrew, would you go upstairs and fetch my briefcase, there's something in it I need."

"Sure Dad," Andrew said, and trotted up the basement stairs.

Once he was out of earshot, I said to the others, "Marco can kill me if he wants, don't think I can stop it. But before he does, I intend to find my sister, Shannon. I just obtained her adoption file this morning from a nun at the Foundling Hospital. I must find her or I will never be right as a man."

Sal and Saverio looked at each other and rolled their eyes. "Holy Jesus, did Don Marco get to your grandfather before he found you or your sister?" Sal asked. "I'm so fucking sick of the mob bosses that wreak havoc into our lives, controlling us with their vile threats."

I felt as if he was talking straight to me—a gangster at his fingertips, and a part of the havoc he despised. "The part of my grandfather in New York is a story we will leave be for now. Again, I don't have all the facts until I give him a call in Ireland. He's never mentioned to me…" I stopped. Details, I thought. It was late and it had to be hashed out another time. "Sal, I've made many wrong turns in my life that I regret. One major one is that girl upstairs. It breaks my heart that we are losing her."

Sal shut the cabinet drawer, locked it, relighted his cigar, and stared into my eyes. "Yes, my Judy loved you, son. We all make choices in life, but I see your regret now. You were just a boy, and boys make choices as a boy would, but once he becomes a man, he sees the path ahead as clear as a Manhattan skyline on a crisp spring morning."

Andrew came tromping down the stairs. "It's never too late to confront our mistakes and to clear the path ahead where the streets aren't named yet. Right Paps?" he said, handing me the briefcase. "And don't worry Signore Russo, there are no gangsters in front of your house or down the alley. I just checked again."

"Good man, son. Thank you," Sal said. "Did you see a tall, slender officer standing on the corner? It's about the time he runs his route."

"Yes, Signore Russo. There was an officer standing on the corner who waved at me."

Sal nodded with a smile.

Back to my agenda, I looked at a clock on the wall and wondered if nine-fifteen was too late to make a call to Buffalo, New York. I pulled out the file and with the three men staring at me, I knew I had no choice but to ask Sal to use his phone to make a long distance call.

I walked over to the brick wall, took the receiver off the phone, and dialed the operator as my hands shook. Meanwhile, Sal, Saverio, and Andrew continued to look at the guns.

"Sir, I have three numbers of O'Scanlon surnames in Buffalo, New York, two residential and one business," the operator said. I took them all down. One was a Jason and Joan O'Scanlon, the next was Jordan and Jaxon O'Scanlon, and the last, O'Scanlon's General Store on Market Street.

I called the last one first; the concept of a business was intriguing, I thought.

A young woman's voice answered. "Good evening, O'Scanlon's General Store. We close in ten minutes. Where may I direct your call?"

"May I have the manager please?" I asked, my heart pounding out of my chest.

"Yes sir, one minute."

I waited on the line and watched the men who moved over to look at a mounted deer head on the wall.

In two seconds, a gentleman answered. "Good evening, Jordan O'Scanlon here. May I help you?" a deep voice said.

"Hello, Mister O'Scanlon. My name is Declan Quinn. I'm calling from New York City. I have a sister with your same surname. You see, I haven't seen her in over thirty years and I'm trying to find her. Her name is Shannon O'Scanlon. She would be in her early forties now," I said, needing to take in a deep breath to quiet my racing heartbeat and whipped out a hanky to pat my forehead.

There was a long pause before the man replied. "You said your name is Declan? From New York?"

"Yes, that's right," I said.

His tone sounded serious. "I have a sister named Shannon O'Scanlon DeAvery. She is forty-two, her birthday is in September. Why are you calling now? Is there some trouble?"

"No, no trouble, not at all, I just wanted to reconnect. It's been too long." I gave him the sad story of our adoption in 1933 and of how we were separated.

Then he drops a bombshell on me.

"If we're talking about the same girl, she doesn't live in Buffalo anymore. After the war ended, she moved away, far away in fact. You see her husband was an Army specialist, he was shot and killed in the third year he saw action overseas."

My heart pounded and I took a deep breath. "Well, could you please give me her address or telephone number? I'd give you mine, but I'm only visiting here in New York and doing some traveling. I understand that I am a complete stranger, but…" I said, pleading.

"No, I'm happy to give you her phone number and address. I know who you are," he said. "Shannon's grandfather came to visit her after the war. A nun from the adoption agency gave him Shannon's name and address. There must be a connection."

"Yes, he's my grandfather as well, Professor Declan Quinn, just like me, but he uses the Professor title," I said, with hope. "We've corresponded over the years."

"I see. So, if your grandfather's known of Shannon's whereabouts since the end of the war, how come he never told you?" he asked, changing his tone. "Please don't tell me you've been in jail for twenty years."

"No. I've never been in jail. It's a mystery to me as well. My grandfather writes me all the time and never once mentioned visiting my little sister. I am confused on this issue and need to call him as soon as I hang up," I said, with hopes for tenderness on the other end of the line.

"Okay. You have me curious, Mr. Quinn. But all the names line up. Sister Mary, the Sisters of Charity, Professor Declan Quinn."

I asked if he needed more hard facts. "Well, if it would help, I have my grandfather's address in Ireland memorized. It's 17 Abbey

Road, Fethard, County Tipperary, Ireland. Check your records to see if they match up."

"I have that address memorized as well, don't need any address book. I protect my big sister as much I can, you understand," he said.

"I understand. Well, let me give you some more information. I don't live in New York. I live in Bridgeport, California. I'm visiting my son who is studying at Fordham University in the Bronx. I got your name from Sister Mary Catherine and am calling you today to get information on where Shannon is living now."

His tone changed. "You must be living under a rock out there in California," he said.

"No, just working, and raising my family. We have a ranch," I said. "Please. Are you willing to tell me where she is? You have no idea how much I miss her."

"I don't need to tell you anything. You already have her address. You just gave it to me, 17 Abbey Road, in Fethard, County Tipperary, Ireland," he said.

"What?" It was difficult to hold on to the receiver. My legs and arms shook and that last shot of liqueur went straight to my head. "Holy Jesus! She's in Fethard? Thank you, I am forever in debt to you, Mr. O'Scanlon. Thank you so much and I promise to get back to you when we are reunited once again," I said, and then hung up the phone.

I looked at my crew of three well-wishers and figured the expression on my face must have rivaled that of a child on Christmas morning.

"Shannon is in Ireland, living with our grandfather!"

"So we're going to Ireland?" Andrew asked, clapping his hands together.

I nodded and smiled. "Andrew you have a degree to complete first. As soon as I can arrange a flight, I will board that plane. Alone."

CHAPTER EIGHTEEN

THE LITTLE BROTHER

The house was quiet when we men returned to the family room at the top of the basement staircase. The children who were sleeping on the floor were gone.

"Please excuse me. I want to say good bye to Judy," I said.

"Would you like me to go with you?" Sal asked.

I nodded my head, grateful for the emotional support and he followed me as we climbed up the stairs. The hardwood flooring on the upper hallway creaked when we walked down to the last door, ajar with a low light coming through. Sal opened it slowly and the old hinges squeaked loud enough to wake the whole Brooklyn borough. Sal walked in and quickly took the arm off of the turntable as it had reached the end of the album and needed to be locked into its base. A candle was burning with the scent of insense on a nightstand as her mother sat, asleep on a sofa chair next to Judy's bed. When she dropped her book on the floor, both women stayed fast asleep. Their faces looked so angelic, I felt as though I was entering the gates of heaven itself.

Sal waited by the door as I walked over and took Judy's soft hand, kissed her forehead and whispered, "Sing to the angels, my dear. They wait for you with all the love of the universe, but it can't be more than my love for you. No one loves you more. Go in peace my Starlight Ruby—go in peace."

We exited the room leaving the door ajar as we had found it. Overcome, I sat to cry on a chair in the hallway. Sal waited patiently, his hand on my shoulder. After a few minutes, I stood and gave him a hug. He escorted me down the staircase to the front door and foyer where Saverio and Zia Anna waited for us with Andrew. My cheeks were still wet with salty tears as Zia Anna kissed me goodbye. "Thank you for coming to see us today,

Declano. God bless you." She turned to Andrew. "You have what it takes to bring our church to the next generation, son. Pope Paul's Second Vatican Council has made many changes, but it's up to you and your fellow candidates in the seminary to put those changes into action. The church is counting on you. Bless you," Zia Anna said, and kissed Andrew's cheeks.

"Declan, it was good of you to come. I haven't seen Judy in such peace for a long time," Sal said, with a hand shake of full gratitude again.

I returned a firm grip in a handshake as well, and looked at him man to man, sharing a common love to the beauty upstairs. "I'm so glad I was able to see her. Every one of you is as kind and welcoming as I remember from those blessed years I lived with the Attanasios. Thank you again for your hospitality, it's late, and I hope we didn't stay too long. If you don't mind my borrowing your phone again, I'll call for a cab to get us back to the City."

"A cab?" Saverio interrupted. "Absolutely not, Frankie will drive you. He lives in Manhattan close to the Brooklyn Bridge. He's waiting back at home for us, and will get you to your hotel boys, no problem. Prego, come with me." Seeing his wife already on her way back up the stairs, taking each step slowly, using the banister for support, he added softly, "Anna's staying another night. Loretta needs her now."

Saverio drove us ten short minutes to his home on the corner of Bay Ridge Parkway and Eleventh Avenue; it looked the same as the day we moved in thirty-nine years ago in 1928. A whispering crowd from the neighborhood gathered to watch us move in that day, as a few men unloaded our belongings from Father Carmen's truck. I heard someone say, "Look, there's some Irish Mick's moving in." All we had was the wood frame of our beds and mattresses, one suitcase, and the wooden wall clock my father made. I had forgotten about that clock until Father Carmen mentioned it, and suddenly wondered if I should take it back after all.

Remembering that morning as if it were yesterday, I recalled how a mover, standing in the bed of the truck, called out to my mother next to us on the sidewalk. "Signora, did you rob a bank or something?" He held up my knapsack full of coins. I jumped onto the truck bed, grabbed the knapsack out of his hands, and ran like a thief back to the front porch holding on to it as if my life depended on the coins inside. It was a grand collection of money for a boy to have, and no one knew I had nailed it to the mattress boards under my bed.

The look on mother's face that day was a mixture of embarrassment and delight when she looked at the treasure trove in the bag. We needed the money badly, yet she wanted to tar my ass for having taken so much generosity from Signore Nusco. "That nice Italian man in church gave it to me every week, told me to hide it from Dad until I could open a bank account." I pleaded. Needless to say, Signore Attanasio took my mother to the bank that same day as I had collected almost six hundred dollars, which at the time, was enough money for more than a year's rent and food.

The day we arrived, Zia Anna greeted us at this same doorway with the 1102 address over the door. She was a friendly, welcoming lady, beautiful, in a bright red dress with large black buttons cascading down the front. The dress was accented with a tight black belt around the waist to match the buttons and Zia Anna's hair ribbons. She looked like the women in the Bloomingdale's catalogue my mother kept under her pillow.

My heart sank thinking about us that day, my shy mother and precious Shannon standing beside me, all three of us helpless and homeless, but alive. Zia Anna's smile that day was like the sun bursting through storm clouds. She opened her heart and the door to her home to us. I thought of Zia Anna as our rainbow's end, holding a pot of gold. She was that same rainbow, still breaking through dark clouds, but on this night, she sat at the foot of my beloved's deathbed. It was a feeling of sadness and gratitude at the same time, along with the fact that I was surly exhausted. It had been a long emotional day.

Waiting for Saverio to find the key to his front door, I jingled the coins in my pocket, feeling for the oldest half-dollar I always keep there. "I bet you won't believe what I have in my pocket, something you gave me years ago," I said, handing him the well-worn coin.

He nodded and smiled holding the coin under the entry light, and I knew he remembered the moment he had given it to me. "Good for you, Declano."

"Does Frankie still carry his?" I asked.

"Let's find out," he said, and opened the door. Frank was asleep on the sofa, small wonder since it was nearly eleven o'clock.

"This is a Walking Liberty silver half-dollar," Saverio said to Andrew, showing the coin to him under the light of a table lamp. She's a symbol of strength and courage. The stars and stripes are flowing over her shoulder with the rising sun at her feet. The flip side has the brave American eagle ready to soar. I carry one of these half-dollars too." He dug in his pocket and pulled out a matching coin. "Here, take mine as an early graduation gift. I know you will appreciate her symbolism, just like your father has. Never forget, every coin in America has the words, 'In God We Trust, E' Pluribus Unum, and Liberty' inscribed on it. We live in a blessed country—just have to make sure those lousy politicians in Washington don't fuck it up."

Andrew laughed in surprise. "Thank you Signore Attanasio. I promise to cherish this coin just like my dad has. This one is shiny and brand-new, 1967, the year says here. But Paps, you always flips three coins between your fingers." Andrew looked over at me. "How do you know which one Signore Attanasio gave you?"

"Because the word Liberty is almost worn off, and the date is 1929. See." I pointed to it, pulled out the other coins from my pocket. "These two have significance for me as well. This one is from the year you were born and this one is from 1933—for Shannon and my mother—the year I last saw them. I have one for your sisters and Frankie, too. See." I held all the coins in my hand.

"Jeez Paps, I always thought you flipped those coins through your fingers just to look cool," Andrew said. "I never knew they had any meaning."

Our chatter didn't rouse Frankie, so Signore Attanasio jostled him until his eyes open.

Frank was slow to wake up as his dad walked away down the hallway. "Hey, you're here." He got up with a half-smile tossing his greasy hair back, stood tall and brawny, with thick arms and firm handshake. Andrew was correct; he looked like a heavyweight boxer and certainly was no one's little brother anymore. He didn't seem overly excited to see me. "Gosh, my long-lost Irish big brother from the past is here. What's new? Is it true you became a badass Nevada gambler? What's it been, Declan, a-hundred years or something?"

"Just a lifetime I think," I said, and acted more cautiously than I had ever talked to Marco.

"You used to be my hero, man, taught me all I know about baseball and the damn Bums before they up and left us stranded here in Brooklyn," he said, shaking his head. "God, I hate the Yanks, and the Mets are still wet behind the ears for me to hustle over to Queens—ah, you'll never see me becoming a bona fide Met fan, never." He looked at me and gently punched my shoulder. "Damn, look at you. You're some rich lawyer type, a casino gambling, woman chasing son of a bitch, right?" he said with a half smile.

If he wanted to make me uneasy by his attitude, it was working. "Not exactly. I…"

"No, no, I wanna hear all about it. See me, I never left Brooklyn. Not much has changed for me. All I became was a fucking pizza dough man," he said, smelling like dough and cheese as he brushed off his clothes full of white flour and stains. "Bet you think that's pretty lame."

"No, not at all. Thanks for offering to take us back to the City tonight. It will give us time to catch up," I said.

"Yeah sure man, and this time we don't have to race over the bridge in our sneakers like we used to at George Westinghouse Vocational. You still helping the lazy ass Nusco bothers cheat their way to the top of the food chain, just like you did in Mr. Poe's math classes?"

"Ha, you remember that? Everyone hated all those algebra problems," I said.

Frank continued finger combing his greasy hair back, looking a foot taller. "Yeah, Marco was a cheating rebel then and is a rich cheating bastard now, screwed plenty others just to gain control over them and to rob guys of their dignity. And fuckin' eh, didn't Tino get shot in the gang wars on the West Side docks after the war?"

I nodded, but said nothing.

He grabbed his keys off the coffee table. "Hey, I gotta an old jalopy truck to drive you, and we'll have to cram into the front seat, hope it doesn't cramp your Nusco style. What do you drive, some fucking Caddy?"

Saverio stepped back into the room and joined the conversation wearing his nightshirt and slippers. "Boys, this reunion was great, but Frank has to get to the shop early in the morning, so better get a move on, gentlemen. Good luck at Fordham, Andrew, and be sure to make this bum father of yours give us a call before the next thirty-year mark comes around and I'm dead and gone."

We hugged him good-bye and headed out. The drive with Frank was quieter than I expected, but I was glad he wasn't drilling me with questions. I wasn't in an answering mood, too exhausted, and emotionally spent. The front seat of his rickety Ford truck bounced under us as we maneuvered through Brooklyn. I used to know these streets like the back of my hand. When we approach the lights of the Brooklyn Bridge and the skyline of Manhattan, Frank seemed to wake up a little more.

"So tell me, you never seemed like the mafia type back when we were kids. You've come a long way from your choirboy, goodie two-shoes days, haven't you? That Nusco family, they're a bunch of murderous gangsters, right? I can't tell you how many days at Westinghouse High I wanted to punch Ricco right in the balls. He was a cocky motherfucker."

I agreed, too tired to make excuses. "Yeah, he never fit in with the choir too much. But, for me, I'm trying to turn a new leaf, if you really want to know."

"A new leaf, huh? So that's why you came back. Hoping to make it up to my sweet cousin, Judy. You're way too late, brother. You know you broke her heart, twice in fact. The first time was when you moved out and wouldn't talk to any of us. How you turned your back on her then is beyond me. Guess you thought the Nusco mansion was better than our place in Bay Ridge, right? Then, the second time you broke her heart, was when you married that girl from Jersey. Judy came to me crying her eyes out after that happened."

I was stunned. "Maybe I should explain."

"Nah, you don't have to explain nothing. I know plenty of guys like you, killers on demand. You hassle hard workingmen like my father and uncles. Sorry to say it, lost Mick brother of mine, but we hate your kind. And we better hope none of your goons followed you to Bay Ridge tonight. I came by Zio Sal's place tonight just to scope it out, but lucky for you, everything looked normal on the street, and Joey Fitz had us covered anyhow."

He leaned over Andrew, who sat between us in the middle, and opened the glove box. I saw a revolver.

I rose up my hands in surrender. "Frank, I want no trouble with you."

"It's not for you. It's for protection. Just last week, my wife's best friend's daughter got raped a few blocks from here. She and her boyfriend made the mistake of walking through an alley behind one of your mob buddy's nightclubs. They mugged her boyfriend, stole his money, and left him for dead, and then they drugged and raped her for half the night. She was found the next day naked and bleeding near death in some filthy hotel room in Harlem, poor thing. Trust me, Declan, we need guns, and it's because of people like you."

"I'm sorry," I said, shutting up, not knowing what else to say.

He pulled to the curb, leaned over Andrew and me again, and opened the passenger door. "Good to see you, brother. Now go fuck yourself, you're no better than what I see on these streets every day. You can take your money and shiny silk suit and stay in the casinos, just stay the fuck out of Brooklyn. Okay? Now, get out of my car."

Andrew and I got out, standing at the open car door. I hoped Frank was just venting for a moment and would reconsider leaving us here, but his eyes were full of rage and I realized he would enjoy shooting me if my son's presence wasn't stopping him.

He held one hand on the steering wheel and draped his arm over the bench seat as he spoke to us. "Don't know how you did it, Declan. You got a nice boy there, studying at Fordham and all. A fucking Nusco wants to be a priest? God is one twisted man upstairs watching us screw up his planet, right? Sorry to wreck your night in Brooklyn, Andrew. You seem like a nice kid, probably take after your mama, I'd guess. Good luck in those confessionals," he said, then leaned over and pulled the passenger door shut.

I opened the door again. "Look, Frankie, I'm sorry about everything that's happened. Maybe someday you'll give me a chance to explain. I'd like to tell you the whole story."

"Not interested," he said. "Now shut the fucking door."

I closed the door then watched him pull away. "Sorry, Andrew. We'll have to go uptown to find a taxi." I put my Fedora back on and fixed my scarf for the cold walk.

Up the street, Frank made a U-turn, came back, and drove slowly alongside us. He unrolled his window and dangled his arm holding a lit cigarette in his fingers. "Hey Nusco. Thought to tell you, I already know your whole sorry story. Marco's empire in the desert is collapsing and the papers say Ricco drowned—an accident, reads the headline. Ha, like I buy that. So are you next? That's why you're here in New York? Hiding from your Don? Word on the street is Marco's looking for you. These lips are sealed on that, but don't think it's out of any loyalty to you. It's to protect my family."

"What exactly have you heard about me?"

"Enough. Like I said, went to scope out Zio Sal's house tonight, just to make sure your visit wasn't going to cause harm to…"

"Tell me. Please."

"What—tell you what? You don't need to hear nothin' more off these fucking streets, you're a dead man and you know it, just leave my family out of it, okay. You can fool my parents and Uncle Sal maybe, but not me. I see who you are behind that fancy suit, a

Nusco through and through, and Don Marco's Consigliere. Since when does an Italian mob boss have an Irish Consigliere? Like I said, God is one twisted fuck." He flicked his cigarette at me, and then burned rubber in a wet slushy gutter, leaving us on the dark street.

In the distance were the lights of the Brooklyn Bridge. We had a long walk ahead as I guessed the trains must be done for the night.

Andrew looked at me, angry, and confused. "He shouldn't have talked to you like that. You're not a Nusco. He's got it all wrong."

"No he doesn't, Drew. Frank is right about it all. I'm no better than any gangster on these streets. Son, you have no clue what I've seen, what I've done."

We walked a long time, heading uptown in silence. Finally we spotted a taxi and waved it down.

"The Plaza Hotel, please," I said to the driver, as my teeth wouldn't stop chattering from the cold. We rode in silence, grateful to the heated cab. When we arrived at the hotel, the doorman opened the door on my side of the taxi. "Take my boy up to Fordham," I said to the driver, and handed him more than enough bills to cover the fare.

"Andrew, I'm leaving for Ireland as soon as I can get a flight out. If you don't hear from me for a couple of days, assume I'm on my way there. I'm looking forward to sitting by the fireside hearing your G-Pap tell stories of the old land with Shannon at my side." I hugged my son and closed the taxi door.

He leaned over and unrolled the window. "But are you going to be okay, word on the street and all?"

"Don't worry, kid. I'm used to this kind of stuff unfortunately. Good luck on your Spina-therapy thesis. I hope my journal will be of help to you."

"Call me when you get there, Paps, airmail takes too long. I want to know when you find her. Shannon. Aunt Shannon, that is."

"Yes, your Aunt Shannon. Still can't believe I found her," I said shivering again. "Okay, now, get going. It's been a long, long day. Go back to school. Do the work, son. I think the world, no, mankind will be better for this therapy of yours once you get it out into the public realm. I'm proof, despite what Frank says."

The taxi pulled away and I jingled the coins in my pocket as I watched its taillights disappear up Fifth Avenue. Damn, I forgot to ask Frank if he still carries the Walking Liberty coin in his pocket. Chances were slim he had them still, and even slimmer that he would have told me. Sad. We were so close once, I thought.

CHAPTER NINETEEN

ACCIDENTAL GANGSTERS

I walked up to the lobby desk to get my key.

"Mr. Quinn, we have a message for you," said the lobby clerk who handed me an envelope.

I opened it at the counter and pulled out a note card that was written in Marco's handwriting, "Meet me in the Oak Room. Marco."

"Shit!"

The clerk began to walk away, but stopped with a look of surprise. "Is everything okay Mr. Quinn? May I help you in any way?" he asked.

"Yes, I need to know what time the Oak Room closes," I said, as I stood frozen before him, staring at the note in my hand.

"Down the hall to your right, Sir. It serves hotel guests all night. Wouldn't you like a nightcap before you retire? I can have someone show you the way."

"No!" I answered harshly, making the man's eyes widen. But with a quick second thought, I reconsidered. If Marco himself came all this way, hiding in my room on the sixth floor wasn't going to do me any good, but having someone with me might. "Sorry, yes. That would be helpful."

The man summoned over a bellboy and I had my escort.

Though well past midnight, the room was full of men talking loud, smoking, and having a drink or two; on any other evening, I would have enjoyed winding down the same way, but not tonight. Tonight, it was the last thing I wanted. I should have gone straight to the airport, I murmured to myself, as my escort departed, and then realized going to the airport would have done me as little good as the bell boy. I never would have made it onto a plane once Marcos' guys were on my tail.

I had been on the other side of this situation one too many times to know running didn't work. Once targeted, you were stuck; once cornered, you were done, I told myself. And the fear in running was worse.

Marco was sitting in a rear booth with two other men, new faces to me, but assumed them to be New York thugs nonetheless as I walked to their booth.

"Marco, you just can't take no for an answer, can you? You know I came here to help my son, and you are fucking out of line following me here."

Marco looked at one of the two men. "Frisk him."

"Fine," I said, rolling my eyes, and stood still while he patted me down. I was clean, but the guy didn't think to look in the briefcase I slid under the table.

"We need to talk in private," Marco told them. They walked away and stood near the entrance. I took a seat and poured myself a brandy from a crystal decanter on the table.

He didn't waste any time. "Quinn, don't give me that fucking story about helping Andrew, seminary studies of all things, I'm not buying it. What family in New York are you working with?"

I put my hands up in sarcastic surrender. "No one. I'm here with Andrew. That's it."

"Come on, you can be straight with me. Don't flatter yourself, not planning to kill you. We need to talk, that's all. I've got a gig ready to take off that means big bucks for the family, and it's all legit," Marco said as he sniffed the blood-red rose on his lapel.

"Sure it is." I used my legs under the table to move my briefcase between them. I figured it'd be easy to grab the pistol inside, as I watched him take the beauty of that rose and stick his greasy nose into it.

Marco continued. "Come on, get on board with me as I'm moving into phase two of the planning stage on this project. You see there's three thousand acres of property northwest of Reno, on the California side near Lake Almanor in the southern Cascades. I want to build casinos up there with golf courses, camping, and an amusement park. Family friendly. See, all legit brother," he said, with a straight face, and put an architectural plan rolled up in the center of the table.

Knowing he was always full of lofty ideas, I opened the roll and halfway glanced at an elaborate set of blue prints as he placed two brass candleholders on either side to hold the plans down. "Casinos and families don't go together, never have, never will, and California will never legalize gambling," I said, dismissing his scheme.

"Sure they will if we play it right. That's why I need you. You have plenty of friends in those mountain regions that trust you, not to mention the Indian tribes who love you, too," he said, and dipped the butt of a new cigar into his brandy like he always did for added flavor.

"You're dreaming," I said. "The Indian lands are sacred, and where are you going to get the cash for a project like this? Labor is expensive, and just getting past the planning stage and permits would be a nightmare. Goddam Marco, do you even realize we'd have to appeal to the public in a general election for something of this size?" I asked, slamming my hand down on the plans.

Nothing fazed him. "Again, that's why I need you. You know how to deal and get the legal ball rolling. You're smooth," Marco said. "And I'd like you to run for congress in your district, as that would help our credibility."

"What? California would elect a slimy, defense lawyer like me in the House of Representatives? Forget it. I'm not interested. I told you I'm done. Besides, Senator Mitchell won't even take my calls any more, not after the dam reservoir we built four years ago. We could have earned legitimacy with that project, but you had to corrupt the whole thing by demanding a ten percent kickback from the concrete supplier."

On a benign level, it looked as if a chess match was beginning, so I eyed him and paused to set up my strategy. As he scowled at me, I refilled my brandy and warmed it with a match at the base of a crystal goblet. He watched the flame flicker over my numb fingertips while I used the act of fire to move his focus in my direction. "Marco, are you aware that all the state representatives in

California and Nevada know you bribed that councilman over the Indian reservation waterways permits? When he accused you, I felt you had it coming, and if you recall, I told you to leave his family alone. But as usual, you went ahead with your pursuit for vengeance and had to go and fuck up his future son-in-law's face just before his daughter's wedding."

Marco just inhaled his cigar and listened. "Ah, his son-in-law was a cowboy schmuck anyway."

I slammed my empty glass of brandy down on the table, trying as I might to put the strategic moves in my favor. "I don't know why you're so set on keeping me around. No politician will talk to me now and you never listen to my advice anyway. You go over the line, time and time again, everyone knows you play dirty. I can't help you. You're never going to get your plans approved. Face it Marco, I'm no use to you anymore. Just let me go live in peace. I didn't lie. I came to New York to work with my son on his research, just my son, no one else."

Marco wasn't impressed with Andrew's work and tried to read my thoughts. "What is it, Quinn? You are different, come on, I've known you my whole life," he asked. "This is about something else, isn't it?"

I shrugged without comment.

He gritted his teeth. "Okay, you think I went too far with Ricco, right?"

I refilled my glass with a shot more of brandy and drank it right down. "I begged you to let him go, but you wouldn't listen. You went too far, come on, you don't take out your own."

He relighted the cigar in his mouth. "Oh, so you and Axel Hauser didn't share the same blood?"

Marco was always cool when aiming for the jugular vein. "This isn't about my father. You know what he was like, but Ricco was one of us," I said, slamming my glass down on his plans one final time. "Read my lips brother. I'm D.O.N.E. Done."

"No, you're not."

"Go fuck yourself Marco," I said, knocking my glass over as the last drops of brandy spilt on the blue prints. I stood up, grabbed my briefcase, and walked away.

His two men stopped me at the door and Marco motioned them to bring me back. Having no choice, I returned and took a seat again, keeping my briefcase close to my hand.

"You son of a bitch," Marco said, shaking his head. "You think you're better than me, don't you. But I hear your mother was sleeping with all the men on the Lower East Side and that's why Father Carmen had to move your asses out."

Enraged, I grabbed Marco by his shirt collar, ready to pull him out of the booth to put my fist into his face. But before I could hit him, his men grabbed and threw me back down into my seat.

Marco straightened his tie and combed his black greasy hair back with his hand. "It's okay, won't try nothing like that again," he told the two bodyguards and they returned to their post.

"Make one more comment about my mother, and I'll fucking kill you right here."

He just smiled, clearly not worried, and refilled our glasses keeping his eyes on me.

"What do you know about Father Carmen anyway?" I asked. "You haven't seen him in over four decades."

"I know you visited him today on Mulberry Street," he said. His rugged face was calm and certain. "I've been watching your every move, think you can run from me, Quinn? You should know better than anyone, no one leaves this family unless I say so, and I say you're going nowhere."

Marco handed the waiter a hundred dollar bill just to get rid of him, ordered another couple brandies, and told him to keep the hotel's security guards away from our table. He dabbed his sweaty forehead and the back of his neck with a napkin, and then tried to mop up the brandy off this plans, before he spoke again.

"We have Patti. The boys won't hurt her, she's just playing with my daughter and baking cookies with my wife," Marco said, unflinching.

I didn't get up but reached across the booth again with both my hands and grabbed Marco's hair and smash his head against the table, cutting his nose between the eyes. "You mother fucker, we always promised to leave our families alone. Where is she?" I said, still holding his head to the table as his blood fully ruined the blue prints.

Marco struggled and I lost my grip due to the combination of grease on his hair and the inept strength in my fingers.

"Oh dear mother of God, why did I ever get mixed up with you?" I said, and took his brandy snifter with the back of my hand and sent it flying off the table across the wood floor. The two guards ran over again. The taller one pulled me out of the booth and trapped my head with his forearm on the table to wait another order from Marco. Marco waved the goons off, and patted his bloodied face with a napkin. One of the men guarded me closer, holding my upper shoulder, and the other stood right next to me in the booth.

I wrestled off the guard's hand on my shoulder and pushed him away. "Tell me right now where she is, and I will call any politician you need. Goddamn it all, you bastard. Your father is rolling in his grave now. I'll never forgive you for this. First Ricco, and now this," I said, and stood up to leave pushing the goons aside once more. I grabbed my briefcase wishing to shoot all three of them as I set to leave.

"Glad we've come to an agreement. Your daughter will be in my office when you arrive. I have a ticket waiting for you at the TWA terminal desk," Marco said, with a bloodied napkin over his nose. "Better hurry, you don't want to miss your flight—your little Patti's waiting."

Fuming, and fixed to kill him, I shouldered past the two guards who followed me out. They watched me enter the elevator and waited while the operator closed the doors.

Back in my room, I called Sofia immediately. It was approaching eleven o'clock in California, and Sofia must be up pacing the floor. I knew she would pick up. No answer. I called the lobby desk to check my messages again, none. Did Marco kidnap them all? I wondered. I grabbed my bag, glad it was barely unpacked, threw in what little I took out, zipped it up, then called the porter to get me a taxi to the airport. One more attempt to call home, still no answer. I called Kitchi in the land handler's cottage. No answer.

"Fuck!" I said, hanging up the phone, and rushed down to the lobby. The attendant at the front desk attempted to call the numbers I gave him. The clock behind him said it was two-thirty in the morning—still, no answer at home, and Kitchi wasn't picking up either. Strange, I thought.

The doorman called out to me, "Your taxi is here, Mr. Quinn." It idled outside waiting to take me to the airport, back to California.

When I arrived at the TWA ticket counter, with my head hanging in defeat, a stranger walked up and handed me a note without a word. As he walked away, I read it. It read: Meet me outside the women's restroom near the International flights boarding area. Frank Attanasio.

Great, as if dealing with Marco wasn't enough, now I had Frank Attanasio looking for me. Perfect. How ironic would it be to be killed at the hands of a good guy? I thought, but paused. Wait, I never even had a chance to tell him my plans. Strange, I thought again.

I took my ticket from the lady at the counter and my heart sunk reading the itinerary: JFK (Idlewild) to LAX non-stop, boarding at 6:45am.

Oh my God, please protect her. Marco said Patti was with his wife, that's a lie as she is a decent woman and wouldn't go along with this—but who had her, I wondered in a panic. She's barely comfortable out of her bedroom, let alone in a strange place. My mind was racing. I thought of her, picturing her dark hair and thoughtful eyes in the cold possession of one of Marcos' guys. I couldn't think of it. She was nothing like her wild red-haired twin, but every bit as precious to me, maybe more so. Shannon and my Pappy in Ireland will have to wait, I thought.

I walked the long marbled corridors to the International flight desk and searched for the women's bathroom looking for Frank. The morning crowd was light as I scanned the crowd of a few scattered people reading their newspapers. I spotted Frank near the lavatory entrance sitting on a chair smoking a cigarette. Our eyes met. As he looked around, he walked to the other end of a huge support beam; it blocked the both of us from onlookers. Frank stood close to me with his hands deep in his jacket pockets. I watched his hands waiting for him to stab me.

Instead of a knife, he pulled out a note and handed it to me. The handwriting was Andrew's. Frank leaned close to my ear. "Andrew told me he has a baby brother named Frankie," he said, and jabbed me with a forefinger. "You're a complex mafia punk that's for sure. Go now. Fix your life brother, and give me a call when you do. I'd like to meet this Frankie character someday. Andrew tells me we're kind of alike." He smiled and walked away.

Confused and tired, I let Frank leave and read the note. It read:

"Dad, this one is on me. Go to the Capitol Airways International desk, an agent has your ticket to Ireland. Shannon Airport (love the name). I sent a telegram to G-Pap to tell him you're on the way. I will check on Mom tomorrow. She, Frankie, and Patti—yes, Patti too, are all well and safe at the country house with Nonna Lavona and Papa Johnny. Tell G-Pap I'll be on my way, too. Love you. Andrew. P.S. Call me before you board. The lady in the Walsh Hall dorm office will fetch me from my room. I can tell you the details then. Just know Mom, Frankie and Patti are safe. AQ.

Though skeptical and worried, I walked down another corridor of marbled flooring to the Capitol Airways International desk, glancing around to see if anyone was following me. An enormous trepidation filled my insides knowing that Marco would soon catch up to me. I approached the woman at the counter. "Do you have a ticket for Declan Quinn—to Ireland?"

She checked her list, then smiled, and handed me my ticket. "Enjoy your flight. First Class, Mr. Quinn. We board in one hour."

I found a phone booth and called Andrew, still looked for any sign of Marcos' goons.

"Hey Paps, I've been waiting for your call. So you saw Frank Attanasio, right, and he gave you my note? Did you get your ticket to Ireland?" he asked me all at once, sounding rushed.

"Yes, yes, but kid you don't understand. Something terrible has happened back home. Marco kidnapped Patti. I must get back to the ranch, so Ireland will have to wait."

"No, Paps, he doesn't have her. I swear. Patti is fine. She's with Mom at Nonna and Papa's house with Frankie, too. I didn't feel right when I left you last night after hearing what Frank Attanasio said was the 'word on the street', so I called Uncle Tony, and asked him if we should be worried."

"You called Anthony?"

"Yeah, Paps, it's all good. Uncle Tony's done with Marco just like you. After we left him on the side of the road, he went back to the ranch and told Mom she better find a safe place to stay for a while," Andrew said. "Marco wanted him to kidnap Patti the day we met on the highway, but he wouldn't do it. So he hitchhiked back to our ranch and told Mom to start packing for Grandma's house."

"Hold on. Patti is safe, with your mother in Pennsylvania? Are you sure? Anthony could be wrong," I said frantic.

"No, he's not wrong. I talked to Mother last night. They're on the road to the Pocono's as we speak. Uncle Tony told her not to call anyone until she was safe. He says Marco's empire is crumbling. Uncle Tony lied to him about taking Patti. The other guys are falling in line with you and Uncle Tony. Guess it's not a job even a goon was willing to do. It seems you have fans in the family, Paps."

I held on to the phone and added more coins into the slot. "Son, Marco was here in New York. I met with him last night along with two tough bodyguards. He looked stronger than ever with his demands. I want to believe she's safe, but I don't …"

He interrupted me. "Dad, listen to me, Patti is with Mom. Kitchi took them all to the airport and waited until they boarded the plane. Marco's people are lying to him. The hotel clerk last night told me you were in the Oak Room. I watched your table the whole time and used a house phone right at the bar to call Frank."

"What, you were there and used a phone…" I paused. "You took a chance of getting killed in some fucking mafia gunfight, before you even graduate, have you lost your sanity?"

"Paps calm down. I'm fine. I keep telling you everything's okay." Andrew seemed hurried and annoyed with me. "Just get on that plane and enjoy Ireland, G-Pap, Aunt Shannon, and everything. I really have to go now; the line for the shower gets so long in my dorm."

I was fully agitated. "Now you just wait one more fucking minute, Drew. How does Frank Attanasio fit into all this?" I asked, and heard him sigh on the other end of the line. "I need to know."

"Okay, okay. Uncle Tony asked me if I had anyone I could trust in New York, and I thought of Frank. Uncle Tony agreed he could be trusted and said I should call him for help," Andrew said. "Turns out, Frank's a great guy."

"Last night he wanted to kill me," I said.

"He changed his mind when I told him you named your youngest son after him. You did, right?"

"Yes, I did, but…"

"Thought so. Then I told him about Uncle Tony, Patti, and about your fight with Marco in the bar, about Aisling and the accident, everything, Father Carmen, your journal, my thesis, and he said, 'tell me how I can help.' Okay? Ask Frank. He called Uncle Tony himself to verify my story if you don't believe me."'

"Frank called Anthony? You must be kidding me."

"It's true. All of it," he said.

I shrugged. "I'm not sure I can board that plane kid, everything is so fucked up."

"Come on, Paps, trust me, our family is fine and you will be too as soon as you get on that plane. When do you board?"

"In thirty minutes." I said, thinking hard, then gave in with a sigh. "It's not that I don't trust you, Drew. You know that. I just needed to be sure, but the pieces do fit I guess." Then I noticed a big man hiding behind a newspaper. I recognized the shoes. "As a matter of fact, Frank still is keeping watch over by the window."

"Good man, good man," Andrew said.

What my son had done for me finally hit home. "Drew, you saved us." I laughed, despite my stomach being in knots. "You sure you want to be a priest? Cause you would make a really great gangster."

I heard him laugh. "Good luck, Paps, and don't forget to call me—guess this makes you the "The Trans-Continental Island Hopper Man, now?" he said proud of himself.

"The Trans-Continental Island Hopper Man…" I tried to respond, laughing, but he hung up on me in haste. Taking the phone receiver and looking at it in disbelief, I nodded nonchalantly at Frank as he acted as my bodyguard, waiting to make sure I boarded my flight without interference. Like we used to cover the whole outfield in the sandlot at St. Ephrem's together, nothing really had changed, as the two of us monitored the whole waiting area at the International gate. No fly balls, no goons would get to us without being tagged out first. When he nodded back, tipping his low brimmed hat to me with his thumb up, I knew my chances to board the plane were good. I smiled and breathed my first deep breath of the day with hopes Marco would assume I was too scared to do anything but fly home to save my daughter.

When boarding started, I exited the terminal and gave Frank one last tip of my hat. The roar of the jet engines was exhilarating—and the excitement inside me, as foreign as the Gaelic dialect of my co-travelers' chatter. I walked onto the rain soaked tarmac in a single filed line with the others. I turned to look at the viewpoint windows of the terminal and saw Frank standing next to the glass, watching me approach the stairway. I felt like Humphrey Bogart in my favorite film, as I too, was on an airport runway in a cause to find freedom over tyranny. With a huge sigh of relief, I waved once more at my faithful friend and smiled, quoting the last line in Bogart's film. "Frankie, I think this is the re-beginning of a beautiful friendship."

I walked up the steps to the airplane and saw the vast Atlantic Ocean at the edge of the runway. There was a huge deep-sea separating me from my past; everything was ahead of me from that point on. Shannon, Ireland, the city after which my sister was named, was my next stop. Surreal feelings came over me, as very soon I would be at the door of my Pappy's home. I was set to solve the mystery of his visit to New York after the war and to unravel his reasons for excluding me from my sister's life.

Getting into my seat, I couldn't believe it all actually happened. I slipped past Marco once more and set myself to venture to Ireland in a single, serendipitous leap. As I watched Frank walk away from his watch at the window, I looked inside my briefcase and slipped out Shannon's file to write a quick itinerary in no certain order: Visit Pappy at 17 Abbey Road, Fethard. Walk his farm. Ride his horses. Smoke his tobacco. Hear the stories of his life. Meet Shannon once again.

I closed the file with excitement, but stopped myself to add one more thing: Write thank you cards to the good people who helped me get this far, adding the names of Anthony and Frank to the top of the list.

How shall I pay them back, I wondered.

PART FOUR

IRELAND

"The sacred earth is where life is found and buried."

~ Declan Quinn ~

CHAPTER TWENTY

A GENIE IN A BOTTLE

As I settled into my seat, I shook my typically agnostic mind and laughed at my unceasing questions. "Did my mother's spirit finagle a way to get me on this plane from the start? And was she up in the heavens patting herself on the back with this accomplishment? I didn't believe in ghosts as such, but her quiet voice of disapproval had always been inside my conscience from day one. Back in the early heydays of my career in the mob, she was easy to tune out while I happily cashed-in and moved up in rank, but as things grew darker, her voice grew louder. Lately, I found myself consulting her while I sat alone in my office or tended to my horses, sometimes Sofia caught me conversing with her spirit out loud into the thin air. My poor wife must have thought I was losing my sanity altogether, and when reflecting back on these days—I admit that madness lurked very close.

Looking out the window of the plane, I felt saner and more purposeful with my newest objective, even though my mind was a labyrinth of thoughts. I heaved a sigh of relief reviewing the last six hours, as Andrew, a would-be seminarian, outsmarted a cold-hearted Don with many kills under his belt. Amateur or not, I credited the entire string of events to my son. He was the reason why the tide changed at my feet. From the moment of seeing Andrew's eyes light up when I gave him my mother's sketch on campus, to Frank's surveillance at the terminal, I felt connected to something good, something purposeful because of him. I hoped in the end, he'd be proud of me to have finally passed through the thorn fields and to be in a position to trek forward, I thought.

After spending the first hour of my flight gazing down over the Atlantic, I fumbled with the coins inside my pockets remembering Signore Attanasio and realized Andrew's black rosary beads were there also. I took them out, reflexively kissed the crucifix, and recited quick prayers for Judy and the Attanasio and Russo families. Had the earth claimed her limbs yet, I wondered, brokenhearted, thinking of the poetic verses we shared.

When finished with the prayers, I decidedly placed the rosary beads around my neck and wore them tucked under my shirt for the duration of my flight. *No Man is an Island* (Merton), I wrote down the title of the book Father Carmen recommended for me to read, grateful he was part of my small army who helped me get this far.

Repeating the words on the page, I felt like a caged bird being set free off an island to soar into the wild, and laughed scribbling down the newly appointed name Andrew gave me. "The Trans-Continental Island Hopper Man, that's me," I said, laughing still.

With a sense of liberation, I got busy and constructed a few of lines of prose:

> In the rush I became something I thought I'd never be.
> Below me, a vast sea,
> Far gone are the nights spent feeling incomplete.
> It's time to return to a life that's waiting for me…"

I stopped and added a few more items to my itinerary. Buy Merton's book and a journal. As at this rate, I will be running out of paper soon, I thought.

What only seemed like forty winks or so, the skidding of the rubber tires hitting the runway in Ireland startled me awake as my pen and paper fell onto the floor. Hurriedly I grabbed them, took hold of my briefcase to check for the gun inside, and slipped the file back in. When I got up, I instinctively scanned the plane to see if Marco slipped into any of the seats behind me. Groggy, with heavy eyelids, I looked out the windows into darkness, realizing a whole day was lost in flight, and then briefly panicked thinking how far away I was from Patti, hoping Anthony had the information correct.

As soon as we exited the plane, I searched for a phone booth and soon discovered the round dial was far different than American phones, so I asked an operator to help me place a call overseas to my in-laws' cottage. It took more time to connect the lines than I had patience for, but finally I was holding a receiver in my hand, talking to my wife.

Sofia was in a complete panic, and upon hearing my voice, began to cry.

"Sofia, no. No, I'm fine. Don't worry about anything. Is Patti okay, and Frankie?" I asked, immediately thinking of his namesake. When she reported to me that they were safe, I wondered once more how I could repay Anthony and Frank for their help—and Andrew, I thought shaking my head, that kid is going to get one hell of a graduation gift from me. Sofia was still worked up, so I fervently tried to calm her down. "You'll be safe there at your parents' home, just think of it as a nice winter vacation. The kids will have fun in the snow exploring the hillsides of Pennsylvania, just like you did as a kid."

She was seemingly through with a patronizing husband and asked for details.

"Yes, I know I've been such a mystery to you, but don't worry, Sofia. Marco's a villain for the history books." She continued to deliver a litany of questions. "Yes, Andrew and I had a wonderful time. We visited old friends and traveled all over the Lower East Side yesterday," I said, wondering if he told her about our tour of Brooklyn.

"Declan. The operator said this call is long distance from Ireland. You're where now?" she asked, confused.

"Ireland. The operator is correct."

She yelled at me, as if she had to convey her voice over a vast turbulent ocean. "What's going on with you? You have been acting so odd, and then Anthony scared the skin right off of me, telling me to take the children and run. The day you left with Andrew, he came to the house with his suit torn to shreds and was covered in mud, obviously having fought off one of Marco's bloodthirsty hit men. No doubt, you are in danger as well."

I figured as much, as Anthony wouldn't have told Sofia it was Andrew who wrestled with him that day. "I'll be fine, Sofia, and you will be as well. You did the right thing to listen to Anthony. You're safe now."

"Safe? What if Marco finds us here?" she asked, starting to cry again as she continued to talk through her sobs. "It was a miracle we had Kitchi at home to help us, not sure we could have gotten to the airport so fast. Maybe I should have my dad take us to the airport now to be with you? I can't believe you're—in Ireland, really?"

I continued. "Yes, being here sounds crazy, but it's the sanest move I've made in decades. I'm here about Shannon, my sister. I found out she lives here with my Pappy," I said. "Sofia, I'm sorry. There's too much to tell you over the phone."

She replied with concern. "Yes, I know. Andrew told me you went into Manhattan to get information on her, she's the woman you…" She stopped herself. "Do you finally admit that we have a lot to talk about? He told me you met with a Father Carmen and a Sister Mary who helped you find records on her—on her adoption?"

"Yes, Sofia, her adoption, it's a long dreary story," I said, and tried to lighten the subject matter. "But you would have loved to meet Sister Mary Catherine, she was wonderful, as was Father Carmen, you'll be happy to know they chatted with Andrew about the seminary."

She continued to cry. "Yes, he told me. But, I'm sorry Declan, a lost sister? Holy Jesus, I know nothing about you, one would wonder if you and I are even married, and now you call me from four thousand miles away."

"Yes, you're right, but I've changed. You'll see. So how does a trip to Ireland sound to you?" I asked, needing to regain her sympathies and trust, but was rushed to finish due to a few other people checking their watches and waiting to use the phone.

She just sighed through the static filled line. "Ireland?"

I turned my back to the others in line and shut the phone booth door tight. "Yes, dear. Ireland." I wasn't planning to tell her about my time with Father Carmen, but she deserved to know, and well, okay—I figured it would help my defense, so I paused to assert my intent to win her over again. "Sofia," I said, and surprised myself when I began to choke up telling her about what happened in the alley. "Would you believe Father Carmen heard my confession and blessed me with sacred oil a few days ago?"

She began to cry hysterically hearing this information, and together our cries added to the muddled telephone wire. "Oh, Declan dear, there have been too many secrets between us. I want to be close to you. Please be careful. Marco scares me."

"Sofia, you have every right to be upset. Please don't worry. You'll be fine where you are for now, just stay with your parents; your father knows what he's doing when hiding out from gangsters like Marco. Remember he went to the cottage when fighting against those guys who tried to put a card club in his city?"

She was silent and had nothing to add on that issue, knowing I was right.

"I will call you—or better yet, send for you when I can, so keep your bags packed and ready," I said, and hung up, opened the door to the phone booth, happy to give the receiver to the next person waiting. Canvassing the new area, I walked straight to the ticket counter to rent a car and purchase three airline tickets. I wasn't going to panic my wife further, but planned to call her after I talked to Pappy about having them come at once. I knew time was running short and had to act fast towards a solution before Marco completely reached his point of madness. I've seen him reach that point many times over and it was never pretty.

I purchased a map and asked for directions to Fethard, County Tipperary. The attendant gave me keys and walked me out to a small lot with a half dozen cars. He chuckled when I automatically walked to the left side of the vehicle to look for a steering wheel. "I love it when you Americans come to drive our cars," he said, with such a thick brogue I could barely understand him. "Ere in Ireland, we do the driving on the right side of the vehicle, Sir. Sit on the right, drive on the left. You'll get used to it in twenty kilometers or so."

I certainly hope so, I thought.

Even in the pitch black of night, I was grateful the attendant was correct, as it was easy to adjust to the reversed method of the roads and to change gears with my left hand on the manual stick shift. The headlights of my car fixed dimly onto white dotted road lines, and flashed on several directional signs towards the first town out of the airport area. Resigning to attempt this drive in the daylight, I folded up the map to concentrate on the road.

As I drove into town, found a bar and parked, I walked into a welcoming pub and asked the bartender if he knew of a room close by. After pouring a beer for one of the boys playing fiddle on a small, improvised stage, he graciously called the cottage across the lane and reserved a room for me.

My body clock said it was time to eat a breakfast of eggs and hash browns, however I accepted a dinner menu instead. A nice basket of brown bread with fresh, creamy butter that tasted straight from the cow calmed my hunger along with a most refreshing pint of Guinness. The drink went down like a glass of milk, so I splurged and had another—well truthfully, I lost count, but looked at the dark stouts as fuel for my tank. The pints went well with a few deep bowls of homemade lamb stew, and hearing improvised folk music eased my soul again, and was initiated to the land before I even saw a sunrise.

After a few hours of a replenishment of food, song, and drink, a friendly cottage waited for me across the street. I entered a small room and dropped my bags on the floor exhausted, yet relaxed. I quickly fell on top a down-feathered bed and into deep slumber again.

In the morning, I woke to the sound of roosters crowing. Lying with my head on the pillow, I listened for them to stop boasting to the sunrise, and had to wonder if the past few days had all been a dream and I was back at my California ranch needing to feed the horses. I pulled back the white-laced curtain, and looked through the window out onto green rolling hills that seemed to go on forever. Overwhelmed by the fields of green before me, I laughed, thinking of what my mother would say as I saw the wet black asphalt roads that framed the greenery.

See Declan, I told you the roads never dried here. The voice of my mother's spirit welcomed me.

"Will you be with me for the duration?" I asked in return, as my eyes lit up as if it were the first time that vivid greens pierced into them. The photo I recently shared with Andrew in my office, the night before we left the ranch, was the large heirloom picture of a cathedral on a hill. The view in my gazing eyes was far from the black and white image I had grown accustomed to; as in an instant, the black and white longings in my heart were replaced with a fresh, new reality. "Is the color green a sign of growth, and if so, are the green grasses of Ireland blowing in my eyes again?" I asked the spirit once more.

I could have fixed my eyes on this view all morning from a sofa chair in the room, but closed the curtain to get back to my agenda, first familiarizing myself with the map. If Andrew's telegram arrived on time, my Pappy was expecting me. I wondered if Shannon were there, along with the cathedral on the hill—soon all these treasures would be in my arms. Overcome with it all, I thought this must be what Pappy meant when he'd entice me in letter after letter to come visit him. "Declan, when will you leave your work and visit me?" he'd ask. "Come, come, Ireland is a burst of surprises."

I smiled thinking of how close I was to seeing him face to face and felt compelled to fully feel the earth, so I stepped outside in my nightshirt, into the rain-fresh air to absorb the splendor of the land beneath me. To be standing with my feet here brought me to wonder if my eyes and body needed to see and feel this sacred soil to be whole again. Then in a whisper, as if I breathed the words into the soil itself, I said, "Is this what Andrew meant about the crossroads of life?" So I took in more fresh air, stretching my arms up, and readying my limbs, wondering about the days when mother and Pappy longed to leave the cramped quarters of the asphalt jungles in New York and to return to these vast open ranges of unblemished earth. Looking around, I flexed my toes in the dark soil and green grass outside the door of my room, bending down to sift some dirt through my fingers feeling an overwhelming peace inside me.

Welcome home son, you're headed in the right direction.

I smiled and felt so close to my mother once more. Coming back inside, I took a quick shower, toweled dry, and then glanced at myself in the tiny mirror over the sink. I combed back the hairs on my head and gave myself a challenge for the day, "I am home, but are you ready to be a decent man again, Declan Quinn?" I asked myself and leaned closer to the image in the mirror, checking to see if the darkness in my eyes that Sofia accused me of had vanished. "Greenies to greenies and decent," I said once more, but panicked, wanting to present my best self to them.

It takes work son, set yourself to the pace of the Irish now—go…

I loaded the silver, boxy two-door car, and checked out of the cottage. My small bag and briefcase could barely fit into the trunk, so I placed them on the passenger seat and pushed a few buttons on the radio to pick a station. The channels on the radio brought me instantly to think of my mother singing to Shannon and me while I enjoyed the brown bread slices the innkeeper gave me.

I fingered the map, southeast towards Fethard, County Tipperary and drove along side low-lying ancient rock and mortar fences that ran parallel to the curvy country road that barely fit my car. Happy I decided to do this drive in the daylight, as I had to fight my instinct to veer to the right when I saw oncoming traffic. More than once, one vehicle had to pull over to the left to let the other squeeze by. My mind was already in a state of anxiety, but reading the map and concentrating on the flipped method of driving kept me focused. Scattered white sheep painted with pinkish red brandings grazed on the misting green marshes. They looked so calm, well fed, and peaceful in the quiet, early morning.

Every twenty-five kilometers or so, I slowed down through a circle roundabout going clockwise to drive through small towns following white road signs written in Gaelic with distances figured in kilometers. Typically, there was a pub on each corner, a schoolhouse, a medieval church, quaint boutiques, a library, and a general store scattered around a cobblestoned main street or center. As I approached the heart of each town, I observed the local peoples riding bicycles in varieties of colored, down feathered rain gear, including a postman delivering mail. Women and men walked with large shopping bags on their backs or pulled rustic wagons carrying a child or two. I unrolled the window to take in the refreshing air, and noticed young children everywhere. Similar to the States, it was apparent that Irish-Catholic families multiplied like rabbits here, too. But every child I passed on these roads had a face and hair like Shannon's. My heart skipped a beat or two when a little girl the age I last saw my little sister caught my eye. I wondered, had I answered Pappy's calls for me in my hospital bed in 1933, would Shannon and I have spent decades in this environment, and been one of these blessed children too.

Feeling the need to be connected once again to both Shannon and my mother, I pushed the steel pistol down deep into my briefcase and fished for the file once again. Rubbing the papers, like a genie in a bottle, I hoped Shannon would pop out to join me in the flesh. "Okay ladies, you will be my newest comrades, we're off on this new adventure together. Mother, feel free to tag along, as you've taken us this far to your beloved country, and Shannon, my little genie-in-a-file, over three decades are between us, please welcome me with an open heart."

There was no audible reply that time, but I felt them next to me nonetheless, as we always were a unit of three—I was the man who took care of them before my father stole it all from me. But no more, as this enchanted place will unite us again and make it right, I thought.

I pulled over off of road M18, then continued to head southeast where I found a small, quaint pub in the town of Limerick. Taking in the foreign morning's pace, I wondered if perhaps there was something magic in the reviving air in my lungs, as I started to feel like writing again—not just an agenda list either, but writing more prose to the verse I had started, a part of me set aside too long.

When in Rome—act like a Roman and toss your old ways aside, Declan, as you can take the boy away from poetry, but you can't take the poetry away from the boy.

I shrugged at my would-be escort, and thought of the fun we had when she'd ask Frankie and me to write prose or Limericks for her English classes at St. Ephrem's School.

There once was a boy from the ridge
Who was set on building a bridge,
When he rose with the sun
Then started to run
He realized he needed courage.

Laughing at myself writing these lines for fun, putting an accent on the last word to make the rhyme work, I accepted a refill into my coffee mug.

Then, as if I were James Joyce himself, I wrote my first poem since entering high school, feeling fully linked to the voice of the spirit as it blended with a voice internal—a voice I thought was dead.

I remember your face, that of a child.
Quietly we faded into sleep, with fear on our minds.
Your cries echo in the embers there,
Bonded of the same angel of love and care.
Save us, can a life turn around?
Alas, alas, tis home I found.

CHAPTER TWENTY-ONE

FRIED EGG SANDWICHES

As if my mother set the stage, the weather was unusually pleasant for the dead of winter; the mid-morning sun glistened over the dewfall on the rolling green fields that surrounded Pappy's property as the air began to warm. I eased my car up a cobblestone lane and stopped in a narrow driveway in front of his cottage, checking my wristwatch for the time. It was close to eleven o'clock in the morning. I looked up to patchy clouds spread across a blue sky, thankful to my faithful guide for bringing me here safe and alive, and thankful more so, to be finally at the threshold of forgiveness.

Before I arrived, I stopped at a quaint market in the enchanting town of Fethard, and filled a bag of groceries with an array of meats and cheeses, brown bread, and plenty of fresh butter. If telegrams were delivered at the same slow pace as the cars on the curving county road I just traveled Pappy surely hadn't expected my visit.

His home was handsomely layered in gray flagstone with white wood-paned windows, surrounded by a sturdy white split-rail fence. Approximately one hundred feet off the main road, it appeared to stand as sturdy as it did when first built, stone over stone centuries ago with the strength of a mason's hands. From the mortar of the entry steps to the high chimney top, the home was replete with a history of fortitude.

I walked up a flagstone path, bordered with flowerbeds full of winter purple irises and white snowdrop blossoms, and stepped up to the front door that was thickly coated with layers of red, lead-based paint. Preparing to knock, my hand was shaking, so I lowered it in haste. I needed a moment more to prepare, so I paused to look around the area, and wondered if all the postcards he sent me over the years were photographs of his own home and surroundings.

Then an animated bark turned my attention around to a furry, wire coated, black-and-white terrier that ran toward me, his tail, white, short and cropped, wagged rapidly, resembling Peter Cottontail instead of a dog. He stopped to circle two Kerry Bog ponies that seemed unconcerned with his antics as he searched through wooden sticks on the lawn, before choosing one to drop at my feet. My curious nervousness had been offset by his bark as he announced my arrival. Nature in all forms had a voice here, it occurred to me, and man must allow it to orate without restraint.

Looking around at this stunning property, I thought it must be the first surprise Pappy warned me of in his letters. One time in the mailings, he sent a box with dozens of leather-bound literary classics, but they were old and worn, so I used a tin of saddle wax to return their ancient leather soft and vibrant again. Like his books, the aging wood framed windows and moss-blanketed flagstone covered in ivy on the façade, gave an appearance of solid authenticity. I could picture him in front of this house reading one of those classics and felt awful that it had taken me so long to get here.

To my surprise no one came to the door to learn why the terrier was barking. I finally had more courage and knocked repeatedly using the heavy black iron knocker on the door. After several tries, I double-checked the address and reconfirmed the correct location. Honing in on the surroundings for clues, I noticed an old faded, red wood barn stood at the rear of the property. When the dog trotted ahead, leading me down a gravel path, he barked at a few ducks waddling down a grass embankment and continued to be my guide toward the barn.

Off in the distance, I saw a young man, perhaps not much younger than Andrew, pulling feed off a huge stack of hay with a pitchfork as he sang a folk song.

"We tracked the Dublin Mountains,
We were rebels on the run,
Though hunted night and morning,
We were outlawed but free men.

Farwell to Tipperary, said the Galtee Mountain boy."

The dog nearly tripped me dropping the stick at my feet again, so I tossed it as far as it would go, which got the young man's attention. Standing tall and brawny, he took off his red and black-checkered cap, flipped his darkish-red chunky hair back, and approached me.

I smiled and was happy to greet him. "Sounded like you're planning on leaving Ireland, you look too young to be bidding farewell to such a grand place."

"Nah, you'll never get me off this island, Sir," he said.

Interrupting us, an even younger boy, maybe sixteen, came running from behind the barn. His jet-black hair hung over the side of his brow and muddied face, with eyes as black as the dirt under his fingernails. His smile was bright as he ran passed me in well-worn overalls to grab sticks for the dog.

I watched the teen play with his pup and continued to chat with the older boy. "Glad to hear you're not heading out soon, who would ever want to leave a place like this anyway," I said. "I'm looking for Professor Declan Quinn. I thought this was his house."

"It is," the boy said, putting his hat back on. "But today is Thursday, so he's up at The Rock of Cashel, teaches a class there 'til three o'clock. I'm Daniel," he said, and offered a firm handshake, speaking with the same endearing accent I remembered from my mother and had heard all over this land thus far.

I shook his hand with delight knowing I had found the right place and introduced myself. "Good to meet you, Daniel. My name is Declan Quinn," I said. "I'm his grandson from California, haven't seen him since I was younger than you boys. I sent him a wire yesterday to tell him I was coming, but…" I stopped there, not wanting to press my case. I was dying to know who these boys were, but I tried to be patient. Details, Declano, I thought to myself, thinking of Signore Attanasio's advice. "Would you mind giving me directions?" I asked, pulling out the map from my pocket. "I'd like to head over there to meet him right away."

The boys exchanged looks, not exactly ones of suspicion, but doubt.

"How could you be his grandson?" Daniel asked confused.

The younger boy interrupted. "Yeah, Mother says the only family we have is her, G-Pap, and our uncles in Galway."

G-Pap—so that's where the name comes from, I thought.

The older boy moved his body in front of the younger one. "He's right. Just the mention of America makes her cry. I could tell you were American, so maybe you shouldn't be here, or maybe I should punch your lights out."

His words and angry scowl made me pause as he fixed the hat tighter onto his head. Daniel was strong looking and serious minded and appeared ready to handle trouble if not cause it. The dog dropped another stick at my feet, so I backed up a bit to throw it aside. I stuttered a little. "Maybe you should. I'm so very sorry. In all honesty, I did abandon my sister many years ago, but it's complicated boys. There's so much that needs to be cleared up, but feel free to punch me if it makes you feel better. I know how it feels to watch your mother cry." I was rambling on, analyzing the faces before me. The older boy had the same fiery green in his eyes, with a facial boney structure on his cheekbones that was a classic Quinn trait, so any more confirmation of who he was deemed unnecessary.

Daniel approached me closer. "I'm thinking now you might be someone who hurt her."

I put the map back into my pocket and shrugged defeated. "No please, you have it all wrong, well yes—perhaps I did hurt her, but we were just kids," I said, with beseeching eyes.

He responded to my plea with little or no avail. "So, mister, you drop in on us out of the blue, unannounced, and then try to make us believe you're family," Daniel said, in disbelief. "Get this, if you're her brother, she's pretty screwed up because of you."

I was shocked, he may as well punched me telling me this, and knowingly deserved every ounce of it. Daniel stood waiting for me to defend myself, but I knew better and let it go. So I simply spoke of his mother from my heart. "I can tell you my sister Shannon was a rare gem to me growing up, and I can tell your eyes are the same as hers," I said, still hoping to soften his demeanor. "This means the two of you are my nephews. I'd recognize your green eyes anywhere Daniel, they're just like my sister's—and our mother's."

It worked. Daniel softened and his fists relaxed as he took a stick to throw, while his little brother ran off with the dog. Together we watched the two of them running around and enter the barn. "G-Pap tells me that too, always singing how 'the green grasses of Ireland grows in my eyes' just like my mum, but not my brother, his eyes are as dark as the night. When he comes home late after carousing with his buddies, riding motorcycles and wreaking havoc in town, I'm the one who has to run and find him, then guess who gets the blame."

"What is his name?" I asked.

"Sean, a real pain in my side. During the week, mum teaches at the university and stays with our father and little sister at G-Pap's flat in Dublin. We work the farm and I take Sean to school in town on my way to University College in Cork. Only on Thursdays, when G-Pap's away, does Sean try to push the limits," Daniel said, and then sighed. "Don't know why I'm telling you any of this. We might be family, but you're still the guy who makes my mum cry."

I placed a hand over my heart. "That's something I hope to fix. I don't want her crying any more than you do. Hopefully we'll get to know each other in the next few weeks, and you'll come to understand." My stomach rumbled and I remembered the food I brought. "I stopped at the market on the way here. Would you mind if we went inside so I can make us all some lunch? Then after you can give me quick directions to see your G-Pap. How does that sound?" I asked, with gentle persuasion.

He nodded and said, "Alright. We were gonna quit soon anyway and you can simply follow us up to The Rock." He called out toward the barn. "Sean, stop with the feeding. The mules can wait, lunch is calling."

The teen came running out holding a pitchfork and then dropped it on the ground.

"Come on, you know G-Pap hates it when you leave tools out to get wet. Put the damn thing back in the barn into its proper hook and bring your blasted pup with you," Daniel said, in a loud voice.

Sean ran back into the barn as Daniel and I started walking toward the house. He and the dog soon returned, minus the pitchfork, and raced ahead of us.

It was a relief to return to the red door, to finally open it, and set my bag inside. The burnt scent of pipe tobacco resting in an ashtray brought me back to the aromas of my childhood, cracking my senses so much a tiny vertigo in my head made me dizzy for a second. I was transported to Pappy's brownstone home near New York University, where he read me one bedtime story after another and sang sweet Irish lullabies. I remembered my mother in the kitchen wearing her housedress humming the tunes and being so happy then.

"Make yourself at home," Daniel said. "I'll be back." He went down the hall disappearing from view.

Surprises indeed, I thought, looking around Pappy's home, watching Daniel walk away. I am shamefully more than just a tad bit late in coming home.

Sean watched me as I opened the groceries on a long plank wood table that looked even older than the home it occupied. The dog panted at my feet, so I gave him a fresh bowl of water and a few strips of meat and cheese. He gobbled down the food first, slurped up a drink, and then found a cozy rug lit by a beam of light from the window to warm himself. "This here's my pup," Sean said, and sat next to him brushing his scruffy fur with his fingers. "His name's Jack, but G-Pap calls him Jack Benny, says he takes after the American actor on the radio who makes him laugh."

I walked over and ratted the pup's wiry coat, laughing at his naming. "Nice to meet you Jack Benny. So, your name is Sean?" I asked, and offered him a handshake.

"Hey there, Mr. Quinn. Yes, you've got it right, I'm Sean, stick around so I can hear all about America, okay? We're off on school holiday until next week, when I go back, the American National Park reports start," he said, returning a firm hand with a smile.

"I'd be delighted to help you with that," I said.

Daniel returned with his face washed clean and hair slicked back. He looked like a giant in the low ceilinged room, three-inches more and his head would have hit the dark wood beams. I set out a six-pack of coke bottles on the table along with sandwiches of sliced brown bread, salami, ham, cheese, and butter.

Daniel watched me working on the cold cut sandwiches. "Looks good so far, but there's something missing. Do you mind me adding a farm fresh topping to those?" Daniel asked.

"Go right ahead," I said, wondering what he had in mind.

He stepped up to the stove and took half a dozen brown eggs out of a bowl on the counter easily holding three in each of his huge hands. Daniel set them gently near the wood burning stove that looked like the same one we had in our tenement apartment in New York. He leaned over where I was stacking the meat on the bread, stole a slab of butter and tossed it into a heavy, dark, cast iron frying pan. With his left hand, he cracked the eggs and fried them up, gently flipping them over with a flip of the pan.

"I like your style," I said, impressed with his skill.

But Daniel wasn't finished. As he hummed the same melody from before, he took the top slice of bread off the sandwich along with the meats and cheese to grilled them for a few seconds in the already hot pan. When finished, he put the top of the sandwiches back on with the fried eggs inside. "There you go, got to have an egg with everything on a farm. Even the dog," he said, then dropped a cooked egg into Jack's dish on the floor.

Sean filled a tall glass with milk and joined us at the table, seemingly ready to chat about my country.

"We'll take one of these sandwiches for my G-Pap. We always bring him his lunch on Thursdays and he gets grouchy if we're late, so we'd best get on now," Daniel said.

This felt like a dream. "How long of a drive is it to The Rock of Casher?" I asked, taking it all in, along with a huge bite of the sandwich.

"Cashel, The Rock of Cashel," Sean said, correcting me.

Daniel interjected putting his hat on. "It's about fifteen minutes or so up the M8 North. G-Pap's friend picks him up every Thursday morning with a busload of college students. He wants me to read them some verses of Keats today. I was thinking about bringing my own verses for a surprise, but I'm not sure they're good enough."

I stopped eating for a second. "Your own verses? I'd be honored to be the audience for a dress rehearsal, Daniel." I readied myself to listen and rubbed my hands together in anticipation.

"No, that's okay. I wouldn't want to bore you," he said.

"Please, son. I'm a closet poet myself. Read me your treasures, then later I'll make you suffer through a collection of mine."

Daniel laughed at that. "Well, the only ones who've listened to me so far are the horses and chickens. Human ears would be nice. Sean sure doesn't give a crap."

"I want to hear. Truly," I said.

"Alright then." He nodded and ate faster.

I couldn't believe this was happening. Here I was in the sanctuary of my Pappy's home waiting to hear my handsome, young nephew recite his own poetry to me. I only hoped my mother's frolicking spirit had stayed along for this segment of my journey. The joy in hearing Daniel read could grant her a passage out of heaven and to sit in the empty wood seat next to me. Daniel finished eating then took a folded piece of paper out of the inner lining of his cap. He carefully unfolded a thin well-worn sheet with smudged handwriting and stood up in front of me, clearing his throat.

"It's called, Epona's Tears."

"Please proceed son," I said, with anticipation.

He cleared his throat once more and readied himself like a confident orator.

Fields vast wait, Epona, o' spirit come to thee.
The flames o' your longings char in kind you see.
Naught ye hide tears as the late moon doth rise,
I hear your cries and see thy eyes.

Soft and tender you sing to me, though you think I'm blind.
Ner to love the piercing wounds, hest they do remind.
Stay awake my faithful heart,
The dreams of love will never part.
Fallen from the sorrows, though joy is best.
Alas, a rising sun's warming dew fairly remains unrest
Aye, glory tis yours as grace spills on the greens.
The flames o' your longings,
Come alive with sunlit streams –
Upon your face yields all your dreams.
Epona, o' mare, o' mine –
Come to thee with thoughts Divine."

Daniel slowly folded the paper and slipped it back into his hat while I sat in stunned silence.

On the floor Sean kept playing tug o' war with Jack. "Epona o' mare of mine—Come to thee with thoughts Divine." He echoed with an overly dramatic flair. "Daniel's been reciting that poem all week, Mister," he said, rolling his eyes.

Without praise or comment, I walked over to Daniel, reached up to take hold of his shoulder. "Daniel, your poem is beautiful. Your G-Pap will love it. Those words came from a heart that is precious and rare. Thank you, for sharing them with me." I felt tears spring into my eyes and wiped them away.

He backed away. "It wasn't meant to be sad," he said, frowning at me. "And not romantic either, Punk." He looked at Sean, walked over and punched his shoulder.

"Hey come on boys, I've got two just like you at home. Daniel, my tears aren't from sadness. I'm overjoyed. You are my precious nephew and your poem will sit in my heart like morsels of goodness in a barren soul." In humility, I held my hand over my heart once more.

He still wasn't convinced about me. "I don't know anything about barren souls."

"Nor should you ever. Oh, I do hope to be your friend, son. Perhaps one day, I can rise to the level of a cherished uncle to you and your brother," I said, but knew my excitement was off putting when my hug went unreturned.

"Mister, I protect my mother first. We'll have to wait and see about the rest," he said.

"Yes, of course. I apologize, my emotions get the best of me these days."

He shrugged. "Anyways, thank you for hearing my poem without laughing."

"Is Epona a girl you know?" I asked, even more afraid he'd punch me for the question.

Instead, he smiled. "No. I'll let your American ignorance go and give you a pass on that. Epona is the Celtic goddess of horses."

"Oh, it just sounded so personal," I said.

He smiled again and glanced toward his brother busy playing with the dog, then lowered his voice. "That's because, in my poem, my mother represents the goddess." He checked to be sure Sean wasn't listening. "It's her glory I speak of. But please, that's between us. One thing is for certain, when you meet her again, you will see Epona in her as well."

He walked to the sink, wrapped up the remaining sandwich, and put it in a brown bag. Grabbing a soda, he walked over to me. "Hey, lost uncle from California, ready to go see your grandfather?"

"Yes. It's been too long," I said, and swallowed my tears.

CHAPTER TWENTY-TWO

A POETRY LESSON

We followed Daniel out of the house and down a rocky path over to an old garage attached to the barn. "I complain about watching my little brother," he said, smiling. "But I love Thursdays, really. Mostly cuz I get to drive G-Pap's old jalopy."

"Does he still drive it too?" I asked.

He shrugged. "Not anymore. At eighty-six he walks with a cane, and has trouble braking with his weak knee, so he has me drive him around now. The back seat of his car is small, so you'll have to follow us," Daniel said, and opened an old rickety wood garage door. Inside was a classic car I recognized.

"Oh my, that's a Dolomite Roadster, isn't it? What a beauty," I said.

"Ah, that she is, it's a 1940. G-Pap says she's mine if I graduate with honors."

The Roadster was a beautiful convertible, two-tone with deep emerald green siding, and black fenders that glided around the large tires and down to the passenger doors, providing elegant steps for entry.

Daniel grabbed a bag of rags and tossed one to me. "Sean, get over here and wash the tires like G-Pap said, and you better not have muddied your shoes. Come on, polish that chrome real shiny this time. Hop to it. It's getting late."

When the boys and I finished buffing the smooth, deep green, nearly black paint and the silvered chrome on the tires, the car sparkled like new.

Sean tried to grab the keys away from his brother. "Let me drive, the sun is out today, so we can ride with the top down. G-Pap will be teaching me after my birthday next week anyway. Let me get a head start, Danny."

"No way. You're still a punk kid to me." Daniel said, fully taller than the boy and held the keys high out of his reach.

Sean pulled at his shirt, fighting for the keys, but Daniel easily won out. "I'll be fifteen and driving soon, you can't stop me."

Daniel bent down to finish shinning the fenders, tossing the dirtied rags in a basket. "Maybe so, but you're not driving today." With a sense of accomplishment, he climbed in behind the steering wheel.

I couldn't help but smile seeing Sean's pouting face as he took to the passenger seat. The dog sat between them like a captain on a ship as Daniel fixed a black and red-checkered scarf around his neck, backed the car out of the garage, and headed down the driveway. I jumped in my small boxy rental to follow.

The country road was narrow and winding, taking us north through lush green landscapes. I watched with a smile on my face as the terrier had his front paws on the dashboard, his long wiry-coat and black ears flapped in the wind. Sean, on the left side stretched his arm like a wing, while Jack seemed to be on a hunt for fowl overhead.

I followed close behind them with Shannon's file still in my briefcase on the seat next to me and smiled thinking of my mother when hearing the accents on the radio again. My heart dropped when I felt inside the briefcase for the file, but touched the steel of the gun instead. In haste, I pulled off my scarf, wrapped up the pistol, and placed it into the glove box. "I won't be in need of a pesky gun on enchanting roads like these, will I," I said, using a mock Irish accent. "Why did I bring this blasted weapon anyway?"

Forget all of that, Son. Just remember it will be greenies to greenies from here on in. You've come to the land of your soul—your sister has called you home.

This had to be a dream and a world away from my troubles with Marco. Had he gotten word yet on how we skirted his thugs. I imagined Sofia and the kids on the ski slopes, but couldn't help to worry about Anthony and what cost he might be paying for siding with me. And worse still, hoped there was no chance Marco would ever travel this far.

I drove slowly behind the boys, thinking of how Marco would seem like a black sheep here on the hillsides full of white wooly ones. But thinking of him made me uneasy, so I decided to take the wrapped gun out of the glove box and stuffed it back into my briefcase again. "Sorry, Mother, no one can ever be assured with a man like Marco on your tail."

We soon arrived at the quaint town of Cashel. The grand cathedral appeared in the distance, a majestic medieval structure atop the crest of a hill over a picturesque village below. The cathedral looked dark and ominous behind ancient stonewalls with garrison watchtowers and a graveyard. I imagined the massive walls laden with a row of weapon-clad soldiers stationed there centuries ago.

Looking up at the hill in awe, I pictured Pappy standing in these ruins reciting special lines of wisdom in a meaningful lecture or poem. From years of reading his elegant letters, I knew him to be a wordsmith extraordinaire, but was so young when he moved away, that I barely remembered his face. Surly my mother would speak as if he were always just around the corner, yet in my heart, it was as if I met him that day for the first time.

We parked next to the bus as I took the briefcase in my hand, feeling unease about its contents once more. The gun. What should I do with this confounded thing, I wondered. So I decided to place it back into the glove box, wrapping my scarf around it in haste like before, leaving the briefcase on the seat.

I met the boys at the base of an incline, and together we hiked up to the cathedral.

"What are you perspiring about Mister? It's freezing out here," Sean asked, as Daniel looked at me with suspicion.

I wiped off my brow, annoyed with myself, wishing I hadn't had the need to bring that damn thing along in the first place. This was a sacred journey and guns had no part in it. Diverting my thoughts with the surroundings, and cooling off with the cold windy breezes into my lungs, in the back of my mind, I wondered how to pose the many questions to Pappy. The first mystery I hoped to unravel was how my little sister came to live with him in Ireland and why he never mentioned it in all those letters.

I breathed in the aromas from the fresh, moist air, as the hairs on my arms stood straight up seeing the grandiose medieval site at close range. Of course, he would pick a setting like this, one representing myth and legend for his poetry lectures, I thought.

The Rock of Cashel, a larger than life edifice filled with history and mystic experience, was a perfect backdrop for our reunion. Even though I had found him while at work, I didn't feel the least bit intrusive dropping in on him here. The enormous wall surrounding the complex had an entrance through a small wrought iron gate. We quietly walked through a Hall of the Vicars and outside again onto the grounds. A cross, unlike the typical one with a ring around the crossbars, had a stone image of Christ wearing a robe on the front.

You are treading on sacred ground, Declan.

Daniel spoke in a hushed tone, hand signaling us to follow him to the chapel area. "Sean, keep a close eye on your pup. If Jack opens his trap or lifts his leg for a pisser, G-Pap is sure to come unglued."

We followed Daniel around large facades of smooth tan and brown sandstone, shaded dark by cloud drifting overhead. I heard a man's voice coming from inside the smaller chapel through an open arched stone door with a lion carved into the stone that carried a bow and arrow. When Jack growled at the image, Sean grabbed his larynx and snout to silence him before we entered.

Approximately two-dozen students sat on folding chairs in a circle along with Pappy as he lectured. We entered, trying to quiet our steps, and stood silently in the back to listen in. His commanding voice, with a strong Irish brogue echoed, making every follicle of hair on my arms stand straight once more. His head was fully grayed and not the brownish-red I remembered forty years ago, I thought absorbing his presence.

"To come close to God, look at the heavens. The stars. They are perfect. The moon, it is constant. Human lives, in contrast, are flawed, unpredictable. Who in this room can say their life is perfect, or that any of the people in their lives are perfect? God wants us to do battle with our flaws, to make a prayer or a poem of our efforts. What we write will seal the cracks in our souls and make the hard soil of our lives ripe for planting new seeds, new thoughts. Thank God for the arts, they are a medium for man to come closer to God, to His perfection," he said, and continued as I meandered behind one of the stone columns with a smile on my face.

"Look at this room we are sitting in. The masons had to get the engineering precise or this structure wouldn't have lasted one year, let alone centuries. Music too can be a path to God. Attend a symphony and you can hear the voice of God, if one string is out of tune, even an untrained ear can hear the flaw. In music, fine art, and architecture, the Almighty must be there when it's perfected. The bible, one of the world's greatest works of literature, is fully inspired by God. Isaiah 64:8 says, 'Lord, we are the clay, you are the Potter; we are all the work of your hand.' When we create, God works through us to form the clay. Yes?" he asked, and looked around the circle of students facing him, then saw us there watching in the background.

He clapped his hands together without restraint and announced at top volume, "Ah, lunch has arrived. Boys, I was starting to worry the road ate you up. I trust you came prepared to recite one of the greats for us today, Daniel." Pappy's voice echoed once more, amplified by the surrounding stonewalls.

He turned to his students. "My great-grandson will sit in for me while I take a short break for lunch," he said to his students, standing slowly with the help of his cane. "Daniel, take my seat. We were discussing the question you asked me the other day. 'Why, if God is perfect, did he make man flawed?' Go on, you are fully capable of leading this discussion."

Daniel sat down, while Pappy walked toward Sean to get his sandwich. He looked shorter and stouter than I remembered, with a beard groomed to perfection, and indeed fully grayed. He leaned on his cane with one hand and took a big bite of the sandwich. Enjoying it, he noticed me, as I stood frozen in the background staring at him. "May I help you with something? The tours aren't scheduled today," he said, through a mouthful as Daniel started in with a discussion.

Words failed me, as I slowly walked over and stood before him, smiling and teary eyed.

"I'm sorry." He swallowed and scowled at me. "Do I know you?"

"Yes, but I wouldn't expect you to recognize me." I tried to squelch a huge smile and whispered to not interrupt Daniel, but the excitement in me made it impossible. "It's been forty years and I was just a boy. But here we are together again at last, just as my mother prayed would happen," I said, with a quiver in my voice. "It's good to see you again, Pappy."

He dropped his sandwich and cane on the floor then grabbed me into his arms and held me as tight as any man ever had. "Declan. Declan, you have finally come. Oh my, oh my! I can't believe it. You're here."

We were crying, reading each other's expressions and exchanged embraces as all eyes in the room turned to watch us.

Finally, he released me and took a deep breath. "Come, meet my students and faithful colleague, Professor Bloom," he said, in his thick accent, and guided me forward. The students didn't get far into a discussion and were staring, entertained having witnessed our emotional reunion. Pappy introduced me with joy. "This is my grandson, Declan Quinn, you don't use the Hauser name since law school, right?" he asked, glancing at me. I nodded, as he opened his hand toward me as if he was announcing me on a stage. "Correction students. Let me present, Declan Quinn the Fourth from America." His smile was catchy.

It was as if I had grown two inches hearing him introduce me. "No more Hauser. I'm a Quinn, through and through—and the Fourth, as you said." I got emotional as I scanned the faces of smiling students.

He held onto my arm, steadying himself without his cane. "Declan came all the way from California, haven't seen him in over forty years," he said, with his deep-set eyes beaming.

"Hey, Sean, fetch my sandwich and walking stick and join our circle. Let's get back to our discussion and end class early today, so I can spend some time with my long lost grandson," he said. One of his students supplied me with a seat and I sat down next to Pappy needing someone to pinch me to tell me I wasn't dreaming.

"Forgive me Declan. I teach this group only once a week and we must finish our lesson before they take to their pens for their poetry assignment this weekend. Sit in. You will enjoy it. And Daniel, I still want you to lead the class. Sean, find yourself a spot on the floor and bring that mutt with you," he said, wrapped up the sandwich and stuffed it into his jacket pocket.

As the boys followed orders, Pappy looked at me in wonder. "I'm in shock seeing you here, Declan, and such a fitting place for our reunion, The Rock of Cashel. This sacred chapel is one of my favorite spots in Ireland. Did you know the King of Desmond, Cormac Mac Carthaigh, consecrated it in the Twelfth Century? But this place is even more ancient than that. It was first a fortress in the Fifth Century." Pointing to the walls on the south end of the nave, he continued his lecture. "If I could have another life, I would unveil the obscured frescos on that wall and up to the ceiling, chiseling away centuries of dirt and waterlogged sandstone. What those paintings need primarily is heat, dry heat to suck the moisture out of the stone from centuries of moisture. If you look closely at the ceiling, you can still see fragments of the frescos. They are beautiful expressions of faith and exactly what we were talking about today. Students observe. What you see there is God's craft made with a human hand, don't you agree?" he asked. Always teaching, he placed his hand over my shoulder. "Students, experiencing this room and the art on the walls and ceiling, what does it challenge us to do?"

The students all looked at each other with blank stares.

Daniel gave a reluctant try. "This room inspires creativity."

Pappy was pleased. "Nice try and you're close." He looked about the circle of faces and waited another few seconds, then continued. "Some of my colleagues will accuse me of blasphemy, but the opposite is true. The art around you, from the frescos to the architecture and masonry, challenges us to express the God inside ourselves, and what comes out of that manifestation, is what I call the voice of God within us."

Sean commented. "If I build a bird cage, G-Pap, does that count?"

The students laughed along with Pappy. "Yes it does, but students don't laugh at this joker. If a birdcage brings comfort to one of God's creatures, then yes, it falls into the art category. Doesn't this very chapel bring comfort to us? The challenge for your generation is to create an art form that provokes dialogue, inquisition, and most of all, a work that inspires growth and shows us a pathway to the Holy."

He watched the students write down notes and pointed his finger upward, using a louder, booming voice. "God's not up there, he's in here," he said, pointing to his heart. "Students, you must read between the lines in your experiences with art. Take that famous movie with the Wizard, for example, he never gave the Scarecrow any brains he didn't already have—and Dorothy, she never even left home, but see what her subconscious brought to her dreams. Home is here, no matter where your travels take you. Don't run away from the God within," he said, pointing to his heart again. "When we say things like, 'we're not good enough', it's just a cop out, a laziness. As it's the God within that scares us the most—you see, tapping into our greatest light is what makes us crap our pants on the stage."

The students laughed and wrote down more notes.

And then he spoke to me. "Declan, today's literary topic is about the use of conflict and tension when constructing a poem. Follow along, you will catch on," he said, and turned to Daniel. "Daniel, would you read the Keats piece you found that illustrates this?" Pappy asked, smiling with pride. "Sean, you can walk the grounds with your dog after your brother is finished, that is unless you've come prepared to read too?"

Sean shook his head. "Not bloody likely, no."

Daniel stood and took the folded paper out of the lining of his cap again. "G-Pap, if you don't mind, I was hoping to share one of my own poems. I think it shows conflict and tension like you wanted," he said, waiting for Pappy's response.

"Oh, I love it, by all means. Please proceed." He turned to me with a devilish smile. "Hey, by the way, Declan from America, I bet you were surprised to meet your nephews today at the house."

I laughed. "I'm quickly finding out Ireland is full of surprises, like you've always promised." The students laughed again, softening the atmosphere for Daniel's performance.

"It would be a gift to hear you read your own piece," Pappy said, and waved Sean over to stand at his side, putting Jack on his lap. "And you gave your work a title, I presume?" Pappy asked, stroking the pup's fur.

"Yes, G-Pap. It's called: Epona's Tears." Daniel cleared his throat and read the poem in a confident voice, reminding me of my own boys at home.

"Fields vast wait Epona, o' spirit come to thee.
The flames o' your longings char in kind you see.
Naught ye hide tears as the late moon doth rise,
I hear your cries and see thy eyes.
Soft and tender you sing to me, though you think I'm blind . . ."

As the students clapped, I was delighted to hear Daniel recite his poem again, but it's Pappy's reaction I was concentrating on.

Pappy dried his eyes and stood, giving the dog back to Sean, and then slowly walked with his cane over to Daniel. Just as I did a few hours earlier, he affirmed his work, holding Daniel's two young hands into his wrinkled ones. "Daniel, clearly, Epona, the Celtic goddess of horses, is someone you care deeply about. With grace and style, she struggled in the beginning of your poem, but finds resolve and hope in the last lines," he said, then turns to his students. "Daniel used archetypes, nature, the elements, and the Holy in this work. Can anyone tell me the points of tension and conflict he used?"

"Ner to love the piercing wounds, thou they do remind," a young, beautiful girl said.

"Fallen from the pains of death, of fear, of life, of youthfulness," another boy said.

"Exactly so. And the tension sets up the climax for the reader. Yes?" Pappy asked. "This is why I ask you all to use the elements and nature in your works to balance the tension. Danny, can you tell the class why you chose the metaphors you used?"

He nods. "Well, I chose fire, 'the flames o' your longings', due to the fact that Epona cannot hide her pain. I chose 'sunlit streams' as an element in nature, because the sun cures and creates growth, and streams have purifying qualities."

"Yes, indeed. I love how you used both fire and water in your work, your choices fit beautifully. You don't have to answer this question if you choose not to, but is Epona an archetype of someone you know or relate to?" Pappy asked.

"Yes, G-Pap. I know her. She's my mother," Daniel said, folding up his poem.

"I suspected as much. Daniel, your work is touching. Well done," Pappy said, and then turned to me once more. "You want surprises, Declan the Fourth from America? You'll find Ireland is filled with them. It's a blessed land you now tread, where no fear—or no boss, keeps a man from expressing the God within."

He looked at me with steel eyes, and then I knew he met my 'boss' on his post-war trip.

CHAPTER TWENTY-THREE

A HOOLIGAN DRIVING CAP

I started to worry about Pappy. He seemed oblivious to the fact he just celebrated his eighty-sixth birthday and that my surprise appearance had to have jarred the stability of his heart. He kept on with his lecture, and then listened as another half a dozen students recited their poetry pieces. His younger colleague, a poet in his own right, sat quietly in the background observing the class with a few books on his lap as he jotted down notes.

The students were a classy bunch of kids in their twenties, clad in the mod fashions, but wore jackets and overcoats as the chapel was cold and damp inside. They were a stark contrast to the medieval chapel surrounding them, and to Pappy, who was dressed conservatively in a thick gray knitted cardigan with a white-collared shirt and a thin, blue necktie, his cleanly groomed gray beard, bushy brows, and wise eyes peering behind silver-rimmed reading glasses, imparted on him a rare, classic look.

Pappy scanned the circle for other volunteers to contribute to the discussion. "Lauren, do you have a poetry piece to share with your class today? I want to hear from all of you before we break for the day," Pappy said. The student recited her verses and listened to comments from the group as the others followed around the circle. When the last student spoke and the critiques were finished, he called Sean to his side. Sitting near the doorway, Sean got up and carried Jack with him in his long lanky arms. Pappy took a ball of rolled up string out of his pocket. "Hand your pup to Nick," he said, as Sean complied. "Now take this ball of elastic cord over to Beau, then grab the starter string and bring the end back here to me."

The ball of elastic unwounded in Beau's hand as Sean returned holding its tip.

"Excellent," Pappy said. "Now pull it tight you two."

We watched Sean back away, struggling to hold on to the string of elastic.

Pappy walked along the pulled elastic with a cane and a limp. "This is tension in the material form. Can anyone tell me what I'm trying to illustrate in this exercise?" he asked, his gaze sweeping around the circle of faces.

"It's ready to snap, G-Pap. I can't hold on too long," Sean said, smiling. His pup barked and created an echo, making the class laugh again.

A pretty blonde in the circle spoke up. "At my sister's wedding last April, we did a limbo dance under a long string. Are you going to lead us in the dance, Professor Quinn?"

He laughed. "What, an old decrepit body like mine, bend under a wire? Never. But, in the spirit of surprises, let's dance. Joni, pick a few friends and show us how the limbo works."

As a hand full of students took turns at dancing under the elastic line, the rest of us clapped to give them a beat. Sean and Beau continued to lower the line until it went so low to the ground that the dancers gave up and returned to their seats as we all laughed along.

When we quieted, Pappy smiled and returned to his lecture. "Now don't go home and tell your parents I encourage you all to dance inside a sacred chapel, okay? But if this is tension in the material form, what am I trying to illustrate here?" he asked again.

The same girl raised her hand.

"Yes, Joni."

"It's stretched to the limit, Professor Quinn. You want us to grow beyond our comfort zones—or bend so low that we win the limbo dance," Joni said, getting the class to laugh with her once more.

Pappy smiled and waited for the laughter to stop. "You're on the right track, Dear. Growth beyond our comfort zones," Pappy said. "Anyone else have an observation?"

The two boys holding the elastic line were struggling to hold on.

"The elastic, its stretching and tension, definitely has our attention focused," a sweet girl with long black hair said.

"Focused attention. Good. Thank you, Briana," Pappy said. "Anyone else?"

"We are anxiously waiting for it to snap," another girl said, looking so Irish with red hair and freckled cheeks.

Pappy smiled. "Yes, Jaclyn. In poetic jargon, the elastic snapping represents what?"

"Are we done yet?" Sean asked, interrupting.

Pappy laughed. "Sean answered the question without even knowing it, but don't let go boys, until someone answers the question. Come on class, it easy. The snap is…?"

"The ending," several of the kids said.

"Right. A resolution after the tension or the climax, that's the term I was looking for, we must use tension as it makes the reader yearn for a resolution or a close."

"G-Pap!" Sean yelled as he continued to struggle.

Pappy laughed. "Good job boys, thank you. You may let go now."

With a snap, the elastic tape flew from Sean's fingers back at Beau, making him and everyone else jump. The remainder of the ball fell off his lap and rolled onto the ground. Jack barked and jumped down to give chase, making everyone laugh, and the walls of the great chapel chamber echoed again.

Pappy quietly walked back to his seat and waited until everyone stopped laughing. "You see, everyone, tension can even keep the focus of a high school freshman and his dog."

Angelina raised her hand. "Professor Quinn. Tension in poetry works, I get it. But I prefer to avoid tension, or the people who create it." Her peers nodded and smiled.

"Ah, 'the people who create it', that brings in another stanza doesn't it? Let's face it; all relationships are intertwined with tension. If someone hurts you, it's best to confront him or her and speak up for yourself. I don't like to hear you have chosen to not use your voice in these cases. I've read your work, Angelina, and your voice is honest and eloquent. Trust this voice, apply it, or better yet, shout from the mountaintops with your point of view."

The girl smiled and her classmates were seemingly grateful to her for the topic.

Pappy continued. "We must strive to be like the brave men who climbed onto the rafters to paint the frescos in this chapel. And like the masons who built this room, laying the stones and mortar without the safety of a net or scaffolding, they stretched beyond their limitations, voiced their passions, and hence, created a masterpiece." Pappy got up again, walked up to pinch Angelina's cheek. "My dear, write about those in your life that bring you tension." He turned and looked at everyone. "Students, it's up to you and the coming generations to continue this quest. Ireland, no—the world, is depending on it. You can choose to stay like an elastic ball wadded up in a pocket or stretch yourself to the stars, creating the healthy tension our world craves. You decide."

Standing next to his students, balancing with his cane, Pappy looked ready to bring the class to a close, and concluded by asking, "Any questions?"

"Yes," a dark haired boy who sat on the far side of the circle next to three other boys, all looking as if they played for the university football team spoke up. "Professor Quinn, I understand what you're saying about stretching ourselves and using our voice, it's easy to talk about that concept here in your class. But once we leave this safe cocoon, and set forth into this world alone, stretching oneself like that becomes scary. Beneath all her beauty, Ireland is a rough place, Sir. I prefer to use a net. What do you recommend for someone like me?" he asked.

"Matthew, you're braver than you think. To be so honest and authentic in front of your peers, shows courage beyond measure and an honesty that is rare," Pappy said, tenderly. "Matthew, your fear tells me what you lack is faith. I believe if you use God as your safety net, you will accomplish the goals you deemed impossible before—and there's the stretch."

"But how do I know God's there?" Matthew asked.

"From having faith. God designed us to doubt, so don't fret there, but do you enjoy music?" he asked.

Matthew nodded.

"It's pleasing, not only because of the sound, but because of the silences that are in it, without the alternation of sound and silence there would be no rhythm. Yes?" Pappy reduced his words to a lecture-styled whisper and cupped his mouth so all could hear. "God is in the silences, without the silences and the pauses, all we'd have is noise. Anyone can play a note, however, the pauses between the notes are where one finds the voice of God."

Matthew nodded his head. "In the silence..." He wrote the notes down.

"I challenge you to find your own rhythm, Matthew. You don't need to go at this alone. None of you do. Reach out and build a community of your own, and always remember—the stacks in the library are filled with the wisdom of the sages. You will never be without a net within the stacks of a library." Pappy walked over to the boy, offering an affectionate handshake. "Good question. I trust you will find that beat in your soul. Make music. Make art. 'Art allows you to lose yourself and find yourself at the same time', so says the American Trappist monk Thomas Merton. And make love too. True intimacy is found in the silence—this we know for certain." The students all laughed at his last comment. He prepared to leave. "Get busy kids. The world is waiting for your imaginations to merge with the silences. Class dismissed."

"Thank you, Professor Quinn," Matthew said, walking over to shake his hand. "I'm going to miss you and this class when the semester is over."

"And I you," Pappy said, returning the shake and brought the boy into an embrace. "I appreciate a man with courage like yours."

"Professor Quinn," a young girl wearing black-rimmed glasses addressed him. "We will let you go so you can catch up with your grandson, but one last thing. It's not a question."

"Yes, Katie, go ahead, please."

"We will chisel away with you on unveiling the frescos in this chapel if you promise to return to us here in your next life like you said."

Pappy chuckled. "Ah, that's a deal, Katie. I'll let you know when we start construction," Pappy said, receiving her embrace. "And Matthew, I'll be sure we have scaffolding with nets when the construction starts." The class burst into laughter.

I took a few steps to the side and let the students say their goodbyes with gentle hugs and handshakes. I could see he had mesmerized them all, just as he had me. With humility, style, and grace, he touched the soul of every student in the circle. I stepped over with Pappy's colleague and we chatted about the class while the students folded up their chairs and carried them out the door.

At last free of his adoring students, Pappy joined the two of us. "Did you see how this guy came upon me today almost giving me heart failure, Stuart?"

"Oh yes. It looked like a warm reunion to me. I can sure see a resemblance in the two Declan Quinns, he even looks like your son, Declan, in Galway—so the Fourth title is apropos." The professor, dressed in a tan, cable knit sweater vest, brown jacket with elbow patches, looked every inch a poet. "Pleasure meeting you, Declan, the Fourth from America. I bet I will see you at the next class, as once you get into this guy's grasps, he will never let you go back home."

Pappy and I chatted with him for a few minutes and then watched him leave with the other students. "He's a good man. We don't agree on anything in regards to politics, but see eye-to-eye on what's important to our souls." After the chapel quieted, Pappy turned to me. "Well, I would love to show you the rest of the grounds today, but I'm afraid your surprise and my enthusiastic students took all the life out of me for now." Cane in hand, he walked towards the exit, with his great-grandsons at his side. "Daniel, your poem was very touching. Does your mother know you wrote it? You described her brilliantly. She is the epitome of Epona, the horse goddess. Well done."

Daniel shrugged. "I took a gamble and won this time G-Pap."

"Epona Tears was a good bet, son, and a lovely tribute to your mother. I have been blessed by so many surprises today. First Declan Quinn comes into Cormac's Chapel, my favorite sacred chapel in all of Ireland, and then Daniel, you bring such beauty and grace with Epona's Tears. I'm an old man, and my days counting down, but this day is one of my very best. I think tomorrow, we might come back here to The Rock for a complete tour, or maybe we should wait on your mother boys." Stopping himself, he turned to look at me again. "Shannon," he said, as tears welled in his eyes.

"Yes, Shannon. I know. She comes in tomorrow on the six o'clock train from Dublin. Daniel told me, but no rush on that subject. We will finish with my fact-finding mission over time. Right now, let's get you to the car," I said.

"Yes. That sounds good," he said.

Sean walked up to us and tossed me the keys to the Roadster. "Here Mister, why don't you drive G-Pap's car, here's the key."

Pappy was delighted. "Good idea, Declan from America needs to drive the Dolomite Roadster. Agreed?"

I was uneasy about the idea but tried to hide it. "Okay, sure. The boys can drive my rental easy enough, but…" I stopped when considering the gun. But Pappy took my hand and firmly held the keys in my palm. I couldn't get the smile off my face and was forced to hold the Roadster's keys and to let my worries pass.

Even though he was old and wobbly, Pappy commanded the lead with ease.

I took it all in, but was disgusted with myself that I had allowed so much time to pass seeing his strong jawbone and high-cheek structure that had been inlaid with dozens of wrinkled lines over the decades. With eyes the unchanging marble-like translucent gray-green color, he had the rare ability in his gaze that would penetrate as you spoke, as if you were the only one in his presence that held the secret answers to the meaning of life.

Enjoying me as his newest companion, I was delighted to give him everything I could offer; there was no use in debating with the boys over the car. "Daniel, you can figure it out with the rental. We will follow you boys to a pub in town before we head home for dinner. How about a nice stout, poured like only an Irishman knows how?" It was obvious that he was used to setting the order of things without room for negotiation.

I acquiesced. "Sounds perfect," I said, with a pit in my heart thinking of the contents of the glove box.

He laughed as we headed toward the downslope. At the top of the incline, he paused. "Declan, if you don't mind, since you're taking Daniel's place today, I need you to hold my cane while I take your arm. It's rocky here and this cane isn't support enough. We'll be a team together, for as long as you stay next to me, how does that sound?" Pappy asked, his eyes filling with tears again.

"You and me from now on," I said, thinking I had so much to learn from him and so much time to catch up on. Wasted time no more, I'm finally where I belong. Pappy next to me, the Irish fields around me, Daniel's poetry in my heart, and Epona—only a night's train away.

I helped him down the incline surprised he was still very sturdy. I inhaled the smoky smell of his clothing and wished to always have its scent near. His arms were strong for a man his age and his back was straight, despite the fact he favored his right knee. Taking my right arm, he walked next to me, relying on my strength, as I absorbed his. Touching him intimately like this put my sentimental senses on overload. Somehow I kept my composure, walking with him slowly down the gravel road and back to his car. Opening the passenger door, with gentle care I helped him inside.

Daniel and I exchanged glances and he gave me a wink before heading to my rental. I thought to take him aside to warn him about the contents of the glove box, but didn't have the desire to interject my past into this scene. The pistol was wrapped, no one would think to touch it, I thought.

Walking around the back of the car, I tossed the Roadster's keys towards the sky and caught them. The afternoon sun peeked out of the clouds overhead, and its streaming beams of sunlight matched my mood. I thought of my mother. Was she sitting on my shoulder like a happy leprechaun? Perhaps she would protect my nephews from the gun, I thought. Imagining her there, I whispered, "Thank you. Thank you for leading me here, for bringing me home at last, please bring us all your protection today."

When I took a seat behind the wheel, Pappy smiled and gave my arm a jovial shove.

"Declan, I realize seeing Daniel and Sean must have you very confused about your sister. It's a long story and I will share it when the time is right. But for now, let's simply enjoy this moment and this beautiful weather. It's not often we can ride my lady with her top down in January. Are you okay with that?"

"Whatever you say, Pappy. I will follow your lead. I'm just happy to be here. I especially enjoyed watching you with your students. They love you very much, as do those two boys. Whatever the long story entails, I trust you used your good judgment." I started the engine, sinking low into the seat of his sports car as the boys waited for us to follow.

"Declan from across the sea," Pappy smiled, and shook his head. "Do you like thoroughbreds? I want to take you to Kane's thoroughbred stud farm while you are visiting." He paused. "Wait, you are missing something vital for the road." Leaning forward to pull out a key from under the floor mat, he opened the glove box and pulled out two hats. "Young man if you're going to drive my lady, you need the proper attire. These are genuine Hooligan driving caps. Do you prefer the gray-tweed with red piping or the solid dark green one?"

I laughed. "You're too much, Pappy. The dark green one, I think." I put it on and adjusted my new cap in the rearview mirror.

Sean shouted at us. "Will you two hurry yourselves up, come on."

Pappy waved him off. "That boy is so intelligent, only he's like one of Kane's untamed thoroughbreds. He needs to be harnessed or he will run wild, jump a fence, and hurt himself."

I let off the brake and coasted down the incline, following the boys. The breathtaking landscapes glided by and the wind whipped around us while the setting sun reflected in the rearview mirror. I was mesmerized being in his presence. "This Ireland of yours is more than anything I expected, Pappy. All I knew of it was from the picture you and Mammy had in your home in New York."

Pappy fixed his gray wool Hooligan and buttoned his sweater. "Ah, I remember that photograph well. It was taken before this road was even paved. I had it rolled up in my suitcase for years, then Axel took it, measured it precisely, and constructed an ornate mahogany wood frame for it." He was oblivious to the sensitive topic of my father. "Wonder what happened to it," he said.

"I have it still. It hangs on the wall in my home office. I never knew my father framed it though. You know, I searched acres and acres of Eastern Sierra Nevada mountain parcels of land to find a replica of it, of this very place. The Conway Summit region is a grand place too. That's where I built my ranch."

I could sense Pappy was delighted I had preserved the family heirloom. "Really? So now that you're here, how do you think your Conway Summit area compares to Northern County Tipperary? In my humble opinion, this is a beauty unparalleled."

"Unparalleled, indeed," I said, wishing he hadn't mentioned the name, Axel.

As if he read my mind he said his name once more. "Axel Hauser—that's a name I haven't spoken in decades."

I adjusted the hat once again. "I don't speak of him, ever. But none of that, as there's so much we need to catch up on," I said, and quickly returned to his benign question. "In truth, Conway Summit runs a close second to the beauty of Cashel. My whole life I stared at that picture, dreaming of coming to this place. It's incredible, beautiful, magical, and majestic, all wrapped in one, and definitely not at all black and white like the photograph. It's vibrant green in countless hues, and the gray clouds overhead, diminish the horizon just enough to matte the canvass, creating a romantic feel, like—like setting candles next to your lover's bed."

I could feel Pappy's eyes on me as I drove, but kept my focus on the road as he spoke. "You are aroused then by the landscape? Good, and you're a poet with that description. It's a shame you studied law. What a tragedy. When I heard that, my head almost spun off," he said, blurting out another hidden topic. "Don't be a stranger to this land from now on, Declan from America. Her love bed is here, waiting for you. This is your land as much as mine. You just took the wrong train home, that's all."

"The wrong train," I said.

I wasn't accustomed to parental advice but absorbed his nonetheless. "You belong here, not out west with the Nusco brothers. That blasted family held you as their prisoner all these decades," he said bitterly.

"A prisoner?" Surprised once more by his blatant comments, but knew he was baiting me, so I let it go for now.

"Yes. Do you see yourself in that mirror there?" He adjusted the rearview mirror so I could see my reflection. "That hat fits you in more ways than one. I promised this Roadster to Daniel one day, but it's yours for now if you want it," he said. "We'll leave topics like Axel Hauser, the damn Nuscos, and your law degree for the time being. Just like everything else. Best to turn the pages when the time is right."

"Hauser. The damn Nuscos—when the time is right," I said in agreement and wondered what exactly happened with my "boss" on his post war search for me.

He pulled a cigar out of the glove compartment, offered me one and lighted his, then continued to talk with it in his mouth. "Ah, time in Ireland has its own odd beat, son. You can't orchestrate time in Ireland, won't find a pendulum on this land that keeps time with the other. If you stick around long enough you'll learn that concept quick."

Just then we heard a shot. Daniel drove approximately thirty yards ahead. He pulled his car over to the left side of the road on a muddy edge next to the pavement. He jumped out of the car and ran around to Sean's side and opened the passenger door. By the time we approached them, the two boys were on the muddy roadside wrestling each other.

Then another shot went off.

CHAPTER TWENTY-FOUR

CALL ME UNCLE DECLAN

As fast as I could, I maneuvered Pappy's car to the left side of the road on a soft embankment, and parked directly behind the boys. "Please, Pappy! Stay in the car," I said, jumping out running to break them up from a fighting scramble. When I reached them, I held Sean down, grabbed the gun out of his grip as Daniel wrestled free.

"Is anyone hurt?" Pappy shouted slowly walking towards us.

"No, G-Pap. Sean was just trying his duck hunting skills that's all," Daniel said, brushing himself off. "What's wrong with him, that last shot almost tagged me!"

Pappy walked over to Sean, who was slowly getting to his feet, and took him by the collar. "How many times have I told you to never take my pistols out of the shed?"

"I didn't G-Pap. I swear," Sean said, wiping the mud off his trousers. "But look, I tagged one over there."

I steadied Pappy by taking his arm in mine. "This belongs to me. I am sorry," I said, and showed him my gun.

Pappy took his arm away from my hold. "There's a side of you I don't know, right Declan?"

I took the bullets out and put the pistol inside my jacket. Looking blank-eyed at the scene, watching Sean trying to catch his barking terrier as it fetched the dead partridge off the pavement, I stepped up to guide two cars around Sean, still in the middle of the road.

Daniel walked up and stood next to me sweating and angry. "G-Pap, are you sure we can trust this American?"

Pappy placed his hand on Daniel's shoulder. "Trust is like a mirror. Once its cracked, the reflection of it hurts only us—so move on now and don't judge."

Daniel gave me a stern look as he helped Pappy walk back to the car.

Sean put his dog back into the vehicle muddied and all, and tossed the kill in the trunk as if it were an everyday occurrence. I thanked God that the only issue to deal with was mud on the leather seats and a bloodied bird in my trunk and not anything dire. Pappy reluctantly allowed Daniel to help him with the uneven grass embankment as he slipped back into his car.

Wanting instead to climb into the trunk with Sean's catch, I slowly moved back to the car and resumed our drive. We followed along once more, listening to Jack barking at the sky with his head hanging out of the window, and proceeded down the road for three miles or so without any more conversation.

Just before we entered town, Daniel slowed the rental alongside us. "Are you okay G-Pap?"

He tipped his hat and grumbled, "Yes, we're fine."

"Is it okay if I pick up Chrissie and meet you at the pub?" Daniel called out, and then pulled away to turn down a side road without waiting for an answer. I watched as the boys disappeared down a tree-lined street with redwood, split rail fencing framing the properties looking again as if we were living inside a postcard.

"Straight ahead," Pappy said, in an uncompromising, yet solemn tone, tapping the steering wheel to get my full attention. "My family comes above all else, Declan, and I know very well that you try to hide much of your life from me—so you better tell me now if you're bringing mafia troubles with you. Shannon is doing fine, very well in fact, without any of your nonsense here."

I took a deep breath, respecting his stance on the issue completely. Knowing trust wasn't going to be easy to earn, I put my hand out to his tender, wrinkled one. "No nonsense of any kind. I bring only goodness and repair—that's a promise," I said, as we shook on it inside the tiny cabin of his sports car.

Marco will never penetrate this zone. Never, I thought with a lump in my throat.

He shrugged and held my hand firmly for longer than a general handshake. "Goodness and repair are reason enough, but why the surprise now?"

"Just long overdue that's all."

"That's the understatement of the century," he said, with suspicious eyes, releasing hold of my hand. "Pull over here. Best we fetch seats before the place fills up. I could use a drink."

I parked in front of Johnny R's Pub, sandwiched between a fabric shop and a tannery, in the middle of a quaint downtown, lined in cobblestone pavers in a circular roundabout with shops around its circumference. It was a classic spot with green signage and white wood lettering with a farm-styled, Dutch door, opened at the half point, inviting people inside, as the live music being played could be heard out onto the street.

"Pappy, remind me to come back to this tannery to have a leather belt embossed with the name Quinn on it," I said, helping him out of the car.

"I will, and get yourself a shoulder holster for that gun while you're at it. O'Farrell's Tannery makes fine leather saddles for just about every horse ranch in this valley. Declan, despite the fact your damn street pistol could have hurt one of those boys, your belt and holster will be gifts from me," he said, as I opened the bar door for him.

When we entered, a man stood behind the counter serving others. "Hey Professor!" he said, offering us a couple barstools as he gave Pappy an affectionate handshake. I looked around the place, absorbing the lively ambiance, and settled in watching the bartender finish the two-part method of settling a few stout beers. Once served, Pappy and I enjoyed the break, starting with quiet conversation underneath a hanging Irish flag and a set of rugby and football jerseys. Team banners decorated the room, hanging across the entire ceiling, as two young men in dark wool sweaters and hats sat in a corner improvising on fiddles with an older man in dressage tall boots singing along.

I decided to squeeze in some self-condemnation before Daniel and Sean showed up. "Pappy, I have no real reason for the gun or an explanation as to why it's taken me so long to get here. But I'm here today to get my family back, as I've let forces shackle and gag me until now. It's true. I have been living like a prisoner as you said, and a dark side consumed me. I thought a journey to this enchanted island was impossible." I rambled on as he listened intently. "It's a long complicated story, maybe even more so than the one you plan to tell me, but…"

"Declan," Pappy interrupted. "I know plenty about your long complicated story. I wanted to be face to face with you decades ago. The few letters you wrote only appeased my soul temporarily, but most of the time, I read them right next to my mailbox, crying, even in the driving rain."

"I too, read every one of your letters and cherished all your gifts," I said, still rambling knowing of his 'decades ago' failed trip to see me.

Pappy nodded. "But you bring darkness with you, even though you promised otherwise. I can see it. A street gun, and now you blame your so called prison guards for keeping you from writing me back, what—did they steal pen and paper from you as well?" he asked, standing up and set his hat on top of the bar. "Take responsibility damn it. It pains me to see a man who cannot stand on his own, let alone my own flesh and blood. No man must take a command from another. Declan, let me repeat, no man can be a real man under the thumb of another."

"He can." I stood to face him. "But it's not a happy man who lives under these conditions," I said, helping him back on a stool.

"Not a happy one, but a fearful one," he said, asking Johnny for another refill. "You said no mafia nonsense—okay, but you've been distant for so long, why? Is it due to a Goddamn mafia boss threatening to hold back your paycheck if your loyalties stray?"

I was stunned by his anger. "It wasn't about money, and I'm afraid of no man. You are wrong on that, and about the gun."

"Yes, the gun. What the hell Declan—time to make a choice—are you here on the rubrics of my planet or yours?"

I sat speechless, as justifying either choice to a master at truth would have been futile.

He waited another minute watching the stout, as if a settling beer clocked the timing of things like an hourglass. "This much I can tell you, Shannon won't be able to handle it if you choose the latter." He gulped half of the beer down like it was his first drink after being stranded in a desert, and then shrugged in disgust. "But let's just forget the issue for now," he said taking down more of the drink, sitting like total strangers in silence for ten more minutes.

After seemingly refreshed, he spoke again while Johnny placed a freshly poured glass next to the other. "I remember pushing you in a pram in Washington Square and around to all the librarians and my colleagues, was so proud when they said you looked more like my son than grandson. Then, when you started school, I adjusted my schedule to walk you to and from kindergarten, and the next year, from the first-grade—we wore matching vests, knickers, and hats that my tailor custom made for us."

"Of course I remember those clothes, my mother cried when I grew out of them after you left," I said.

He laughed. "Indeed, you must have grown out of those outfits the following year, and the hats too." The image I have of you wearing those clothes is how I think of you always. He picked up the Hooligan hat off the bar top and placed it back on my head. "Wear this one now, boy." Thankfully, he laughed and found his smile again. "Declan, I will go easy on you. You are good to come, no matter what history has passed or what darkness you bring along. Look at me. My wife and my daughter are gone, and I have lived with a heart full of empty spots for decades—until now. Tonight, it's overflowing, so let's not burden it with our flaws. I trust you had your reasons for staying away—reasons for bringing that…"

Not being able to hear him speak of the gun again, I interrupted. "It pains me that I've waited so long to see you." I took out a handkerchief as tears began to well in my eyes.

His eyes filled with tears when seeing mine. "Ah son, pain creates a void that only can be filled with love," he said motioning to the bartender. "So let's not waste any more time. Johnny, bring us a few shots of whiskey, we need your elixir to start the process of healing."

The tall and strong-bodied bartender put two short crystal cut tumblers in front of us. "Ah, the process of healing huh, let me know if you need any help with that Professor Q," he said, giving me a cautious look.

I stared back at him without flinching. "I am game, Pappy," I said, and gladly accepted the shot.

"Not so fast Declan from America. Of course before love can enter a void, a purging must happen," he said.

"Oh, a purging?" I asked still wiping my eyes, thinking of Andrew's thesis.

"Yes, time to till the soil a bit," he said, loose and eager.

"Ha, my son Andrew calls this process 'pulling thorns'.

"Good, he's right to say that—in his honor, let's start with a pruning then."

"I am ready. Shoot," I said, regretting my metaphor, wishing we could simply discuss Andrew's thesis project.

He jump-started our discussion with a passion. "I will start in. It was a shock to lose your mother. A tragic wickedness took her life. It haunts my nights thinking of her dying on a filthy New York tenement apartment floor. I can't forgive myself for not being there, for not protecting her. I left you abandoned, in poverty, thousands of miles away with a frozen ocean between us."

This wasn't the pruning I expected. "Please, let's save this topic for another time," I said, and put my drink down.

"No. I must tell you this face to face now, any attempt at this topic in our letters only frustrated me, so I ended it, and simply wrote to you about better things," he said.

"Yes, of poetry, of astronomy, of philosophy, of…" I could have gone on and pushed for more of his 'better things' topics, but he obviously wasn't in a mood for it.

He interrupted. "No, now I must speak of it. When her parish priest called telling me of her death, I contacted my colleagues at the university, and asked them to find out what happened. They talked to an Italian neighbor at the tenement building, a lady who gave them the whole sad story even though they barely could understand her."

"Ah, that would have been Signora Aimerito. She taught me how to speak that crazy Italian dialect of hers," I said, trying to lighten the mood.

"Declan, the story we heard was how you ran into the streets, angry, looking to kill your father for what he did. That night wouldn't have happened if I hadn't left your mother behind, pregnant and alone in the crazy jungle of New York," he said, pounding his fist on the table. "I was blinded from a rebels fervor, all for some blasted Civil War we're still fighting on this land. If I'd stayed, my Aisling would be alive today."

"You couldn't predict what would happen," I said, and took a deep breath, hearing his words, knowing exactly what fervor felt like. It was my own blindness he described. How could I argue with pitched strikes buzzing right by me. It was true. Had he stayed, my mother would be alive and my life would never have turned dark. I've always believed my life changed forever at the age of thirteen, but hearing him say this, the vital change happened when he left mother pregnant with Shannon, and me a six year old.

Nevertheless, I had to lift his spirits. "You did what you had to do," I said. "Mother always said she had to share you with her two brothers. But for what it's worth, I cried for months after you left, as you were like a father to me," I said, tearing up.

He smiled. "Yes, like a father, thank you. You're mother named you well, I suppose. At least she won that argument with your father."

"Oh, they argued over naming me Declan?" I asked.

"Oh, yes!" He bellowed for the whole bar to hear. "Axel despised me from that moment on. He wanted you to be named after his father in Germany. Otto, I think his name was. Then, to cap it off, seeing us together all the time really got under his skin. When we began to dress alike, it put him over the edge."

"Interesting." I said, remembering my parents fighting about this issue.

He shrugged. "Seeing the jealousy in his eyes should have been a red flag warning, as his bitterness grew from there and eventually consumed him."

"It wasn't pretty, I witnessed the whole downfall," I said.

"Not much of a childhood for you, right?" he asked.

I shrugged. "Right."

He continued, keen on telling his side of the story, shaking his head. "I'm so sorry about that, about everything. What could I do, as on top of dealing with the post war issues here, I got the call about your mother in 1933, and lost my mind," he said. "When you went missing, my former colleagues put a search team together to find you, ten students tried to help, looking all over the many blocks and buildings of the Lower East Side. They learned some Italians found you in the basement of a school building, sick with fever, and took you to a hospital. You nearly died. I'll never forgive myself for what you went through. Nor should you forgive me—I called the hospital everyday, but how could you have known that, being so sick and drugged up?"

He held up his empty pint glass to the bartender as I slid mine over to him as well.

I told Pappy details of the night my mother died, of my eye infection, and having to wear the constricting eye bandages, but had no words of comfort to offer. My own guilt was too heavy to help him with his. Then it was he who spoke of forgiveness—how did I ignore his calls? I thought. "Please, don't get upset about this now. I don't need to forgive you for anything. Please. I was just a screwed up, angry teenager."

"For good reason, son. But these words must be said." Pappy pointed to his chest. "They're embedded right here, on the crest of my heart. I have no energy to keep them inside anymore. I'm too old to allow life's pains to eat away the few good years I have left." He finished the drink. "Sorry for dropping all of this on you on your first day, guess that damn gunshot riled me up." He laughed. "Blame it on this damn brown barley juice as I'm rambling on about issues from the dark ages."

"Seems this juice works like a truth serum," I said, still trying to keep it light, but knew all too well he too had thorns to pull before peace could come.

He shrugged. "These are the sorrows of my heart, waiting to spill for decades. Your father was a stubborn German, too proud to come to Ireland, and I was too obstinate to stay. Everything would've been fine if one of us had given in."

Pappy paused, took another shot of whisky Johnny put in front of him, and continued. "That kindhearted Italian family in Brooklyn, who took the three of you in after Axel got thrown in jail, saved you. Your mother told me you worked two jobs to help support her and your sister." He pounded the wood bar top again. "You were just a boy taking on the role of being the man of the family, holding down two jobs at the tender ages from eight to thirteen years old."

"Ah, I liked the work, don't worry about that."

"I bet you did, son. Your mother wrote to me bragging about you all the time. Then, after she died, it was impossible to travel during the depression years, so knowing the Italian community helped you in 1928, I figured five years later, the Nusco family would do the same."

I was fascinated to hear his side of the story, so I let him continue.

"When the parish priest called to tell me of Shannon's adoption and the two of you getting separated…" He stopped and pounded the bar top once more. "God help me, Declan. All my students are full of praise for me. 'Oh Professor Quinn', they say, 'you are a wise and wonderful man'. But what kind of man leaves his family behind to struggle in poverty?" Pappy said, shooting down the rest of the whiskey.

Before I could think of anything to say, Sean and Daniel burst through the entrance with loud conversation and laughter as a pretty blonde held on to Daniel's hand. I regretted the intrusion, but seeing them safe and not hurt on the road put a smile on my face. That gun, I thought again, why did I bring that thing along.

Daniel shouted from the entrance. "G-Pap, we better put the rooftop up on your Roadster. It looks like rain's coming in. Throw me the keys, Uncle Declan. I'll take care of it."

I walked over to him and handed him the keys. "I'll help you."

"No, I got it, Uncle Declan. I'm used to it," he said.

"Uncle Declan," I said, walking back, echoing Daniel's greeting with a smile and sat back down. "The sound of that is sweet music."

"Eh, what's so special? You're their uncle and that's the proper way to address you," Pappy said. "I wish Shannon could join us here tonight. You'd be proud of her. She teaches music and works with the chamber chorus every Thursday and Friday at the Catholic University in Dublin. She comes in on the Friday night train. She met her husband, Paul, there in 1952, while she was earning her music degree. He's a professor as well. Before we knew it, she asked me to walk her up the aisle. Sean was born the next year, and then her beautiful daughter four years after that. They named her Aisling, too," Pappy said, as my heart nearly stopped.

He didn't know about the death of my daughter. I never had the nerve to write him about her accident. Shannon's daughter would be around ten—the same age as mine. Hum, no mention about Daniel being born though, as he's over twenty and must have been born in America. I let my thoughts go without questioning.

"Does my sister even know I'm alive?" I asked.

"It's complicated. I will tell Daniel and Sean not to tell her anything about your surprise visit if she calls them tonight. Best not to hear of it until she arrives, but will most likely pass out at the sight of you."

I tried to speak, but he waved me quiet. Sitting curled over his drink, my heart went out to him. "It's good you've come, to set the story right," he said, dabbing his eyes.

"The story?"

"Yes, there's always a story attached to our lives, Declan. We neither can control the telling of it nor the timing of things, anymore than we can control the tides—you're late in coming, but I'll take the crumbs," he said, glancing over at my nephews with the pretty young girl. "Maybe we should go keep an eye on them before they create a story that needs a diaper."

I laughed and nodded in agreement. Together we grabbed our beers to join them at the tables near the musicians playing, only staying for another half an hour enjoying the band, until we headed back to the cottage.

CHAPTER TWENTY-FIVE

BUTTER ON A DINNER ROLL

It was dark on the drive home, so I was grateful to simply take directions from Pappy. When we passed the local grocery market, I offered to prepare us dinner. "Oh, that's the same place I went in for our lunch items this morning. Let me stop to get some meat for sauce and I can fix us a spaghetti dinner. Or perhaps you'd like a nice grilled steak tonight, Pappy?"

He smiled and shook his head no. "Son, you're in for a treat once we get home. The nice ladies from across the lane cook up a dinner to feed an army."

"Really. Okay, I will do dinner tomorrow when Shannon gets in."

"That's a deal. Remind me to show you a historical marker on this road in the daylight. The site shows when President John F. Kennedy graced us with a visit back in June of 1963. Our whole family came out to see your president's limousine drive through this route on his way to Galway. I quoted him in the Tipperary Historical Journal when he spoke at Eyre Square on June 29th. 'If the day was clear enough and your vision good enough and you looked west, you would see Boston, Massachusetts. And if you did, you would see down working on the docks, there's some Dougherty's, Flaherty's, and Ryan's, and some cousins of yours who have gone to Boston and made good,'" he quoted Kennedy word for word. "How I wish your grandmother had still been alive to see that day. Your president's visit was a golden gift to all of us here in Ireland. I was happy to report on it. I sent you the article, hope you saved it," Pappy said, smiling at me.

"I've saved everything you've ever sent me. Your letters are all in a wooden embossed box an American Indian tribesman made for me, and the John F. Kennedy article is framed on the wall of my office. I was so proud to see your name in the byline."

"So was I to write it. It's a shame what happened to him," Pappy said. "A loss felt around the globe."

When we arrived at the cottage, I helped him out of the car and together we walked up to the front door. "I've got to have Sean cover these winter flowers before the frost kills them, my bones tell me a moist frozen air is on the way," he said, holding my arm and opened the door.

I felt this day was a dream as I entered the cottage with him latched to my arm. We inhaled amazing aromas of roasted lamb, rosemary, and mashed potatoes, as two ladies were over setting the same table I used to make our lunch earlier.

"Declan, meet the Marion sisters from across the lane. Francis and Helen fix us dinner every Wednesday evening when Shannon and Paul are at the university," Pappy said.

Frances and Helen watched us enter and continued to work in the kitchen full of energy. Helen gave me a smile as she had Sean follow her to fetch pans and plates full of meats and breads, while Frances fussed in the kitchen over a counter already filled with enough food to feed the rebel army for weeks. I looked at the variety before us with amazement.

"Frances, let me present to you my long lost grandson, Declan Quinn the Fourth. He is Aisling's oldest child. Miss Marion's husband's great-great-grandfather and my great-grandfather worked this land together. She and I traced the history of this land from the 14th Century. The Quinn's and the Marion's have gravestones here dating back nearly three hundred years," he said.

Frances was glad to get into the story of the old land. "It was our duty to trace the ancestors and to pass our heritage on to our children. We didn't fight those lousy English all those years for nothing," she said, wiping her hands with a towel then throwing it back on her shoulder. "Sorry if I sound bitter, but our youngest son, who's around your age, was just an infant when his father died in a fire set by the Black and Tans in 1921. David was hiding ammunition in the basement at the factory in town. They knew he was in there and set the whole building ablaze, the dirty cowards. He loved to tell the stories of growing up with your mother before they all left for the States in 1910," she said.

"Ah yes, your mother was a horsewoman like no other, they used to take the horses to jump the creeks and race until they'd come home all muddied," Pappy said.

"Indeed Professor, and now the earth has taken them both, David in bloodshed in the Isle, and dear Aisling in the jungle of New York. Oh my, the soil is unforgiving at times," she said, and wiped her tears with a napkin.

"I'm sorry about your husband," I said, taking her hand. "Thank you for mentioning my mother. It's refreshing to hear you speak of her as a child."

"I'd be happy to share more stories with you over tea anytime, son. I sit with Shannon all the time speaking of those days." She handed me a plate of boiled spiced apples to carry out. "My sons, Aaron and Mike are like uncles to her boys, they teach them so much about fishing and hunting," she said. "I'll have them drop by to meet you."

Pappy sat in his seat at the head of the century's old table, now covered in a white-laced cloth, and insisted we wait to eat until Helen and Sean returned. When they walked in carrying bowls and platters, somehow squeezing it all on the table, they took to their seats. The two Marion sisters sat next to me, while Daniel and Sean sat across from us the on a bench seat. I was beginning to recognize the routine in this home, and realized that I was quickly becoming a part of it.

"Now, who would like to say the blessing?" Pappy asked.

"I will," Daniel said, then clasped his hands together and bowed his head. "May this food restore our strength, giving new energy to tired limbs and new thoughts to weary minds. May this drink restore our souls, giving new vision to dry spirits and new warmth to cold hearts. And once nourished and refreshed, may we give thanks to He, who gives us all and makes us blessed." He looked up with a grin and grabbed the plate of mashed potatoes.

Sean added a few comments. "And thank you Uncle Declan for coming so far to be with us today. It's great to meet an uncle we never knew about."

Daniel interrupted and shrugged. "Ah, you're just happy he has brightened G-Pap's spirits. He isn't so hard on you with him here."

"Which means you better keep in line," Pappy said, winking at me. "Hey, come to think of it, Uncle Declan, you're here just in time to help. Sean needs to do algebra practice problems before classes start again next week. He hates doing those, but he must finish a few word problems after dinner. Don't forget, in the morning, someone has to fix up the barn early before your mum's inspection."

Sean shrugged, but was too busy eating to argue. Daniel passed me the potatoes and grabbed another dish. I was grateful he hadn't held any grudges on me from the roadside.

"I'd love to help. I miss doing homework with my son, Frankie. He's vacationing with his mother in the Pennsylvania ski resorts," I said. "He's fifteen, close to the same age as you, Sean. Boys, you'll get to meet Andrew, my oldest in June. He graduates soon and is going to County Donegal on a pilgrimage, then coming to meet you all after his tour."

"Great. So, two sons, any girls?" Sean asked.

"Yes, twins," Pappy said, with great enthusiasm. "They must be what, ten years old now?"

I nearly choked on the food in my mouth.

"One's named Aisling just like your sister, boys." Pappy looked at me again. "Our little Aisling goes to school at the Saint Attracta's National School in Dublin. I can't wait for you to meet her. Tomorrow will be a day full of surprises. Frances and Helen, you're going to hear screaming from across the lane. Declan hasn't seen his sister Shannon since 1933. Boys, when Uncle Declan last saw her, she was younger than your sister is now. But remember, it's important to keep this a surprise, so please keep your mouths shut when your mother calls tonight."

"Of course, G-Pap. We won't say a word." Daniel put a lump of butter on a warm, flaky dinner roll. "Where in California are you from?"

I managed to swallow and answer. "In Northern California, on a farm not too different from this one, the only difference in the landscape is the majestic Sierra Nevada Mountains in the background; they peak at over 12,000 feet. My farm is located at the foot of them," I said, missing home a bit.

"So G-Pap, how come you never told us about Uncle Declan before?" Sean asked.

Pappy's smile turned to a frown. "It's complicated. Boys, trust me—there were good reasons I have kept this information from you."

Daniel spoke to Frances under his breath, giving me a cold stare again. "Our American relatives, this one right here, abandoned us."

Pappy tapped his fork onto the side of his water glass. "Daniel, our neighbors don't need to hear about our intimate family dramas. Besides, that's between your mother and Uncle Declan."

A long moment of uncomfortable silence followed.

"Declan, perhaps you should bring out your wife and kids for a visit after their vacation, seems they're already halfway here if they're in Pennsylvania," Pappy said.

I nodded, withstanding the fact tickets were bought already, his idea fit perfectly.

Daniel added to the conversation, confused. "A Pennsylvania ski resort? You said the 12,000-foot Sierra Nevada Mountains are in your back yard. Don't they have ample ski runs?" he asked, serving himself more potatoes. "Been studying United States geography throughout my life, it's great Theodore Roosevelt set aside land to preserve it for your National Parks. The way you Americans do things, you'd probably put skyscrapers smack in the middle of Yosemite," he said, clueless to the fact that Marco just showed me architectural plans to infiltrate the southern Cascade regions to do just that.

"True point. With peaks that high, why did they travel all that way to go skiing?" Pappy asked.

"Yeah, if I had ranges like that at my fingertips, I wouldn't be getting on a plane to go skiing," Daniel said.

"Well…" I said, and changed the subject. "Boys you have cousins your age. So Pappy, what do you think, a Quinn family reunion is in order I feel?"

Pappy was delighted. "The sound of that is music to my ears," he said, adding butter to one of the dinner rolls.

One of the ladies clapped her hands together. "Oh, what a wonderful idea. Declan, when your family visits, you and your family can have my house to yourself. My sister and I will move into the cottage in the back and cook for all of you."

Excited over the whole concept and to get my family safe, I put this idea in motion. "Could we make this happen, next week even?" I paused, not wanting to sound over ambitious.

"I don't see why not. I love the idea. In fact, I want you to arrange it as soon as possible. There are grandchildren out there I haven't met, such a travesty. I will pay for the tickets, no argument, and forget worrying about the kids missing school. I will tutor them myself." Pappy stood up and pulled a large chalkboard out from behind the refrigerator. "Tell your Uncle Declan boys, your G-Pap is a tutor like no other."

Sean stood up and carried his plate to the sink and grabbed one more roll. "Sure G-Pap, you are a tutor like no other, that's for sure, but let's not chase my new cousins off this island before I get to know them better."

CHAPTER TWENTY-SIX

BLACK HOLES IN THE SKY

After finishing dinner and cleaning up, we gathered at the table again. Frances Marion served the warm spiced apples with fresh whipped cream. Sean took off, as Helen made us coffee and tea. When my nephew returned with his math assignment, I flipped through his textbook and readied to help.

"So Uncle Declan, can you really help me with these word problems? I'd love to see the shock on my mother's face when I show her they're all done," he said.

"You've come to the right place, son. Have a seat," I said, giving Pappy a wink.

Pappy and Daniel eased over to the living room joking how they should leave the two of us alone. As Sean and I went over the practice problems, I was happy to be familiar with level of algebra required, but realized he needed little, if any help. He worked out the problem while I sat back considering placing a call to my wife. After a while, the two women emerged from the kitchen to say good night.

"Daniel, please see the ladies home," Pappy said. When they started to protest the need, he wagged a finger. "You never know what critters are out this late."

Daniel rolled his eyes at me as he escorted them out the door, and I got the impression this same argument occurs every Wednesday night.

Minutes later, I saw Pappy trying to wobble his way to a chair without the aid of his cane. "Damn it," he said, coming to a stop in the middle of the room, clearly frustrated. "Can one of you please fetch me my stick over there? I forgot it again."

I got up from the table and fetched the cane for him.

"Daniel might be a while across the street, so come sit with me, and please supply the fire. The temperature outside has dropped tonight; my bones tell me rain is on its way. The wood is just outside this door."

"Sure." I looked to Sean. "Let me know if you need any more help."

He nodded and smiled, and then went back to working. Pappy followed me outside to the woodpile, watching as I filled my arms. "Don't worry about that boy, Declan, he's plenty smart enough to do his own homework, just needed you to get him started. All he needs is to apply himself the way you did at that age," he said, glancing over to Sean. "Your uncle here held down two jobs when he was younger than you, survived the streets of New York on his own from age thirteen on."

I shrugged trying to disregard his comments.

He continued as Sean looked at me with interest. "Let's look at the facts. He was on his own without parents at your age, graduated high school the highest in his class, finished college magna cum laude after serving two years in the war, earned a Silver Star for his service, and then obtained a law degree," he said, walking over to his seat pointing his cane at me. "Now he tends to legal needs of a major crime family in Nevada, not many could handle that kind of pressure."

His final complements almost knocked me into the woodpile, the last thing I wanted to talk about was my career as a mafia lawyer, and so I simply ignored him and set the wood inside.

Before I could interject to change the subject, Pappy pressed on grumbling. "Declan, you see this knee, this wobbly joint of shattered bone?"

"Yes, what happened?"

"It's been like this for twenty years. Wish I could say it was due to a moment of misjudgment during some pleasurable risk-taking adventure, like when I used to run my quarter horse, Max, along the River Suir. Then I could tell you a hair-raising story of how he threw me into the river rock. But sadly, my tale isn't a pleasant one, no it's far more sordid."

"Oh," I said, adding starter twigs to the fire.

He paused to grab his pipe and tobacco tin. "I was beaten by a pair of thugs and left for dead. It happened in the spring, 1946—near your home on Ocean Parkway in fact."

I was afraid he might say that, knowing what Judy told me, but I had to hear it from him nonetheless. "Someone at the Nusco house did this to you?"

He raised his hand for me to stop. "Patience, son, let me tell the story in my own way."

I waited with angst, as he took time to tamp tobacco into his pipe. He lighted it, took a few puffs, and then pointed the pipe at me to emphasize his next words. "I waited and waited for that bloody war to end so I could come get my grandchildren once and for all. Two times on that trip I attempted to find you."

I got the fire going and walked closer to Pappy as he continued with his story. He talked with the pipe in his mouth as the scented aromas filled the room. "Regrettably, there was to be no Declan for me that year. I knew you were living in that big white, brick house on the corner with a black iron gate keeping everyone out, but was told to go away or get shot."

"All they had to do was to tell you I was up at Fordham," I said, clearly agitated.

He shook off my comment and wouldn't allow me time to talk. "On my second try over there, two thugs threw me into a car and beat me raw, dumped me on a coastal road, and left me for dead. I ended up lying next to the Atlantic Ocean on the beach like a dead whale, ice cold and bloodied. Lucky the police found me at sunrise and took me to the hospital, shivering, and could barely speak."

"What—left for dead? I've heard enough and promise whoever hurt you will be punished," I said, trying to keep composure as my heart pounded out of my chest, but with Sean working an earshot away, this was no place for an outburst.

"Punished, how? Please don't come here with your mafia tough guy bullshit." He stood up and tapped his pipe into my chest. "Declan, do you want justice or do you want peace?"

"I believe peace follows justice," I said, staring into his eyes with fuming anger at who did this to him.

"It can, son, but rarely. More often the price of justice is too high, and brings no peace."

Pappy grabbed my arms tightly with his strong grip. "What happened to me wasn't your fault. You were caught in the crossfire as was I."

I succumbed to his touch and felt powerless to argue with the truth of his statements. "Pappy, I…"

"Come sit down and listen," he said. "Let me finish. I've never been the type to mince words, and I don't plan to go easy on you. I'm sure you can take the heat, right?"

I sat feeling the blaze of the fire on my back, my gaze fixed on him.

"For everything there is a season, and tonight isn't the time to review twenty years of history, not to mention, your talk of revenge is senseless. So right now, with you here right in front of me after decades of absence, I'd prefer us talk about the emptiness you bring," he said, shocking me. "Tell me about that and show me some real toughness, son."

Not having the stamina to hold his stare, I turned to look at the fire. "Tonight is a night of happiness, though. Let's leave all our flaws…"

He stopped me. "Please face me, Declan. Please. You can't hide it from me anymore. As soon as I mentioned the Nuscos—your eyes turned as empty as black holes in the sky."

"How can you see my emptiness?"

"Your eyes. They confess your sorrows and losses. I know those eyes, Declan," he said with his captivating Irish brogue. "I can read them like the poems of the sages."

"My greenies?"

His face crinkled into a thousand deep lines as he smiled. "Ah, you remember that song your mother and I sang to you when you were a boy. I taught it to her when she was a young girl. 'Oh the green grasses of Ireland dance in your eyes—your eyes, please no cries, no cries, not in my baby's greenie eyes, because the green grasses of Ireland dance in your eyes—oh, the green grasses of Ireland dance in your eyes.'"

It took all my strength to keep from succumbing to full emotional breakdown hearing him sing their lullaby in the tender Irish accent I loved. "I remember it well," I said, as he inhaled more scented tobacco. I heard Sean humming the tune as he worked his math problems.

Pappy smiled. "Your surprise visit is a dream come true, but you've come so sudden for a reason, yes?"

"To get my family back, I told you, and to see the green grasses of Ireland for myself."

As if I were his star witness on the stand, he questioned me further. "But why now, unannounced? There's more to it, what is it?"

I shrugged. "Please forgive me, I'll tell you the long complicated story after you tell me who hurt your knee. Again, I promise whoever hurt you will be punished."

"Declan, sometimes no response is a response—and it's why poetry is written, art is sculpted, and ballads and operas performed. They are all that's left to do the job of the lamentations of our souls. The biographies of our favorite artists and authors often reveal checkered paths full of turmoil, suicide, and heartbreak, and even revenge—but little peace. Without that sense of injustice we'd have empty libraries and museums."

I began to massage my fingers, thinking I hated poetry after all.

"Wringing your hands together won't help. You say you want justice, justice now. I prefer to leave it to the universe to decide what is just. It seems to do a fair job of it without my help," Pappy said. "The problem with Americans is that they have no patience. You want everything now, rushing ahead with your rose-colored vision of the future." He paused. "Look at me son, I don't have a daughter today as I believed that type of ideology once."

I shrugged. I don't have a daughter today, as I believed that type of ideology once too, I thought, repeating his words in my mind. Aisling is gone today having paid the price of my ideology of seeking justice—he was right completely, but I argued the matter nonetheless. "Someone has to step up when the universe doesn't. What would the world look like without Americans jumping into the fight?"

"Ah, no argument there. You were part of that fight as well. Americans saved Europe—perhaps the world." He threw his hands up in disgust. "But now, they march on again, trying to sell the war in Vietnam using a lame theory of dominos, sure let's use young Americans to stop the Communist takeover. I don't buy it…"

"Maybe, but someone has to put an end to its spread on a mere humanitarian level," I said.

"Seeking and rushing to justice more often than not causes more harm, more dead sons and daughters," he said.

"Yes, saw many of my fellow troops killed right in front of me in the cause for good and for justice in France," I said.

"Yes, you did. Is that the cause of the emptiness I see?" he asked.

"There are many causes for it," I said. "The main cause is why I'm here. Now. To reconnect with you and Shannon," I said. "You didn't realize this, but that picture you sent me last year triggered much sorrow in me."

"Oh? In your letter you said how much you loved it, I thought you should have it instead of storing it away in the attic," he said.

I smiled. "Indeed. We loved it, but the scene behind that drawing was full of sadness for me."

"Oh, I see. I left you and your mother a few years before she sent it. No doubt those years were difficult for you both," he said, and listened intently.

"I have many sleepless nights staring at that picture, missing her, missing you, and missing Shannon—and remembering the night she sketched it…"

He interrupted. "So at least I can say, the picture served us well in getting you here, it was one of my favorite pieces she sketched, as you looked so valiant, so brave, ready to take on all the evil in the world."

I listened, but shrugged. "Yes, a brave boy who stood over the drunken body of his father," I said, and considered telling him how

Andrew was using the picture for his thesis presentation, but decided to wait, as I needed to stay focused and on topic.

He stood and walked over to a shelf full of books and papers, swaying in front of a huge selection, thumbing though scrapbooks full of newspaper cutouts and pictures. "Oh, it kills me to think of what you went through after I left," he said, skimming through the books. Finding what he wanted, smiling with a sheet of parchment paper to his chest, he added, "If that picture of you as a boy conjured memories of sadness, would you like to see another picture your mother drew of you during a very happy time?"

Delighted I said, "Absolutely, I do."

As he grimaced in pain moving toward me, coddling the paper like a priceless treasure, I wished to find out who mugged him. Anthony would know, I thought.

"What do you have there, Pappy?" I asked.

Then he showed me the most amazing piece of artwork I had ever seen. "This sketching your mother drew in my office at NYU, must have taken her an entire semester to get our faces right." He laughed through tears as I gazed at it stunned, as if he presented me a rare artifact in an archeological dig. The image was another charcoal sketching, but this one was of Pappy and me, drawn with the mediums of a harmonious collection of pastel colors of tans, pinks, and browns. Dressed in matching outfits, we wore brown knickers, white shirts, blue vests, brown striped ties, and brown Hooligan hats, as we sported rosy-cheeked smiles full of bliss.

"Why is this hiding in a scrapbook, may I have it please? I'd like to frame it and display it for all to see," I said, with tears welling in my eyes.

He cried along with me. "Let's take it into town, have it copied and framed as a memento of those times we had together," he said, standing the photo up against the crystal goblet on the buffet table.

"Great," I said, watching him grimace from his knee, adjusting himself as best as he could to get comfortable in the chair again, forcing me to move pass the nostalgia and to press him further on the injury. "And now I see you suffering—your knee Pappy. One last time, I beg you to give me the truth of who did this to you."

He got comfortable and continued to enjoy his pipe tobacco. "You say you want the truth from me. How about yours? What are your truths, Declan? Come on, you're not that darling little boy anymore." He fixed the picture of us upright, but sneered at me. "Are you ready to be a man who can reveal his truths to me? How many lies have you told? How many promises have you broken? You can't pass through a void inside you until you take a hard look at your deep holes first. Look here," he said, as he searched through a classic selection of pipes carved in various wood types, handing me a cherry colored one out of his collection. "Your father promised me he would bring you and your mother to Ireland after Shannon was born. That pipe in your palm was carved out of a fine block of solid mahogany straight from Germany, hand-made by your father. Axel gave it to me the day he asked me for your mother's hand in marriage."

I was quickly learning that the more I tried to avoid a topic in this man's presence, the more it came to the surface. Gripping the pipe, I tempted to throw it into the fire and to end the issue of my father for good.

Nevertheless, he eyed me once more, and I knew the truth I tried to hide about my father was too heavy to hold any longer.

CHAPTER TWENTY-SEVEN

AISLING'S CODE

The elephant in the room had exposed itself.

"You heard he hung himself in his jail cell?" I asked.

"I did. A sad ending for a bitter man who chose to drown his talents in the drink." Pappy shook his head and walked over to the small bar table with a cut crystal decanter holding dark liquor I couldn't identify.

I walked over and stood next to him. "Let me help you," I said, taking his arm to help him back to the chair.

He waved me away sipping his drink. "I've been managing just fine without your help for too many years to count. Declan Quinn the Fourth from America, fix yourself a drink, but please, don't treat me like an invalid." He put the drink aside and set to walk over to the other end of the room. "Let's leave any talk of your father for a moment, as I want to give you something I wrote years ago for your mother, she's the one who can help you fill that emptiness I see. Now, just stay here while I get it."

Taking his cane, he wobbled over to the overflowing bookshelves lining the far wall. He looked back at me with eyes narrowing, telling me that he didn't want any help again. He stepped up three rungs on a rickety wooden ladder at a snail's pace and reached over his head to fetch a dark brown colored, leather-bound book from the top shelf. I watched him dust off its cover, flip inside its pages, and then descend the ladder gingerly, as my heart fell onto my lap. Finding the floor, he managed to make his way back to sit in the chair next to me without falling, using his sweater sleeve to finish dusting the cover. "Declan, I've been wanting to send this journal to you for a long time, but held back, because deep in my heart, I knew one day you'd come here and I would give it to you in person," he said, handing it to me. "Read the title on the first page."

I opened the book and was surprised to read, *Aisling's Code.*

Sounding like a classic storyteller, he began to tell his side of grief. "Those words came to me on a cold winter's night in February of 1933. As not long after your mother's death, I heard a voice from heaven—it was the voice of my angel. I wrote down every word and it saved me, perhaps reading these words now will save you as well."

"I don't understand," I said, flipping through more pages.

"Patience, Declan," he said, returning to his seat. "After receiving that terrible call from her parish priest, all I could do was to walk the floors of this very room as your grandmother cried the nights away upstairs in her bed. Night after night, I would try to grapple with our daughter's death. I was filled with hate and despair. Like you, I wanted justice and demanded to know the truth. I heard what happened, and justice was eventually served, but I found no peace. Aisling's Code came out of that pain. It was as if she shook me and said, 'Do life right, do it for me, because I can't.' Her Code tells us how to live in her honor. We owe her that."

"You really believe she spoke to you?" I asked.

"Oh yes. Your mother's spirit is a strong and persistent one. She had something to say, and my pen was the conduit. Once her words were written down, I felt at peace again though confess I do not always succeed at it, we are frail human beings after all. Son, this can be a guideline to move you out of the emptiness you carry. I'd like you to read it. Out loud, please."

"All right." I respectfully stood to face him, removing my hat. Out of the corner of my eye, I saw Sean put down his pencil and leaned back to listen.

"Aisling's Code." I cleared my throat.

"Live each day with purpose and meaning.
Concentrate on the positive—even when life gets you down.
Never hold back when speaking the truth.

Shoot for the stars.

Always act with honor and refuse to fill your heart with hate.

Remember to be your genuine self—and if there's a song in your heart, sing.

Never take those you love and who love you for granted.

Be strong, but lead with the heart.

Seek peace and understanding in conflict.

Practice the art of forgiveness, especially toward yourself.

Know that life itself, and each breath we take, are gifts to treasure.

Be happy, even when life gets you down.

Thank God for each and every day."

Pappy stood with cupped hands around his mouth like a megaphone. "Let it known that a message from Heaven has been passed down to new ears. Take your mother's words to heart. Share what you know and practice Aisling's Code in everything you do. When truth speaks, there is no denying it."

I walked over and thanked him. "This here is proof of the spirit. I'd like to copy it."

"That journal is yours to keep. The rest of it contains my poems along with excerpts from my favorite poets. I want you to have it, and there's plenty of blank pages inside for your own lamentations of the heart," he said, as I flipped through the pages in awe.

I caressed the leather cover as if it was a long lost sunken treasure, looking once more at the meticulous handwriting on the pages. "You're right—this Code can save me. My hope is that living by these words will bring me out of the emptiness you see."

"Never take those you love and who love you for granted." See, you've followed the Code already in coming home," Pappy said.

My eyes began to well with tears once more. "Yes, home," I said, as I placed my finger on the page next to line five of the Code and read it another time, as it convinced me the essence of her spirit was here—here with us. "Don't fill your heart with hate," I said the same words she whispered to me in the cemetery, again feeling taken aback by words on the page. "Pappy, my mother's voice is real, she speaks to me often, these lines are proof of it, it's she who called me here. She spoke the exact same words to me a few days ago in New York, at the cemetery. I thought perhaps I was hearing things, or worse yet, losing my mind, but now reading her Code, I see it all in plain sight."

He bellowed. "Indeed, you're not mad, believe it, as you can see—her spirit has a lot to say."

I admired him for many reasons, but it was the brightness of his eyes that was so appealing. "Pappy, you have a sparkle in your eyes that I admire. How can I follow her Code and be rid of the hate in my heart once and for all—to get that light back like I see in your eyes and heart?"

He smiled. "It's doable, and now you have a cheat sheet in your grasp. You've got the Code now, son. It won't be easy. I fail often, but we can strive for it—together now." He placed an encouraging arm over my shoulder. "Declan, it's time you snuff out all the hate and be the light you want to see."

I listened, feeling I could be with him for the rest of my days and not learn everything he had to teach me.

He added more twigs to rekindle the fire. "One Christmas, several years ago, Shannon and the kids surprised me with Aisling's Code framed with a picture of your mother when she was a young girl. It hangs on the wall in my bedroom."

"A picture of my mother?" I asked, immediately curious, since I had never seen one of her as a child.

Placing his arm around my shoulder again, he smiled. "Yes, come let me show it to you and give you a tour of my little cottage," he said, and then hesitated. "But before it gets too late, I know you have questions about Shannon. As you know, she's coming in on tomorrow's evening train."

"Yes, tomorrow."

He laughed. "Hah, Declan, here's an American metaphor just for you: It's best we cover all our bases on that issue tonight before she arrives."

I smiled. "I've already hit a home run reconnecting with you and meeting my nephews, and now reading her Code. When I see

Shannon, it will be a grand slam for sure—she'll bring it all home for me."

He laughed, but his eyes looked worried. "I hope so, Declan, for both your sakes." Pappy fished in his drawer for a pen and paper. "Here, I want you to pen a note to your wife for me, tell her about the reunion being planned."

This is where he must have penned the many letters to me, I thought. "Were the Marion sisters serious?"

"Oh, they meant it, my boys stay at their place when they're in from Galway. Please son, write to Sofia now. Don't hesitate to take everything they offer. They'll probably insist you stay the entire spring in their home. Change your citizenship while you're at it, or at least apply for a dual citizenry."

I threw my arms up. "Whoa, slow down, Pappy. I think we might be getting a little ahead of ourselves."

"Ah, maybe so, maybe so, but I'm serious, son. I knew you belonged here the first moment you put that green driving cap on your head."

"Thank you," I said, straightening the cap again. "Being here is like a dream come true for me and the idea of moving here permanently is appealing, but truth is, I haven't come close to living up to Aisling's Code. It's as foreign to me as if it was written in French," I said, hesitating and wondered if I should tell him how I had bought tickets for Sofia already, or how I'm on the run from Marco, or how badly I need to find a new life. No, not yet, I thought.

As usual, he missed nothing. "What is it, Declan? I can tell you're holding something back from me," he said, making me feel transparent. He sat, emptying the burnt tobacco into a small tin box. "Remember, I'm trained to read between the lines, tell me what's on your mind, son."

"You say I need to speak of my emptiness before I can pass through it, right?"

He nodded. "I believe that very much, yes."

"Well, I might not be suited to be reunited with my sister after all, as I'm not the man you think I am," I said. "Yes, I'm my mother's son, your namesake, the boy who wore the same knickers as you, but a darkness overcame me after my mother died. That Code tells me I'm moons away from the boy she knew, moons away from being the type of brother Shannon needs, and moons away from being a good role model for my nephews, it's why I let Shannon go in the first place years ago—as I, I…" I said, stumbling over the words.

He listened.

I couldn't tell him the real reason I abandoned her. "Ah, let's just forget it, perhaps this emptiness has prevailed in me so long I can never get back home," I said, tossing twigs into the fire.

"One can come home, only when they're willing to face the crux of their problems, then the door is always open. Declan, the emptiness I see began as you said, when your mother died, and rightfully so—but you turned a corner and never came back to us—to yourself, for that matter, and you let bitterness win. You weren't born to be that person. It's time to be a real man who is able to discipline his desires to make the achievement of good possible. You see, too often in life, one gets consumed with the ways of the world, be it materialism, greed, vanity, lust, sin, or ego, and yes—even vengefulness. These things can intercept messages from the sages and can alter our life's journey all together."

I sipped a glass of the sweet fruity brandy, and then warmed it with the candle on top of the table. My father's mahogany pipe was still there, so I picked it up again, and noticed how soft and smooth its cherry colored wood felt under my fingers. "I changed when my father…" I stopped, and set the pipe down again.

Pappy picked it up. "Yes, seeing evil like you did as a boy had to change you, it did me as well, for a long time I sat full of anger and hate, thinking how could he have taken the most precious gem from us?"

"He was a bitter, angry drunk," I said.

Pappy didn't comment, but continued to stare at the pipe. "You want to know something about Axel Hauser?" he asked.

I shrugged.

"He never drank when I first met him and was a master at wood carving—go visit the library at NYU sometime, you'll see his mastery woodcraft there."

I began to feel ill. "Toss that blasted thing into the fire, please."

Pappy sighed. "I won't do that—kept it this long for a reason, as a reminder. You were too young to know this, but I wanted to loan him money to start a furniture shop and clock business right here in Fethard. Of course he refused from too much pride."

"I've always wondered if that story was true. Mother used to talk about that all the time," I said.

He nodded. "It's true, all of it unfortunately," he said, handing me the pipe again. "Go on—try using it. Fill it with some of my fine rum flavored tobacco blends over there."

My hands were shaking. "I'm having difficulty even holding it."

"Spoken like a man with a guilty conscience. What is it? There's something you need to tell me about your father, isn't there?"

I shrugged. "Can't talk about it yet, sorry, especially now, given what you've just told me." I put the pipe down next to the decanter and returned to my seat by the fire. "Just let me enjoy being here with you. What about that tour of your cottage you were going to give me?"

Pappy exhaled fresh smoke thoughtfully and looked toward Sean at the kitchen table. He gave the boy a look, and my nephew closed his book, left the kitchen, and walked outside.

"There now, no more barriers. Declan, you're a grown man and I'm an old one, which means it's time you put your childish fears to rest and not waste any more time of mine. I will speak honestly to you, and I insist on getting the truth from you in return. Admit it. You purposely ignored my calls and letters after your mother died. You were set on avenging her death. You set out to kill your father yourself, but are afraid to tell me this. You think I don't know the urban myth told of his hanging was in large part—tale. You believe I would think ill of you because truth lay within the story. Had I been there, what do you think I would have done? You better believe I would have tried to kill him myself. How can I blame you for wanting to do something I wanted to do as well."

"You're just saying that. You're not a violent man. You're a poet, a professor."

"So you think I have no capacity for revenge? Believe me, Declan, I can hate as much as anyone else. I'll never forget the look on Axel's face the day your grandmother and I left for Ireland. He was so happy to be rid of us with never an intention to come here, as the competition for our daughter and grandson's affections were too great for him to bear," he said. "I was never so glad as the day I learned he was dead. I'm only sorry it was by his own hands, and not mine."

"Pappy, you're no killer. You are a decent man."

"Declan, did you read the sign over the front door of my cottage?"

"A sign. No, I didn't notice," I said, confused.

"It's written in bold letters: NO COWARDS ALLOWED. You must understand, that brave men run in our family, so you may as well climb on board. I'm no coward and neither are you, but I can tell you're afraid to be honest with me and I want to know why."

CHAPTER TWENTY-EIGHT

CLARITY IN THE CHAOS

His comments hit me like a fist to my stomach, giving me an instant need to swallow. As my shames rose, I could see this man standing before me knew the truth; he just wanted me to substantiate the facts.

"The story you heard of my father's death is an urban myth you say. If you want the truth, I will tell you about my father," I said. I told him how when I couldn't kill him myself, I contracted with the Nusco mafia family to do it for me. I explained the whole story, starting with ignoring his phone calls at the hospital to letting Shannon depart on the orphan bus without me. I said how my father's fate was set when Signore Nusco's men on the inside were ordered to rough him up and of how he hung himself from fear a few days later.

He listened without a comment and stared at the smoke rising from his pipe, as if there was a message written between the vapors. "I see. No wonder you didn't answer my calls or want to ever speak of this with me." Pappy frowned and looked away. "Well, dead is dead. He was doomed by his own sins, whether at your hands or mine, or someone else's—or from the bottle. He was good with a wood carver's tool and could have made something of himself, instead he wasted his God-given talent, and made others suffer for it."

He picked up the pipe my father carved and filled it to the brim with some of his juicy tobacco, and then handed it back to me. "Smoke this damn thing and keep it as a reminder not to waste your talents like he did."

Pappy watched as I lighted the pipe.

"Aisling's Code says, never hold back when speaking the truth. So now that you've heard it, what do you think of me now?"

He contemplated my question seriously. "You were put in a tough place for a boy so young, and then hooked up with the Nusco family who killed men for sport," he said. "A boy makes a decision as a boy would and suffers the consequences later. However, I believe even though when a truth is a painful reflection of ourselves, it still needs to come out in the open, or deception persists—to the point where we deceive ourselves in the end."

"I've lived like this for decades," I said, with my head low.

He listened without comment, provoking me to continue.

Then as if the force of entropy worked in reverse, creating a force to build up as opposed to breaking down, I had to speak against the primary source of my darkness, lay it out on the table and into the tobacco scented air around me, with hopes a new light could gain access to the dark holes of my being. "There's one more truth I haven't mentioned to you," I said, as my heart pounded hard inside my chest.

"What is it, son? Please."

I began to speak, but fumbled over my words. "It's wonderful you sense my mother's spirit. Indeed, I too believe she is caring for us from the heavens, so then, maybe—maybe my Aisling is not alone, maybe…" I cleared my throat. "You see something terrible happened last year at my ranch, there was an—accident—my daughter, Aisling—we lost her." I couldn't go on and cried into my hands.

Pappy stood up abruptly, his face lost all color as if he had just seen a ghost and started wobbling again on his cane. I could sense he was glaring at me. "Holy Mary in heaven, how did this happen?"

When I found my voice again, I told him how I found her drowned in our icy pond, dug her free, and why my hands have never been the same, nor my heart. "It happened a year ago. I've been trying to quit the Nusco family ever since." I took another deep swallow of my brandy, hoping its warmth would burn away my guilt.

He threw short twigs into the fire one by one. "Damn it all, Declan. If only you'd broken free of the fucking Nusco's and come to Ireland decades ago." He began to pace the floor and took off his cap. "This is very difficult for me to hear. I'm sorry, first my Aisling, now yours? Our innocent children paid for the crimes of their fathers," he said, walking grief-stricken with short steps back to his chair.

I choked on my brandy and dropped my father's pipe on the wood plank floor after hearing his comments, gathering enough strength to speak. "Yes, I believe that as well. Her death was punishment for me, for neglecting my family. I aligned with the Nuscos and turned away from everything real and true in my life, from Shannon years ago—and from you. It started with my father's killing, and I've been turning away ever since. My innocent child paid the price for all of this, it's a guilt so great, even the universe can't fix." I paced the room. "But I can't live like this anymore."

He listened. "It's a wonder you made it sane this far, shoving down all your pains and truths, like solid rocks into your belly."

I nodded. "Pappy, you're a wise man, beloved by your family and your students. You suffered so much, but somehow found a way to survive it all. Tell me how to get out of this hellhole I'm living in."

"Through hard work, Declan," he said, reaching over to take my hand into his stronger one. "The first step is to take full responsibility for your actions, face the truth of it, then vow—as if your life depended on it—to change your life for the better. The way I see it, you're halfway there, son."

I shook my head with frustration. "Halfway there. I hope you're right, but I haven't figured out the second half yet. I want to be done with all the killings, the crime, but I'm on the run from Marco as we speak."

He let go of my hand, stood up once more. "On the run—a Quinn—on the fucking run? Running makes you a coward of the worst kind, Declan."

"I am not a coward."

"You're better off killing Marco than running from him." He walked away and picked up my father's pipe from the floor. "I suppose this explains the gun and why you are in such a rush to send for Sofia and the children. You're afraid he'll use them against you."

"It would be hard for him to find them at her parents; they're in Pennsylvania remember."

"So it wasn't a ski trip after all."

"Right. They're there because Marco recently attempted to kidnap my ten year old daughter."

"What? Little Patti? When did this happen?" he asked.

"Last week, don't worry, I took care of it before I left," I said, thankful to Andrew, Anthony, and Frank.

"This boss you have is more vicious than I thought—kidnapping a child!" He tapped his cane onto the edge of the stone fireplace. "So, you're not the coward, but a mouse in a maze looking for a way out, but you only keep bumping into walls and dead ends." He paused. "Fuck the Don of West and get out."

"Exactly, been working on that."

"Moving to Ireland can bring you new life—it's not too late to come home, son," he said. "That bastard will never find you here, nor would he even try."

"Please Pappy, understand this—please, as it's important to me that you know this—I didn't come here just to escape. I came for Shannon—and for you. My issue with Marco and my desire to reconnect with you and Shannon are like two different plays using the same stage."

"But with the same protagonist," Pappy said. "This is quite the epic journey, but in proper mythology, the hero must confront his nemesis. You must stop running. You are Declan Quinn the Fourth. You come from brave Irish blood. Face him, tell him you're done being his legal counsel."

I stood up. "I have faced him. I've done all of that, got into it with him in New York when he came looking for me, practically broke his nose…"

He interrupted. "You owe them for the help they gave you with your father, don't you?"

I stood up to face him. "Yes, been indebted to them ever since. Been outnumbered and outgunned and have had to speak the language of the tribe—or else."

He nodded and listened, once more provoking me to continue.

I shrugged. "I'm a lawyer, not a hit man. Respectfully, you don't understand that no one defies the Don. He wants total control, uses manipulative ploys, and won't let go until I comply. As you can see, he makes my family live in fear."

Pappy enjoyed his brandy and I watched his eyes squint as he seemingly began crafting a scheme. "I see. Then I suppose that must be the final scene in your melodrama. You simply need to die. I will send him a telegram saying you were stampeded by a herd of wayward sheep," he said, with a wry grin.

I scowled at him. "Why are you making light of this?"

"Light? I'm serious." Pappy said. "You don't have to confront the bastard, or run, you just have to outsmart him."

I wandered around the room and gave a quick look at his walled bookshelves. "He's not going to fall for a made up story. Not for long at least."

"Damn it all Declan. We'll write him a story he can't refute," he said, taking out a pen from his pocket. "Let me repeat. You should have broken the hold that Goddamn family had on you and come to Ireland decades ago. Who says some small minded goon can't be fooled?"

"Says me, from long experience dealing with him."

He walked over and we stood like prizefighters readying to spar with each other. "Then you truly don't know who you're talking to. Son, I am a conductor of words. I tell stories for a living, stories so good my audience thinks they're real life. It's easy. Come up with a tall tale, son. Let's have some fun with your mafia friends and give them the ulcers for a change." He shrugged. "I don't like this hold they seem to have over you."

The idea of trying to convince Marco I was already dead and out of his reach was appealing, but didn't feel like a real possibility. "I don't see how fiction would work," I said, staring back at him, waiting for his counterpunch.

"Maybe it won't, but it's worth a try, don't you think? Show me your backbone, son. Prove to me you can stand on the mound burning-in fastballs," Pappy said, laughing. "Together, we'll pitch a curveball so well, your greasy mobster brother will strikeout looking straight at it. That's my Irish storyteller guarantee," he said, with the devil in his eyes.

I laughed. "You catch on pretty quick to using baseball metaphors, Pappy. I think it's a crazy idea, honestly, but I'll give it some thought."

"And you will think quickly, as you have me worried about your family in America."

I walked away again and guided him to his chair once more. "Well, you're right on that, it won't take him long to hunt them down," I said, but knew my father-in-law was familiar with protecting himself from the mob since the early days of the century. It was why he had a house in the country in the first place with guards of his own.

Pappy sat down and rolled up his sleeves. "Yes, we must start this right away then," he said, taking out a pen and a small journal in his pocket. "We could make it dramatic. Come on Declan, let's craft a scheme and fool that gang of thugs in the west. They're not shrewder than the Quinns of County Tipperary."

I had to chuckle seeing the excitement on his face at the prospect of fooling Marco, as I held onto Aisling's Code and poetry journal in my hand. "Does this journal or mother's Code hold any wisdom for a grieving father?" I asked flipping the pages.

"What words of wisdom can one give a man in that amount of pain?" he asked thoughtfully. "Sometimes son, there are no words, just tears." Pappy got up again and wobbled over to the fireplace to add another log. It's difficult for him, but he managed it without my help. "Remember, Declan, you're talking to a man who knows exactly how it feels to lose a daughter, an Aisling—a perfect soul. There are no words, just tears, son. The River Suir flows with your Irish ancestors' tears." He turned to look at me. "Have you cried for your loss, Declan—or aren't gangsters allowed to cry?"

"It doesn't lessen the pain," I said.

"No, it just helps you live with it." He looked up at a clock on the wall. "Ah, look at the time, here I'm adding more logs to our fire and it's already late. Daniel prepared the guest room upstairs for you," he said, walking back to his chair. "But there's more we need to discuss."

"Agreed." I was ready for more insights than to think about sleep, was done discussing gangsters and crumbled knees, or schemes to fool Marco, but still needed to hear about my sister. "I worry my visit has exhausted you—you were getting to Shannon's story, remember?" I asked.

Looking as if he'd be prepared to sleep right where he sat, he suggested, "Maybe we should wait to finish that in the morning. It's been a very long day for you, with all your travels and revelations."

I was frustrated we ran out of time. "I don't sleep well anyway, and this will prey on my mind until I get some answers, but I suppose we can sleep on it…"

He interrupted. "Buried topics are difficult to bring to the light, your sister's tale is full of mystery, her story is a sad one indeed," he said, handing me his empty brandy tumbler, suggesting he wanted to continue.

I walked over to his counter and set the glass down without refilling it and returned to my seat next to him.

Pappy's voice was tiring as he continued with a soft whisper. "I met that nice family in Brooklyn when I came looking for you after the war. Signore Attanasio and his cousin did everything they could to help me contact you at that fortress on Ocean Parkway. The Nuscos told him to put me on a plane back to Ireland. However, as you might guess, I answer to no one. So instead of returning home, as ordered by your mafia Don, I went to the Foundling Hospital the next day to get information on Shannon. That's when I visited the cemetery to set your mother's memorial and to set her headstone."

"Yes, I saw it—you carved that yourself? It's beautiful."

"Whose Name Was Writ In Song. Fitting, don't you think?"

"Very much so. But I don't understand why you kept it a secret from me. You never told me anything about your visit, the headstone, or finding Shannon. Why, Pappy? I need to know why?"

He closed his eyes. "When something is painful to tell, and the telling will serve no good, then there is no point in telling it."

I shook my head. "I'm not buying that. You said this is a place for truth."

He opened his eyes slowly. "Ah, that it is. Then, I must tell you this story exactly as I remember."

I readied myself for the telling.

"The morning I went to the Foundling Hospital, I shared a taxi with a young beauty from the Attanasio family, a cousin of theirs. It was a blissful ride on a clear spring morning, shared with a beautiful opera singer going off to an audition on Broadway. Sweet girl—I don't recall her name though," he said, scratching his forehead, perking up a bit.

"Judy," I said, with pain.

"Ah, that's right. Judy. Indeed. I often wondered what became of her. Do you know if she ever got to see her name in lights on Broadway?" he asked.

"She did," I said, with a sinking heart. "But we can get to that story later. Shannon's story—please."

"All right," he sighed, and continued. "I met with a Sister Mary Kate, or something like that, at the Foundling Hospital, who told me Shannon was adopted by the O'Scanlon family in Buffalo, New York. I boarded a train north that very day out of Penn Station, and in two days time, found the O'Scanlon's home. To my relief, the father turned out to be a good Irish-Catholic man, who loved Shannon very much. He was recently widowed and owned a mercantile outlet with his sons in the center of town. When I gave him the adoption file, he knew I was legitimate. He told me Shannon lived in a small rural town about thirty miles west—close to the Niagara Falls," he said, and paused. "Declan, I need to warn you. What I found wasn't good."

"Just tell me, Pappy. Don't try to spare my feelings."

He continued. "Shannon was already widowed, only twenty-years old, and left alone to raise a young child. Her husband, a Specialist in the US Army, was killed in action. George Avery was his name. He never got to see his son, as she was pregnant with

Daniel when he left to go overseas. When I got there in 1946, Shannon was alone with Daniel. It was like seeing Aisling and you all over again. There was no way I could leave her there. It would have been like abandoning another daughter of mine."

"What about her father in Buffalo?" I asked, confused.

"Yes, Charlie O'Scanlon, a respectable man as I said. He visits here with Shannon every other year or so. He was very concerned about her. He said she spent month after month indoors, refusing to take his help or to let her brothers tend to the ranch they owned. The day I arrived, he drove me to Shannon's home. The ranch was falling apart. Daniel was well loved, but Shannon was in no condition to care for him. The pair of them looked like pale loners. For a long time, she couldn't seem to grasp who I was. We visited for a few days, and went to see Shannon's husband's memorial at a beautiful little cemetery nearby."

I had so many questions to ask, but let him continue.

"He was an Army Specialist Rank Four, it said on his headstone. Shannon talked about George and the life they had planned before the Second World War broke out. His dream was to become a Master Sergeant and she wanted to be a music teacher. That damn war destroyed their hopes to build a life together. As it was, she tried to take care of the ranch and taught riding lessons the best that she could."

"Ah, a horsewoman, of course," I said, thinking of my own daughter.

"Yes. Other than Daniel, it was the one good thing in her life, but she was a single mother of a one-year old, destitute, with a 125-acre horse ranch to manage. Her father suggested she sell the ranch and move back home with him. She said no, she couldn't ever live in a big city again. That's when I told her I had a house for her in the wide-open hills of Ireland. I described how green it was here, wild and open so she could ride horses and raise her son. It was all here waiting for her. All she needed to do was say yes," he said, shaking his head.

I wondered, had he found me on this trip, he would have offered me to move to Ireland with him as well. "Fethard, you wanted us to both move there with you, didn't you?" I asked as gently as I could, knowing how my mother used to tell me of his dreams of building all of us homes on the Fethard farm.

He shrugged. "Truth is, yes. I brought blueprints to show you, ones I designed myself—they consisted of duplicate structures for both you and your sister to build homes on the prime corner of this parcel, right here where you sit tonight." He looked away with a defeated look and glanced over at the buffet table with the brandy decanter.

I got up to pour him another shot.

He took the drink and stared into the dark liquid without lifting it to his mouth, as if he were reading the brandy droplets like tealeaves. "Some dreams never become actualized in this life, we step in the mud and muck them up time and time again I'm afraid."

"Well, I'm the one who mucked up your dream. But what about Shannon's side of it, how did you actualize that?" I asked.

He smiled and sipped the brandy. "It was a perfect fit, and the timing was from divine providence. You see the O'Scanlons emigrated from Galway in 1861. Her adoptive father was excited at the prospect and encouraged Shannon to accept my offer. I caught her when she was searching for an answer, so after a few days of work, she agreed when I told her you might build a house next door to hers. Charlie even bought a ticket to come along for the journey. He wanted to help her settle in here and to see his aging parents in Galway. It was a good plan, but it didn't work out too well at the start," Pappy said, giving me back the drink, and asked me to fetch him a tall glass of water from the kitchen.

I walked over and returned with two glasses for us. Handing him his glass I said, "I still don't understand why you never told me any of this."

"You were never told because Shannon had deep psychological issues. Declan, I regret to tell you, but her problems stem far beyond the grief of losing a husband, a mother, and a brother at a young age," he said. "At the time, I thought it best to not burden you."

I frowned, but decided not to press him until I heard the rest of the story. "Okay. Keep going—please."

"Remember, Declan, I was also on a mission to find you."

"Please tell me that Shannon wasn't with you when you got your knee busted," I said.

"No, you think I'm crazy?" Pappy asked, annoyed. "Shannon was very apprehensive about traveling to New York City and very protective of young Daniel. They stayed at the hotel with her father, while I took a taxi out to Brooklyn to find you. That was the night I became a cripple—and those beautiful blueprints are probably still laying on the beach." He pounded his cane on the floor. "Goddamn, I worked so hard on those just for you. Not to mention, we had a glorious tour of Manhattan planned, but those damn thugs ruined it for us."

Trying to rush the story, I pressed on with the questioning. "How'd you get back to Manhattan?" I asked, thinking of who could have been the thugs who did this.

He continued. "When the police found me left for dead, I asked them to take me to the hospital nearest to the hotel. I ended up at Bellevue," he said, nonchalantly.

I stood up and began to pace the room again. "Oh no! Not fucking Bellevue!" I said, and removed the hat on my head.

Pappy kept on with his story. "I wanted to be close by, so Shannon and her father wouldn't have to come far to see me. I didn't think it would be a problem. The next morning, when I heard a woman screaming down the hall, it didn't occur to me that it was Shannon."

I continued to pace the room. "Pappy, that's where our mother died," I said, feeling nauseous.

His eyes opened wide. "Ah, I didn't realize." He paused to remember more facts. "At the time, Shannon couldn't explain her terror. She still doesn't remember anything about your mother's death. When she and her father walked into the hospital, Shannon panicked. I'll never forget the look of terror in her eyes. She wrapped herself and Daniel in a blanket, huddled in the corner of my room, and wouldn't let anyone get close. Her father and I didn't know where her fear was coming from. He had to restrain her so the nurses could give her oxygen as she was blacking out. We had to give her smelling salts to snap her out of it.

"Oh my God," I said, shaking my head some more.

He took a sip of water. "I hated America at that moment. Its golden promises were all a farce. My Aisling was dead, you were trapped in a mob war, Shannon was certifiably crazy, and those bastards had made me a cripple for life." He pounded his fist on the arm of his chair and shouted the last few words loud enough to shake the whole room. "This damned knee kept me from riding in the fields and dancing with your Mammy. Every day it reminds me how that mob family stole my health and my own flesh and blood from me!"

Thankfully, we had the house to ourselves, as I sat down in the seat next to him again. "I know this is hard for you." I urged him as gently as I could and struggled with patience to hear the rest.

He looked grim, but nodded and continued. "The nurses administered her some pills with difficulty, but once the drug took effect, they convinced Shannon to at least take-in some oxygen. It was awful. She never settled down completely, so I ordered the doctor to release me." He closed his eyes again. "She never let go of Daniel the whole time there. We left the hospital together, with my broken knee untreated."

"I'm so sorry, Pappy. There's so much you don't know. Belleview was an awful place for Shannon and me the night our mother passed away. We were there alone for a long time before Father Carmen picked us up."

"And I invited her back to relive the memory of that trauma," he said, shaking his head as he put his hand over his eyes.

"You didn't know, you couldn't have known," I said.

"I wanted it to be a surprise, to have you see the plans, and to help me place the headstone at the cemetery. I was curious—no, truth to be told—I was suspicious of the Nusco family who adopted you, with their name splattered all over the New York Times," he said.

"Bellevue, Bellevue," I said, mumbling and shaking my head.

He tapped on my shoulder until I raised my head up. "Declan, fuck Bellevue. You didn't order those thugs to beat me. Your mother didn't die because of you, and you're not the cause of Shannon's mental illness. Stop blaming yourself. Stop blaming yourself for your daughter's accident, too. Life deals us blows with no explanation. It's up to us to keep up the good fight in this blasted world. Yes?" he asked, still trying to get me to raise my head.

"Yes, Pappy, but my first sin planted the seed to all of this…" I paused and began to cry. "Had I not abandoned my sister, this would have never happened to you."

"Stop. Just seek clarity now, despite the chaos."

I took a sleeve and wiped my eyes dry. "Clarity in the chaos—is it possible? If so, I must fight to find the light somewhere."

"Good, it starts with the light—first find it inside your core son. Find it soon Declan, as this fight's not over. You need to know that Shannon's been troubled ever since she moved here, and may never truly be well. She has no real understanding of what caused her to have that emotional breakdown."

I tried to consume everything he was saying. I was so looking forward to seeing her again, but realized she may not want to see me. I had no idea how to deal with mental illness. Still, there are things from her past that Pappy didn't know—things he needed to hear so clarity could come to the chaos.

I took a deep breath in preparation of the telling. "Pappy, I think I can explain why Shannon had that breakdown at the hospital, but we're going to need some coffee first."

CHAPTER TWENTY-NINE

A SEAFARER ON THE CELTIC SEA

By the time I returned to the living room with a fresh pot of coffee, Pappy was slouched, chin down in his chair with the pipe on his lap about to burn a hole in his gray trousers.

Assuming he was asleep, I tried to take the pipe without waking him. To my surprise, he jumped up out of his seat shouting deliriously. "Declan, why has it taken you so long to come visit me? Why all this pain—why this fucking knee? Bellevue? Why is life so messy? The damn English taking our land, making us battle for our homes, burning them down, killing our boys? Why Declan? Tell this old man why God had to take my sweet Aisling and let her die on a dirty tenement floor, why? Tell me why you had to pull your child out of the frozen ice? A child of all things—take me instead Lord."

He grabbed my arms for support, sobbing. I held him for a moment, and then walked him to his bedchamber. The room was crowded with books and papers covering the dressers, with over-stacked bookshelves lining the walls. One of the windows was opened a crack, letting a breeze in, causing papers to be blown onto the floor. His solid oak bed was adorned with layers of bedding with a green and gold patchwork quilt similar in style to the ones on his chair in the living room. Helping him get his sweater off, I watched as he slowly unbuttoned his shirt and took off his vest. I dimmed the light, as he slipped on his nightshirt and crawled into bed.

"Don't get old, Declan," he told me. "You have too much life to reflect on when you're old. Do your housecleaning now son, or the voices of the past will haunt you in your old age. Sleep becomes a horror when death is near. I feel it coming. Can you sit with me tonight? It's been too many years that we have been apart."

Of course," I said, as he crawled under the covers.

"Best close that window, storms coming in," he said, as his eyes closed.

I walked over to the window and closed it completely, then took a seat in a cozy leather covered armchair next to his bed. Watching him breathe, and reviewing the day's events, my own eyelids grew heavy. Before I knew it, morning was seeping in through the sheer white-laced cotton window coverings, and my spine and neck were stiff from falling asleep in Pappy's small bedroom chair. The early morning light softly illuminated a picture on the wall.

Is that the photo of my mother that Pappy mentioned last night? I wondered.

Trying not to wake him, I tiptoed over for a closer look. Thankfully, the wood plank floor was covered with fluffy woolen rugs and my steps were muffled. In the dim light, I had to lean close to see the picture clearly. It was of a little girl sitting on a spotted, white pony. She couldn't have been older than ten when the picture was taken. She had the same hair Shannon did as a child, and similar to my own daughter. Her face looked soft, bright, and innocent. The photographer painted it with sepia tones and a soft rose tint on her cheeks. Her hair was splashed a pale gold with curls that bounced like a cascading waterfall down her back. Just a girl, but I recognized her. Lit in the soft morning sunshine, she radiated joyfulness and hope, just as she did in life. Next to the photo, Pappy's Aisling's Code was wood-framed and scripted in a Gaelic style scroll on parchment paper, giving it an ancient artifact appearance.

It was so perfect. I was almost tempted to steal it, but shook my head that I even considered such an idea. This belonged to Pappy. She was my mother, but his daughter—and he loved her first. I remembered what Nick Russo told me about Judy, and wondered how was sweet Judy doing. Nick loved Judy before me and Pappy loved my mother from the first moment of her birth as well—I was simply the lucky beneficiary of their love.

Sneaking out of his room, I closed the door quietly as the embers in the fireplace were completely cooled from last night, leaving the room icy cold. I sat down on the sofa and wrapped one of the quilts around me to guard against the chill, debating whether I should go start some coffee or try to get a few more winks in the feather bed upstairs I was promised earlier.

The next thing I knew, I was being prodded to wake up as I slept on the sofa in front of the fireplace. "Did you stay up all night listening to G-Pap's stories? It looks as though you never made your way upstairs, Uncle Declan," Sean asked.

I sat upright and rubbed the sleep from my eyes. "This is Friday, right? I get to meet your mother tonight."

Sean laughed at me. "Did you think you slept the day away?"

I smiled embarrassed and started folding up the blanket. "Can you give me one word to describe your mother for me?"

He thought for a moment. "Hum, one word. How about three? She's strong, she's feisty, and she's gentle—all at the same time," Sean said with a smile, reminding me of the delightful Irish accents again. "She's also the best horse woman in all of County Tipperary."

I smiled at his bright and youthful mind. "I can't wait to see her. Perhaps we can go together to the train station and meet her tonight."

"Sounds good to me." Sean said. "Where's Pappy? He's usually up by now."

"We stayed up very late last night. Why don't you go check up on him to make sure he's okay?"

Sean returned shortly. "Snoring peacefully. We should just let him sleep. Daniel's out front warming up the truck to go into town. He promised to take me fishing this weekend and I need bait. Want to come along?"

Still feeling overwhelmed from last night's deep conversations, a tiny vertigo returned as I masked it with a smile. "Would you mind going without me? I'd like to wait here for G-Pap to wake up."

When the boys left, I grabbed my bag that was still sitting next to the front door and went upstairs to find the dormer room I neglected to sleep in last night. The bed Daniel made up for me looked inviting, but I felt the need to take a shower. After I dressed in fresh clothes and quickly brushed my teeth, I decided to lie down for just a minute. Instead, I fell asleep. When I woke and headed downstairs, the boys were back and Pappy was sitting at the kitchen table eating a sandwich.

"Declan, I'm glad you found your bed upstairs. I trust you took liberty and took a shower, too," Pappy said.

"Indeed. Made myself at home in County Tipperary," I said, refreshed.

"Good for you. I want you to feel at home here. Even though you've showed up at the bottom of the ninth inning, you are family nonetheless—remember that, okay," he said with a triumphant smirk.

I laughed. "Thanks, Pappy, seems the next thing we need to do is play a nice round of baseball with the boys. I'm happy you seem to be none the worse for wear," I said, relieved to see him awake and bright-eyed. "I was a bit worried about you last night. Did we overdo our storytelling session?"

He smiled with his eyes so bright once more. "No, Declan, these bones have travelled rockier roads than last night. But thank you for sitting up with me. I get morose like that occasionally. Perhaps I miss my sweet Laura more than I let on these days. She was quite the woman, my Laura—talk about a voice from heaven son, any time she sang, "How Great Thou Art," the world just stopped for me. Pappy turned to the boys. "Boys, have you taken care of your chores? Your mother gets home tonight and it's already past noon."

Daniel popped into the kitchen. "All done, except Sean has to finish with curry, dandy, and soft brushing Frey's Eclipse. You know he won't listen to me, so you have to be the one to tell him to clean her hooves. He walked her all over the muddy path this morning and never remembers to check the hooves, then mum yells at me for it."

I was delighted to just watch the order of things in Pappy's home and smiled. "I'll come help with the horses after I have some coffee with your G-Pap and enjoy some more of that delicious bread from last night." I winked at Daniel, as he smiled and went outside. Sitting at the kitchen table with Pappy, drinking coffee, munching on breakfast bread and some hardboiled eggs, I felt as if someone needed to pinch me again to prove this setting was real.

Reluctant to disturb the peace of this moment, I knew far too well that we had more to discuss. "Pappy, we never finished talking last night," I said, trying to ease into the details.

"True. I nodded off, and then you had to help me to bed. That's the trouble with getting this old. You never know when sleep will grab you. Son, did you tell me last night that Bellevue Hospital was the place where your mother was taken the night she died?" he asked. His eyed pierced into mine.

"Yes. What happened in that place wasn't good. Perhaps Shannon was too young to remember, or maybe it's such a painful memory she put up a mental block. I think…" I stopped.

"Go on," Pappy said, listening with all ears.

"We need to talk straight. You see, I know walking back into Bellevue Hospital, with the scent of death and illness, triggered her into having that breakdown you described."

He sat, sipping more coffee and thought about my memory. "Probably so. I feel terrible for asking them to meet me there. We had such a nice city tour planned. She and her father were looking forward to attending an opera and seeing the symphony halls of Manhattan. We even planned to see some Broadway shows together with you and bring Daniel to the top of the Empire State Building," Pappy said. "Obviously none of that happened. So what can you tell me of that night at Bellevue with your mother? I, for one, have a hard time thinking about what could have happened there."

I put my food aside and took a sip of coffee. "It brings up a lot in me—makes me ill really. So Pappy, please bear with me if I struggle in telling you what happened," I said, staring into his eyes.

Pappy took my hand. "The parish priest told me some of it, but that was a thousand moons ago."

"I will tell you everything—can't forget any of it, no matter how hard I've tried over the years. Father Carmen and Sister Mary Catherine tried to help, but they got there far past midnight and didn't see what happened to us."

He got comfortable and listened. "Yes. Of course, I need to know everything."

I got up to refill my coffee. "Okay, please let me tell it the best I can," I said, slowly returning to my seat. "Did you know I was the one who found my mother? She was on the floor, unconscious, bleeding. Shannon was sitting next to her sobbing…" I proceeded to retell the entire, horrific story. "Shannon's breakdown with you, Pappy—relived that night all over again."

"The horror and the trauma of that are at the root of all her paranoia." He stood, walked to the sink to splash his face with cold water. "You can help her now, Declan. She needs you, your strength and indeed, your clear memory."

"Pappy, I lie awake nights hearing Shannon's screams from that night—from the nurses who…" I had to stop, thinking of the needle they poked her with—and of the straps on the bed that tied her down. And even though it pained him to hear the story, he listened, asking only the necessary questions, allowing me to move through this dark night, with him at my side and my mother's spirit in my heart.

Don't fill your heart with hate, no matter what this world will take, our love must not be disgraced. Her whispers sang inside me as the hatred and pain evaporated like magic.

Oblivious to her presence, Pappy sat at the table and reached over, covering my clasped hands with his aged ones. "Trauma carves memories into our minds like a sculptor's chisel, making sure we never forget. I see more tears coming to you now. Such tragedy hit you both. Declan, don't forget, you were just a child as well. You have every right to mourn for this boy inside of you."

I squeezed his hands over mine then wiped the tears from my face.

"Rehashing this night is difficult for you," Pappy said. "But you show me a love for your sister that is very deep and selfless. And, most importantly, it explains everything to me about her phobias. In my day, giving birth at home was commonplace, but most people of your generation choose a hospital. Not Shannon. She gave birth to Sean and little Aisling right here in this cottage, with only the help of a mid-wife. To this day, she refuses to take her children to doctors in town and we have to summon a private nurse to make a house call when one of them comes up ill. Thankfully, the births had no complications and my grandchildren are all healthy."

"I see," I said.

He smiled. "I remember the day little Aisling was born here, just like your mother. We came full circle that day."

Delighted hearing the history, I smiled. "Are you saying that my mother was born in this house? Now that's poetic, Pappy," I said, hoping it was going to be a beautiful day from here on in.

"Ah, yes, poetry at its finest. That it is, Declan, at least now the mystery is uncovered. We've always wondered why Shannon fears hospitals, and now you've shed light on it, no—better yet, you've shed love on it."

Shedding light and love instead of darkness and hate was appealing to me. "I hope to help her through this trauma, to tie the loose ends in her mind. I will be her memory, her strength. But, I still don't understand why you didn't tell Shannon about me. Or better yet, why you didn't tell me about her."

He crossed his arms. "More loose ends. They need to be tied up," he said and continued. "That morning at Bellevue, the hospital threatened to commit Shannon into a mental institution if we couldn't calm her down. We didn't want that, of course, as those places were worse than prisons in those days. So we took her back to our hotel immediately. Shannon held onto Daniel all night. Her father and I didn't know how to handle the situation. She spoke gibberish about how we couldn't let the nurses take her son and begged us to return to Buffalo that night."

"So what did you do?" I asked.

"It was quite a scene. Me, an invalid, and mere stranger to them, trying to save my young granddaughter and great-grandson, while her adoptive father was steaming mad, threatening to punch me for bringing them to New York in the first place. Thankfully, George finally thought to call his mother. Apparently, she was familiar with my column for the Dublin newspaper and with my work at the university as well. She had the ability to calm Shannon down when these panic attacks happened, as seemingly it wasn't the first time. Shannon's adoptive grandmother talked sternly to her and was adamant that she not return to the depressed, Buffalo farm." He pause and smiled. "And, by the grace of God, Shannon listened. By the time the phone call ended, Shannon stopped hyperventilating and agreed to get on the plane to Ireland in the morning," he said, sighing and sipping a cup of coffee.

"Has Shannon ever talked to you about her breakdown?" I asked.

"No. She never has, refuses to. We don't bring it up."

"What about me? Has she ever asked about…"

"Yes," he sighed, cutting me off with evident reluctance. "I wasn't going to mention this to you, Declan, but we've opened Pandora's box, so let's have at it all out, right here. The morning of her breakdown in the hospital and on into that night in the hotel room, she was calling your name over and over, crying non-stop—blabbering about the moon of all things."

For a moment I couldn't speak. The memory of her crying the night of my mother's death was still fresh in my mind—and now she still calls for me and speaks of the moon. "What did you tell her about me?"

"Almost nothing. Shannon didn't need more complications. I wasn't about to tell her you were mixed up with the mafia. I had to protect her first and foremost."

"But you must have told her something when she asked."

He shrugged, yet pressed on with the telling. "Don't hate me, Declan. Remember I had just been beaten and left for dead by men close to you. So, I told her you did not want to see her, that you were one of those overly ambitious American businessmen on Wall Street and didn't care to know your Irish family."

"Oh my God. She must hate me. Why would you tell her that? It's not true." I stood up and pounded my hand on the plank table.

His eyes peered into mine. "Isn't it? Remember, you chose the Nuscos over us."

I couldn't respond, so Pappy continued.

"You said it yourself last night. You turned away from your true family. Sorry Declan, but you will see that I did right by Shannon when you see how well she's doing," Pappy said, without shame. "I purposefully left out the details and I've never told her that you and I have been corresponding all these years. It was a topic to leave buried. It's worked for twenty years—until now."

I was not happy. "Come on Pappy, you're the storyteller extraordinaire. Why couldn't you make up something?"

"What? You think I should have told her some fanciful tale so she'd go off and search for you like I did? Perhaps I should have said you were a seafarer gone off on a world quest for treasure, never to return."

"I would have preferred the seafarer story," I said.

"Declan, she was not a child. She needed some form of the truth. I just simplified it. I made a decision and never looked back. I can't say I regret it. I wasn't going to lie to her, but I couldn't tell her the whole truth either, and how when I tried to see you, your Italian mobster family crippled me and left me for dead on the beach."

Standing up, he limped over to the coffee pot and brought it over to the table to refill his cup. "She has a fiery side to her, our Shannon, and a fiercely strong will. I was always afraid that she would try to find you. If she thought there was any chance you wanted to see her, she'd walk right in to enemy territory. I couldn't risk it. I had to make sure what happened to me never happened to her."

I nodded. "But after what you told her, how is she going to react when she sees me? Do you think she can handle it? I don't want to cause her another mental breakdown. Perhaps I should leave now and let her live with the story you gave her."

He took a minute or two to revue our options.

"No, it's time for this to be settled, and those boys could benefit from having an uncle like you. However, it won't be easy for either of you, but maybe the angels will be on your side. This is what your mother would have wanted, for the two of you to be reunited," Pappy said.

“Yes, our mother…” I couldn’t speak, and was sickened by the story just told.

Don’t fill your heart with hate…

Pappy tried to ease my thoughts, and placed the plate of food I put aside back in front of me to eat. “I believe you did the right thing to come here, Declan.”

I listened to the spirit and to her earthly assistant, taking the food with gratitude and smiled. “Even though I’m running from a mob boss?” I asked.

“Yes,” he laughed. “Even though it’s the bottom of the ninth and you’re running from a mob boss.”

CHAPTER THIRTY

EPONA – THE CELTIC GODESS

The heavy conversation between Pappy and me had left my stomach in knots, so when Sean came in looking vibrant, it was a welcomed interruption. "Hey Uncle Declan. Come, see, everything I've done. I cleaned the stables and have Frey's Eclipse all spruced up for mother."

I was eager to take a break, but looked to Pappy first to make sure he didn't feel like I was running out on him. "Pappy, how are we doing on our loose ends project? Is it okay if I head out to the barn with Sean?"

"Go ahead," he said, "We've pretty much covered it all. I think you can piece together the rest on your own. Just keep in mind our Shannon is a complicated one, and very sensitive. You'll need to go easy on her. And also remember, she's Daniel's Epona. He just might take you down himself if you upset her."

"You don't need to worry, Pappy, I was, and still will be Shannon's most dedicated protector again soon. She's my baby sister; don't think for one moment I've ever forgotten that. Protecting her was once my privilege and primary goal in life, and now it will be again." Emotion threatened to overwhelm me, so I looked around the room and took a deep breath, knowing Shannon would soon be standing here with me. "This living room of yours is turning into an arena for full-circles." Tears threatened again and I quickly walked out the door to follow Sean, glad to have had an excuse to collect myself.

Sean grinned when I entered the horse stables, but then he stopped, and I knew my face had given me away. "Are you okay, Uncle Declan?" he asked, as he was sweeping clean a trail of random pieces of hay.

"I'm fine. Nothing to worry about." I tried to smile, but had to wipe my face dry.

"G-Pap can stir up tears in the toughest of guys, believe me. I've gotten his line of questions far too many times. Sorry, but I listened in on you last night. He laid it down on you pretty heavy," Sean said.

"Sean, last night was a collection of many issues over the years between your G-Pap and me. I deserved every ounce of his interrogation son." I looked around the stables and changed the subject. "Oh my, this place looks shiny and new. Great job."

"Thanks. I swept up the stalls, added new hay to each one, and smoothed out mom's little prince's face and mane. Check around and tell me if you see anything I missed," Sean said.

I walked through the eight stalls in the barn, four on each side, looking around closely inside each one and shook my head. "Young man, you are a champion. I couldn't have done a better job myself," I said. "So which of these fine horses is your mother's favorite?"

He walked me to the stall of a young gelding, a gray Irish Sport Horse with a white-speckled body. As I was admiring the animal, Daniel came into the barn and joined us. "Meet Frey's Eclipse, he's the best jumper Ted Kane has ever seen," Daniel said.

"I can see why he's her favorite. Tell me, do you boys know how to braid a mane?"

They both shook their heads no.

"Let me show you how my American Indian friend, Kitchi, taught me to do it back home." Is this my home now, I wondered?

I proceeded with the braiding lesson while the boys then tried it themselves. Under my tutelage, they soon mastered the skill.

"Hey, you want to see where we live?" Sean asked, when we finished.

"Is it close to your G-Paps?"

"We've got our own house out back," Sean said.

As we went out the back door, I was surprised to see a lovely cottage sitting behind the stables surrounded by trees and green lawn.

"Our uncles built it for us, going on ten years ago now," Daniel said. "If you and your family decide to move here like G-Pap wants, they'll probably build you one, too. Want to take a look inside?"

The boys raced ahead before I could answer.

"Come on," Sean called out and I trailed after them. The boys went into the house and left the blonde-wood paneled front door open for me. Peering inside, I saw a cozy wood paneled living room that looked like an equestrian museum. Horse themed pictures covered the far wall, mostly of Shannon receiving awards and participating in various dressage events. Dressed in a blue and white riding jacket, white pants, and tall black boots, she was on horseback, jumping over fences or guiding her mounts into fancy side-steps and working trots. Next to the wall of photographs was an award case full of colored ribbons, riding trophies, and chamber music certificates.

It was too much for me, and I backed away. To look inside her home without her expressed permission would be like spying. I needed to wait for Shannon herself to invite me in.

"It looks like a really nice home," I told the boys who were waiting inside for me to enter, "but I think it's your mother's place to give me the full tour."

Daniel nodded solemnly. "Yeah, now that you mention it, that's probably a good idea. You still planning to come with me to meet her at the train station?"

I shook my head. "No, I've changed my mind. It's better if I wait here. Let her get home and settled a bit before she sees me."

Sean walked past us and exited the house. "I don't know why everybody's making such a fuss, she always had us look towards the west when a rainbow was in the sky. I think you're the pot of gold she had always wanted, Uncle Declan," Sean said.

Daniel and I shared a look of common understanding. "Uncle Declan's right not to surprise her at a cold train station," Daniel said.

Sean shrugged.

When I got back to the house, it was close to three in the afternoon and Pappy was waiting for me. "Son, we still have a few hours before Shannon gets in. Let's go into town. I want you to meet Jimmy Van, the tanner, and have him make those belts with the Quinn name embossed on them. And I want to get some more tobacco, too. Galvin's smoke shop has the best in the County. You've got the whole Emerald Isle at your fingertips now, and you're looking at the best historian you could ever have as your guide. I am all yours, Declan the Fourth from America," he said delighted.

"Why don't you let me pick up something and prepare dinner for all of us tonight at that nice grocery store in town," I asked.

"You must mean AMC's Market. They carry the best meats; short ribs are Shannon's favorite. We better head out now if we are going to get back in time to put them in the oven," he said.

Pappy and I ran our errands in town and wasted no time in returning so that I could slide the ribs into the oven to be browned and ready when they arrived.

While everything cooked, Pappy had me sit down at the kitchen table to pour over maps of the region while he pointed out places of interest he planned to show me.

"I'm leaving now," Daniel announced, popping his head inside the front door. "Be back with Mum and Dad in an hour—don't worry G-Pap, my mouth is sealed shut on Uncle Declan, I know."

My heart climbed into my throat as Daniel went out the door. This was really happening. I was really going to see my sister. Finally, I thought.

Pappy touched my hand, bringing my attention back to him. "The last hour of anticipation is always the hardest. Let's go take a look at something I've been waiting to show you since the day you were born," he said, and then called out for Sean. "We're going to drive along the property boundaries. Get the truck."

He was trying to distract me from the up and coming event and I was grateful for it. Sean brought an old green truck around to the front of the house. The truck looked well used, but also well maintained. The three of us had room enough to sit next to each other in the front seat. With the wheel in Sean's hands, and the clutch pressed as he set it into gear, we took off. He drove over a combination of graveled and dirt roads taking us all around the vast acreage while Pappy pointed out the property lines outlined in ancient, low-lying rock fences. He had Sean drive up to the top of a grassy hill approximately seventy yards behind his cottage where several gravestones lay encircled by a rickety black iron fence.

"We don't have time to pay our respects right now Declan, but many generations of your ancestors are buried here in our private Quinn family graveyard. It's sacred ground we tread now." He whispered and tapped Sean on the knee. "Don't let me forget to have you drive me back here in the morning to bring your G-Mum her favorite winter lilacs." We paused in silence for a minute until he asked Sean to drive further on the trail. Driving another two hundred yards or so, we stopped near an open green field sprinkled with trees and decorated with a creek running through its center. There was a small stone structure sitting alone in the distance.

"What's that?" I asked.

"A well, for drinking water," Pappy said. "I've waited a long time to show you this piece of land. I never wanted to tell you about it unless you came to see it for yourself. You and your family can build a home here if you want, son. It once belonged to your mother. Now it belongs to you," Pappy said, smiling.

Looking at the land, I smiled at its beauty in amazement, realizing my family could actually live here.

"Why don't you and Sean go take a look?"

Sean turned off the engine, jumped out, and I followed from the center seat. We left Pappy waiting in the truck while we walked the property. He unrolled the window and pointed to the road on the south side of the property. "That's the access road there, Declan. We can move a hefty tracker through easily enough for the grading and foundations, my nephew, Nolan, can draw up the architectural plans anytime you're ready."

I clapped my hands together, so excited with the high quality of land. "Sean, seeing this land makes me want to start construction now. You will help me build it, together with my boy, Frankie, we feasibly could finish construction in six months."

"Consider it done, Uncle Declan. I have my own tools to start, too."

"And you know how to drive on your own as well," I said.

"Sure, I've been driving that old truck since I was ten, the stick shift is kind of stiff today, but it does the job moving haystacks around. Mum got upset with G-Pap when he gave me the keys the first time, but now she's glad I know how to drive it."

"Gosh, my two new nephews are an impressive pair that's for sure," I said.

"Well, you must be special, too, Uncle Declan. G-Pap gave you prime land here. The creek runs all year, right down the middle. If you decide to build here, I'll help you, practically built the entire barn with my dad." He tossed his black hair back and looked as if he was born straight out of the earth. The descending sun behind him told me the time was nearing for his mother to arrive.

"We better head back and clean up for dinner," Pappy shouted from the truck. "Does this parcel suit your fancy son? No high Sierra Mountain peaks behind it though, only soft and romantic rolling hills that absorb the sunsets to the west like candles near a lover's bed. Right?"

I laughed. "Hey don't go stealing my poetry lines Pappy." I hopped back into the truck, grinning ear to ear. "I have never seen a parcel of land more beautiful in my life."

"We can break ground as early as the sun rises, say—tomorrow?" Pappy said.

We needed a diversion, so the topic of construction carried us back to the cottage. Sean drove the truck back in front and helped Pappy out while I ran inside to wash up and to check on the dinner in the oven. I splashed my face with water, and then looked into the mirror quickly searching to see if light had returned to my 'greenies'. "Well, it's show time, Declan Quinn the Fourth from America—let's pray I pass her inspection."

I ran back into the kitchen and checked the dinner fixings and started to prepare a variety of homegrown vegetables. Is this the right time for us to be reunited together, I thought, or have I waited too long? While I worked in the kitchen, Pappy started some coffee on the stove, acting unusually quiet.

When Shannon and her husband walked in the front door with Daniel holding her portfolio, I nearly dropped the chopping knife on the floor. Holding my breath, I stood in the back of the kitchen to give her due respect and space.

"Dinner." I reminded myself in a whisper, and turned back to open the oven and basted the meat inside.

Just listening to her voice put my senses on overload.

"Oh my, G-Pap. Is Pope Paul coming for dinner tonight? Looks like you brought in personal catering for the occasion," she said, looking over at me in the kitchen. She was everything I pictured her to be, with long auburn hair pulled into a side ponytail dancing over her right shoulder in gentle curls. When she looked towards me, I saw her deep green eyes, and a bolt of love shot straight out of my heart.

"Come on in here little Aisling, show me what you worked on this week darling," Pappy said, as his precious great-granddaughter hopped onto his lap.

Shannon surveyed the room. "This is quite the welcome after a week of grading papers and dealing with unforgiving college students. The barn shines like new and Eclipse looks ready to walk in a parade. Daniel dear, did your sweetie Chrissy braid his mane for me?" Sean just grinned taking his dad's briefcase while Daniel set down his mother's things and put the keys in a ceramic dish by the front door. He looked at me with stark eyes, but said nothing while he stirred the gravy.

Shannon walked over to kiss Pappy on the cheek, whom was still busy with her young daughter, another red-haired Aisling wearing her hair in a ponytail draped to the side like her mother's, the spitting image of her mother as a youngster. When finished talking about the child's week at school, Pappy took a seat on his chair next to the fireplace as the little girl fetched a book for them to read together.

Shannon's husband smiled, then walked passed me in the kitchen to look into the pots on the stove and stirred the potatoes, all without asking me who I was, as cooks seemingly worked in my spot often. Sean opened the refrigerator and poured himself a tall glass of milk watching us both expectantly, waiting for something to erupt.

Pappy called out from his chair using a booming voice. "Everyone into the living room. Boys, take a break from the cooking and come in here."

Shannon bellowed. "Oh, so now you're telling me your caterer is teaching my sons to cook? I'd have to see that to believe it."

I sighed, took a deep breath and waited on Pappy's lead.

"I'll have to read to you later," he told little Aisling and put her off his lap. "Why don't you go play while the grownups talk before dinner."

When the child ran upstairs, my heart sank as she whisked by me, it was like seeing my own daughter again. That's yet another family member I can't wait to get to know, I thought with a long-forgotten warmth in my heart.

See my son, it's good you've come home—not tuning me out anymore, are you?

I smiled like a kid readying for a day at the fair, overwhelmed, yet anxiously game for anything.

Pappy stood and walked over to Shannon, took her hands in his while I came closer to the scene.

"My darling granddaughter, I have lied to you for too long. Today I must make amends. Please, come sit next to me," he said, and led her to the same chair I occupied last night. She sat, but looked puzzled, and then saw his tears.

At once, she got up to put her hand on his cheek. "Come now, it can't be that bad." She smiled, as she wiped his tears away from his high cheekbones, putting the pad of her thumbs right under his eyes. "The worst lie you've ever told me was when that horse I loved got sold so cheap in the trade show. You said it sold for double the amount she was worth," she said.

Her husband added. "Yes, Professor, and gave Shannon twice as much money as you got paid, with the excess coming right out of your own earnings."

They were sweet, trying to lift his spirits, but frustrated, as they weren't too successful.

Shannon's husband poured a drink and handed it to Pappy. "Yeah, I don't think you've ever lied about anything your whole life. So what's really troubling you?"

Pappy sighed. "As I said. A lie. Told to protect Shannon from the truth."

Shannon scowled and glanced over at me, taking a seat again. "So this is why you brought in a caterer, to soften the blow?"

Pappy stood up and walked towards me. "He's not a caterer, Shannon. He's family," Pappy said, and then held out his hand for me to grasp.

All eyes followed and I felt as if a giant spotlight had been pointed in my direction. Summoning my courage, I took Pappy's hand and shook it, then walked over to my sister and took a knee. "Shannon, I've waited my whole life to see you again. And now, here you are—in all your beauty, right in front of me." Placing a hand over my heart, my eyes filled with tears. "You're my dear baby sister, Shannon. I'm Declan, your long lost brother. At last—we are reunited."

She stood up, handed her husband her drink, practically knocking me down, and then backed away. "Pappy—please. This is Declan? My brother, who hasn't cared about any of us my whole life? That's no lie. It's the truth. And now, you invite him into your home; tell me he's family, because he suddenly shows up with tears in his eyes, proclaiming brotherly devotion?"

"Shannon, please." I begged, and got to my feet.

She backed away from me. "Go away. I don't know you and I don't want to. All I know of a brother is that he doesn't exist in the world I live in. He never cared enough to find me in my darkest days. When I was crying for his protection, he ran away never to return. The boy who guarded me before that, ceased to exist. As far as I'm concerned, he died the day…" She couldn't continue.

I stood in the middle of the room frozen.

Then looking at me she said with cold eyes. "Whoever you say you are—leave now."

Stiff and unable to move, even on a demand, I said, "I'm your brother, and I'm here. If you'll just let me explain…"

"There's nothing to explain. I remember it all." She walked to her husband's side, spoke to him and took his arm. "I was thrown on a cold bus full of crying babies and scared children. Boys with shined shoes and little girls with bows in their hair, and all of them with tears in their eyes, shushed by ugly teachers wearing black dresses. I was so scared, so alone and barely eight-years old." She turned to look at me once more. "Now, finally I have my life in order, with a husband who cares for me, and you come here claiming to be my brother. Why bother after all this time? Will you just want to walk out on me again?"

Her husband moved to stand between Shannon and me. "I don't know if you're who you say you are, but you're upsetting my wife. You need to leave this room now before something happens," he said, putting his hand on my forearm.

"Please, I didn't come here to fight," I said.

"All those years, not even one letter." Shannon stepped forward again, her voice shrill and accusing. "And now you decide to show up and surprise me? Did you think I would welcome you with open arms?" She turned to Pappy who had since returned to his armchair. "This isn't right. He shouldn't be here. Why would you let him into your home like this after what he did?"

I answered before Pappy could. "I didn't know you were here. I never knew what happened to you. If I had known…" I tried desperately to explain, but stumbled over every word. I reached for her hand and she threw herself away from me once again.

"Don't touch me!" she screamed, and for a moment I feared I had pushed her over the edge into madness, but then she took a breath and lowered her voice again. I was relieved to see only anger in her eyes. "Don't pretend to care. I've done just fine without you all these years. Just leave. Go back to America where you belong."

She stormed out, passed Sean and Daniel who were standing motionless in front of the fireplace, then walked out the front door into the night as her husband raced after her. The door slammed shut behind them, leaving me stunned, with no words to say.

Only Daniel stood next to me with eyes that wanted to kill.

CHAPTER THIRTY-ONE

WHISPERS NEAR THE WELL

Shannon's wild eyes haunted me all night.

As my tired limbs woke with the rising sun, I fixed the bed coverings, grabbed my bag and set to leave. Putting the journal Pappy gave me in the inside pocket of my jacket, I was grateful he gave me the liberty to fill the few blank pages in the back and wondered if my own prose would be worthy enough to share pages with his.

All I had left to do was to leave here and comb the country roads alone. Perhaps I should head back to the airport and hide out with Sofia in the Poconos, I thought. Discrediting that option on this said morning, my trek to the southeast coast of Ireland posited only two choices: to drown myself in the waters at St. Delcan's Well or to wash away my guilt there.

Bag in one hand and briefcase in the other, I walked down the stairs and found Pappy sitting with a cup of coffee at the kitchen table. Alone. He stood up when he saw me, looking grim and tired.

"I'll call you tonight from my hotel. I'm hoping Shannon just needs some time, and we could talk it out in a couple of days," I said. "And Daniel?" I questioned, shaking my head remembering his eyes from last night as well. "He stormed out of here last night pretty angry."

"Yes, he guards his mother like no other," Pappy said.

Strapping my bags over my shoulder, I walked to the sink for a glass of water. "I'll leave—give you all some space. I surely have caused turmoil around here, I am so very sorry."

"Forget the apologies, son. We Irish boil it up a plenty. But this is a big one indeed."

"I hope to fix this," I said.

"I hope so as well. You have a difficult battle ahead of you."

"One I can win?"

He pushed his ratted gray hairs back and fingered his beard with a defeated expression on his face. "One can never predict the outcome of battles on this land."

There was nothing left for either of us to say or do. We both knew we couldn't rush the outcome of my melodrama. It was time for me to go. I gulped down the water, walked to the door, as he saw me out. Pappy watched as I loaded my bags into the backseat, got in, and adjusted the seat and the rearview mirror, realizing Daniel, who was far taller than me, last drove the car. I looked at Pappy from the mirror, and saw that he was crying. Shaking my head, I saw how my visit had only brought him grief, as disgust with myself grew exponentially.

How could I have burdened him with the excess debris of my life, I thought. He could have gone to his grave peacefully having never seen me, but after my visit, he and my sister had to deal with the stinking load of crap that I dumped on them.

As I exited the rocky driveway, I watched Pappy wave good-bye while heading down the approach. With no one to quiet me, I shouted to myself after I turned around the bend. "What was I thinking? Barging into their lives without warning, expecting Shannon to welcome me back after I deserted her. Of course she hates me. Who wouldn't. I come barging in, saying hey Sis, it's your charming brother, the one who disappeared for forty years without a word, thought I'd drop by and say hello. So come on over here and give me hug."

I threw my hat on the dashboard disgusted and sat low in the driver's seat the whole way with utter disdain for myself. The gray clouds in the sky blended with my mood. A slow rising sun battled against the thick cloud cover, but the sky remained dark. Fitting I thought, as darkness had fallen on me once again.

Don't fill your heart with hate… I had to shut her voice out somehow, so I turned up the volume on the radio.

"Declan Quinn the Fourth from America, your life is a fucking mess. Go climb into a hole and die." I mumbled bitterly and struggled to put the hat back on to stay warm.

Despite my mood, or maybe because of it, I recalled the stories my mother used to share about this vast land she loved. She'd tell of a cave in the cliffs at Ardmore where she drank her last tea and carved her name into the limestone, before she set sail for the west at the turn of the century with her parents.

Decidedly, I headed south on Route 706, to trek to a place I had heard about my entire life. Yesterday, when Pappy and I were pouring over the map, he showed me the location of Declan's Stone and Hermitage. Of course, I had hoped to go there with him and Shannon, but on this day, I resigned to settle for a solo run.

"Declan's Stone and Well is a beautiful spot," Pappy said, yesterday with hope. "Only eighty kilometers from here. The winter sea there is always alluring, yet demanding. I've done some of my best thinking listening to the hum of the waves off those shores. One day, I will tell you of St. Declan's bell and of his wells, a place all Ireland calls blessed. It is said that the well waters help those whose vision is hindered. Perhaps a fitting pilgrimage for a man with struggles like yours."

I was neither surprised he'd suggest I needed restored vision, nor insulted, as when someone knows you as a child, then meets you again as an adult, a change, for a good or for a bad, is startlingly obvious. If an evolution had not occurred in one's persona over time, the flaws lie on a cutting block to be manipulated and sorted. Hence, I knew I was on trial that first day we spent together, and I ended up here—guilty and alone. He wasn't about to let a man with flaws like mine ruin the peace he had worked so hard to create for Shannon and her family.

Nevertheless, I was fine being alone on this morning, as I too needed to confirm my worthiness to reenter my sister's life.

So taking a day to figure out things was apropos. Unrolling the window, I let in the fresh rainy air, without a care of the elements coming into the car, as childhood stories of Irish tales and mythology filled my head. I pondered on the tales of Declan's sacred golden bell that miraculously floated back to him on the waves, and how the massive stone was placed on Ardmore's shores by the mighty hands of St. Declan himself after his long journey from Rome to bring Christianity to Ireland. Mother reminisced often with her fanciful Irish accent many stories of her days in Ireland. "Your Pappy carried me as a baby on his back all the way from Cashel down St. Declan's Pilgrim's Path, he carried me for eighty kilometers over the pass of the Knockmealdown Mountains that climbed almost two thousand feet, to receive the blessings of his well every year. One day, you and I will make this pilgrimage together and bless ourselves with the waters. The secret is to take the salt waters from the Celtic Sea and mix them with the fresh waters of Declan's Well, and then a special magic happens." I remembered it all, and despite my mood, I enjoyed traversing the same roads she did as a girl.

I drove on and thought back on the many summer days with my mother when we'd walk through Battery Park every morning. With the help of her telling and retelling, the stories of Ireland remained fresh in my memory as if told to me yesterday. Many nights, Shannon and I would lie in bed with our mother while she shared stories of her homeland. When we slept in the convent dorms, she would whisper the stories to us as if one of the nuns might overhear. "This must be our secret, as the sisters at St. Patrick's will be upset if we tell them the truth about who first brought Christianity to Ireland, as it was St. Declan from Ardmore in the Fifth Century, not St. Patrick."

As the kilometers went by, I began to question whether there was any point in continuing my journey after all. Judy was gone and Shannon rejected me. My wife and children would be better off without me putting them in danger from Marco. If I ended it now, they'd be safe, I thought, turned the radio off, rolled up the window, and fetched the gun in my briefcase.

I thought how Pappy said I was a coward for running. Would he think me even more cowardly for taking my own life, or would he understand it was to protect those I love. My coming here had thrown everyone off kilter. With me obliterated, it would bring balance to the universe again.

Conflicted, I held onto the gun as I weighed in with my team: there was Andrew, the one who saved my life; and what about

Frank and Anthony. I owed them as well. And Judy, what must I do about my last promise to her? And Pappy? Shannon? Or my mother's spirit watching from above… I tried shaking all the thoughts off, but couldn't quiet them and scratched my head—didn't I just leave New York a few days ago? I asked myself the list of questions, thinking I must be on the brink of insanity, but in exhaustion, set the gun down on the passenger seat defeated.

Andrew said, "Pain begets truth, and the truth will set you free." Well, I had done plenty of his Spina-therapy and reliving out the past, all at the feet of two special people I loved, but it hurt them and I was still not free. I just wanted to be dead. A man like me shouldn't live a life of crime and mayhem, and then one day on a whim, cross the Atlantic, turn a new corner, and fix it all. That was the truth I faced, and the darkness continued to resurface inside me, as routine as putting butter on bread.

So I contemplated a solution. I resolved to end my life, but how? I didn't want to make more of a mess. I needed to just disappear. Maybe I would just walk into the Celtic Sea and drown. No, my body would wash up somewhere, then there would be investigations and a funeral and… No, they mustn't find me, I thought. I picked up the pistol once more. This damn thing wouldn't work, too messy again. I punched the steering wheel, instinctively slipping the gun into the lining of my jacket, and got busy reading the road signs through the rain splattered windshield.

A plethora of perfect plans were playing Ping-Pong in my brain as I thought of one after the other. A freighter off the shores of the Celtic Sea was only miles away, I could sail off to a far, distant place, jump over board, and no one would know what happened to Declan Quinn the Fourth from America. Yes, that was what I would do, becoming that seafarer who never returned just like Pappy suggested. I liked that plan. There was no point in going back to America to endanger Sofia, and Ireland was only a hopeless dream. This enchanting place would never be my home after all.

Marco thought he could hold my family as ransom to get me back. He wanted to keep me around as his tool to negotiate deals for him, but didn't realize when Aisling died my debt to the Nusco's was paid in full. He would never give up until I were dead, and I knew he'd continue to use my family to force me to return. The only answer was the final one.

I had to die and disappear.

When I came to an intersection in the road, I was uncertain which way to go, so I pulled off to the side to fumble with my map. The car idled under a torrential downpour as I figured the proper direction. Easing back onto the highway, I turned south to follow the white painted road signs in Gaelic, stating Ardmore was still thirty kilometers away.

The sun was hidden behind thick gray clouds, busy emptying their contents of rain in already saturated landscapes. Again, the weather fit my defeated spirit, so I kept driving. Six more kilometers to the sea, another sign read where I followed the markers showing St. Declan's Church and Hermitage.

I drove on, battling to find resolve, while the sun continued to fight the heavy clouds in its search for an opening to shine its light on the earth below. Finally, the vast Celtic Sea waters appeared beyond the cliffs ahead. As the rainfall slowed to an easy drizzle, streaks of sunlight pierced through cracks in the gray sky. Seeing the long streaks of light streaming through, I thought of paintings depicting heavenly light shining down upon upturned faces like mine, seeking guidance from above.

Journey on, son. Don't fill your heart with hate, no matter what this world will take—our love must not be disgraced. Her voice was like a song, and as real as if she were sitting next to me. My spirit lightened, with hopes the next cloudburst waited long enough for me to walk the sandy beach and make the same pilgrimage I heard so much about.

The excitement I felt in approaching this sacred site told me I was just a disappointed man with a battle ahead, not a lost soul looking for final departure. So, as if discarding an old worn out shoe, I dumped my defeated spirit once and for all. It was out of the question that I shame my mother here by ending my life at her sacred spot. I was no coward like my father. I was a Quinn. Taking my own life, whether here on the grounds or far out at sea, would only disgrace my Pappy and sister once again, and break all the promises made in good faith to those who helped me get this far.

The sunbeams and spirits called me to live on and to fight to get my family back. I would not give up until my sister's favor became mine once again. I would bring her to these shores and talk of our heritage and chat about our mother. The keys to the mysterious causes of her anxieties and phobias have been locked away and I could be the one to help resolve them, I thought with hope.

As I eased my car towards the seaside, I saw a market and stopped to grab a few boxes of crackers and two candy bars to hold me over for my morning hike up the cliffs. The air smelled moist from the freshly fallen rain as I hopped back into the car and drove on, getting as close to the beach as I could.

The sea beyond was calm, rolling in gently, like a bay protected from an ocean. Fishermen nearby were readying their small fishing boats, which made me laughed at myself for wanting to vanish overboard on a giant freighter. "This isn't the New York harbor, Declan from America, it looks like no huge freighters are at the waterfront to transport goods from these shores."

Sort out your troubles. Let the fresh rain cleanse you. Bless yourself three times at St. Declan's Well. Then you will be prepared for the battles ahead.

I heeded to the call of that spirit once more, packed a day's bag, and took off down the rocky beach with a smile—the first one of the day. Looking up from the beach at the cliffs above, I wondered if I could find where my mother and Pappy carved their names next to caves embedded into the limestone. The beach was quiet and the trail going up the cliff was deserted. I paused for a moment to unwrap a candy bar, realizing how hungry I was, as I hadn't eaten anything since lunch yesterday. Storing the rest of the food into my jacket pockets, I felt the rectangle shape of Pappy's journal still there. I wanted to write notes, so I left it in its place.

The stairs leading off the beach were worn, and took me to a path of dirt carved by foot traffic. Just before I left the beach to begin my trek upwards, words formed in my head. *Remember the pebble, Declan;* she spoke to me again. I looked about and found a sea-worn stone that fit into my palm and slid it in my pocket.

Remember the seawater, too. Mix it with the well… her voice whispered with the wind.

I used my Styrofoam coffee cup, dumped its contents and walked down to the sea, and filled the cup with frigid, salty Celtic Sea water. The gravel-lined path stretched and weaved between the green marshes covering rolling hills above and all around me. Looking at the vastness of green, all I could do was think of my mother's refrain, 'Greenies to greenies. I can see the green grasses of Ireland in your eyes…'

Humming her song, I began to walk up the path and took a deep gulp of the fresh air into my lungs. Looking over the edge, I realized I should have brought some rope if my goal was to find an earthen cave on the side of these cliffs. When I come back next time with Shannon, we will bring climbing rope, I thought. I continued my trek for approximately fifty more yards of winding path, grateful for the dry warmth of my winter boots that were covered with sea water, sand, and brown mud.

I smiled for the second time that morning, seeing the sun win its battle with the gray clouds as it pushed through to construct a rainbow over the sea. Surveying the grounds, I mapped out my morning walk, and could see that beyond the ruined façade of the church was the tall circular oratory. At the start, I realized Declan's Well was set at the beginning of the grounds, with two framed stone exteriors covering the wells inside them. No one else was around this early in the morning, and I wondered if I should tour the entire grounds first and perform my mother's ritual at the sacred well upon my exit.

So I paused in front of the well, dipped my fingertip into the cup, and rubbed some of it on my forehead with a tiny sign of the cross. I was tempted to indulge, but trekked on. When I reached the top of the path and approached the ruins of the oratory and the graveyard surrounding it, I thought of St. Declan finding this site in the Fifth Century for his mission to spread Jesus' gospels. I felt the pebble in my pocket and took it out, being careful to not spill my cup of seawater.

The signage posted showed this was St. Declan's Hermitage and ahead of me stood St. Declan's Cross. Along with mixing the seawater with the well waters to bring special blessings, mother told me of the tradition to bring a pebble from the beach to carve deeper into the stone cross using the same grooves that St. Declan started centuries ago. I set the cup down with care, and placed the pebble into the indentation, carving out my cross exactly as centuries of pilgrims had done before me. In that moment, I felt a connection to my Irish roots like never before. Adding my pebble to thousands of others on the ground when finished, I slowly hiked the path ahead up to the church ruins. This was no time to rush, I thought, though wished again, with all my heart, that Shannon were up here with me.

The view of the Celtic Sea was vast and beautiful from atop the path, an inner bay lie eerily still below, tranquil enough to reflect the gray and white puffy clouds overhead. I enjoyed the scents of wild garlic herbs that were dispersed on the hill and took another hour to walk the grounds munching on some crackers. After looping the entire site and reading the historical markers that spoke of St. Declan in the Fifth Century, I set to return to the entrance where Declan's Well stood.

When I reached the stonewalled well, I set my cup down and instinctively knelt, leaned inside the stone frame, and dipped my hands into the water below. I drank one handful, two, and finally took my third blessing of the cold and refreshing water into my mouth and swallowed, grateful for it, but a bit ashamed that this sacred purity helped me wash down a few chocolate candy bars and crackers. The food could have waited, Mother and Pappy would have fasted, I thought.

Not quite ready to leave, I remembered my cup of seawater.

Mix it with the well water, Declan.

I put my hands in the ice-cold deep well water once more as it appeared to have no bottom, added a handful of the well water into the cup of seawater until it overflowed, and splashed my face half a dozen times. Gluttonous, one might say, but no one was here to judge me, except God. I didn't care and believed God didn't either.

Smiling once more, it became a permanent fixture on my face for the rest of the day.

Renewed, with such peace, as I was blessed on holy ground, I saw a bench nearby and took a rest. Here, I indulged myself in peace-filled contemplation as more pilgrims arrived and partook of the well. I prayed, surprising myself. "Please, if there is a God in heaven, please Lord, bring forgiveness and acceptance into Shannon's heart once again."

An elderly lady approached and sat alongside me. When she began to recite the rosary in the ancient Gaelic language, the same prayers memorized from my childhood, I joined in her recitation of the prayers. She smiled at me in encouragement as I stumbled along. I kept reciting with her, trying my best to remember the Gaelic version of the prayers.

After another hour passed, I continued down the path, back onto the sandy shore below. Shannon's comments lingered in my mind. "When I was crying for his protection, he ran away never to return. The boy who guarded me before that, ceased to exist. As far as I'm concerned, he died the day." These were her words, but her eyes are what pierced my heart the most.

And Pappy's comments as well. "The innocent pay the price of their fathers. You are like a mouse in a maze looking for a way out—bumping into walls, dead ends. Declan, Ireland can bring you new life. It's never too late to come home, son."

My mind replayed them all, continuing with Father Carmen's in that stinking alley in New York. "So your suffering is useless then. Both your mother's death and your daughter's are all in vain, and now Judy's, too? You've turned your love into hatred. Have you learned nothing?"

And another came to mind, the voices of Sal and Saverio, "Every Italian in New York who wants peace has to confront the mafia bosses first to get to the greener grass on the right side of the fence."

And then, sweet Judy's, "Would you promise to let your guilt go—to forgive, to forgive yourself."

And of course, Frank Attanasio's parting words to me at the terminal chimed in, "Fix your life, brother, and give me a call when you do."

And last but not least, I couldn't leave out the wisdom that started my quest in the first place, on the dedication page Andrew wrote for me on his Christmas gift. "A wound is a place where light can enter."

The wisdom of those I admired, mixed together with the salty smell of the ocean, my Gaelic prayers, and the blessing of the sea and well waters on my skin—something magical occurred, just as Pappy and mother had promised. I saw a new life opening before me, one of hope and newness. I was neither whiner nor coward. It was becoming clear to me that the dark and barren soul I knew was losing the battle with the good I imbibed.

As the afternoon sun began its rose-colored descent over the earth to the west, I realized I had spent my whole day here in contemplation. Another rainbow appeared from the west, and I hoped Shannon was looking at the same prism of light with the similar new hope. Perhaps Pappy had had a chance to bestow some of his wisdom on her by now—enough to forgive me, I thought.

She's calling for you, Declan. The voice was so apparent I had to look over my shoulder to see if anyone was there. *Go to her, son. Make it right.* Again, I spun around to search out the voice.

I fetched Pappy's journal out of my jacket, to give an effort to channel the voice through my pen, the way Pappy did with the Code, but stopped when I felt the steel of my gun there.

Leave your troubled past and start anew.

If her message didn't say what I needed to hear, I would have shouted at the voice to tell her to stop nagging me. But she was right. This was no place for a gun.

Hence, I trekked back up the path to the well, looked around for any other witnesses. No one was around except for my elderly prayer partner from earlier. So I pulled out the pistol, felt its heaviness once more, and then dropped it into the deep ice-cold well water. Once the few bubbles came out of its barrel and stopped rising to the surface, I blessed myself again, more gluttonous than before, but feeling fully renewed with a drowned past behind me.

I sat next to my prayer partner again, taking in the salt of the sea as refreshed as a man would feel after trekking across the barren desert and views his first sighting of water.

So I opened my journal and flipped it to the back pages to read some scribbles from last night. "In the rush I became something that I thought I'd never be…" Taking out my pen, I added one more line. "But now, as our mother has died…" I stopped, crossed out "mother" and replaced it with "as our parents have died, we must hold on to each other in their place."

Closing the journal and taking some of the water on my hands to buff its smooth leather cover, I thought, perhaps another day I would finish the poem. I knew there would be many more days ahead to connect with the spirit and channel its message onto the pages.

Breathing in more of the fresh Celtic Sea atmosphere, I sat and fully submitted myself to an entity greater than my own ego—and wept. And like the tatter-skinned snakes I'd find on my ranch, I, Declan Quinn the Fourth from America, shed my skin at last and replaced it with a helmet of faith and a shield of goodwill. Smiling, watching the sunrays battle through the clouds and permeate through my being, I listened.

Go home and make it right again.

It was time to walk down from St. Declan's grounds to face life again. I adjusted my hat and made my way down the trail along the cliffs and back to the car.

It was only a few short driveways up to the Cliff House Hotel, where the friendly clerk greeted me at the front desk. She gave me the key to my room, a quick weather report, and wished me a nice stay. After I settled in the room and took in the view of the Celtic Sea from atop the cliff where the hotel stood, I looked at the phone on the nightstand and made a call home—to Pappy, and he answered.

Clearing my throat, I spoke into the phone. "It's me, Pappy—yes, I'm all right. I was hoping you had some good news after talking to Shannon."

His voice had strength, but his report wasn't a cheerful one.

"No Declan. We haven't heard from Shannon. Not yet, no good news. Last night Paul tried to console her, but despite his efforts, she stormed off to bed like the wonderfully passionate soul she is, and cried in her pillow until sunrise. But please persevere, as will I."

"She's gone? Left the farm?" I asked.

"Yes, you see, Paul packed the horses before dawn, and they were gone to settle it the only way they know how, on the back of their two thoroughbreds, combing the trails of the Isle as far as it takes to set her mind right again."

My heart sunk. "The rain was coming down like a typhoon when I left this morning. Did they wait for it to clear at least?"

"No. That is what concerns me. According to Paul, she ran off after they stopped to make camp halfway up the Galtee Mountains. She's done this sort of thing before, only to resurface back at the farm in a few days with a load of lilacs and field roots to plant in her garden."

"She took the truck without him?" I asked, assuming they trailered the horses into the hills like I did near my ranch.

"No. You are indeed a stranger to your sister, aren't you. She took her horse and left the truck at camp. She's on her gelding, Frey's Eclipse, the best mud runner we've got in County Tipperary, but we're still worried. Paul's been searching for her. Daniel is coming back from his classes in Cork with a team of his friends to help look as well. If you can get here in an hour, you can join the search. Sean is saddling up the horses now."

"I'll get there as soon as I can." I told him, but it didn't seem to sink in. He kept talking, begging me to come back.

"Declan, she needs you here. Please. We can figure out this mess and be a real family again. Please. Come home, your sister needs you. She needs you—you're the only one who can help her."

"Pappy, I'm on my way." I told him and hung up. I ran back to the lobby, handed the room key to the hotel clerk who just gave me a confused stare as I took off running to my car.

CHAPTER THIRTY-TWO

A PRAYER OVER THE CLIFFS OF MOHER

I watched the setting sun stretch its last rays onto the ground between dreary cloud covered skies on my drive back to Fethard. Who was the character that dropped breadcrumbs to find their way back home, I wondered, feeling like that person as I followed my way back to Pappy's farm easily reversing my trek from earlier. A light rain was falling again and it was nearly nightfall by the time I arrived at his cottage.

It appeared as if the rebel army was gearing up on the front lawn, as a half a dozen men on horseback gathered in full gear, carrying flashlights and lanterns. Blankets and plastic sheets covered their bodies to protect them against the impending storm. Three hound dogs barked excitedly, sniffing at a black sweater one of the men showed them. I could halfway understand what the riders were saying, but they sounded heated and hurried as though heading out for battle in the mountain range.

Sean stood in front of his horse, holding its reins while his pup ran circles around the yard, barking at the gathering troops of men and animals. As I approached, I saw Daniel was one of men mounted on horseback while Pappy stood with him, one hand under the neck of the horse and the other balanced with his cane.

"This storm looks serious, Daniel." I heard Pappy saying. "I wish you would stay back at the cottage with me and your brother."

Daniel was handing out lanterns to the group. "You know I can't, G-Pap. You'll be fine here with Sean. I need to show the others where to look and know this land better than anyone."

"Ah yes, you do. All right, but be careful out there. In this terrain at night you could easily step into a crevice. I don't want anyone getting injured. You'll need to go far afield in your search.

Your father already checked her favorite spots. Stay together and don't take chances," he yelled through the crowd.

I interrupted, coming up behind them. "Please wait while I saddle a mount."

"Take mine," Sean said, and handed me his reins. "G-Pap insists I stay here with him. It's probably more important that you go anyway." The tall roan was saddled and ready with a saddlebag. Checking the contents, on one side of the horse, a bag was empty, but on the other side, a satchel was packed with emergency supplies. I thought it odd he didn't balance the weight, but this was not the time to deliver a lecture on horsemanship.

"Thank you, Sean," I said. I checked the cinch, and then flipped the reins up over the horse's head.

"Jaxon's only two-years old, but well trained and faster than any other horse in this group." Sean told me as I mounted up and settled onto his horse's back. I set my feet in the stirrups and found them the right length.

Sean whistled and his dog came running and leaped into his arms. "Take Jack with you. He's the best hunter we've ever had."

I looked to Pappy for approval, but he waved his hand in annoyance. I grabbed the pup, wondering how to position him on the saddle, but he wiggled free and crawled into the empty saddlebag and sat with his head out as if he'd done it thousands of times.

"Be good, Jackie boy, listen to Uncle Declan, now." Sean patted his pup's head, and then produced a plastic bag holding a green wool scarf.

Pappy stood next to Jaxon as I tried to settle him. "G-Pap, excuse me," Sean said, almost knocking him down as the boy handed the bag to me. "Let Jack smell this when you think you're ready. Those ground-sniffing hounds over there don't know how to hunt a horse girl whose feet never touch the earth. Jackie here will follow my mum's scent from the air. Just listen to what he tells you, Uncle Declan. Don't worry. This Isle isn't vast enough for anyone to hide from him. He'll find her for you."

I frowned at the little dog, doubtful, but I was not about to question Sean's good intentions.

"Show them the way, Jackie boy," Sean said, his youthful confidence reminding me once more of my own boy back home.

Daniel took charge of the search, pairing the men. "Bobby, you and Anton go back to camp and see if your dogs can pick up a trail from there. They set up camp just on the east side of the crag at Rosegreen. Robert and Hugh, you guys head south along the River Suir." Two others ventured off listening to directions. "Look for horse tracks, broken branches, anything that looks like someone's been there recently." Daniel pointed out the areas on their maps. Initially, we rode out together toward the back of the property, northwest, away from town, then split off in our different directions.

As requested by Pappy, Daniel and I stayed together. He motioned for me to follow him up a steep grade, but rode ahead and didn't wait.

I hurried to catch up with him. "Does she go on horse rides with your dad often?" I asked, hoping to learn more.

"Ah, sure she does, but she never stopped crying all night and Dad thought it might do her good. They had already planned to go over to Rosegreen today. When they were packing for the ride this morning, I begged her to talk to G-Pap first, but she refused. Saying it wouldn't change how her brother left her before and would only end up doing it again." He paused to give me a look of suspicion. "You know, I had a feeling you were trouble when I first saw you, but you said you were my uncle so I tried to give you the benefit of the doubt. Seeing those eyes of yours, I should have known better than to let you get near her." He rode on ahead.

I kicked Jaxon to keep up. "Daniel, the last thing I wanted to do was upset her or to hurt you. I came here to heal the past. To make amends."

He shrugged. "Amends. Guns can't amend anything, your piece of shit, loose triggered street pistol practically killed me."

I shrugged and wished to tell him everything had changed and that the damn thing was sitting at the bottom of St. Declan's Well, yet we rode on, as I proved my horsemanship by riding Jaxon at a good speed. Showing him I could handle keeping up, I shouted over the hooves on the muddy, rocky terrain, as the pup bounced happily in the satchel sack. "There's so much I need to tell her and to tell you. Simply put, I wanted us to be a family again."

"Your plan didn't work too well, now did it?" Daniel yelled back at me over his shoulder. He kept shouting to overcome the sound of the wind and the horse's hooves on the rocks, but anger was driving him. "Hey look, the only reason we're riding together is because G-Pap wants it that way," he said, then pressed his horse into a lope. "You don't know my mum. She is tough in some ways, but when it comes to family, she's fragile."

"I want to spend the rest of my life getting to know you both."

He shrugged. "Right. We'll see about that. All I will tell you is that my dad said he had her settled by the fireside at their camp, when out of nowhere, she stood up shouting, 'My dear mother's calling me beyond the crag—calling for Declan and me. I must visit every well on this island to find her,' she told him. 'Don't you hear her? We need to go. Please, I need to pray and bless myself with the well's sacred waters.'" He shrugged. "Of course, Dad said no, it didn't make any sense, but she begged him over and over. I've seen her like that plenty of times, and now I know you are the root cause of it all." He rode on, whipping his horse hard.

We had to be a team to solve this, but how was I going to gain his trust, I thought.

Daniel kept on riding ahead, seemingly over us staying close together, but I caught up with him finally. "Please son, I can help you with your mother, if you can try to trust me."

Desperate, he paused and looked at me with a frown on his face. "Okay, if you betray us even one time, it won't be pretty."

I listened as he retold the story from last night.

"Last night, she was crazed, like I've never seen her before, screaming at us with her wild eyes, and I swear her hair gets more red when she's angry. I saw my dad do something I had never seen, an unthinkable thing coming from him. He's always been so gentle with my mother." Daniel hesitated, and looked back at me with caution. "You're a stranger and probably more trouble for us, so I probably shouldn't be telling you this—but, he slapped her, right across the face, and pretty hard too. It was as if a force from God made him do it, to bring some sense to her again."

I was not sure how to respond to that, angry that anyone would hit her, but the last thing I was ready to do was to judge. "So, what happened after he slapped her?"

"What do you think happened? She was as shocked to be slapped, as I was to see it, but it stopped her screaming. After that, she cried herself to sleep. I went to bed as Dad kept watch over her all night. In the morning, she actually seemed okay, packing up, and tending to the horses—still angry, of course, but acting fairly normal. They go for overnight rides all the time, rain or shine, so I didn't think much of it and helped them put the horses in the trailer."

I followed Daniel on the muddy dirt path through low grass while he processed his thoughts and evaluated the terrain ahead using our lanterns.

"Dad already searched her favorite places to ride, but when he told me of her talk about going to all the wells in Ireland for blessings, it got me thinking about this one place she took us to as kids. You're not from this country, so you're not aware to the fact that there are over three thousand sacred wells in Ireland. She'd have to be daft to think she could bless herself at every one. But this well was one of her favorites and within a couple hours riding distance. She took us there a number of times until Dad found out. He said it was too dangerous and put a stop to it."

He told the story with hope, but was mixed with worry in his voice, as he recalled them visiting this place years ago. "It's not a typical well, it's high up in the mountains, north of the crag at Rosegreen. The horses can only go so far, and then you have to climb on foot the rest of the way. Sean was still little when we went, so I had to carry him over the rocks, and little Aisling was just a babe in bunting on my mother's back."

The narrow path widened into a flat clearing, and we pressed the horses into a gallop, thankful the rising full moon was sufficient to light the way. When the trail narrowed and climbed again, we had to slow back to a walk allowing Daniel to continue his story. "The well is enclosed inside a low ceilinged stone house, you can barely stand up in it. She had us shout our wishes down the well, then listen for them to come back in an echo. We'd sing hymns and watch the sun set over the Cliffs of Moher. 'Pray to the western setting sun, boys,' she'd say, 'America is in the west. Hope comes if you pray to the west.'

I smiled picturing the scene. "Sounds like you enjoyed going there."

He shrugged. "Ah, she'd beg us to sing the harmonies with her there all the time—called it, our Harmony House. But, to be honest, the darkness inside used to scare Sean and me, especially when a sudden storm trapped us up there. She always told us not to be afraid. 'Don't worry boys, the darkness protects us…' One time the rain trapped us up there overnight, that's when Dad found out. We stayed inside the rock-sided well and sang song after song. Then we said hundreds of Hail Mary's praying the rain would stop." He laughed at the memory. "Yeah, whenever we tried to recite them in English she'd tap our hands and make us do them in Gaelic. Even later when we didn't go up there anymore, whenever we got scared, she would bring us outside our cottage to stare at the dark side of the moon, telling us to imagine hiding from the bad guys there. Guess you can say she has a certain affection with the moon, always going on night rides when it is full."

"The dark side of the moon, interesting," I said.

He nodded at me as our horses picked a path up the rocky slope that was even more bathed from the increasing moonlight, giving an unearthly tone to the landscape. "She's likely blessing herself at this special well right now." He looked up at the bright light in the sky. "Speaking of moons, good thing there's a full one tonight, we're going to need it."

We continued to urge the horses up the trail, climbing steadily for another half an hour. Their hooves slipped on the slick wet stones, and I thought of Shannon lost out here somewhere on her own in the black of night. The whole time, Jack rode quietly in the saddlebag, sniffing at the air as the wind ruffled the black and white fur on his head making his ears flap. I guessed he was enjoying the ride, but doubted he would be of much help. This pup had no more sense of smell to find Shannon than I had a sense how to regain her trust, I thought.

The sky was completely dark when we reached the crest; the only light came from a sky filled with a blanket of stars that surrounded the full moon, hence I was grateful to the lanterns we carried. The trail ended at the base of a steep stone footpath disappearing into the dark above us.

Daniel and I were disappointed to see the wooden hitching rail was empty.

"Looks like I was wrong," he said. "Her horse isn't here."

"We've come this far," I said. "Shouldn't we go up and make sure of it?"

Again he shrugged, defeated, with lost hope. "Not much point. The wind's coming our way down the mountain and Jack's not barking. Damn, Sean and his stupid dog, we should have taken one of the hounds."

That's when I realized I hadn't done my job. "Wait, I haven't let him sniff the scarf yet." I pulled out the green wool scarf and held it up to Jack, who happily buried his nose into it.

"Can you find her for us, Jack?" I asked. "Find her, boy."

He leaped out of the saddlebag onto the ground, barking like mad and ran straight up the footpath, vanishing into the dark, only the white parts of his coat reflected off the moonlight.

"That's it. He's on to her!" Daniel shouted and we jumped down, quickly tied off our horses and trekked up the path after Jack.

It was no easy climb and I could understand why their father wanted their adventures up this steep rocky path to end. As our warm breath misted in the cold air, Daniel looked like a valiant rebel storming the breach with his riding hat on and his lantern's light being a sign of hope.

"Almost there," Daniel said, nearly as out of breathe as I was. When we got to the top, his lantern revealed the ruins of an ancient, old medieval church made of large bricks of brown and ashen rock held together with centuries old thick browned mortar. "The well, it's over there, see it? To the right of the church."

I looked ahead then saw Sean's pup waiting in front of the ruins for us. He barked at us as if commanding us to hurry and then ran off like he was chasing the sticks in the garden.

The whites of Daniel's teeth glowed as he smiled. "He's picked up her scent. She's probably singing her songs or praying inside the well house right now," he said, with a grin and took off after the dog.

I hurried after him. The pup ran ahead of us, passed the church in ruins, and around the hill to disappear into a stone-wrapped, vault-like structure. From inside, he barked wildly, and I heard a woman exclaim in surprise.

Before we reached the well house, Shannon emerged from its entrance with Jack in her arms, his white-cropped tail, like a cotton ball, wagging as he licked her face. "Jackie boy, what on earth are you doing out here, you crazy little thing. I heard a bark, but thought I was hearing things." She then saw Daniel walking toward her and again cried out in surprise.

"You gave us quite a scare." Daniel called out, cupping his mouth like a megaphone. "Are you all right?"

She kissed Jack and petted his ears. "Oh, I'm fine Daniel. I'm so sorry. Forgive me. I just needed some time alone to think."

She looked dirty and muddy, but her face and smile glowed white in the light of the lantern. We came up to her, Daniel ahead of me. "I suppose your father thinks I deserve another slap across the face, but Daniel dear, I had a right to be upset."

"Yes, you did," I said, winded, walking closer to her.

Her eyes opened wide in the dark and the whites of them reflected once more off the light of the lanterns to where I stood. She recognized me, then gasped and handed the pup over to her son.

She walked toward me, wiping her tears with the front of her shirtsleeve. "Declan. I have so much, so much…" she stumbled on her lack of ability to convey her emotions. "I thought you were gone forever…" She wiped her eyes again, creating a streak of thin mud on her cheeks.

I walked closer. "No, forever didn't work for me. I won't give up on us. I'm sorry for the pain I caused you, but you need to know I never meant to hurt you…"

She interrupted. "But Declan, why? Why so long?" she asked, her voice catching in sobs as she ran off into the darkness behind the well house.

I ran after her and Daniel came after me shouting. "Mother, stop! Dad is worried sick and G-Pap is…"

I kept on after her, but it was windy and pitch black away from the lanterns. Then the rocky wet surface caused me to slip off my feet and I cracked my skull in the back. Daniel passed over me carrying the lantern, without asking if I needed help to stand and continued after his mother, begging her to stop. After a few minutes, I heard them shouting to each other as I struggled back onto my feet. But my efforts failed me when the terrier kept putting his nose into the scarf I still carried, licking the salty sweat from my face as a small line of blood streamed down the back of my neck.

I stayed sitting on the rocky surface gathering my breath, holding the dog for another minute, when Daniel walked up to me, set his lantern near my feet, and gave me his hand. I accepted his youthful strength and stood up to brush the muddy dirt off my clothes.

Shannon stood behind Daniel, but was watching me. She approached, fixing her long mane, combing it haplessly with her hands, as she put it in place over her right shoulder without thinking. From the light of Daniel's lamp, I could see her face as it held the soft glow that she had decades of pain to express.

She didn't hold back. "It's been so long Declan. I was ready to live the rest of my life without you. Again, why now? I'm no fool. I know men like you, carousing around, causing havoc in people's lives, and then come back around when you need something. What is it that you want from me or from Pappy?"

I handed her the green scarf. "I don't want anything from you or him. Not one thing. If you want, I will go back to the States and leave you alone. For a long time I thought you were better off without me, but I've never been right without you. It took a tragedy…" I said, but stopped, not wanting to use my loss to benefit the situation. "Shannon, I just know it was time to make things right between us."

Wrapping the scarf around her neck, she hesitated to continue, and started to cry. "This well is my safe place. I can cry here in the dark—alone, until I feel right again."

"Sounds like when we were kids, remember when we used to hide on the dark side of the moon?" I asked, fully knowing already what her answer would be.

"Hum, when we were kids..." she said, and continued to cry. "The dark side of the moon, it was the only time I felt safe."

Daniel stepped up and put an arm around his mother's shoulder. We headed back to the front of the well house; my ankle was a little sore and the back of my head still bleeding, but I managed to keep up. When we got to the dark stone enclosure, she leaned up against the façade and covered her eyes, beginning to hum a soft melodic tune.

Daniel took a lantern, set it at her feet, and placed another lamp at the opening of the well.

I walked up to them and gently tried to get her to look at me. Then, as one would remove petals from a rose bud, I slowly pealed her hands off her face.

She started to cry and turned away, placed her hands over her face again, and hummed louder.

Without a thought, I tried to kiss the side of her cheek, tasting the salt of her tears.

She stopped humming. "You were thirteen when we were separated. Younger then Seanie, right? And now, you're what, five, six years older than me, yes?" she asked again, tired and dazed.

"Yes, I was thirteen, and in February, I turn forty-seven," I said, and added in shame. "It's been over thirty years…"

She interrupted and shook her head. "Then you were just a boy when…" She paused. "But why now Declan, after all this time?"

"It's a long story. I want to tell you every chapter of it, but somewhere warmer, out of this cold wind," I said, thinking of Pappy's cozy living room.

"It's a long story you say brother. My story is longer I'm afraid," she said, defeated.

"Indeed. I am sure of it. Perhaps you and I could…"

"What? You and I could do what together. Talk? Be a family again?" she asked.

"Yes, a family again. That would be a good start," I said, with my hand over my heart.

"Fine," she said, looking stronger. "We can talk. Come with me."

To my surprise, she grabbed my arm and guided me into the stone house and well chamber. Daniel stood at the opening with Jack in his arms and set another lantern inside the stoned door entrance.

I bent my head down and walked inside the well chamber. "Sit," Shannon said, as if it were an order, and pointed at a stone bench inside the enclosure. She stood resilient and with irrepressible eyes, I knew she was prepared to stay all night to talk this out. "This is my family's Harmony House, my boys loved to play up here with me when they were young. We came here to sing mother's music and to pray to the western setting sun—to America—and to you—in the hope that my brother would come back to me."

I sat stunned listening to her as she leaned a tall torch light on the wall next to the seat; the lowlight set a perfect tone for us to begin to heal.

"Paul thinks I'm crazy, but I heard mother calling for us to be together," she said, as her eyes stayed fixed into mine. "I know I heard her voice calling me, calling your name, too. Do you think I'm crazy, brother?"

I sat and answered, staring at her wild beauty. "No. I don't. I've heard her too. She's been whispering…"

"You have?" she asked, interrupting and was stunned.

I was held spellbound having her this close in front of me again, and saw how she resembled my mother at her age. For a moment, it was as if I became a boy again with my mother, and was put into the same scene—but in different time warps, like déjà vu. This time, I saw a genius working once more, like my mother drawing me as the Warrior Boy, Shannon stood in her own realm of creativity; this was her creative space—her genius. They both put chaos into an order, and I watched as they found their souls in the process.

I was in awe of witnessing genius in action, so I honored her space and listened.

"It's her spirit. I'm convinced of it," Shannon said.

"Yes, and we need to listen as I believe our mother has a message for us," I said.

Shannon listened intently and nodded.

I continued. "Her message is why I'm here, in my dreams I—I missed you so…"

Out of habit, it seemed she fumbled with her long mane when she was upset and interrupted. "If that's true, Declan, I don't understand why it took you so long to come see me. All these many years I've needed my brother. When mother died, I was so frightened, and again after the war, I was in such a bad way. If Pappy hadn't found me after my husband died, I don't think I would have ever gotten any joy back in my life. Daniel was the only thing that kept me going."

I tried to stand and to walk towards her. "Shannon, I…"

"Stop, it's my turn to talk. And sit, please. I have decades of words to say to you. You need to hear me out," she said.

I sat as if I was the accused on the stand at a trial and she the prosecutor. Daniel took Jack away from the well's opening, set him free to bark at the moonlight.

"I was so young, Declan. You were supposed to be my protector. Why did you leave me alone, alone after mother died, and alone after I moved here? Pappy told me you wanted nothing to do with building our homes side by side together. Why?" she asked, her beseeching face radiated in the flickering light of the lantern.

"Shannon, I have no reasons that suffice. I am not a decent man, just a sorrowful one."

She stopped. “Not decent? You’re a Quinn—like Mother and Pappy. Decency should be in your blood. What have you done to make you say such a thing?”

“Like I said, it’s a long story, but that’s all in the past. Shannon, I want to learn to be a Quinn again—to be a good man again.”

She stared at me with her hauntingly, deep green eyes that looked so much like our mother’s, I hesitated, stunned again by their resemblance and from her wild beauty. “I’ve missed seeing your beautiful eyes, sweet little sister. They light up like shining emeralds.”

She poked her finger into my chest. “Stop it with your bloody poetry.” She snapped at me. “You sound like Pappy, and what do you see in my eyes? A light, you said?”

“Yes, a light so beautiful, Pappy has it as well—as did our mother.”

She still wasn’t impressed. “I don’t remember her—not at all.” She paused and looked at me for a long while in silence. “You should see your own eyes at this moment, they are filled with a green so dark and sad, it hurts me to look at them. What is this long story of yours that’s left so much sorrow inside you?”

I wanted to stand, but didn’t dare move. “Shannon, you are my little sister. I want to protect you, so you don’t need to worry yourself with all of that. Seeing you has brought light to my darkness. Let me be a brother to you once more. I beg you. You can see my pain, it’s deep in my soul—it’s true, but a fresh light lies somewhere deep inside me too,” I said. “I believe you can help me find it again.”

She listened quietly to my plea.

“My wife is coming here with my children. She’s a good woman. They are coming to meet you. We can be a family together again. But Shannon, I’ve lived as a broken man without you. There hasn’t been one day that’s ended without me longing to see you again.”

She sat down next to me and took my hand into hers. “It’s been like that for me as well. I feel as if I’ve been waiting for you in the dark too long—of course I remember ‘the dark side of the moon’, you taught me to hide there in our imaginations night after night.

As a little girl, when…" she stopped, trying not to cry. "And then, when we hid in the closet from…" she stopped again, and couldn't continue. She tried to bear her thoughts to me through more sobs in her breath and hid her face in her hands again. "You said the dark would keep us safe, but the dark never worked for me the way it worked for you."

I removed her hands once again gently from her face. "My darling little sister, darkness never worked for me either."

She then turned to me and put her hand gently to my forehead, as she pushed back the hairs on my reseeding hairline. I closed my eyes to absorb the joy of her touch.

She spoke softly for the first time to me. "Open your eyes, brother. No more darkness. Greenies to greenies, Declan," she said, and smiled so pure. "Do you remember our mother saying that? Do you remember her songs—her steadfast love?"

"Yes, I remember." I looked into her eyes again, and as if a primal instinct was awakened in us both, our childhood bond became transformed with our tears. "Greenies to greenies, Shannon. I can see the green grasses of Ireland in your eyes, dancing in the wind, can you see them in mine, too?"

Her smile illuminated my entire world.

"I hate to intrude," Daniel said, poking his head inside the well house, "but it's freezing out here and by now G-Pap must be near ready to have a stroke. We still have enough light to get down the trail while the moon's high, but we should leave now."

"You're right. We need to get back." Shannon agreed, and gave me her hand as I stood up.

Daniel poked his head once more inside the well house. "Mother, where's Frey's Eclipse? He wasn't tied up below."

"Hmmph," Shannon said, looking indignant now. "A rabbit ran out of the brush and spooked him. He dumped me in the mud forty meters back and took off running. I'm surprised you didn't pass him on your way here. He's probably munching on hay in the barn by now, all nice and cozy, leaving me to make my way on foot in the mud and rain."

"Guess we're riding double then," I said, charmed, allowing her to exit the well chamber ahead of me. "That is, if you don't mind hanging onto your big brother."

She smiled at me even bigger than before. "Declan, that's exactly what I'm going to do, and I'll not be letting go of you ever again."

CHAPTER THIRTY-THREE

SOFIA'S TRUTH

One week later, I was waiting at the airport bouncing on my toes searching the faces of arriving passengers for my loved ones. Frankie and Patti were the first to greet me as they ran over to give me hugs. I looked at Frankie and thought this kid had to meet his namesake in Brooklyn one day. Sofia waited, looking shy and worried. I stepped forward towards her with my hand over my heart, almost as if I were asking for permission to kiss her for the first time. When she smiled and began to cry, I grab her into my arms, swinging her off her feet. She laughed in shock and kissed my neck. When I put her down, I kissed her, like I never had before, reminding myself of Signore Attanasio kissing Zia Anna. After we unlocked our ten-second kiss, she gasped my name in surprise. "Declan, is it this fresh Irish air or is it being away from me that's transformed you?" she asked, tipping the brim of my green Hooligan hat. "You seem like a new man."

"Yeah, you even look different, Paps," Frankie said, smiling, trying to steal my cap. "Can you get me one of these?" he asked, successfully putting the green Hooligan cap on his head.

I laughed. "Anything you want kid, it looks great on you, but give it back."

He handed it back with a smile.

"What do you think of my new belt?" I asked, showing him my Quinn embossed tan leather one.

His eyes got excited. "Cool, Paps. Did you make me one?"

"Yes, one for you and Andrew, and two more for your cousins that you are soon to meet."

Sofia gave me her bag and smiled, put her arms around Frankie and Patti. "It must be the air, darling, you seem poles apart from my old man of the west."

With a wink at Frankie, giving him the signal that I was going to teach him something, I hugged my wife once again, leaning her back to plant another passionate kiss on her. We kissed like we were young lovers again. "Now that's a kiss no western boy could pull off," I said, proud of myself. Then announcing to the whole group, I made a proclamation. "Ireland is a place for new beginnings." As Sofia stared at me with wide eyes, I lead the group to the car. "Let's go." Grabbing their luggage, I walked over to the parking lot and opened the rear door for Patti as she squealed in delight seeing the new doll waiting for her in the backseat, a gift from her cousin. I was not ready to mention the other Aisling yet.

Driving away from the airport into the countryside, I pointed out the local sites like a seasoned tour guide. "These Galtee Mountains peak to three-thousand feet or so, they are tiny hills compared to the high Sierras, but just as beautiful. Don't you think?"

Sofia nodded. "I've never seen so much green in all my life."

"Well if it rained at our ranch at home as much as it does here in Ireland, we'd have green like this, too," I said.

The kids pointed out the windows, laughing at the traffic driving on the opposite side of the road and me driving on the right side of the car. They talked non-stop, asking questions in their excitement, mostly about what I had been doing here and about finishing the last of their school year with a tutor. I hadn't yet told them the plan was for their G-Pap to guide them through their lessons, but figured the news would be like icing on the cake for them.

"You are going to meet your Irish family soon and two nice ladies across from your great-grandfather's farm. I have never shared much about my mother's family, but you are about to meet them—her father is an amazing man, you may call him G-Pap. He has a beautiful little cottage home on his ranch, kind of like the ones you see off the road here. The ladies I mentioned are lending us their home to live in for now. At least until Daniel, Frankie, and I finish building one of our own on the south end of Pappy's acreage." I waited for a big reaction from Sofia and the kids.

They didn't disappoint me, all exclaiming at once. "Our own home? Here?"

"Really Paps? We're going to build a cottage like that one over there?" Frankie said, pointing to a quaint house along the roadside.

I glanced over at a cottage up on the hillside. "Yes, or even bigger if we like, but I want ours to have a flagstone façade to match Pappy's cottage. You'll soon see what I mean, your G-Pap's friend, Nolan, is working on the topography of the land as we speak. All that has to be done before we form the foundations, but there's plenty of room for whatever we want to build. He has fifty acres with a plot set aside just for us," I said, excited and looked at Patti in the rearview mirror. However, she was scowling and clutching the new doll, and Sofia wasn't all too game herself.

"You want us to live here? Forever?" Patti asked, holding back a cry.

Sofia took my hand as I spoke to her via the rearview mirror. "We can if we want to. Depends on how much you all like it. You'll have cousins to play with. Daniel is about four years younger than Andrew; Sean is Frankie's age; and their sister—she's your age, Patti." It takes me a moment to find the courage to say the rest. "Her mother named her Aisling, too," I said gently.

Sofia took a deep breath, looked at me, and I saw tears forming. "But what about our Aisling, Daddy?" Patti sniffled behind me. "We can't leave her all alone."

I pulled the car over, got out, and walked around to open the door where Patti was sitting. I knelt on one knee and took her hands. "Darling, you are my sweetheart. Your sister was my little girl from heaven, just like you. I would never leave her behind. I promise everything will work out, you'll see," I said, and took the handkerchief out of my sweater pocket to dry both our tears.

Sofia sat silent in the front seat, staring ahead. Even as I climbed back into the driver seat and continued the journey, she kept her eyes fixed on the road and said nothing more all the way to Fethard.

***

For the next week, my family settled into the two sisters' cottage, and I was soon feeling more relaxed and at home with my family than I had in years. My family was safe, and Marco almost six thousand miles away.

One afternoon the following week, we all set off for a night in Dublin to hear Shannon's chamber orchestra and choir. Frankie and my two nephews took the train into the city, planning to meet us there, while Pappy, Sofia, Patti, and I took the car to pick up young Aisling on the way. She was at a parish school on the outskirts of Dublin. I drove us though towns heading northeast towards Dublin while Pappy gave directions, played tour guide, and told stories about his homeland. Next to him, Patti listened in rapt attention the whole time. My sweet daughter looked adorable, dressed in a powder blue dress for the concert with matching bows in her hair. Arriving at Aisling's school, I pulled up and parked near the school entrance.

Pappy immediately opened the car door and struggled to get out. "I don't need your help," he told me, as I was opening my door. "Patti dear, come with me," he said gently, intent to do this alone with my daughter. "You can help me up the stairs as your cousin wants to show you her classroom. You know, if you move here, you might go to this school as well."

Despite his protests, I got out and helped him out of the car. Sofia waited in the front seat as we watched Pappy and Patti walk up the stairs together. Pappy smiled, encouraging his shy great-granddaughter, while Patti beamed looking at her G-Pap, helping him up the steps.

I stood on the sidewalk and waited for them to return, smiling at other parents walking by us with their children.

Sofia unrolled her window to talk to me. "You belong here in Ireland, Declan. I can see why you want to stay. Your family is wonderful. I've never met nicer people. G-Pap is an amazing man, and your sister—such a delight. It's such a shame you were separated all these years."

"Well, I'm making up for it now. This will be a wonderful night seeing Shannon on the stage leading her chamber singers. The sad days are behind us. Please know how grateful I am to you for coming here and being with me tonight at this concert," I said, and kissed her through the open window.

As I watched for Pappy and the girls, Sofia leaned out the window and grabbed my arm.

"Darling wait, you must tell me what's made you so different. You are like a new man I have never met. What is it? And don't tell me it's something in the air or your being done with Marco—or even the idea of a new start here in Ireland. What's happened to you? I must know."

I leaned in the window and kissed her cheek, breathing in her rose scented perfume.

"You need only to know that the thorns in my side are gone, Sofia—plucked out, one-by-one from the telling."

She placed her hand on my cheek. "The telling? Of what?" she asked, confused.

I smiled at her. "The truth," I said, simply and kissed her hand. "The truth I told to Andrew, Shannon, and to Pappy—and in that crazy journal you had me work on for Andrew's thesis. 'We feel the thorns of the past—we remove them with the telling,'" I said, stealing the first of my lines.

Sofia listened, but sat back into her seat defeated. "The truth was told—but not to me, Declan. You haven't told me. I've been patient long enough—too long. I am your wife and deserve to know about these 'thorns' you speak of."

Kissing her hand once again I said, "No, Sofia, you deserve much more than that. You deserve my protection."

She gave me a look I had seen before, a frustrated glare telling me I must be the stupidest man who ever lived.

She pulled her hand away from a quick, gratuitous kiss I offered to her, while the deep brown in her eyes pierced into mine. "Keeping someone in the dark isn't the same as protecting them."

Her denouncement sucked the air from my lungs and for a moment I had no words as the truth of what I had done to her unfolded in my mind all too clearly. I had been trying to protect her the same way I protected Shannon as a child, and with similar results. These years of denying Sofia the truth had been every bit as damaging to our relationship as if she'd been locked away in a dark closet.

"Dear Lord," I said, aghast at the realization. "Sofia, I'm so sorry. I never realized. I've been so wrong. I kept my secrets to protect you, but it was wrong of me. You're my wife, the mother of my children, and loyal to me all these years. You are a smart, strong, and incredibly beautiful woman. I don't know how I failed to appreciate what I had. Please, let me make it up to you. You deserve my devotion and all my love."

"And your honesty, Declan?" she asked, with tears in her eyes.

"Yes, absolutely."

She took a lace handkerchief out of her purse and blotted her eyes. "Declan, until all the walls fall, we'll just keep being strangers."

Her statement was like a fastball up the middle of the plate that I never saw coming. I refused to strike out this time. "Yes. You are so right, Sofia. As soon as we get home tonight, we'll find a quiet place alone, and I'll tell you everything, answer every question, I promise. No more secrets, no more walls up."

When she continued to scowl at me in disbelief, I opened the car door, took her hand to help her get out. With my hand, I gathered her soft, long curly hair and brushed it softly to the side, kissing her neck. "I swear this, Sofia. I swear my life on it."

I promised her with all my heart, and that night, after clapping my hands sore at Shannon's concert, we returned home, and found that quiet corner for the two of us. Pouring out my confessions to Sofia until late into the wee hours of the morning, I answered fully and honestly every question put to me. It wasn't easy. By the time we finished, the sun rose, and many tears had fallen, but we found a new peace in each other's trust—and a new passion in each other's arms.

***

The following week, Frank Attanasio called to tell me of Judy's passing. It was awful to have it final and to hear that her beauty and love were gone off of this earth. But he had more to discuss, and he wasn't happy to talk about this topic as well. He kept pressing me about being on the run from Marco and of how I compromised the safety of his family by coming into Bay Ridge. "No one is safe, Franco's goons in Bensonhurst will spread the word to Marco about us, and no matter if there's the Atlantic Ocean as a separator—he'll find out we helped you."

"Franco and the Bensonhurst gang are long dead or in jail after the NYPD cleaned house in the boroughs, and don't worry about me. I will be okay," I said.

He was agitated. "Don't flatter yourself Declano. It's not you, but my family who I'm concerned about. I spend many nights seeing those thugs snooping around. You have us involved now, how can I have a guarantee that Marco won't be after me or my family for this?"

Mafia guarantees were like gluing a house together instead of using nails. There was nothing I could say to ease his worries, so I asked him to call Anthony. He would be the only one we could trust.

Frank made the call.

Two days later, he called me back with his report. He said Anthony was able to save face with Marco concerning the incident on the highway and the botched kidnapping. But he was still trying to out smart him and to leave the family for good.

"Good work," I said. So I asked Frank for one last favor: to hand deliver a package to Anthony, telling him doing so would clear any fears of vendettas coming from Marco.

Frank met with Anthony in Virginia City, Nevada, a few days after he received the package I sent him, airmail from Dublin. It contained a safety deposit box key and a copy of the Irish Times of Dublin. Dated: February 4, 1968.

By the time Frank contacted me after the meeting, happy to be pocketing a fresh stack of one hundred dollar bills he found in the safety deposit box, which if he counted—and he did I'm sure, amounted to be one hundred, one hundred dollar bills inside the stack. There were two more equal stacks Frank distributed for me—one for Anthony and the other for the Attanasio and Russo families.

He then gave me an account of Marcos' reaction to the headline and boxed contents.

I was curious if it was not simply a tall tale, recalling what Pappy had said about urban myths that were formed off of the streets of New York, and wondered if his report was a mere falsehood.

Nonetheless, I listened, as Frank's story came with certainty.

The tale goes as follows: It was a dark and stormy night in the Sierra Nevada, mountain lake regions of Nevada, the snow coming in was so thick the Nevada State Police had to escort cars in rows of ten through the passes that approached and encircled the lake. Marco stared out the windows of his swank penthouse office and stood stiff as the wall of blinding white snow shut down the city below. No one in their right mind would be brave enough to leave his office that night, let alone attempt to drive the icy mountain roads.

Don Marco and a hand full of his trusted men, watched a newly appointed Consigliere open a black, legal file-sized box on his desk. The mafia Don dipped a cigar into his brandy snifter as he walked over to his apprentice. He set the glass down on his desk and sifted through the pile of papers in the heavy box, and then picked up a revolver.

The documents contained mounds of evidence tying Marco to the killings of Ricco Nusco and countless other murders over the last three decades. The lawyer flipped through the stack of papers. "The prosecutor already has witnesses lined up to testify against you Don Marco, if that isn't enough, here is a letter from the Internal Revenue Service. It seems they are investigating you for tax evasion, along with a similar letter from the State of Nevada, stating that all of your assets have been frozen. It looks like you have many enemies in…"

Don Marco was not happy, interrupted, and grit his teeth. "If Quinn were still here, he could have found a way to get me out of this fucking mess and hide all the evidence. He's the only Consigliere to trust in a time like this!" He looked frustrated at his new lawyer who didn't know how to grease palms and blackmail judges.

Then, he looked over at the copy of the Irish Times of Dublin on his desk, hand delivered a few days ago via special courier. The headline read:

Declan Quinn IV of Fethard, was found dead on the shores of Waterford this morning, drowned after his fishing boat capsized on the Celtic Sea. Declan Quinn IV leaves behind his wife, two sons and a daughter. He lived in the Western United States where he was an attorney and only recently arrived in Ireland for a visit with his grandfather, a well-known local, Declan Quinn II, Literature Professor at Catholic University in Dublin from 1926 to1961.

Private services will be held for the immediate family at St. Augustine's Church chapel, County Limerick, in the province of Munster.

Marco ripped the rose off his jacket and tossed it across the room, slamming his Smith and Wesson revolver on top of the photo of the wrecked ship in the newspaper, and crushed his burning cigar into the black and white page over Declan's picture.

"Damn it, Quinn, you look like a fucking Irishman wearing that stupid hat on your head. How dare you up and die on me when I need you most? What did you do—jump overboard like the coward you are? I should have killed you myself when I had the chance!" he yelled out in the fancy room filled with his goons, one—a friend of Anthony's.

There was a knock on Marco's office door and a deep voice asking if he was ready to come out. Marco's Consigliere announced the news to the men in the room. "The hotel manager is here. He said the police are on their way to make an arrest. Don Marco, what shall we do now?" he asked.

"I'll be damned if I'm gonna end up in some fucking jail cell," Marco said, with clenched teeth.

The young attorney walked over to Marco, took his keys to lock the door behind him, and picked up the phone. "I know a guy, Nunzio—he can make your bail. I will get on it, don't worry bout' a thing. You'll be out in no time. Trust me."

Marco picked up the revolver again. Feeling the weight of it, knowing it was fully loaded, he slid back the safety latch and looked at himself mirrored in the ceiling to floor windows. Without another thought, he pointed the revolver at his reflection and pulled the trigger, shattering the glass into a million pieces to the frozen ground eighteen floors down.

A dozen police wearing riot gear busted open the door. Weapons drawn, they ordered him to drop his gun.

Marco let it drop to the floor and then struggled with the two SWAT officers who forcefully handcuffed him.

A detective stood in front of the dejected Don. "Marco Nusco, you have the right to remain silent …"

***

Four Years Later

Downhill from where I stood, the diesel engine of a dilapidated school bus full of students from Catholic University rumbled idle on the road adjacent to my property. The bus door opened and Andrew stood on the first step. When he spotted me in the distance, he cupped his mouth to amplify his voice. "Come on Paps, did you forget today is Wednesday and we go up to The Rock of Cashel for class? And don't forget to bring the picture of The Boy Warrior, "Aisling's Code", and Aunt Shannon's record album, "The Dark Side of the Moon". I need them for today's lecture," he said.

I waved and shouted back. "Okay son, I haven't forgotten anything. Give me a minute. Let me grab my things and I'll be right over."

I visited the east end of our property early every morning, and that day was no exception. I was a free man, but one in a continual mode of repair. Before me was a small wooden wagon full of flower baskets, my journal, Andrew's recently published book titled, *Spinatherapy: Man's Extraction of Past Traumas and Regrets.* Written by, Dr. Andrew Quinn. In my hand was the rolled up sketch of me as a boy in an art tube as well as a copy of Aisling's Code. Shannon had recorded an album a few years after Pappy found her—it was another expression of genius I held in my possession and cherished.

I pulled the wagon behind me as I climbed to the graveyard. The air was sweetly fragrant here, as Shannon collected a basket of garlic bulbs to plant from the shores near St. Declan's Well. She and Sofia also planted climbing pink and red sweet pea vines around the newly painted white iron fence that surrounded the graveyard. The flowers and wild garlic were just starting to bud on that fresh spring morning.

We buried Pappy at the top of the hill. I looked at his headstone, crafted by my own hands, that closely resembled the one he arranged for my mother those many years ago. The stone engraving read:

Declan Quinn II
November 12, 1882 – May 3, 1972
Herein Lies One Whose Truth Was
Writ in Story and Rhyme

On that morning, I opened the gate and pulled the wagon with the three baskets of white snowdrop flowers and daffodils with me. With the books and album under my left arm and the art tube in my hand, I placed one of the baskets in front of Pappy's headstone. The others were placed in front of the same styled headstones for my mother and daughter—two Aislings side-by-side with Pappy. They belonged here in Ireland with him, as did I. And one day, I will lie down beside them all, and Sofia when her time comes as well.

I opened my journal and read out loud Andrew's dedication again—it rang true every time I said it. "A wound is a place where light can enter."

One day, my own epitaph will say these words.

I would remain here in Ireland, freed of the past, by the telling of my truths. I didn't doubt that there would be many more generations of Quinns to come. I would make sure they too would know their heritage and to live a life that embraced the truth while extracting the pains therein.

Tears filled my eyes as I stood at the graves of my mother, daughter, grandfather, and many generations of Quinns that preceded them. I missed them so much, but just as the losses threatened to overwhelm me, my mother's voice whispered once again in my ear.

Greenies to greenies, Declan. Grieve not, my son, because your eyes and soul are lit with the fire of redemption.

THE END

AUTHOR'S NOTE

Although this is a work of fiction, I have inserted personal true stories throughout. The Attanasio family of Brooklyn is my family who lived on Bay Ridge Parkway. The use of fiction allowed me to blend names and personalities in order for me to include everyone in this work. Granted, many of my aunties will say, "Donna dear, you got all the names wrong and the generations mixed up"—but this was my purpose. I combined three generations of family into one generation living in the Sixties, and had a blast doing it. Hopefully, when *The Consigliere* lands on the laps of my loving family, they will read and laugh along. And at the end of the day, I will propose we drink anisette in our coffee with Ricotta Pie together in honor of the Attanasio family—with a special toast to Judy and Anna. A primary motivation of this work was to have an opportunity to put Judy Winslow under the lights of stardom and to write about my mother, who is the character of Zia Anna. They both passed away from us too soon.

On the mafia connection, my father and grandfather were both chased out of New York, my maternal grandfather Mike, in the early Nineteen-hundreds and my father, Saverio, in the Nineteen-fifties, due to the fact they would not abide by the rules of the corrupted unions or pay fees to the mafia bosses. Sure, we have a mafia connection. It sounds something like, "so-and-so was in so-and-so's wedding", that kind of thing, but I don't want to blemish our name just to spur interest. The mafia is not the glamorous world that screenwriters want you to believe. They are murderous fear mongers who disregard any notion of human decency and independent hard work.

My grandfather Frank Masotto and father, Saverio Masotto, could have easily joined the ranks of the mafia in the early Twentieth Century, but chose instead to give the latter generations like myself a life of peace and goodness.

I am forever grateful to Grandpa Masotto and my father for that.

ACKNOWLEDGEMENTS

First and foremost, I'd like to thank my circle of friends and family whose encouragement always kept me going with this project. Each and every one is my cheerleader extraordinaire, especially my husband, John, and my three amazing kids, Joni, Angie, and Matthew, who patiently watched me devote so many hours to this project. Without these motivational partners on the sidelines, this work would have ended up into the trashcan many times.

A theme intertwined in this novel is of the notion of the spirits amongst us—the angels who linger on the sidelines and cheer us along despite our life's struggles. My mother, Anna Masotto and cousin, Judy Attanasio are the celestial women who inspired me to write this book. The first seed was planted when I heard Judy's voice on an old recording and knew her story had to be told. My beloved grandson, Jaxon James Moravec was the angel that inspired me to live by a code of positivity—it's his spirit that wrote Aisling's Code. I wish to hug them in the physical sense today, but know they'd have to leave divine bliss to return to me. So, I will settle for the virtual hug from the heavens for now.

Wayne Dyer's work, *Wishes Fulfilled* was the motivational book that got me away from simply talking about my dreams to finally working them with the fervor of a Mt. Everest expedition. Granted, I yelled at Dyer through the first two or three readings of his work, but he asked his readers, "Why did you pick up this book in the first place? The title attracted you for a reason." Dyer posits we all have a light inside us to cultivate—but are too afraid to allow it to shine. There is no guarantee for success, but the joy one receives from accessing this light is how happiness is found.

I'd like to thank Dr. James Fisher from Fordham University for graciously responding to my questions and verified the historical aspects of university life and academics at Fordham in the Sixties. I must take my hat off to Dr. Stuart Bloom and Mary Franz's *Character and Conflict* courses and leadership training at California State University, Fullerton. Their group-teaching approach and trainings changed my life—it's their classroom settings and lectures that inspired G-Pap's teaching style.

My full gratitude goes to the La Jolla Ladies Book Club and to their gracious host, Kandee Bondee. Hugs go to Chris D, Chris S, Cheryl, Bonnie, Pam, Marleigh, Laura, Mindy, Diane, Shelly, Laura Kane, Sam Masotto Jr., Joan E. Moravec, Angelina T. Reyes, Elizabeth VandenAkker, Donna Rodgers, Marie Caldiero, Denise Masotto, and CMC Hugh Isbell, for being the best beta readers ever. A special appreciation goes to Doreen DeAvery whose coaching and friendship kept my mind sane on many days. Her expertise in formatting copy into an ebook is why you are reading it on your readers today. Monsignor Robert Ecker was the man who became my spiritual guide through this process, he never preached to me on matters of faith, but he made me laugh, and hence, believe again. I'd like to give a special hug to David Reyes from Carousel Agency, he created the outstanding cover and website for this project. David and my son Matthew Rullo were my team when launching and promoting this work, without their assistance, this most likely would have been lost in the stacks in cyberspace. I will be forever grateful to David Larson, J.D. Wallace, Marla Anderson, and Mike Gibbs, from the San Diego Writers Group, they graciously coached me at the many levels in the writing process. Further, I can't speak more highly about the *Robert McKee's Story Seminars*. I devoured Mr. McKee's lectures and became obsessed with his books, videos, and weekend crash sessions. I will forever be a student Robert McKee.

Last but not least, this work wouldn't have been possible without my editors, Brian Tibbetts from MacGregor Literary Agency, Marla Anderson, and Helen Chang from Author Bridge Media. Their editing expertise and professionalism brought this manuscript to its polished end.

A READER'S GUIDE

1. The opening quote of The Consigliere is from Holocaust survivor, Dr. Viktor Frankl. In his prolific work, A Man's Search for Meaning, he writes, "There are only two races of men, the descent and the indecent." Do you agree with this statement?

2. Declan as a boy made a decision that changed the course of his life. What choices as a child did you make that would be different if given this same choice as an adult?

3. Two themes used in the novel are Crossroads and Choices. Share your experiences with life-changing crossroads and choices in your life.

4. Childhood trauma is embedded into our psyche and is manifested in various forms in life. How do you deal with the past and do you believe it needs to be investigated and expressed?

5. Existential therapy, as practiced by Dr. Viktor Frankl, is based on a philosophical approach known around the world as, Logo-therapy. One of Logo-therapy's basic tenets is that life has meaning under all circumstance—especially in the midst of suffering. Is it unrealistic to believe an individual can possess happiness in the throes of despair?

6. Declan was grief stricken and subconsciously, had an internal desire to change. Do you think Declan could have attempted this journey alone without his son's challenge? Who is your 'Andrew' in life and can you make changes without an accountability partner?

7. One of the themes of the book is the concept of forgiveness and second chances. Do you think Declan deserved the blessing from Father Carmen? Do you think Sofia was right to give him a second chance?

8. Declan had a love other than his wife. Judy told Declan, "Love is only for the stars in the sky to figure out. Life on earth is too imperfect to experience a perfect love. We can't have the love promised us in fairy tales—at least, not on this planet." Were Judy's statements on love correct?

9. Do you think fairy tales create a false sense of love in young children's minds?

10. Did Judy make the right decision when she chose to chase her dreams over love?

11. Declan worked three jobs as a boy to support his family, but was happy. How do you find balance between work and finding meaning in your life? And are you one of the lucky few who create meaningfulness within your work?

12. Do you believe God designs our destiny? Or, do we fall into our paths by random chance?

13. Pappy said, "The innocent pay for the crimes of their fathers." Do you believe this statement to be true? Does Declan's pilgrimage to St. Declan's Well make you want to make a spiritual pilgrimage/retreat?

14. In his lecture at The Rock of Cashel, Professor Quinn used an elastic ball to explain how the usage of tension in poetry causes a reader to focus on a theme. If this aspect works in poetry, why does man tend to run away from conflict (tension) in life?

15. About conflict: How do you approach your nemesis in life? Like Declan, do you believe in order to have peace one must, as Sal Russo suggests, "confront the mafia bosses first to get to the greener grass on the right side of the fence"?

16. A major theme in the novel was the therapeutic tool of a fictionalized theoretical approach called, Spina-therapy—the art of pulling out the thorns of our past through the telling of our stories. Do you agree that engaging with painful memories helps to expel them or does the telling resurface the pain all over again to cause more sadness?

17. The author chose to end the story with a lie with an embellished story in the Irish Times of Dublin—an ironic element in respect to the major theme of the story: The pursuit of the truth. In your life, are there times when fabricating a story or putting on a mask is necessary to achieve a peaceful existence?

18. Declan wasn't fully whole as a person without the key women in his life. Do you believe our society encourages division between men and women? Discuss ways to bridge this issue, if so.

19. Write your epitaph.

An Existential Personal Evaluation

1. As you come to the crossroads of life, how do you evaluate which direction to take and how do lessons from the past influence your decision?

2. What defines you as a man/woman: Goodness, success, community, or service?

3. What brings you happiness: Pleasure, purpose, work, or love?

4. Is happiness found within you or from extrinsic rewards?

5. Do your sufferings lead you towards humility or rebellion?

6. Do you believe your body is a temple of the Holy Spirit or a temple of pleasure?

7. Do your sufferings turn you away from God or do they unite you to the Holy?

8. When faced with conflicts, do you confront them or flee?

9. Do you believe that you make choices or do choices make you?

10. What in life causes you restlessness? And it can't be hunger, thirst, or lust.

BIOGRAPHY

Donna Masotto was born into an Italian-American family of eleven children. As the middle child she was the consummate observer, and hence, the family historian. Her writing reflects a first hand view of how the mafia infiltrated the neighborhoods where her family lived in Brooklyn, NY. Sure, she has a mafia connection, it sounds something like, "so-and-so was in so-and-so's wedding," that kind of thing, but it's far from a topic she'd be inclined to boast about. Her viewpoint of the mafia is real, raw, and dirty, but true and bold. Ms. Masotto's perspective provides readers an insider's view of life within the mafia that has never been told before. Crime isn't glamorized in her work—truth is.

Donna is a substitute teacher for San Diego Unified School District and for SD Diocesan schools. When not driving the back roads in Italy to collect ceramics for her import furniture business, she enjoys the San Diego area with her husband, John, three kids, and two Jack Russell terriers, Benny and Topaz. Most often you will find Donna teaching her six grandchildren the fantastic game of tennis at San Diego Tennis and Racquet Club.

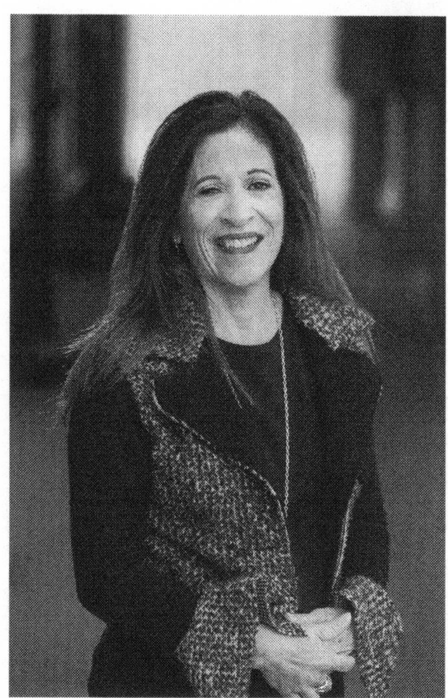

For more information:
www.westmarketpublishing.com
www.theconsiglierenovel.com